STAMPEDE!

The storm strode down the flats toward the big herd, rattling flashes that illuminated the land. Matt Hazelwood could read the wind, knew there were riders this side of the herd, one circling counterclockwise and others coming from the windward side toward him. So far the herd was still on its ground.

Then a cannon burst in his ears. Blinding light was all around and he seemed to float in it. He swung around, dazzled eyes ranging the distances of what was now a rolling, shifting sea of running cattle, a sea that bobbed and thundered and clattered, awash with the glowing whitecaps of foxfire. He slapped rein and the bay bounded away, running parallel to the flowing thunder of the herd.

"Stampede!" he yelled, but the word was lost in the din.

THE WAY TO WYOMING

Dan Parkinson

ZEBRA BOOKS
KENSINGTON PUBLISHING CORP.

ZEBRA BOOKS

are published by

Kensington Publishing Corp.
475 Park Avenue South
New York, NY 10016

Second printing: October, 1989

Printed in the United States of America

1

On a gray hillside bleached by glaring sun the man with the arm-sling drew rein—the merest touch of pressure on oiled leather—and the big blood bay slowed to a walk and then stopped. It was lathered and panting, and like the man who rode it, matted and grimy with gray dust.

He had ridden two hard miles along a downwind gully before doubling back and taking to the hills. It was an old trick. The fretful wind, tumbled by canyon walls, roiled the dust of his passage and carried it with him to deposit its burden of dust in his passage. It didn't obliterate his tracks, but it softened and obscured them. At a distance in high sun they would be hard to see.

Now from the hillside he scanned the lands north and east, searching for sign of movement. He had doubled back twice since his last glimpse of the two riders following him. The first time it had been almost a parallel backtrack. He had gained distance on them in a flat-out run, then dropped down into limestone breaks, heeled around and crept southward at least a mile, wanting to get behind them. When he found the wide, silt-bed canyon running eastward he veered into it and ran, with the wind, riding just ahead of the low, thick dust that boiled up and settled behind him. The canyon and the wind covered him for nearly two miles. Then he doubled back once more and headed northeast.

If he was lucky, he would not see the pair again. By now they should be far to the north, wondering where they had missed him.

He knew they had shadowed him from Three Rivers, and he knew why. One way or another, they had learned about the horses he was bringing down to sell to Valdez—twelve thousand dollars worth of top-notch horseflesh. Good riding stock was at a premium in Texas, and a herd moving through the lonely plateaus might be an easy target. They didn't know where he had left the herd, but they knew about it and had followed him.

He was hampered and frustrated by the crippled arm held in a sling across his chest. It was a clean fracture, healing nicely, but it was a nuisance trying to get by with one arm. A man driving forty-four young and sassy Arabian-cross horses seven hundred miles in lonely country needed both his hands. Even with Pepe's help, it was a chore. He had learned in recent weeks to throw and cinch a saddle one-handed, to build a fire and boil coffee, to roll and tie a bedsack one-handed. But it was pure hell to get his boots on of a morning. As often as not, Pepe had to help him with that.

The herd was safe with Pepe, so long as he could

6

avoid bringing horse thieves down upon them. Pepe was holding them on good graze in a little backwash meadow boxed in by tumbled limestone bluffs, a good place to rest them while he went on in to Three Rivers to make his deal with Valdez.

Pepe had waved him off with a reassuring grin, and would be waiting for him. He had left by one route and was returning by another, just to be safe.

Three hundred dollars a head, Valdez had offered for the stock. Twelve thousand dollars for forty-four horses. But Valdez would not be disappointed. Jim Tyson knew horses, and the years of perfecting the breed had paid off. Eastern Arabian stock crossed with tough Mexican ponies, they were everything a man could want for the practical conduct of cattle ranching.

The blood bay Tyson rode now was a fine example, combining the intelligence of the Arabian stock with the size of Mexican *caballo grande* ancestors and the quickness and staying power of mustang forebears. For travel, for general riding and for cow work, a nearly ideal animal. The rest were as good, and Valdez was a shrewd buyer. They would both come out all right.

Were they still back there, on his trail? Not likely, but possible. Tyson climbed down, rubbed the horse's muzzle and knelt to inspect its feet. It was breathing rapidly from the run, but it was a strong horse and not yet tired. It had plenty of go left in it. Bred true and hand-gentled through long days, weaned on gathered oats and barleycake from the wrangler's hand and on the lush graze of flinthills bluestem, it was his horse and it would serve him.

Valdez's offer, wired from Austin, had come at a perfect time. Tyson had just returned from Wyoming to Kansas, with a brand new dream in his mind.

Building his Arabian-cross breed in the flint hills had taken years, but now it was done and the breed was established, and he had found in Wyoming the thing he wanted to do.

He had sold his breed stock at Abilene, paid off his debts and headed south, he and Pepe moving the herd easily and taking their time. They backtracked the big cow trails, down into Texas, and the only problem all the way was when he cracked his arm in that fall. But even that was minor, although a nuisance. Jim Tyson had been a wrangler since the day he had returned to Texas from the war, an eighteen-year-old veteran with a head full of hard memories that could only be put away by looking forward and never looking back. And he had hooked up with Matt Hazelwood, and with Mr. Price and Soapy Green, and seldom had time after that to look back.

Satisfied that the horse was in good condition, he stepped to his saddle again, slapped the blood bay's rump and ran another zigzagging mile, through rough breaks. He was sure now that he had eluded them. A pair of young hardcases out on the prowl, there was no doubt they had intended to follow him to his herd and take it. But now he guided the blood bay to a ridge top and looked out on the wide land, and they were nowhere to be seen. And just beyond the ridge was the hidden meadow, and Pepe with the herd.

He stepped down, loosened the cinches slightly, took up the reins and walked, leading the sweated horse. The high south Texas sun crept past zenith to bleach the land with brilliance and made the far hills shimmer like ripples on a stream. Seeing Texas again was like seeing an old friend, but it would be a brief visit. Wyoming waited for him, and his dreams now were there.

He had toyed with the idea of swinging a few days east, to see Matt Hazelwood and the rest. It had been a long time. He hadn't seen Matt in . . . what? Ten years? Not since they all made the drive to Abilene and he had found the lease range up in the Kansas flint hills where all his ideas about breeding horses seemed to come together. It was horse country, a place where a man could throw a herd of Mexican mares on good pasture with a couple of select sires from eastern stables . . . Arabian crossbreeds, he had decided . . . and breed up a line that men would bid high prices for.

Matt had shrugged at his idea, then grinned that slow, hard grin of his. "You may be crazy, Jim Tyson," he had said, "but I guess you're no crazier than the rest of us. If it's the thing you have to do, then do it. I don't know how Rafter H will get by without you, though. We'll all have saddle sores from trying to ride rough stock."

"There are plenty of wranglers," he had told the older man, seriously. "Just be sure the one you find can think like a horse."

"Yeah, I know," Matt was still grinning. "'There aren't any bad horses . . . just bad trainers.'"

It was an old line between them, but once more,

for old time's sake, Tyson had repeated his pet theory: "The only thing wrong with any cowpony is poor education, from a wrangler who thinks about horses the way a drover thinks about cows."

And Matt had followed the old line: "Any drover who forgets that cows are the enemy is a step away from being gored and stomped."

"And any drover who forgets that his horse is his friend is just a toss away from the same thing."

Matt chuckled, ending it. "I know, Jim. I know. That's why folks ride horses and eat cows and not the other way around."

They had laughed together, not at the stale humor but at the nostalgia it produced, and Soapy and Mr. Price had come to join them for a handshake all around.

"We'll miss you, Jim," Soapy said.

"But not as much as you'll miss my biscuits," Mr. Price added.

It was the last time he had seen them. He had leased his spread in the flint hills and the years had passed. It had been hard at first. He had made mistakes, and learned the hard way about the horse breeding business. But gradually a strain emerged that was the strain he wanted, and they began to sell.

Pepe had come to him with a herd of good brood mares from Mexico, and stayed to help him work his stock. He was the fourth in a string of Pepes, and Jim had learned secrets from all of them. A Mexican who knew horses knew more about horses than anybody else.

Then Katie had come into his life. Two years

ago? Was that all? It seemed she had always been there.

Morgan Toliver was a New Englander who had made money in ships and invested it in Wyoming mines, and Katie was his daughter. They had stopped at Wichita on their way west, and Toliver had heard of Tyson's horses. He came out to look, and stayed to buy, and in those two days the sun had risen in Jim Tyson's world. That sun's name was Katie.

Toliver paid top dollar for a young stud and seven fillies. Six weeks later Jim Tyson delivered them personally and stayed on for almost a month, seeing Wyoming, seeing Toliver's new mines and seeing Katie.

Katie. From the range stock on Toliver's spread, Jim selected a gentle mare and spent days teaching it to respond to a rider as no horse had ever responded before. Every skill he had, he used. And when he was satisfied he put her saddle on it, and his own on his favorite blood bay, and led them to her door.

"Come out, Miss Kate," he called. "Come ride with me. I've a thing to ask you that's best asked out where the land is clean and the morning sun plays songs among the wildflowers."

They rode together and he led her to a place he had found, a valley where sparkling streams met among tall grass meadows, and the hills around were alive with larkspur and prairie buttercup.

"This is horse country," he told her. "I've learned to build a strain, and with what I can get for my stock I could start afresh here and make a good life

11

of it."

She looked out on the valley and her eyes shone with his dreams. "It's beautiful," she said.

"But a good life is only good if it's shared," he told her. "Would you share that life with me, Katie?"

They had wandered through the valley, and she had thought about it. And she had agreed.

When time came for him to go, she had fretted over his leaving, but he put his arms around her and held her close. "A few months, Katie. That's all it will take. I need to sell my stock . . . find the right buyers. When that's done I'll be back here with a ring for your finger and we won't be parted ever again."

"Promise me, Jim," she murmured. "Promise me you'll be back."

He had promised.

The ring in his saddlebag now was a fine gold band that he had carried since the spring, and its presence where he went was the promise he had made.

Leading the blood bay, he walked along the hillside to where the land fell away to lacing canyons, then found a game trail winding downward. In the distance, water glinted in a shelf-rock tank, and beyond in the distance were his horses.

There was no further sign of the hardcases who had trailed him, and he guessed they were miles to the north by now, maybe angling westward. Despite his fatigue and the time he had lost, he felt no particular animosity toward them. He felt nothing toward them at all. Their kind were always around, flat-eyed young men on the prod or on the prowl, men going nowhere and gaining nothing. They would be hanged as rustlers eventually, or waylaid by a posse, or shot down on a street, and their passing would be no more than dust on the wind. He didn't pity them. They chose their way. But their way had nothing to do with him.

His injured arm throbbed and itched, and the glare of Texas sun made his eyes ache. But thoughts of Katie, waiting in Wyoming, put these irritations to rest. Born a Texan, Big Jim Tyson had soldiered when he was sixteen. At eighteen he had driven wild cattle out of Texas to the markets and at twenty-two he had begun the breeding of fine saddle stock up in the flint hills. He had done his share of roaming and more than a little fighting. But now, at thirty-two, he knew what he wanted of life and was content.

The blood bay followed closely at his shoulder, nuzzling him for reassurance now and then, scenting the water below and wanting to be there.

"Easy, sport," he crooned to it, rubbing his whiskered jaw against its muzzle. "It's a long way to Wyoming and we've only just started."

The words brought to his mind other words, and he could almost hear Soapy Green, riding night-herd on the high prairie, singing to his cows.

"As I walked out one morning for pleasure . . ." he murmured, remembering, *"I spied a cow-puncher all riding alone . . ."* It had been a lot of years since he had heard that sung on the trail, a poignant old Irish tune with words put to it by men

who tended cattle. *"His hat was throwed back and his spurs were a-jinglin', and as he approached he was singin' this song . . ."* He grinned at the old memory and raised his voice, sounding to himself thin and rusty in the vast, empty land. *"Whoopee ti yi yo, git along little dogies. It's your misfortune and none of my own. Whoopee ti yi yo, git along little dogies. You know that Wyoming will be your new home."* Wyoming. Not Dodge City. Singing it pleased him.

The horse shook its head and snuffed. Big Jim grinned again. He had never been noted for his singing voice. "Sorry, sport," he said. "But the words are right. We know Wyoming will be *our* new home."

So far away, Wyoming. And yet, so near because Katie waited there. He had been tempted to swing east, just to drop in on Rafter H, to see Matt Hazelwood, and Soapy and Mr. Price. But the Dry Creek range was a hundred miles away, the wrong direction. He had written to Matt about Wyoming and the need for beef up there. Maybe he'd see Matt up there one day.

Coming down from the hillside he crossed a brace of dry washes and runoff gullies, bleach-white limestone eroded in a maze of cuts and ancient runnels, dropping down toward the living stream.

Abruptly the blood bay shied and sidestepped, showing the whites of its eyes. He controlled the animal, then looked to see what had startled it.

Half-hidden in drift under a limestone bank was a scattering of odd shapes, and he squinted, peering at them. There was the eroded remnant of a saddletree, standing half-out of a sand drift, surrounded by mute shapes. He knelt for a better look.

Bones. Bones of a man and bones of a horse. Old, sun whitened bones, scattered by the elements but still contained in a curve of shallow gully. The horse's jawbone . . . it had been seven or eight years old, judging by the teeth . . . lay half-upright, lodged between shards of stone. And back in the shadows under the bank was a human skull.

Tyson removed his hat, kneeling there. "Pard, I wonder what happened to you," he muttered.

Near at hand a precise dark shape protruded from the sand. He brushed sand away from it, then held it up. An old belt buckle, worn and crusted, erosion obscuring its design and the faint marks that had been chiseled into its brass shield. Idly, he turned it over in his hand, then dropped it into his shirt pocket.

"How long have you laid out here, Pard?" he asked the bones. "I bet there's somebody, someplace, that's wondering where you are."

Standing then, he backed away and replaced his hat. Someone's trail had ended here, abruptly, a long time ago. Maybe Indians had killed him. Or outlaws, or lightning or flood. A man and a horse. They fell here and still lay where they fell. He considered burying the bones, but it would accomplish nothing. They had probably been buried a dozen times over the years, buried and exhumed and reburied by the wind and the rains and the changing land. He picked up the blood

15

bay's reins. "Let's go find that water," he said.

It was a limestone bowl between scoured banks, a natural tank fed by a spring. He filled his canteen, then bellied down on warm stone to drink beside his horse. The water was cool and fresh. He splashed his face, dipped his hat and poured water over his head. Beside him the bay's head went up suddenly, ears alert, and it turned.

For a moment Big Jim Tyson didn't notice. *"We know that Wyoming,"* he sang happily, *"will be our new home."* Then a sound caught his attention and he rose to his feet and turned. Twenty feet away a young man stood on a rock, pointing a gun at him. Flat eyes glittered beneath a wide hatbrim, and stringy yellow hair whipped in the wind.

Tyson's hand started toward the gun at his hip, and the younger man's gun flared. He felt the shock of the bullet striking him, slamming him back, heard the roar of the discharge, and then he was falling, tumbling slowly, slowly, white sky creeping past his eyes. Again the man fired, and he felt the bullet burn through him as he fell. Shock like pounding waves roared over him and the world went dim. Remotely he heard the bay's cry, the flurry and clatter of its hooves as it spun and ran. Then dim coolness closed about him and there was nothing else to wonder about, nothing to hope for, no reason to care.

Hard hands dragged the body from the tank, flopping it face-down on limestone outcrop. The gunman stood, turned and called, "I got him, Maynard! Over here!" He crouched, hauling up the tail of the shot man's shirt to expose the belt and

16

wallet beneath. Smiling grimly, he ripped the wallet free and opened it. Beyond him another man came around a shoulder, mounted and leading a second horse.

"Is he dead?" the second one called.

"Hell, yes, he's dead. I shot him twice. He fell in the water. Look at this, will you? Must be three-four hundred here. Did you get a good look at those horses down there?"

The second sat his horse, his head high, scanning the hills around them. "Yeah. Better'n forty head. One man with 'em, is all. A Mex, I think."

The shooter scrambled up and headed for his horse. "Wish you'd seen him fall," he laughed. "Like a horse had kicked him."

"All right. Are you sure he's dead?"

"Of course he's dead. How could he not be dead?" He swung into his saddle, clutching the stolen wallet.

"You ought to make sure," Maynard said. "Shoot him in the head."

"I'm already mounted up," the other complained. Then, "Oh, well, if it makes you happy." He drew his gun again, levelled it at the body by the tank and fired. Tyson's hat flew away into the water, and blood dripped onto white limestone.

Only a silent, circling buzzard heard the shots a few minutes later below the rocks, and it climbed higher as riders pushed a herd of horses eastward, then circled back to swing on gliding wings over the body of Pepe, face down in high grass.

2

For an endless time there was nothing, then a sense of time and place grew slowly, brightening imperceptibly as he floated there, vaguely aware of wind and water, of heat and the buzzing of insects, aware without knowing it of the buzzard circling above.

Whoopee ti yi yo, git along little dogies . . . the tune had no sound. But it hung there around him, lazy and unrelated, a song with no meaning, simply being a song. *We know that Dodge City* . . . no, that was wrong. The song corrected itself. *We know that Wyoming will be our new home.* That was better. It seemed to make some sort of sense that way. And yet, it meant nothing, because there was no one there for it to mean anything to.

Was there? He wondered about that, vaguely. Wind and water, heat and little sounds . . . insects, a shod hoof on stone, dripping of pooled blood into clear water.

Whose blood was it? And why did shadows move

where there were no shadows? Questions came, and with the questions a dim awareness . . . a sense of something needing to be done, or at least considered.

He floated above it all, remote and not wanting to change anything, yet the questions hung there, like the song. *We know that Wyoming will be our new home . . .*

He fought against awareness, because it was associated with intense pain. Better just to float, to ignore everything, to just wait for it all to go away. Yet, it nagged at him. *We know that Wyoming will . . . who knows? I know.*

"Do tell." The voice came from nowhere, and it shattered the world in which he floated. Pieces of reality erupted, then fell together in half-remembered patterns. Immense pain pounded over him and through him, and he lay on hot limestone sticky with his own pooled blood. He clamped his eyes tight-closed as more waves of pain stabbed at him, explosions of agony that seemed to come from everywhere and roil around him. He felt as though he were drowning in pain.

"I swear! I surely thought you was dead." The voice seemed to come from a great distance, but when he eased his eyes open the thing he saw was the toe of a scuffed boot, inches from his face. The boot drew back a step and he refocused and there were two of them . . . scarred, down-at-heel boots with someone standing in them.

"I heard what you was singin'," the man said conversationally. "Do you know the way to Porterville?"

He tried to turn his head, to look upward, and a wall of pain smashed into him. The world before his eyes flared red and dissolved into blackness, and even in the darkness there was the voice, quiet and taciturn.

"You're bleedin' like a stuck pig," it said. "Ought to do somethin' about that. By the way, my name is Clifton Flowers."

Time was an erratic thing then. Sometimes it existed and sometimes not. Odd dreams that might not have been dreams flitted about like insects, each molded around a sound or a sensation. There was heat and motion and coolness and scuffling noises and pain that came in a thousand shades of color. A sensation of effort—someone struggling desperately to reach some goal—shrouded itself in visions of Arabian-cross foals playing on flint hill pastures. That, and terrible thirst which demanded further effort, which brought pain that hid itself under waterfalls that choked him and drowned him again and again as he drank. He fought blindly and was cold. He hurt and was warm again, slowly, and the rhythmic, throbbing pain in the center of him was his heart, beating with exertion.

There was something wrong with . . . what was it? . . . his left arm. Part of what was wrong there was familiar, as though it had been wrong before and he had adjusted to it. But something else was wrong, too, and that was unfamiliar.

He tried to stay out of his head. The pain there was too intense. Each time he approached it time stopped again and then, sooner or later when it returned, he had to start all over.

He saw Katie standing in the valley by the juncture of streams, and she was waving at someone. Who was she waving at? He wondered and didn't know.

Promise me, Jim . . . It was her voice, and the wind sang it to him. *Promise me you'll come back.* He hoped someone had made that promise to her. Maybe someone had. But who? Jim? *Promise me, Jim.* Yes, she said Jim. He reached inside his head, probing, and the pain drove him back. *Whoopee ti yi yo, git along little dogies* . . .

Do you know the way to somewhere? Someone had asked someone that question. Yes. Clifton Flowers asked that question. Scuffed, old, run-over boots, with somebody standing in them, had asked.

Horse country. The flint hills. A valley in Wyoming. *Where?* he tried to say. *I know the way to Wyoming.* Like Pepe knows the way to Mexico, I know the way to Wyoming, because Katie is waiting there . . . for somebody. I tried to go to Chicago once. *We* tried, me and the others, and those wild cows. We didn't make it, but we made money. And money was Mexican mares and Arabian-cross studs from eastern stables, and foals becoming colts on the lush flint hills grass. And then Katie. Money for Katie . . . but then something happened to somebody, and the bones of a man and a horse lay bleached in a limestone draw, and that was the end of that.

He opened his eyes and wondered what had changed. He had to get into his head to think about

22

it, and that hurt, but he persisted this time. He lay on his back on cooling limestone, and his right hand was numb with cold. The sky was huge, a canvas of pastels above him, painted with setting sun. He raised his hand and cool water dripped onto his face. He licked his fingers with a dry tongue, then let his hand go for more water.

Movement caught the corner of his eye and he turned his head, flinching at the pain the motion brought. His blood bay was there, still saddled, and when he saw it he remembered it. At his motion it ambled toward him and stood over him, looking at him curiously.

"Where you been, sport?" he whispered. "Did you try to go to Chicago?" He blinked his eyes. No, that was wrong, he told himself. It was someone else who set out for Chicago, with a herd of wild cows, and it was a long time ago. Matt Hazelwood knew about that. He was there. He was . . . where?

Confusion wheeled about him and he concentrated on the horse. Could he get on that horse and ride? It was a long way to the top of that horse. And where did he want to go?

"I know the way to Wyoming," he whispered, and tried to raise himself on an elbow that wouldn't work right. He gave up and rolled over, fighting the waves of pain. When they receded he clawed at the stone with his good hand, dragging himself around, and raised himself to half arm's length, panting with the effort. Star clusters of pain danced in his chest, and his head ached terribly. Yet he managed to hold on, and after a time he was upright, on his knees, clinging to the horse's front leg. From there he managed to reach the cinch ring and release the latigo, then grabbed the stirrup as he felt himself falling. He went down and the saddle smashed down upon him, and he heard someone scream thinly.

Darkness came and went.

"You're probably wonderin' whether you're dead," a familiar voice said. He raised his head. The man named Clifton Flowers squatted on his heels a few feet away, gazing at him with mild curiosity. A long, lanky man, he seemed as totally in his element here as did the hills around him. Lank hair with bits of gray in it lay about his ears, and his old slouch hat shaded a face that was like old leather, creased and brown, with a nose that had been broken a time or two and pale blue eyes that seemed never to blink.

"By all rights, you ought to be," the man said laconically. "'Cept if you're dead, I don't see why you're hurtin' that way." His gaze shifted to the blood bay. "Nice piece of horseflesh there," he commented. "Looks like a stayer."

Half conscious and aching, he dragged himself from beneath the fallen saddle and waited for the horse to approach him again. When it did, he coaxed its head down and slipped off its bridle. When it raised its head he clung to its muzzle and found himself sitting up, swaying. His chest ached fiercely, and his head felt as though he had been kicked. He found that his sore left arm was bound in a sling, and remembered that it had been broken . . . somewhere, some time. Fresh blood trickled from a hole in him—a long, rough slash

24

just in front of the armpit—seeping through dried blood that clotted his shirt.

"That ain't so bad," Clifton Flowers assured him. "Bullet just scored the meat. It's the one on your head that near done you. That an' the one dead center. *That* bullet was true."

Bullet? Yes. He remembered a face, and a roaring gun. He had been shot. He had been shot dead from twenty feet away. He raised his hand to his aching chest, and the fingers touched something hard there. He fished it from his pocket. An old, crusted-over belt buckle, fresh-creased where a bullet had slammed into it. A buckle from a bone pile.

"Feller did his best to shoot you to pieces," Clifton Flowers suggested. "But he didn't stop to check his work. Your hat's yonder in the water. He figgered it had more head in it than it did, is how come he only creased your skull."

He stared at the taciturn man. "Did you see him? Did you see who it was?"

Flowers shrugged. "I don't know. Might have. Generally I don't pay much attention. But you said you know the way to Wyomin'. Do you, for sure?"

He thought about it, as best he could. "Yeah. Yeah, I think I do. Don't you?"

"Don't seem like it," Flowers shrugged again. "Don't seem like I know the way to much of anyplace, 'cause if I did I'd go there."

"Where?" Confusion hit him again, and trying to think was agony.

"Oh, anywhere," Flowers drawled. "But mainly it seems like I ought to get to Porterville . . . if I can

25

find the way. That's where I'm supposed to be, seems like. Then again, maybe I'll just foller along with you, if you do right."

"I have to get some help," he whispered, fogging over again.

"All right," Flowers said. "You figger out someplace to go to get some help. Anyplace is all right with me. You just do right an' I'll maybe tag along. I ain't in any particular hurry."

He slept then, and woke to exhaustion and dimming pain, tatters of clamoring dreams trailing him from sleep—parading chaotic dreams of Katie's smile, money in a wallet, colts playing in tall grass, cattle on the move, old bleached bones in hidden places and a bent belt buckle.

"He saved my life," he whispered, noticing that his mind was patchworked like a quilt. "That old belt buckle . . ."

He opened his eyes and raised himself on his good arm, fighting dizziness. His bedroll had been lashed to his saddle. Now it covered him, more or less. Had Flowers covered him? He didn't remember. Maybe he had done it himself. Dawn light showed the blood bay grazing nearby where runoff from the tank fed a little stone-enclosed pasture. Flowers was nowhere in sight.

What had happened to him? He recalled having horses . . . fine bred animals to be sold at Three Rivers. A lot of horses, and someone had trailed him for them. Two men. And he had found a scattering of old bones and put a belt buckle in his shirt pocket. A man long dead, bleaching up there in a hidden gully, had saved his life.

He was going to Wyoming. Katie was in Wyoming, waiting. And he had been thinking about going somewhere else first, to see . . . who? Wild cattle . . . open range, herds and drives and money to buy horses . . . Matt Hazelwood! Rafter H was east! So many years had passed. Yet he recalled the look of those brush ranges now . . . someplace he could find help. And someone he didn't know—Clifton Flowers—meant to tag along with him if he would do right. Do what right? Maybe Pepe would know.

Pepe! What had become of Pepe?

Confusion that was like waves of vertigo spun his thoughts around. Do what right? I don't know what that means. I don't know where I am. I don't even know *who* I am. Do I?

Yes, he thought, I know that. And suddenly he did.

"I'm Jim Tyson," he said aloud.

"Pleased to meet you."

He looked around, his head swimming. Clifton Flowers hunkered beside the stone tank, just a few feet away. "You didn't say, before," he pointed out.

"Rafter H is east of here," he said. "Maybe other places, too. I can get help there."

"You know the way?" Flowers asked, not seeming particularly interested.

"I can find it."

"Then you been blessed," Flowers observed. "A man that knows the way to anyplace is a lucky man."

What in blazes was he talking about? It made no sense. But then, not much seemed to now. "You want to go along with me, Mr. Flowers?"

Flowers shrugged. "Long as you know the way."

"He saved my life. That man." Carefully, he dug out the old buckle and looked at it again.

"Who did?"

"That man up there. The bones in that gully. You didn't see them?"

"Nope, can't say as I did."

"This was his buckle. It saved me." He turned his hand to show it, but Flowers was gazing off across the hills. He put the buckle back into his pocket. "I should do something for him. I owe him." He managed to get to his knees, and the world shifted and swam. For a time he knelt there, fighting waves of confusion and dull pain. Distantly he heard Flowers' boots scuffing on rock, and when he looked up again the man had gone off somewhere. Jim Tyson gritted his teeth and began the task of getting to his feet.

By the time the sun was high he had moved around a little, eaten a few bits of food from his pack and quenched his thirst at the tank. Little by little he seemed to be finding the missing parts of his aching head . . . some of them, anyway.

He wished Flowers would show up. At least he might get him to saddle his horse for him. He waited, and was still alone. He tried to hoist the saddle and could barely lift it one-handed. He decided to give it another hour, for his belly to digest the food he had eaten. He needed strength.

Testing his legs, he walked up from the spring,

fell and rested on a shelf, hallucinating, then walked on. Without really having intended to, he arrived at the hidden gully and looked again at the pitiful litter on its sandy floor. A man and a horse. They lived once, he thought. They were here and alive . . . then suddenly they simply weren't, and all that was left to show for it was weather-whitened bones. On impulse he knelt, reached under the stone ledge and lifted out the human skull resting in the sand. The jawbone was gone, but the skull was intact, and it looked at him with eyes that were only bone cavities. Carefully, he scooped a hole and buried it.

He saved my life, he thought again. I owe him.

A darkness closed over him, full of wild dreams and murky images, and then he found himself beside the stone tank again, holding the old buckle in his hand. He put it in his pocket, wondering whose it was.

The horse came to drink, and through a long series of errant times he negotiated with it. Bridle and bit . . . blanket . . . dim wrestling with a saddle . . . bedroll and gear . . . a good horse, well educated. It knew him. Half conscious, he climbed into the saddle. His chest was heaving, and every movement was an agony.

High sunlight quartered behind him when he rode away from the tank, heading east. The steady rhythm of movement was excruciating, but in a way it soothed him and helped to clear his eyes.

He heard footfalls on stone and Clifton Flowers caught up to him, mounted on a scruffy gray horse that had the look of mustang about it. He won-

29

dered where it had been.

"You know where we're goin'?" Flowers asked.

"East," he nodded. "Rafter H is over there somewhere, over on the Dry Creek range."

"Good as any for now," Flowers allowed. "Long as you know the way."

3

On the last day of roundup, Matt Hazelwood rode a tough line-back grulla to the cap of Spanish Mound for a last look at the Dry Creek range. From the mound on a clear day a man could see more than twenty miles in any direction, one and a half thousand square miles of flats and brushlands, low ranging hills to the west and rough breaks to the east, bracketing the range they had worked in the weeks just past.

Dust haze hung in the air to the south—a flat, dun colored cloud that drifted across the land, obscuring the activity out on the grass flats where they were throwing the herds together.

He removed his hat and wiped a sleeve across his eyes, smearing the mask of fine dust and sweat that layered his face from nose to hatline, from ear to ear. The gather had been methodical and thorough, nearly three weeks of eighteen hour days under the south Texas sun, following Sam Price's chuck wagon, riding out in teams mile by mile to work the brush and the draws, hazing cattle out into trail groups, cutting and trail-marking the stock in herds of two to three hundred, then moving each herd toward Spanish Mound and the gather ground and moving on to work another mile.

Ten men, riding five horses each per day, they had done it in a week less time than anyone had expected, and Matt Hazelwood was pleased. It might be two days before the surrounding spreads got their reps in to cut the herd for strays, and by that time there would be damned few unmarked critters for them to argue about. Dave Holley would see to that. Holley was a top hand, and a careful one. Like Gabe Sinclair, he could read a brand or spot an earmark from a hundred yards. Anything out there that didn't sport the Link brand, or Colter's half-dozen town marks or Triple Seven or one of the shotgun outfits' brands, would be Rafter H stock by the time the reps got into them.

Wind across the brushlands beat down the dust haze to the south momentarily and Matt Hazelwood shaded his eyes. The herd was spread loose and easy, grazing over two sections of good grass, a handful of riders working it, just enough to discourage straying beyond reasonable limits. A half-mile eastward, downwind, Holley and the Sinclairs worked the branding camp while drovers shuttled cows, calves and mavericks across from the main spread.

The chuck wagon had made eight miles a day for seventeen days, its path a sweeping double-S track from corner to corner of the Dry Creek range, spanning more than thirty miles from Rafter H to Spanish Mound. In that sweep, 300,000 acres of range had been combed for stock. Most of what was Rafter H or unbranded, and probably a few strays, were down on those flats now, almost ready to move.

Ninety thousand head of cattle, he estimated, had been looked at by Rafter H riders in those seventeen days—Links, Triple Sevens, T-bar-T stock and Colter town brands mainly, with a scattering of Flying X, Rainbow and other shotgun outfits—and about one animal in ten had been choused out onto the grass flats.

Grimly, he recalled the fury on the face of Herman Link when the old man rode out with five men at his back to see what was going on. The Rafter H riders had not been especially careful about how they scattered Link stock in rounding up their own brand. Matt suspected some of them might have gone out of their way to drift Herman's cows as far and wide as possible. It was no secret that Link had arranged to have Rafter H blackballed by the association. Matt Hazelwood and Herman Link had been at war since the spring—since the day Hazelwood drove Herman's sons, Maynard and Rodney, out of the Dry Creek range and promised to hang them if they ever came back.

Tip Curry and Stan Lamont had backed his play, and the boys had never returned. Matt wondered sometimes whether Herman Link's hatred of him was because of losing a pair of outlaw sons, or because he had faced them down, made them turn tail and run.

At any rate, Rafter H was blackballed. When the association ranches rode circle, spring and fall, working their stock, Rafter H was excluded. Herman Link meant to force him out. And he could. On pool range, even a modest range like Dry Creek, no one outfit could afford the cost of working general roundup alone for very long.

Matt had protested the decision, but Link had them in his pocket. So Matt Hazelwood did what they didn't expect. A month ahead of the association's fall circle, he had launched his own roundup. And everything that was not branded became Rafter H. By the time they knew what he was doing, he was half done. Now all they could do was send their reps, cull the strays and count their losses—unless they wanted to make a fight of it. Triple-Seven and Link both had gunhands on their payrolls. They were big outfits, and could pay the wages—though there weren't many who would face Tip Curry.

They might decide to fight. Like on the day Herman Link rode into his camp over at Bear Tanks. Link had been so mad he could hardly talk. He and his five had circled the gather, looking at the fresh brands, then had come in.

"Damn you for a rustler, Hazelwood," he had shouted. "On this range we share the green stock."

"That's an association decision, Link," Hazelwood pointed out. "I'm not association any more.

And if you intend to use the word 'rustler' again, I suggest you either have proof to show or your gun in your hand. Now get out."

Gabe Sinclair had almost started the ball then. He stood beside the wagon, munching on a biscuit, and gazed up casually at the intruders. "Mornin', Mista Link," he said. "Y'all might ought to do somethin' about your critters, 'cause I believe there's a bunch of 'em been wanderin' clean over into th' Nueces range. I seen a lot of 'em with my own eyes, jus' a-hightailin' that direction."

Link turned and stared at him, white-faced.

"Doggonedest thing," Gabe drawled. "I didn' see no other brands strayin' off like that, jus' Link critters. They mus' have a pow'ful urge to wander, do you suppose?"

For a moment Herman Link had sat stone-rigid in his saddle. Link had been a cotton planter years before, and the shock of being baited by a Negro was plain on his face.

Matt's hand hovered at his Colt, ready for anything. But the others had gathered around then, Tip Curry facing them in that quiet way of his, Stan Lamont openly challenging, hand on his gun, Dave Holley and Soapy Green crowding in on them, Sam Price lifting a shotgun from the chuck wagon.

The Link riders looked plainly unhappy.

Herman Link had controlled himself with visible effort. Then he pointed a shaking finger at Matt Hazelwood. "You won't get away with this," he promised. "There will be other times."

35

Matt shook his head. "I don't think so, Herman. The climate in these parts has gone bad. And so has the company. You and the association can have Dry Creek. Rafter H is pulling out."

He had, in fact, been toying with the notion for months. There was nothing for him in the brush country these days, nothing to keep him. He had been content enough in the early years, and the memories were there. Some of them were fine and bright, but those were the older ones.

Like the time when he had moved his first herd. There had been four of them, he and Jim Tyson, Soapy Green and Sam Price. Fresh from the war, footloose and ambitious, they had met in San Antonio. Sam had been about thirty-five then, Matt and Soapy maybe five years younger, and Jim Tyson was a kid of eighteen, but they talked and made the rounds and found things they had in common.

And out of it came the drive. They had worked like slaves and lived like Indians for months, gathering wild cattle from the brushy draws between the granger frontiers and Comancheria. Then with four hundred wild longhorns and twenty-two half-wild mustangs—owning nothing else except the clothes they wore and the guns they carried—they had set out for Chicago, where Soapy assured them their beef would bring at least eight dollars a head.

They had fought their way through East Texas, past paid badges and Yankee patrols, vigilance committees and nightriders. They had snaked those cows through the hills of the territories and Arkansas, often not quite sure where they were, then fought most of the way through Missouri, besieged every step of the way by organized farmers and disorganized outlaws, never realizing until a long time later how fortunate they were that it was not the other way around. They had walked the herd across the Mississippi River on crust ice so thick it never even crackled, then lost half the herd to the northern winter somewhere between Star City and Springfield.

The cows never got to Chicago. They sold the surviving herd at Springfield . . . for thirty dollars a head!

Six thousand dollars, split four ways.

Soapy had lost his share at Cairo, and Sam had taken off for New Orleans. But Matt and Jim Tyson had other ideas. They came back to Texas and started again, this time with a little capital.

They never tried a drive to Chicago again, and they avoided East Texas after that, skirting around past Denison, then up through the Choctaw Nation to parallel the Overland Mail Road, heading for the rails at Sedalia.

They learned about range cows from the devils themselves, and they learned how to work them from the vaqueros they could hire, and most of what they learned came from the doing of it.

Soapy Green showed up again and threw in with them, then Sam Price, never saying a word about New Orleans. They drove stock up to Baxter Springs. They made enough money on that one drive for Matt Hazelwood to buy Texas land and for Jim Tyson to buy Mexican mares and blooded stallions from the east.

When it came to horses, no man could match Jim Tyson. He had a natural way with them, and what he didn't know he picked up from vaqueros along the way.

They fought Comanches, rustlers, hard winters and dry summers, and Rafter H grew.

Those were the days of Matt Hazelwood's memories. But now he looked out from Spanish Mound and little was the same. Times changed. The rules changed and the reasons changed, and a man changed in the process.

Out on the flats, gusting wind flattened the dust again and Matt could see them working at the branding camp. Past the camp was the chuck wagon, and beyond that a rope corral where Ollie Sinclair was sweetening the remuda. Ollie was a hand with horses. The young Negro could short-tail a bronc in an hour and a half if needed, but he took his time with them, and a horse educated by Ollie Sinclair was a cowpony. He was as skilled a wrangler as Matt Hazelwood had found, except maybe for Jim Tyson.

It was Tyson's letter last spring that suggested Wyoming. Jim had been up there, had seen the miners and their need for beef.

With one more long look at the Dry Creek range—stub hills in the distance that were the boundary of Triple-Seven, vague green of willows along the wash where Link began, boundaries that had little meaning because cows didn't care about them, so it was all pooled range—Matt Hazelwood snugged his hat on his head and guided the grulla down from Spanish Mound, to go back to work.

The reps came out a day early, but Rafter H was ready. Pinto Boyd and Lou Campion came representing the Colter town brands, Marcus Flood and Will Bower from T-bar-T, Johnny McGraw and Corky Lassiter from the Dominion Cattle Company which was the Triple-Seven brand, and a few of the shotgun ranchers came representing their own small outfits. They came together, riding out from Colter, led by Herman Link and a pair of gunhands. At a nod from Matt Hazelwood, Tip Curry and Stan Lamont attached themselves to the Link gunnies like shadows, keeping them honest.

All through the day they worked the herd, each team accompanied by a Rafter H hand. The plain cuts numbered a few over two hundred as Dave Holley kept tally, and there were thirty-nine contested marks, most of them town brands that had been poorly burned. Matt Hazelwood looked them over and let them go. And nowhere in the herd did any rider find a Link brand.

Herman Link swung in beside Matt Hazelwood, circling a drift. "I guess you have pulled a fast one on us, Hazelwood," he frowned. "The boys tell me there are nearly a thousand fresh marks in this bunch. That's more than all of us together branded last fall."

"We've all been lazy," Matt told him seriously. "My boys have branded three-year-olds these past

39

weeks. But it's by the rules, Link. You know that."

"I know you've pulled a fast one. At least you think you have. I also know it's a long way to wherever you think you're going with these cows . . . and by rights, they're not all yours."

"I'm no rustler, Link." He turned his mount and halted, studying the older man. There was no friendliness in his eyes, but neither was there any hostility . . . only a hard-bitten acceptance of things past. "Your sons went bad, Link. You know that, just like everybody else. If I hadn't stopped them, somebody else would have."

"You shamed me, Hazelwood. I won't forget that."

"Another man would have hanged them."

The two ranchers stared at each other, but neither had any more to say. Herman Link turned then and rode away, ramrod straight. Some of the reps hung around to sample Sam Price's cooking and drink his coffee while they compared tallies, but Link rode out across the sundown range and never looked back.

In the evening Matt Hazelwood saddled the grulla. He had gone a mile, southeast, when he heard hoofbeats behind him. Soapy Green and Stan Lamont came up to him and pulled in on his flanks.

"Thought you might want company," Soapy said.

It was nearly midnight when they came to the deserted Rafter H headquarters. By moonlight Matt Hazelwood paused at the gate and pried loose

the sign, a slab of weathered plank marked by Jim
Tyson fifteen or sixteen years before. Using a
running iron, the wrangler had inscribed it.

Matt handed the plank to Soapy.

At the house he paused, gazing at its squat
ugliness in the moonlight. Somehow, he knew, this
house had been the death of one of his wives and
the reason the second had left him. The house, the
barren grounds, the cattle business and everything
it meant. It was no life for a woman.

They waited by the old corral while he rode out
to the fenced cemetery and stepped down in the
moonlight. There were eighteen wooden markers
there . . . more than one for each year of the Rafter
H in Texas. He walked among them absently,
tallying them the way a man tallies longhorns . . .
the way a longhorn man tallies everything.

Eva was there, at peace now. And three babies.
Johnny McGraw's brother Al, caught afoot by a
bad bull. Eb Smith, snakebit when he went
barefoot to the outhouse. Will Gillespie, drowned
in a flood. Tommy Ainsworth, Chad Martin and
Pete Furness, gunned down by rustlers. Earl Chase
and Benny Sasson, killed by Comanches. Old Ward
McMann who had died of heatstroke. Lengthy
Simon, the tall wrangler who was kicked in the
head by his best horse. Two with no names, rustlers
caught and hanged, then given Christian burial.
Pedro Chaka, trampled in a stampede during
roundup. And a drifter named Chicken Willie who
had been thrown into a corral rail and died of a
pierced lung.

Matt Hazelwood tallied them in his mind, then put them away. He mounted and rode back to the compound. He found a jug of coal oil in the smithy, and walked across to empty it randomly on the walls and floors of the deserted house. He struck a match and dropped it, then went outside. Soapy handed him the grulla's reins.

Flames licked upward around the window sills. The house breathed prairie air to feed its flames.

"What will be the count?" Matt asked.

"More'n we thought," Soapy said. "Maybe seven thousand. We'll trail count after we get them lined out tomorrow."

"You're the ramrod, Soapy. Let's see how fast we can get through the Outlet and off Dry Creek range."

Seven thousand head of cattle, brush-wild and snuffy. Moss-horns and mavericks, ten million pounds of lethal, erratic meat to be pushed north by ten men. *Seven thousand cows!*

Cold fingers of uncertainty touched him. He had underestimated himself and his outfit. Reacting to the association blackball, and to Link's constant prodding, he had launched an all-out sweep of the Dry Creek Range. "Let's get 'em all," he had told his men. But somehow he hadn't counted on them pitching in like they did.

He was proud of them, every one. Yet now he wondered what he had gotten them into. Gathering seven thousand cows was one thing. Driving them would be something else.

It dawned on him that, except for Soapy and

42

Sam Price, the rest did not even know where they were going. They rode for the brand, and none of them had ever asked.

Could ten men push seven thousand cows from south Texas to Wyoming? He didn't know. It had never been tried.

4

The flare was a beacon. In the town of Colter, nine miles to the east, Pinto Boyd stepped out of Paisley's place and saw the glow in the sky. He walked out into the rutted street, away from the lamplight of Paisley's window, tipped back his hat and cocked his head, staring out across the dark miles. Rafter H was burning.

At first he thought of Herman Link. But, he realized, it would have gained nothing for Link to fire Hazelwood's abandoned headquarters. The place was already abandoned, and Link was as likely as anyone to move in and establish a claim by possession. It would give him a bigger share in the range pool. He wouldn't burn the buildings. He would move men into them. For that matter, anyone who decided to pick up Rafter H would need those buildings. So who had fired them?

The flame was a tiny spot of brilliance on the horizon, crowned by an orange glow that seemed to light the whole range.

For that matter, Pinto Boyd thought, where did it say that Link had first grab on the Rafter H holdings? Matt Hazelwood had not sold out. He had simply pulled up stakes and abandoned the place. By this time tomorrow he would be long gone with his herd, and there would be a spread just sitting out there, waiting for someone to say it was his and make it stick.

Where did it say that only the big spreads had the right to claim? Anybody could claim, who had stock on the range. And as one of the partners in the Colter Town Cattle Company, Pinto had stock. Not much, but some. That, and the firepower to hold the claim.

Pinto Boyd had never been long on ambition. He had been on both sides of the law in his time. He had done some jack-leg rustling up on the Brazos, and had helped Walt Strickland knock over the bank at Cedarville, and no one the wiser. But it had all been penny-ante. Then after Strickland and three of his gunnies were hanged at Post Oak, Pinto had decided on another kind of life. He had hired on as a deputy over in Harris County, had run for sheriff twice, first in Harris and then in Fort Bend, then run afoul of the Frazer brothers and left that part of Texas in the dead of night. He had worn a star for a few months at Lewiston, and put lead into the wrong man there. Eventually he had drifted to Colter. Being town marshal paid a dollar a day and a cut of the fines. Still penny-ante.

But now, looking across the night-dark miles at distant fireglow, a new idea came to Pinto Boyd. Who was to say that he couldn't have what Matt

46

Hazelwood had? Who was to say that he couldn't have his own brand? That was where the money was. The ranchers had it. Even the little shotgun spreads were better off than Pinto's dollar a day and cut. And the big ones—those with spreads like Link and Triple-Seven and the rest—those men made their own rules. With Rafter H and some luck, he could be one of them. He could claim a share of the pool, and with some gunnies behind him he could make it stick. He could pick up some cattle somewhere—why, supposing Hazelwood got stampeded and lost a couple of thousand, who was to say they weren't abandoned stock? It would be easy to find some hardcases to back him up if the other spreads contested his claim. Who knew better than a lawman where to look for hardcases? He could send Garth to stampede that wild herd. . . .

Pinto Boyd stood alone on the dark street of Colter, gazing at a spark on the horizon, and the spark seemed to become a fire within him. Why not? he asked himself. Why in hell not?

Thirty miles away, to the west, Herman Link climbed to his captain's walk and extended a telescope to study the glow to the east. Rafter H headquarters was burning. Hazelwood had probably done it himself, he decided . . . one last insult. The man would know that he planned to recoup some of his losses by expanding to Rafter H, and burning the buildings just made it that much harder for him.

A hard resolve formed in his mind. He had no intention of letting Hazelwood get away with those cattle, but he could wait. It would take days for

Hazelwood to push those cows past the Outlet . . . and the boundary of Dry Creek range law. Beyond was no law that mattered to Herman Link—a few local sheriffs, but they didn't interfere in trail disputes. They knew better. He ached to get started. He employed four gunhands on Link, just in case he should need them, and they seldom earned their keep. Hazelwood had Tip Curry, but Curry was only one man.

But he put it aside, for now. Looking at the fire reminded him, if he were going to claim Hazelwood's abandoned spread, he needed men over there. That's where the gunnies need to be, he decided. He didn't really think anybody was going to contest his claim. Link was the largest and most powerful of the near neighbors, and he had adjacent boundary. Still, it wouldn't be good business to put it off. So he had need of all his men. Between the daily work of keeping the place up, and the need to send every hand he could mount out to pick up his drifted stock and turn it back in time for the pool circle, and the job of claiming Rafter H's spread, he had no men to spare. Hazelwood would be there when he was ready.

Nearly a day's ride northeast, Corky Lassiter was just putting a tired horse away when one of the nighthawks came in and told him about the fire. He had seen it from the top of Wild Horse Mesa. It was at Rafter H.

Corky mulled it over in his mind, then went up to the big house and rapped on the door. Most of the household was asleep, but a lamp burned in Colonel Nelson's office window.

When Conchita came sleepy-eyed to let him in and escort him to the Colonel's room, Corky dusted his britches with his hat and followed her.

The Colonel was an Englishman, one of three partners in the Dominion Cattle Company. The Triple-Seven was only one of several spreads they owned. Nelson was a remote, severe man with drooping mustaches and pale eyes that never told a man a thing. Corky Lassiter was uncomfortable in his presence, but he cleared his throat and made his report as concisely as he knew how. Rafter H was pulling out, with maybe seven thousand head, more than a thousand of them fresh brands. Hazelwood and his crew had swept the range clean. And now Rafter H headquarters was burning.

Colonel Nelson blinked. "Burning?"

"Yes, sir," Corky nodded. "The ranch headquarters. There's a fire down there."

"I see." Nelson frowned at him. "Why are you telling me this, Mr. Lassiter?"

"Well, sir," Corky fumbled his hat, thoroughly uncomfortable. "There's talk that Mr. Hazelwood has pulled up stakes . . . that he's abandoning his spread and his pool claim, and won't be coming back. And now that fire . . . well, sir, you know there's bad blood between him and Mr. Link. So I figure maybe Mr. Hazelwood fired the place, just out of spite, so as not to leave anything standing for Mr. Link to claim."

"Reasonable assumption," Nelson admitted. "So?"

"So . . . well, sir, I was just wonderin' . . . if Rafter H is up for claim, well, why should it be Link that claims it? I mean, why not Triple-Seven?

49

It's part of the pool, and you have as much right to claim as anybody, I guess."

The Colonel was silent for a moment. Then he nodded. "Most commendable, Mr. Lassiter. Of course it warrants consideration." The pale eyes fixed him abruptly. "Do you have something special in mind?"

"Well, just that there might be trouble, of course, but sir, I know this range. Let me have my pick of the crew, and I think we could occupy Rafter H and hold it long enough to establish a claim for you."

"I see." The Colonel looked thoughtful. "And then?"

"Well, sir . . . ah . . . well, I *am* a top hand, sir. Johnny McGraw will tell you that. And if Triple-Seven *was* to take over Rafter H, well, there isn't any adjoining boundary, so you'd have to have two headquarters. And . . . well, sir, then you'd need another foreman. And I believe I'd make you a good one, sir."

Eighteen miles southeast of Triple-Seven, on a hill behind the corrals of T-bar-T, Marcus Flood stood watching the glow in the distant sky. Will Bower had awakened him by pounding on the door, and now he was dressed in hat, boots, gunbelt and nightshirt, standing on a hilltop watching a fire. And the more he looked at it, the more certain he became that he had been a fool. They had all been fools. Herman Link had bulldozed them and got them to blackball Hazelwood, so that Hazelwood had moved out, and now Link was moving in to claim Rafter H. The fire was probably a haystack or something, Link's declaration to the world that Rafter H was his and the rest of them were out in the cold.

"I'll be damned if we are," he muttered. "If anybody is gonna grab anything around here, it's gonna be T-bar-T doin' the grabbin'."

He turned on his heel and strode off toward his headquarters. Herman Link would find out what it took to hold a spread against T-bar-T.

In the dark hills that bordered the Dry Creek range on the west, rough men came awake and gazed eastward at the flare on the horizon. Killers and rustlers, predators who roamed the badlands because there were good places to hide out, who lay in wait for cattle herds to spook and cut or for lone travelers to waylay, they stared now at a distant fire and wondered what it was. One thing they agreed on: where there was fire, sometimes there were easy pickings.

By the light of the outlaw moon, they saddled their mounts and headed out, snaking down toward the wide range, going to have a look.

As the three riders neared the bed ground, Stan Lamont turned to look back. The blazing ranch was clearly visible, even from here.

"Sure is somethin' to see, ain't it?"

Soapy Green glanced back, then turned to Matt Hazelwood. "That sure is some bonfire you left back there. Any particular reason?"

Hazelwood didn't look back. He rode straight-backed and brooding, his eyes fixed on the shadow forms of cattle here and there, night-bunched and ready for travel. In the distance somewhere, they heard Bo Maxwell singing to the herd.

"Interesting thing about fire," Hazelwood said. "People just can't help looking at it, and the more a man looks at fire the spookier he gets. Folks looking at fire think all kinds of things, and the more it makes them think, the harder it is to take their eyes off of it. You know, I wouldn't be surprised if there were folks around thinking about these cows we have here, and how busy ten men can be trying to move a green herd, much less a herd this size. There might even be folks that would make problems for us."

"So why the fire?" Soapy had known Matt Hazelwood long enough to know that whatever he said, there would be a point to it . . . eventually.

"Fire doesn't generally make folks think about cows. Fire makes them think about property. How many folks do you suppose there are around here, that wouldn't mind having a piece of a nice pool range?"

Soapy thought about it. "I just figured Link would take up claim on the spread," he shrugged.

"Maybe. But maybe some others might be interested, too. Anyway, when there's fire, people go to it and look at it. Anybody who's busy looking at a fire isn't going to be looking at a herd of cows."

Soapy thought about it again. "I guess you know you could have just started a range war, Matt."

Hazelwood glanced at him. "There's just no accounting for what people might do," he admitted.

"But whatever happens next, it will be back there. Where we're going is the other way."

In the hour before dawn, Dave Holley came awake and lay for a moment orienting himself to his surroundings. It was a still morning, dry and cool. Stars by the hundreds spangled a cloudless sky, and what breeze there was carried the warm scent of amassed cattle, still bedded, a half mile out on the holding flats. Nearer at hand, there was an occasional waft of coffee boiling, bacon frying, and the quiet sounds of Samuel Price and Nacho Lucas hustling breakfast at the wagon.

Quickly and by habit, he identified the sounds and scents, read the message of the breezes and did a quick review of who was where and what was going on. Tip Curry and Jesus Gomez would be on the herd now, with Gabe Sinclair circling farther out, crooning softly, reminding the cattle that they were not alone. Nearby he heard the rustling of a tarp being rolled, and knew that Soapy Green was awake. Matt Hazelwood also would be up by now, either studying his day-chart by firelight or, maybe, already out at the herd, circling with Gabe Sinclair. Ollie Sinclair would be out with the remuda, moving among the horses, talking to them.

Dave recounted his own string and decided on the little steeldust for his sunup mount. What the steeldust lacked in size, it made up in cow-sense. And for the first morning of a drive, throwing a wild herd off bed grounds and stringing it out for the trail, he wanted a real cowpony under him.

He peeled back blankets, sat up, and put on his hat. It would be a good day for driving. He shook out his boots, snugged them on his feet, then stood, pulled on a wool shirt and tucked it into his britches, put on his old leather vest—it was cool now, but the day would heat up—and strapped on his gunbelt, hauling out his Colt by reflex to get its heft and thumb-check its loads.

Around him, others were coming awake. A short distance away, men were silhouettes around the lantern on the box of Sam Price's chuck wagon. Stan Lamont was breaking out coils of rope to stake a catch corral for the remuda when Ollie brought them in.

He made up his bed, packed and rolled it, hoisted it to his shoulder and walked to the wagon to toss it aboard. Sam Price was pulling fresh biscuits out of the dutch oven, each biscuit the size of a man's fist. Nacho was frying sliced bacon, mounding it on a tin on the tailgate. Dave helped himself to a biscuit, broke it open and layered a half pound of bacon between its halves. "Is that coffee ready, Mr. Price?"

The old cook glanced up at him. "Check it out yerself," he said. "Toss a horseshoe in the pot, see if it floats."

Dave grinned. It had always been Sam Price's contention that the best way to spoil good coffee was to be too generous with the water. With his breakfast in one hand and a tin cup of scalding, strong coffee in the other, he lounged against a wagon wheel while he ate.

Bo Maxwell strode into the lamplight, knuckling

sleep from his eyes. He had worked nightherd until four hours earlier. Dave nodded at him. "Mornin', Bo. You look a little bent out of shape. Tryin' to carry a tune for a bunch of cows all night can do a man in."

"I can think of things I'd rather try to carry a tune for," the younger man said. "But that ain't the problem. It's plain worry that's doin' me in."

"What are you worryin' about?"

"Why, I been tossin' and turnin', tryin' to figure out how to keep from tellin' y'all that today is my birthday."

Dave sipped scalding coffee. "Is today your birthday?"

Bo gazed at him with eyes the color of innocence. "No. Where'd you get a notion like that?" He tossed his bedsack into the wagon and went to get his breakfast, while Dave Holley choked on his coffee.

At first light, a faint paling of the eastern sky, Ollie Sinclair brought in the remuda and Stan Lamont helped him push them into the rope corral. Dave went for his catch rope and returned, eyeing the milling horses until he spotted the steeldust. He formed his loop, a tight four-foot circle of rope thumbed tight against the honda, and waited for the steeldust to circle the rope corral. As it approached him again he spun the loop once in a fast hoolihan catch and dropped it expertly over the horse's head. The steeldust shied once, then stood, and when he took up slack it came sedately to him. It was one of Ollie Sinclair's educated horses, and the black wrangler knew his business.

Saddled up and set for the day, Dave rode out toward the herd, marveling at the sea of cattle out there on the flats. As a top hand, he had worked plenty of drives for Matt Hazelwood, but nothing ever of this magnitude. Soapy Green had tallied more than seven thousand critters after the cuts. Dave Holley had never seen a drive of more than two thousand head before. He wondered how they were going to manage seven thousand head.

But then, as Soapy had said, "It don't matter how many critters it is, a herd's a herd. All we got to do is take these seven thousand of God's gentle creatures and make a herd out of 'em . . . and don't let them kill too many of us in the process."

In pink dawn he entered the bedding ground and walked the steeldust among them. Here on the flats, in among the cattle in uncertain dawn light, they were a sea of shuffling, grazing forms, bunches and clusters and singles, skittering aside as he passed, tossing great horned heads and lowing their dumb protest at his presence.

A big, slab-sided longhorn pawed sod and threatened him, then lowered its head and lunged, angling its head to spear a four-foot shaft of sharp horn toward the bulk of horse and rider. The steeldust pivoted and dodged nimbly aside, then turned at its rider's leg pressure and went on.

Make a herd of them, Soapy said. Well, they weren't a herd yet. At the moment, they were seven thousand lethal brutes, most of them brush-wild and salty.

Angling through the bed ground, he met Matt Hazelwood and Gabe Sinclair and fell in with

56

them, heading back toward the chuck camp.

The others were saddled and waiting for them.

They gathered, all but Sam Price and Nacho Lucas who were battening the wagon and hitching its team.

"Soapy's the ramrod," Hazelwood told them. "On the trail, you take orders from him. Dave," he turned to Holley, "you take first point. Did you spot a lead critter?"

"I reckon," Dave nodded. "A big brindle longhorn, back yonder. He's full of piss and vinegar. I guess he'll do."

"All right. See if you can chouse him out without milling the herd. Get out there about half a mile and keep his attention. We'll bring the rest of 'em to you."

Holley touched his hatbrim and reined the steeldust. Behind him he heard Soapy Green calling off herd assignments:

"Gabe Sinclair and Stan Lamont, work swing. I'll back you until they get lined out, then I'll ride point 'til we come up with Dave and his angel. Bo Maxwell and Jesus Gomez, ride flank. And spread wide, 'cause this ain't any bunch of kitchen cows you got to funnel. Tip Curry, you and Nacho head out down there to work drag. Start 'em nice and easy. No hurry about it. Just get it into their heads that it would be a nice idea if they'd sort of point north. If any of them break and run, just notice where they went. We'll come back and get them later. Everybody set? All right, let's line 'em up and move 'em out!"

Dave grinned, heading back into the massed

57

bedding ground. What with Sam Price busy with the wagon, and Ollie Sinclair tending his remuda, Soapy Green was fixing to begin the process of turning seven thousand critters into a trail herd, with seven riders to do it.

It didn't seem right, somehow. Those boys had a thousand cows apiece to manage, and he had only one.

But then, all they had to do with their thousands was just sort of point them north and thin them out in a line. He and one longhorn steer were going to get better acquainted than that. By the time the herd came up, he had to have that mossback broke of sucking eggs and ready to act like a leader of cows.

5

When Dave Holley had his irritated longhorn well away from the herd, the steeldust dancing around it, baffling its attacks and keeping it moving, the rest split up. With Gabe Sinclair and Stan Lamont at his sides, Soapy rode wide around the bed grounds to the north. They spread there, Gabe dropping off at what would be the east point of a shield of riders, Soapy taking position at its center, almost a quarter mile away, and Stan going on another quarter mile to become the west point.

They stayed far out from the waking cattle, not alarming them, merely establishing a presence of moving mounted men out on the flats, riding back and forth, occupying an arc of almost two miles.

The rest went south. Jesus Maria Gomez dropped off about mid-point of the herd, young Ignacio Lucas farther back, well past the flank of the main bunch. Matt Hazelwood gave himself center drag position, and rode to a point due south of the mass of cattle. From there Tip Curry and Bo

59

Maxwell continued, Tip to drop off at the west flank, opposite Nacho Lucas and almost a mile away, Bo going on around to a position west of the herd.

The area they ringed was more than a square mile, and contained the bulk of the herd. In the time it took for the upwinders to get around the herd, those already dropped off began the job of throwing scatter bunches back into the main herd, horses and men working patterns of drive on wide areas of the grass flats, beginning to push them, to close them up, to persuade them to bunch . . . always drifting them inward and northward. Here and there a few broke and ran, and they let them go for the time. The flats were wide and they could recover them later, once the herd was formed.

A half-dome of brilliant sun stood above the eastern breaks when they began their concerted push. Matt Hazelwood on his grulla staked out a widening half-mile of territory south of the herd, riding in long sweeps, a lope that sometimes became a gallop, pushing the cattle inward and forward, turning them, making them move. To the east and west, Nacho Lucas and Tip Curry were doing the same, riding extended arcs that closed tighter and tighter against the mass of cattle, pushing them forward and inward. On the flanks, each aboard his best cowpony, Jesus Maria and Bo rode fast zigzags along the flanks of the herd, worrying them, crowding them.

Slowly, inexorably, by twos and sixes and hundreds, the cattle began to move, crowding in on those ahead, narrowing down and lining out as the flankers increased their pressure, beginning to funnel from a bedded herd to a narrowing line. And as they narrowed and moved, Soapy Green pulled back, still presenting a worrisome presence ahead, but stopping just short of anything a cow might interpret as a direct threat. To the east and west of him the swing riders, Stan and Gabe, closed in and began a series of dashes diagonally, narrowing the herd still more, throwing them in upon themselves.

The great, bedded herd drew in upon itself and edged northward, becoming a teardrop of bawling, shuffling beef, extending a bubble toward the north, the bubble becoming a point.

By the time the sun was well above horizon, the herd was a thinning oval, most of them facing north, those on the front perimeter stretching out toward the prancing Soapy Green. Minute by minute, those out front were on the verge of stampede. But always, just short of running, they were cut off by swing riders. And always there was a mounted man directly ahead, not too close, but confusing and worrying them. They were surrounded by riders, pushing from three sides and retreating from the fourth. They moved that way. One of the things they had to learn was to follow a rider.

Far out on the flats, Dave Holley saw the herd beginning to bunch and move, and he swore at himself for his choice of a lead steer.

He was tired and sore, sweat-stained and bloody from a fall, and the little steeldust was lathered and heaving. The longhorn had given up all thought of getting away from him. It knew now that it couldn't escape. So its entire bovine attention now was focussed on killing him. And it had come close, several times. Twice he had drawn his gun, ready to shoot the critter if he had to. The steeldust bled from a horn-cut on its haunch, and its rider's leg on that side was bruised and throbbing.

The horse dodged another charge, and Dave unslung his catchrope. "I didn't intend to bust you, you damned wall-eyed road turkey!" he shouted at the steer. "But you ain't left me a hell of a lot of choice, is how I see it!" Stupid thing didn't even know it was a steer, he thought. He'd seen bulls easier to get along with. This critter seemed to think it still had its oysters.

The beast snorted and pawed, then lowered its head for another charge.

"All right, dammit!" Dave snarled, shaking out his loop. "Come ahead on and get yourself busted. We ain't got any more time to waste on you!"

The steer charged, head down, going for the horse's belly. At the last instant the steeldust danced away, and Dave brought its head around in a haunch-down turn and spurred hard after the hurtling steer. Before it had a chance to slow, he was on it, above it, whipping its rump with his loop, shouting curses. The animal's charge became a race to escape. Anger turned to panic, and it stretched long legs in a belly-down run. He held to its flank and drove it on . . . then veered aside, swung his loop backhand and dropped it under the steer's front feet. At the touch of reins the cowpony skidded to a halt.

Rope played out, tightened and sang. The steer's

chin hit the hard ground as its back legs overran it, and it somersaulted to land flat on its back. The sudden pull on the rope almost jerked the pony off its feet, and Dave clung to his saddle.

A moment passed in heaving silence, then Dave squared his seat on the saddle and edged the steeldust forward, wrapping slack on his line. The steer lay still, legs up, head turned back, one horn propped like a fencepost holding it at an impossible angle.

He rode to it, reached down to retrieve his loop from its forefeet, and rubbed his hand across his stained face. "Just had to do it, didn't you?" he accused. "Had to make me bust you, and I guess I busted your neck while I was about it. Now I'm goin' to have to find another piss and vinegar critter and start all over, and Sam Price will have to cut you up for chuck, and there won't be any more biscuits and bacon for breakfast 'cause we're all gonna be livin' on sonofabitch stew."

Angry and defeated, he snugged his coiled catchrope on its hornstring, patted the steeldust on its neck, and turned away. Not so distant now, the herd was in motion—at least the point of it was—coming toward him, Soapy Green out ahead of the bunch, bringing them on.

Dave felt deeply embarrassed. Mr. Hazelwood had sent him out to educate a lead steer . . . not to kill it. And what was Ollie Sinclair going to say about the steeldust? At twenty-eight years of age, Dave Holley took pride in being a top hand. He had worked for it, he had sweated for it and he enjoyed it. He was the equal of any stock hand, anywhere. He was a top hand. But this . . . killing a steer by busting it, and riding a good cowpony to a lather because he couldn't outsmart a stupid longhorn . . . this was kid stuff. At that moment he felt no better than the rankest greenhorn, and he was ashamed.

Still, there was nothing to do but face up to it, and try again.

The steeldust's ears came up. It turned its head, looked back and shied violently, and Dave's hackles rose at the snort from just behind him. In a single motion he drew his Colt and swung around, aligning it . . . then raised its barrel and let the hammer down carefully.

The steer was tagging along, placid as a housepet, content simply to follow him wherever he went. It had met its master and changed its attitude.

"Sonofabitch," he muttered, trying to quiet the steeldust. "I'd have sworn that you was dead."

Now the herd began to stretch out, a giant hammer of meat on the hoof, its handle in motion, lengthening northward, its head a condensing, tightening mass harassed by sweeping riders. The animals out in front, trudging toward the elusive and worrisome Soapy Green, still were a wall of beef a hundred yards across, but Stan Lamont and Gabe Sinclair worked them inward, paring them down. Both were seasoned swingmen, well-mounted on sturdy ponies chosen for speed and endurance. They raced along the lengthening column, swinging manila coils and shouting, their presence a fury of sight and sound just beyond each cow's instinctive defense perimeter. The cattle pranced, closed tighter in column, lowed and tossed horned heads . . . and began to get the idea of following those in front of them.

On the downwind side Gabe pulled a bandana high on his nose and blessed his little brother for the sweet responses of the short-hocked bay beneath his saddle. It was a cowpony.

He could barely see Soapy Green, working point on the fresh herd, holding the leaders from running, and when he looked back he could hardly see Jesus Gomez riding flank. They were much too far apart. There should have been a drover every hundred yards or so, not every quarter mile.

If anyone other than Matt Hazelwood had told Gabe Sinclair that ten men were going to move a herd of seven thousand snuffy brush snakes, he wouldn't have believed it. He completed a sweep, calling on all his cow sense to put him at the right place at the right time, and turned to head back. Behind him a steer broke ranks and hightailed for parts unknown. He turned again, circling and waving them back, barring the way of any others who might be tempted to follow. He didn't know how many they had lost just in getting the herd started. Dozens, at least. Maybe a hundred or more. But the task right now was "hold what you have," and the bunch-quitters would have to wait. The line bulged toward him as Stan Lamont pressed from the other side, and he swept in, yelling and waving, throwing them back.

"Don't go to runnin'," he breathed. "Y'all's God's critters, so just act right, an' runnin' ain't right."

A clot of cattle far too dense was coming at him

now, a society that had formed on the bed ground and intended to travel as a club. "Cows," he muttered, swinging the bay.

He saw Jesus Gomez coming up fast from flank, to help him narrow the clot. Across the herd Stan Lamont and Bo Maxwell were doing the same.

From middle drag, Matt Hazelwood couldn't see what was going on ahead. But he knew, from the shrinking of the drag mass, from those beginning to fall into step, from the increasing prevalence of tails instead of horns facing him, that the herd was moving. And when he saw Tip Curry and Nacho Lucas swing out around the flanks, working wide, he knew that his flankers, Bo and Jesus, had gone forward to help with the narrowing. He was satisfied. Out of seven thousand cows, at least six thousand now were pointed north and walking. He backed off from the drags and widened his sweeps, alone for the moment with the bulk of the herd.

He glanced back. They had left the bed ground. Not yet fully strung out, the herd was nonetheless in motion, and some of the drags had begun to notice that. It made them edgy. Here and there among the crush of them, some were taking a notion to turn back.

Where there should have been at least three riders, for the moment there was only one. He hung back, watching them warily, reading their minds, staying on the move. Too little pressure now, and a lot of them might abruptly turn and spill back toward the bed ground. Too much pressure and the herd could split and run. There were no "holdups" in this herd—no tame cattle thrown among them to calm and reassure them, to show them the way. These were brush cattle, wild animals whose instincts for herd and trail were nearly forgotten. This first mile was critical. It would take a lot of days to get the herd anything like "trail-broke," but that was still in the future. What counted now was to make them be a herd.

From south Texas to Wyoming was a long, long way.

Over in the left drag, a few were trying to turn. They were getting snuffy. He aimed the grulla that way at a lope. Across the broad mass of cowflesh he saw Tip Curry reining around. Tip had seen it, too. Suddenly, in left drag, hundreds of cattle were beginning to mill.

Off to the east, Nacho Lucas was coming around the herd, riding fast to pick up middle drag.

Slowly and carefully, Matt guided the grulla in among the cattle, aiming for the center of the slow, swirling vortex of motion that was the mill—a hundred tons of beef going around in circles. Tip was doing the same from the other side, and beyond him Bo Maxwell was swinging around the perimeter to sweep up and turn the stock that spilled.

By the time they broke the mill, several dozen head had broken free of the drag and were scattering on the flats. But now the drag was in motion, animals lining out to follow the beaten path of those who had gone before.

Nearly a mile to the east, Samuel T. Price drove the chuck wagon northward, Ollie Sinclair coming along behind with the remuda. Unlike the cattle,

Ollie's riding stock were under good control, content to follow the pinto mare tied to the trailing stove cart. As he drove, Price looked out across the flats at the panorama of cattle in the distance and shook his head. He was surprised they had gotten them moving at all, but there they were, stringing out, a distant, massive worm of dark bodies shrouded in dust haze, drovers working alongside, darting back and forth in erratic bursts of speed.

He could see neither the head of the drive nor the tail of it. It seemed to just go on and on, and Price felt a deep, nagging concern. Though Matt Hazelwood would never say so, Price knew the Rafter H owner was surprised at the sheer number of cattle they had gleaned from the Dry Creek range.

They had talked it over—he and Matt and Soapy—and Price knew that none of them had expected anything like this herd. He, personally, had calculated before the roundup that they might wind up with three thousand head or a few more, and he suspected Matt had thought the same . . . maybe two-thirds of those the Rafter H had under brand, and a few hundred new marks. But this . . . !

Even with the drags still lining out, the herd was more than two miles long. In all his fifty years, Sam Price had never seen anybody try to move a herd of this size. The largest pooled herd ever moved off Dry Creek, aiming at the railroad at Dodge City, was just over two thousand head . . . and that had been with twenty-three drovers working out of two wagons.

They had talked about signing trail hands—

at least a few extras—a few days ago when they saw how it was going to tally. They had thought about it, but somehow they hadn't done it. Sheer cussedness, maybe, he thought. It just seemed so right, that Rafter H on its own had scoured the range ahead of the blackballers, that Rafter H crew and nobody else had shown all the rest of them how to do a gather, that Rafter H didn't need anybody else's help . . . they had convinced themselves—all of them—that it was true.

But that herd out there . . . seven thousand, they had rough-tallied, and they had grinned and winked at one another and enjoyed the gaping reps who came out to see. But seven thousand—seventy knots on a tally-string—was just a number.

It wasn't a tally-string he was looking at now, not a vague number. He was looking at what would be three miles of cows when they were all strung out. And not a critter among them broke to trail.

We're all crazy, Samuel T. Price decided. We are as crazy as a bunch of loons.

6

Of all the crew of Rafter H, only Tip Curry drew
gunhand's wages. Matt Hazelwood had offered
them after Tip's first Rafter H drive, and Tip had
agreed.

That had been a pool drive to Dodge City, five
years before. Tip Curry had been nineteen at the
time, a fair drover and rough-string rider who
had drifted down from the territories riding grubline, then had signed on with Rafter H. A quiet,
rawboned kid, whipcord slim and soft-spoken, he
never talked about how he went adrift. He rarely
talked much at all. The hand-worn Colt .45 at his
hip was no different from the hoglegs most Texas
hands carried, and there was nothing especially
noticeable about him unless it was his dark, curly
hair and a pair of wide, brown eyes that women
always seemed to notice. But there was a quality
about the youngster that Matt Hazelwood noticed
early on, and watched carefully. It was just a way

71

he had about him—the way his eyes never turned away when he faced a man, but seemed to be measuring distance and reflex.

They had taken the trail with twelve hundred head and a mixed crew from Rafter H, T-bar-T and Link, five drovers from each ranch and Triple-Seven providing the chuck wagon, cook and wranglers, with Hazelwood as ramrod for the pool.

West of the territories, in No Man's Land, rustlers had hit them just before dawn. Tip Curry had been on night-herd at the time, along with a T-bar-T hand named Willis. Willis had been thrown in the stampede, and trampled. But Curry had stayed with the herd.

They had found him three hours after sunup, holding eight hundred and fifty cattle in a box draw. Between the camp and that draw they found three dead stampeders, and two more right in the mouth of the draw where they had tried to put Tip Curry down.

The kid was a gunhand.

They had retrieved those cattle, bedded them under tight guard, then spent three days finding and bringing back another two hundred and fifty . . . and a pair of bruised and hog-tied rustlers that Stan Lamont and one of the Link hands caught crossing the Beaver with branded stock. They hanged the rustlers side by side from a wagon tongue, then pushed the drive to Dodge City eighty-six head short.

Tip Curry was twenty-four now. He wasn't quite the cowhand that Dave Holley was, or Gabe

72

Sinclair. He wasn't as big and mean as Stan Lamont, nor as deadly quick as the kid, Ignacio Lucas, and he probably wasn't a better shot than half the others in the outfit. But he was a gunhand. The difference was simple. Another man might hesitate to shoot. Tip Curry did not.

It was why he rode drag now. If trouble came—gun trouble—it likely would come from behind.

Matt watched him now, as the drags thinned down and the great herd put its first plodding miles behind it. With the herd behaving itself for a time and the press of throwing them onto the trail relieved, Curry now hung back, spending part of his time keeping an eye on their backtrail.

Matt didn't expect trouble of that sort, at least not this soon, but Tip drew gunhand wages and he was doing his job. The rancher's eyes twinkled when he noticed that young Ignacio Lucas—Nacho—was also keeping an eye on Tip Curry and was mimicking his moves. It was just the way that Tip Curry had mimicked Matt Hazelwood's moves in the first year or two that he worked for him.

The sun was high, and Matt noticed that the grulla was beginning to fade. It had been a long time since he'd worked a horse this hard.

Ahead of him, the beeves moved steadily but raggedly, most of the run worked out of them now, but still wanting to stray more than they wanted to follow.

Soapy's plan was to push them to water at Sands Hole by midafternoon, then a few more miles to high ground and bed them dry and loose, with good graze. They wouldn't be much easier to start tomorrow than they had been today, and pushing them off water after bedding them would be more than any outfit could handle.

And even though the outfit was critically short-handed, Soapy meant to drive those cows hard. It would be several days before they were off Dry Creek range, and the ramrod planned to make it in as short a time as possible. If they could cover sixteen or eighteen miles a day, that was what he intended to do.

It would be hard on the cows. They would lose weight and they would drive spooky. But they would be less likely to spook on the bed grounds at night if they were exhausted. Until they got through the strip of range known as the "outlet," the last stretch of Dry Creek claim, Soapy meant to keep them that way.

If it would be hard on the cows, it would be hell on the men and their horses. But it was the best plan he had. Matt had no argument with it. He had played a fast game with the association, and he knew that some of them would react once they got the new rules straightened out. He wanted to be well away when they did.

Off to his right, Soapy Green appeared out of the downwind haze and hauled in next to Nacho Lucas, gesturing. Lucas nodded, reined his mount around and headed east. Soapy was on a fresh mount, a long-winded gray from his string. He choused a few laggers, dressing up the rear flank of the drag, then worked his way toward Matt.

"How's things back here?"

"Busy," Matt assured him. "We've ridden thirty miles for every mile these cows have covered."

"Same way up front. Matt, I never seen the like of this bunch. Half these cows is crazy and the other half is bug-eyed mean, and not a one of 'em's ready to settle in and travel. The only thing that's got 'em movin' is they think there's fifty of us."

"You get a good lead?"

"Yeah. Dave had to bust the brindle steer to make a believer of him, but he got 'er done. Keeps callin' him 'Sonofabitch.' Good a name as any, I guess. I believe that steer would climb a tree if Dave was to want him to. Anyhow, Dave's got the point, and as soon as Nacho gets back I'll spell you so you can change mounts. Dave's already remounted, and Bo's spellin' Stan. It's gonna be a three-horse day, at least."

"It's already been a three-day day, and it won't be noon for an hour."

"Yeah. Well, that's somethin' we got to talk about, Matt. You ain't seen the spread of this outfit yet, but I have. I rode a flat two miles gettin' back here, and that with you all comin' the other way."

"Two miles?" Matt stared at him, startled. He had been at center drag since daylight and had seen little except cow-butts and dust.

"Or more," Soapy assured him. "'Course, we can bunch 'em a little more once we get it through their skulls that they're supposed to be a trail herd. But shoot, Matt, we plain haven't got enough hands."

"We're doing all right so far."

"Sure we are. Five hours, six miles. And we've probably spilled a hundred head so far, and we're nowhere near the end of Dry Creek yet. At this rate, I don't see how we're goin' to make it to Wyoming."

Abruptly, for no apparent reason, a half-dozen animals at right rear took a notion to head south. They came out of the herd at a trot, and others turned to follow them. Instantly, Tip Curry saw the problem and swept in toward center drag, freeing Matt to turn back the followers while Soapy, on a fresh horse, went after the escapees. It took several minutes to get the drag closed up again, and by that time new trouble was brewing over in Tip's section.

"Only mosshorns and brush snakes would mill on the march," Matt grumbled, racing the tired grulla to help curb a third bunch of quitters.

For a moment the three drag riders came together and Soapy shot Tip Curry a wave. "Nacho's bringin' out a remount for you," he called. "I said get that black that you favor. Mr. Hazelwood can take that'n back to the remuda when he goes."

Curry nodded and touched a finger to his hatbrim, then wheeled to go after a spotted cow just breaking rank, leaving the older men to talk about whatever older men talked about. He was grateful to Mr. Green for sending for a remount for him, and especially glad it would be the black horse. It wasn't his best cowpony, but with the herd moving now there was less need for a cowpony. The black horse was tall and fast, and could outrun most of the animals in this territory. He had a worrisome feeling, and would feel better aboard a fresh, fast horse.

Tip had seen the flames the night before, flames of burning buildings at Rafter H headquarters. Talk was, Mr. Hazelwood had fired the place himself. But even so, Tip was acutely aware of the bad blood between Mr. Hazelwood and the Dry Creek pool, and the fire in the night had left him with a disquieted feeling. His instincts told him there would be trouble, and he wanted to be ready for it. He had followed the Link reps—men who drew gunhand wages just like he did—during the cut, and had heard their talk. It wasn't anything they said, so much. It was what they didn't say . . . and the way they looked at one another, and how they held themselves.

Mr. Hazelwood didn't think there would be trouble from Link, at least while they were on Dry Creek range. Tip Curry wasn't all that sure, and had decided long since that a man drawing gunhand wages had better pay attention to his own judgements. When it came down to it, he felt, the defense of Rafter H was his responsibility. And *if* it came down to it, he would play it as he thought best. He would no more expect Stan Lamont or Nacho Lucas or even Mr. Hazelwood to do his job for him—though they would back him in a pinch, he knew—than they would expect him to do theirs. A man was paid to do a job and he did it, the best way he knew how.

He got the spotted cow and a few tentative

followers thrown back into the drags of the herd, yelling and flailing with his coiled catchrope, then rode a sweep around to where he could see Bo Maxwell on left flank, then heeled out from the herd a little way to look back across the heat-rippled miles of grass flats, feeling strangely lonesome.

Maybe that was the other thing about that distant fire last night that bothered him, he realized vaguely. He thought about the fire, and little things went through his mind—his slat bunk in the bunkhouse, where he had carved his initials alongside other initials of past occupants, the tin dipper at the covered cistern, where the water was always cool, the hole in the roof where rain came in sometimes but most times he could see the stars to go to sleep by—and he realized he didn't know where they were going. No one had said. Maybe to Dodge, or some newer railhead west of there. He didn't know. All he knew for sure was that this trail herd now was all that was left of Rafter H, and wherever they went they wouldn't be coming back.

That fire hadn't been much of anything—just some old buildings on an abandoned spread. But it had been the only home Tip Curry could remember.

There was nothing to see back there now, only receding miles of grass and heat mirage and the tapering, receding swatch of trampled ground that was the trail of the herd.

He wondered if he should have told Mr. Hazelwood that it was him—and not Mr. Hazelwood—

who had in fact run Maynard and Rodney Link out of the Dry Creek country.

He had been there when Mr. Hazelwood ordered them out . . . them and the three owlhoots they had been running with, "sleepering" calves before roundup and then rustling them later to sell to the Finch bunch over at High Nueces. Tip and Stan were there, but they stood quietly aside, just backing the boss.

But the five—he didn't guess Mr. Hazelwood ever knew about the three drifters, or there would have been some hangings—hadn't gone. They had just hid out, and made some loose talk around Colter about what they were going to do to Matt Hazelwood. Tip had heard that, and went and found them. Two of the drifters he had left face down in a wash. The third one had high-tailed, and Tip had made sure the Link boys did what Mr. Hazelwood told them to do. If they ever showed their faces within a hundred miles of Rafter H, he assured them, he would find them and kill them.

He hadn't told anybody about all that. There had seemed no need to. Mr. Hazelwood had told the Link boys to leave. They had gone. It was that simple. All the rest of it was just the details of the transaction. Tip was Mr. Hazelwood's gunhand, and he was paid good wages to see that things were right.

Nacho came out from what Sam Price called the "rolling camp"—chuck wagon and remuda— mounted on a fresh horse and leading Tip's tall black. With a quick sweep of the left drag, just to

79

remind the critters to keep pointing north, Tip followed him out several hundred yards from the herd to switch his saddle. Nacho watched him intently as he shucked his old iron-horn rig and blanket off his tired mount, then eased off its headstall and replaced it with a quick "come-along" hackamore which he fashioned from a light tie-rope.

The kid had taken to wearing his gun low, just the way Tip did. He even wore his hat the way Tip did, flat-crowned and dip-brimmed to shade the eyes from straight ahead. Both of them—slung holster and eye-shadow hat—gave a slightly disconcerting appearance to him, as though they were at odds with his short, square build and pudgy Irish-Mexican features. But Tip knew the appearance was deceptive. He had watched Nacho practice drawing his gun . . . he used to practice by the hour out beyond the corrals. He had never seen a human who could clear leather so fast. He had never seen him actually fire the revolver, but the way the kid could come up with it bordered on magic.

Tip handed the hackamore rope up to him and took the black horse's lead. Holding it low, he patted the animal's head, stroked its ears and crooned softly to it, saying the things a man says to a fresh horse he is about to ride. Then he slipped off its hackamore and snugged his own bridle onto it. Keeping the reins, he tossed his blanket and saddle on it and snugged the cinches.

Nacho still sat there, lounging in his saddle,

watching him intently. Tip glanced up. "Give this one to Mr. Hazelwood, Nacho. He'll take it to Ollie."

"All right," Nacho said. But still he hesitated.

Tip looked up again. "Well?"

"I been wonderin' about somethin', Tip. How do you feel when you kill a man?"

Tip squinted at him, then stepped to his stirrup and swung aboard the black. It sidestepped once, then accepted him. "How come you to ask that?"

"I was just wonderin'. You've done killin', Tip. How did it feel?"

Tip thought about it. "I don't know. It doesn't feel any way, to speak of. It's like cuttin' a calf or dehornin' a cow, or anything else. If you got it to do, you just do it, that's all."

Nacho seemed to be stirring over something in his mind. He pursed his lips, then asked, "How was it the first time? Were you nervous about it, or anything?"

"The first time? Hell, yes. I lit out that same day, and never went back."

"No, I mean before you done it. Were you nervous before?"

Tip shook his head, wishing the kid would just drop the whole subject. "Wasn't anything to be nervous about. I never knew I was going to, 'til I had."

In the distance, moving slowly away, he saw Soapy Green turn to glance back at them. "Come on, Nacho," he said. "We're supposed to be movin' cows."

When the drovers were all fresh-mounted, Matt Hazelwood rode out a way from the herd, forward toward the upwind swing, then reined in to look at the endless parade of plodding, shuffling, quarrelsome beef snaking past. Harsh, flat light of a high sun bleached color from the scene. There was only dust, pale grass and cattle, moving slowly northward on a bleak land under a dust-hazed sky that hid horizons and masked the distant cedar hills.

From where he sat, a quarter mile out, he could see Stan Lamont a long way off to his left, putting a mile's worth of sweat on his fresh mount for every hundred yards the cattle moved. Back on the flank, just as far off the other direction, Bo Maxwell was hazing cattle, pushing drifters and riding hard to cover more ground than a drover should ever have to cover. Beyond Bo, barely visible in the hazy distance, the wide mass of cows in the drag was like an anchor on the herd, bunching wide and heavy, massing too close for easy travel.

He couldn't see the point of the herd. It was too far away.

Soapy was right. They didn't have enough hands. It was a miracle that they had got this bunch lined out and moving, even in the best of conditions. And conditions would get worse.

The herd would spread at first water, a few hours away, and its organization would dissolve. Then they would have to do it all over again. And if they got them bedded tonight—and could hold them

82

through the night—then they had it all to do again tomorrow.

He had let his anger think for him. He had been stubborn and foolish. Three days of this and they would begin killing horses. A few days more and they would be killing men.

7

"They always said I was fiddlefooted," Clifton Flowers commented.

Clinging grimly to his weaving saddle, Jim Tyson raised his head and blinked. He kept lapsing into wild, meaningless dreams, and a couple of times he had fallen off his horse. Now Flowers was talking and he wished he would keep talking because it gave him something to concentrate on.

"Who?" he asked.

"Who what?"

"Who said you were fiddlefooted?"

"Well, most everybody. That's what they always said. Clifton Flowers is fiddlefooted. They said that."

Maybe this was the second day since leaving the limestone breaks. It seemed to Tyson that a night had passed among rolling hills, when he lay beneath a cedar tree and tried to focus his eyes on stars through its foliage, except that they kept spinning away and people kept walking up behind

85

him in the sunlight and shooting him. *Whoopee ti yi yo, git along little dogies . . .*

He grimaced at the pain that kept slipping up on him and pouncing when he tried to think.

"Why did they?" he asked.

"Why did they what?" Flowers turned to look back at him, peering judiciously from the shade of his hatbrim. "You best set straight there. You're a-fixin' to slide off again."

He steeled himself and straightened his perch on the saddle. He needed to watch that more closely. Carrying a shifting load like he was could saddle-gall the blood bay.

"Why did they say you were fiddlefooted?"

"Plain powers of observation," Flowers explained. "They all probably noticed that I was, so that's what they said. Folks talk about things they notice."

"Well, I wish you'd noticed the honker that shot me. Where were you, anyway? I didn't see you."

"I don't know," Flowers shrugged. "I was around someplace, I guess. Don't know where else I'd have been. Sure enough thought you was dead, though. Never saw a man that had a better right to be. I wonder how come he shot you up like that."

Vaguely, Tyson had been wondering the same thing. Now, riding a fresh wave of pain, the memory returned. He tried to reach around behind him with his injured arm, and whimpered at the pain of it. Then shifting the reins to his left hand, gingerly, he reached around with his right. His wallet was gone.

"My money's gone," he said, dizzily.

"If you had money those fellers musta' took it. The two that killed you," Clifton Flowers shrugged. "Been known to happen, many's the time. You said they took your horses, too."

The casual comment irritated him. "They didn't kill me," he rasped. "I'm not dead."

Flowers glanced around at him, sardonically. "So far, so good. But you ain't all that far from it, either. Besides, bein' dead might not be the worst thing can happen to a man. Just the last."

"You don't make any sense, Flowers!" He tried to shout it, but the effort set off running waves of vertigo and he clung to his saddlehorn. "I'm not dead and I'm not about to die, either."

"That's the spirit," Flowers nodded. "Be stubborn. Many's the man that's kept hisself alive on pure cussedness. All I was sayin' is that I've saw a few dead folks in my time, and none of 'em complained."

Tyson shook his head, blearily. He didn't know whether he wanted Flowers to keep talking or to shut up. The world wavered between light and dark, and he was afraid he would fall again. "Well, I'm not about to die," he insisted.

A discordant, irritating sound caught his attention, and the world steadied itself. Clifton Flowers was singing.

"O bury me not on the lone prairiee-e-e . . ." he dragged out the word, letting the wind catch it. *"Where the wild coyotes will howl o'er mee-e-e . . ."*

Tyson shook his head, gritting his teeth. "Flowers—"

"In a narrow grave just six by three-e-e-e . . ."

"Mr. Flowers, I—"

". . . *O bury me not on the lone prairiee-e-e.*"

"Flowers!"

"What?"

"Do you mind?"

"Not at all. How's about: *A cowboy lay dyin', all lost an' alone, way out on the dusty plain . . .*"

Tyson's head began to swim again and he moaned softly. Flowers glanced at him, scowled thoughtfully, then tried a different tune. *"He's worked his last roundup an' rode his last ride, an' now he's a-crossin' that great divide. A cowboy's sad endin' an' painful to tell, 'cause only the buzzards will know where he fell. O farewell an' goodbye, all you—"*

"Flowers!"

"What?"

"That's enough! Can't you sing about anything else?"

"Don't you like my singin'?"

"No, I don't. Not when you—"

"That's all right. They used to say I could aggravate the nails right out of a church-house wall, just be singin'. So I don't sing much except when I'm alone."

"Well, you're not alone now."

His irritation seemed to have steadied down the world somewhat, and he could make out landmarks. They had veered south of east, and he corrected course.

Flowers peered at him from beneath his hatbrim. "You sure you know the way?"

"I do if I can concentrate on it."

88

"Well, then, pay attention."

Slumped and dazed, Jim Tyson clung to his saddle and tried to concentrate on where he was going. Horizons danced insanely each time he raised his eyes, and sometimes images divided so that instead of one of anything there were two. Time passed and he relaxed his vigil, wondering whether the dark oblivion that hung just beyond consciousness might in fact be preferable to the agonies he felt. He had about decided just to let go and float away, when again he heard a rasping, nasal voice near at hand, singing.

"... *Beat the drums slowly and play the pipes o'er me. Play the death march as you carry me along. Take me down to the valley an' lay the sod o'er me, for I'm ...*"

Tyson took a deep breath and thought about shooting Clifton Flowers.

Was he dying? he wondered. His mind seemed to have come unstrung. It went off on journeys of its own and only now and then did he have control of it. And he hurt. He hurt in ways he had never hurt before. He was weak and shaky and dizzy, and sometimes he felt feverish, and it was all he could do to hold a lucid thought for even a few seconds. And yet, his bleeding had stopped, so far as he could tell, and he didn't think he had any bullets inside him. How many times had he been shot? Was it three? The top of his head was a caked mass of dried blood and he didn't know how much damage had been done there. But the old belt buckle had stopped one bullet. Maybe he had a cracked rib, but that bullet had not entered his body.

Maybe he was dying, but he sure as hell didn't mean to if he could avoid it. Katie waited in Wyoming.

Flowers pulled the scruffy mustang close beside him. "Where's that place we're tryin' to go?" he asked.

"Rafter H." Fevered confusion had set in again, and Tyson felt as though he were listening to his own voice, a long way off.

"Rafter H," Flowers repeated. "Seems like I've heard about Rafter H. Sort of a new spread, 'way out by its lonesome? Bunch of brush-busters snakin' Spanish cows out of the hills?"

"It was that once, a long time ago. But it's an established ranch now. Matt Hazelwood's place. I helped him get it started."

"You did?" Flowers seemed confused. "How long ago was that?"

"I don't know." He was too tired to think about it. "A long time ago. Few years after the war."

"You're not makin' any sense, you know," Flowers decided. "But you know the way there, do you?"

"I know the way." Something was wrong with somebody, and he wondered whether it was him or Flowers.

"Did I ever ask you if you know the way to Porterville?"

"I don't know."

"Do you?"

"Not that I know of."

"Oh. Thought maybe you might. If you did, we could go there."

90

Tyson squeezed his eyes tight shut, waiting out a new wave of blinding pain that started in his head and seared through him all the way to his toes. When it had subsided he looked around, dully. "I never heard of Porterville. Why do you want to go there?"

Flowers removed his hat and ran fingers through thinning gray hair. Above the hatline the skin of his forehead was startlingly white, contrasting vividly with the sun-leather skin below it. He screwed up his face thoughtfully, then put his hat on again. "Don't rightly know," he said. "It just seems like I ought to go there, first chance I get."

Tyson toyed with the response, wondering what it meant. "I guess you could ask around," he suggested.

"I did. I asked you. I said, 'do you know the way to Porterville?' and you said no. But you do know the way to Wyomin' and the way to Rafter H. That's better than nothin'."

The sun seemed to have scooted around behind them and now it lay low upon the distant hills back there. Shifting around to see it caused a wave of vertigo that almost dumped him off the horse and scattered his lucid thughts like so many antelope with a wolf among them. Katie waited in Wyoming . . . his horses . . . somebody had his herd . . . he didn't have it anymore. He lay on limestone beside a hill country tank and his blood dripped in the water there, and he had reached the end of his string, but Katie waited in Wyoming . . . *Whoopee ti yi yo, git along, little dogies, you know that Wyoming will be my new home.*

91

"What're you tryin' to do, ride backwards?" Flowers' sardonic voice mocked him.

"The sun's going down."

"Do tell."

"We have to stop soon. I need to rest."

"All right by me. I ain't in any particular hurry."

Tyson managed to right himself in the saddle, gasping as he willed away pain and confusion. Ahead in the distance was a watercourse, its path marked by occasional groves of cottonwood and chinaberry. He could stop there for the night. A little food and a little sleep, and maybe he would feel better in the morning.

"Where is Rafter H, anyway?" Flowers asked.

"It's east. I told you. Ahead of us. I don't know how far now."

"How far would you guess?"

Tyson tried to think about it. He looked for landmarks, and found them. "Forty miles, maybe. I think this is the Nueces valley here, so those hills out there ahead must be the ridge where the Dry Creek range starts. Rafter H is another fifteen-twenty miles past those hills."

"Them hills got a name?"

Tyson shook his head. "Not that I know of. Who names hills?"

Flowers shrugged. "Folks do, sometimes. Floyd an' Mary Hill had theirselves fourteen babies, an' they named ever' one of 'em."

Tyson decided that he had never met a more exasperating person than Clifton Flowers. "Then maybe those are the Hill hills," he rasped.

92

"Can't be," Flowers said. "The Hill hills are someplace else."

Tyson's mind spun off on various courses. *Whoopee ti yi yo, git along little dogies . . .*

. . . It's your misfortune and none of my own . . .

Things had changed remarkably. One minute he was riding along, with the sunset at his back . . . now bright stars twinkled overhead and a cool breeze played in his bristling whiskers and Clifton Flowers was sitting cross-legged beside him on the ground where he lay, and he was terribly thirsty.

"Thought for a while there that you'd give up an' died," Flowers said. "I told you a dozen times to sit straight on that saddle."

"I hurt," Tyson whispered. "And I'm thirsty."

"Canteen's right there by your hand," Flowers told him. "Help yourself."

He managed to swallow some tepid water, and cherished it.

"Have a nice rest?" Flowers asked, drily.

"What happened?"

"Same old thing. You fell off of your horse. I been lookin' at your head, tryin' to see if that bullet might have cracked your skull."

"Did it?"

"Can't tell for sure. But it sure enough scrambled your brains. You're in about the worst shape of anybody I ever hooked up with. Can you get up?"

"I guess I can try." He drank some more water, slowly, letting it soothe the parching of his throat.

Then he gritted his teeth and sat up. Every muscle in his body seemed to be bruised. But the world didn't spin as wildly as it had before. "Where's my horse?" he asked.

"Yonder by that little river. You reckon you can walk that far?"

"I guess I can try."

Clifton Flowers backed away and stood studying him critically as he got to his feet, staggering and weaving. He was terribly weak, and his legs trembled.

"I could use a little help," he said.

Flowers shrugged, a blur in the gloom. "Yeah. Couldn't we all." He turned away, whistling a discordant tune, and walked off into the darkness.

Tyson swore under his breath, then took a deep breath that sent lancing pain through his chest, and fixed his attention on the dark line of vegetation in the distance. With legs like rubber, he started walking. After a time he heard sounds behind him and Flowers rode up on his mustang. He fell into pace alongside. "It ain't very far. You can make it."

"If you're trying to help me," Tyson rasped, "then how come you're on a horse and I'm not?"

Flowers didn't respond for a moment, and when he did his voice sounded puzzled. "Am I supposed to be tryin' to help you?"

"Seems like that would be the thing a man would do," Tyson snapped, stumbling and fighting to regain his balance.

"Oh. Well, what do you want me to do to help?"

Tyson felt as though he were dreaming. "I'm injured," he said slowly. "I'm weak and I'm dizzy.

How about if I just hang onto your saddle for support, and you lead the way?"

"I don't know the way," Flowers said. "Like I told you." He raised his head then, his eyes distant, like a person hearing faraway sounds. "It does seem to me, though, that if you was takin' us to Rafter H you might ought to veer north just a little."

8

On the eastern slope of the little range of hills where brushy draws ran up from the Dry Creek range as though a giant had drawn great fingers into a pile of sand, greasy smoke lifted above a little brushwood fire to disperse in darkness on night breezes. Rodney Link lay spread-legged on a thrown bedroll nearby, fingers laced behind his head, and grinned at the stars.

Such horses! Money horses! They'd known the big man had stock. They'd heard about it in Three Rivers, about a horse deal. But they hadn't known how much. It was no ordinary saddle herd that the big wrangler was pushing to Three Rivers. Blooded stock. Money horses. They'd lost a few, but they had most of them. Again, slowly and deliciously, he recalled the scene there by that limestone tank. The wrangler thought he had lost them. He didn't know there was anybody around for miles, and Rodney chuckled, remembering the blank, stumped look on his face when he turned and saw Rodney's gun pointed at him, the way his eyes widened and his mouth dropped open when the first slug hit him. Man! Dead center, right through his shirt pocket. It had slapped him back, and Rodney's second shot had taken him falling.

The big jasper had never even reached the gun at his belt. Again and again he recalled it, carefully, delighting in each detail—the way the first placed shot had knocked him back, flopping, the little spray of blood when the second one hit him . . . the way his hat flew off and the top of his head erupted when that final, useless shot hit him. Maynard had wanted that. Maynard was cautious as a turkey in short brush sometimes, but Rodney didn't mind. He liked to shoot, and twelve thousand dollars justified a lot of cartridges.

He wished Maynard had been watching, especially that first shot. He wondered what his brother would have thought, the way it took the wrangler dead on, right through his pocket. Why, there wasn't a man in a thousand could place a shot like that just shooting freehand. But I can, he thought. Maynard's slick enough, but he can't shoot like that. Nobody can shoot like that. But I can. Then the Mex herder the same way—dead center.

It was Maynard that had let Tip Curry run them off the Dry Creek range. Bide our time, Maynard said, his eyes smoldering. We'll just bide our time. No gain in getting gunned down by a hired gunny. It's Hazelwood's fault, anyway.

I could have taken Tip Curry then and there, Rodney thought. I'm better. I knew then that I was better. But Maynard had said no. Just wait and bide time. Tip Curry has killed men, Maynard said. Have you?

There hadn't been a good answer to that, so they had left Dry Creek ... snuck out like a pair of coyotes with their tails between their legs. The grin of a moment ago faded from Rodney's face and he glared at the stars above. Maynard always had to be so damned cautious. Well, that line wouldn't ever mean anything again. Rodney had killed now, and there wasn't any more room for doubt about whether he could.

Those two weren't the first, either, he reminded himself. There was that old Mexican outside of Tres Palacios. Maynard was about to let him go, but Rodney was still mad about being run off from Dry Creek, and he had to take it out on somebody. The old man hadn't had but a dollar and two dimes on him, and that made it worse.

"You think I ain't up to killin' a man?" he had shouted at his brother. Then he drew his Colt and put four shots into the Mex so fast he hadn't hit ground when the last one took him. With two loads left he swiveled toward his brother. "You see that? Did you just see that? *Now* what do you think about it?"

Maynard had just stared at him in that slow way of his, then nodded. "All right. You killed him. Now what are you gonna do, Rodney ... put a notch on your gun? That old wetback wasn't even armed."

Like Maynard thought that might make a difference. But he had proved his point at that little dive in Tulsita. Two greasers in the place and both of them packing iron just like white folks. Rodney had left them lying in their own blood on the dirt floor, and Maynard hadn't said any more about whether Rodney could handle a gun.

And when Rodney decided it was time to go back to the Dry Creek country, Maynard didn't argue much. Stopping off at Three Rivers and hearing about that herd had been a stroke of luck, a sure sign that they were right to be heading back. If they hadn't been lining out for Dry Creek, they never would have been in Three Rivers in the first place.

Right through the shirt pocket! Rodney grinned again, feeling good, wondering how he could make it known about that shot without getting law on their tails. Folks would walk wide around a man that could put lead through a fellow's shirt pocket . . . if they knew about it.

But then, he figured it wouldn't be long before he showed them. Maybe if he put a hole in Tip Curry's shirt pocket, a lot of folks might sit up and take notice.

Brush rustled and he sat up, his gun in his hand. But it was only Maynard, coming into the firelight.

"Put it away," Maynard said. "There's nobody around but us." He hunkered by the little fire, rubbing his chin the way he always did when he was thinking about something.

Rodney put away his Colt. "Those horses restin' quiet?" he asked.

"Just fine," Maynard said. "But I saw some more stray cows in a draw. They're Link brands. Far as I can tell, every one of them is."

"The old man is gettin' careless," Rodney shrugged. "Time was, he'd have busted a man that let his cows stray off like that. They don't put on beef in these hills."

"Yeah." Maynard still looked thoughtful. The firelight on his cheeks didn't reach his eyes, but Rodney knew something was troubling him. It was Maynard's worst habit. He thought too much. He'd take a notion and pick at it for hours sometimes, just the way an old turkey buzzard would pick at a carcass, looking at it this way and that, backing off to see it first one way and then another, then stepping in again to rip at it.

"I don't like it," Maynard muttered now. "It's just not like the old man not to have these hills combed out by now, with fall circle comin' on. I think there's somethin' goin' on."

"Like what?" Rodney cocked his head and curled his lip. "Maybe the old fart got sick and died."

"Then some of the other spreads would be out here chousin' these cows so they could get the jump on brandin'. No, it's something else." He raised his head and looked at his younger brother. "Rodney, those cows we saw earlier, back in that first draw—"

"Those were Link, too."

"Yeah, I know. But did you see any mavericks among 'em? Did you see anything not carryin' a mark?"

"No . . . no, I guess not. Why?"

"And do you ever remember any of our cows driftin' up into these hills in a dry year before? I don't. It's almost like they'd been pushed."

"So what? No skin off our hides. The old man knows you and me ain't gonna work cows for him. What difference does it make?"

"Maybe none," Maynard shrugged. "I was just thinking. From here it seems like the roundup's already been done . . . and like somebody got awful careless about Link-branded cows while they was doin' it."

"Still doesn't mean anything to us. Forget about it."

"I don't like it. It smells funny. Something's changed."

"You're just like an old woman sometimes, Maynard, you fuss so much. Like an egg-bound, old hen. Are you goin' with me or not?"

"It's plain crazy," Maynard shrugged. "There ain't a thing on Dry Creek range that we need. What good does comin' back here do?"

Rodney stared at him, bristling. "It does me good! And when I put bullets in some folks down there it'll do me better."

"Yeah, you're just itchin' to face down Tip Curry, ain't you?"

"I'm gonna kill him," Rodney growled. "Nobody runs Rodney Link out of anyplace and gets away with it. I'm gonna do like I did to that wrangler back there. I'm gonna put a bullet right through Tip Curry's shirt pocket. And when that's done I'm gonna do the same for Matt Hazelwood . . . yeah, and maybe Stan Lamont, too."

"You get started like that and somebody will gun you down," Maynard said flatly. "You can't kill them all, Rodney."

"You think I can't? You *still* think that?"

Maynard shrugged. "That gun has sure been talkin' to you, brother. Like now that you've tried killin', you just can't get enough of it."

"It was you that wanted me to shoot that wrangler in the head."

"He saw you, Rodney. We had to be sure he was dead."

"I was already sure. Right through the shirt pocket. You don't know it yet, Maynard, but there isn't anybody in Texas that uses a hand-iron better than me. Maybe not anybody anywhere. But that don't matter unless I prove it, so's everybody knows. That's what I aim to do. Are you with me or not?"

"That's crazy talk, Rodney. What will that get you?"

Rodney stared at him, and firelight burned in his eyes. "What does it get me? Why, anything I want, brother. Anything I want."

Maynard shrugged. "So do we ride in and see the old man, or what? Maybe see if he'll buy some of those horses?"

"What for?" Rodney was enjoying himself now. Things had changed between the brothers since he had killed men. It made a difference . . . almost like *he* was the big brother now, and Maynard stepped easy around him. He wondered if Maynard was afraid of him now, and the idea pleased him. Casually he drew his pistol again, looked at it in the firelight, and drew back its hammer. Then abruptly he swung it to point at Maynard. His brother flinched and stared at him. Rodney grinned. With elaborate disdain he raised the muzzle toward the sky and let the hammer down. "I said, what for?"

Maynard relaxed slightly. "Sometimes I wonder if you're playing with a full deck, Rodney. Put that thing away."

"Why would we give the old man first bid?" His curiosity satisfied, he holstered the Colt.

"I don't know. But if we don't, just how are we gonna play it?"

Rodney really hadn't thought it out, but now he made up his mind. "Come first light we head for Colter. I need me a drink of whiskey, and then if Tip Curry ain't around I'm gonna send for him. And I'm gonna wait there for him, right out in front of Paisley's. And when he comes, I'm gonna kill him right there in the street, just like I killed that wrangler out there. I'm gonna put a bullet right through his shirt pocket. Then after that's all settled, and we got their attention, then we'll sell horses to whoever offers the best price."

Thirty-five miles away, lanterns burned in Paisley's place, washing the dirt street beyond latticed windows with sullen light where armed men waited, watching the darkness beyond and watching one another. Inside, the Dry Creek Range Association was meeting.

The floor beyond the bar had been cleared, except for three tables set in a row to accommodate eight chairs, as was the custom. Three of the chairs this evening were not in use. Rafter H was gone, and the customary place of Matt Hazelwood was empty. Pinto Boyd was not present, and only Lou Campion represented the Colter town brands.

Marcus Flood had refused to come in. The T-bar-T owner had a crew out at Rafter H, holding a perimeter at gunpoint around Corky Lassiter and the Triple-Seven outfit dug in around the burned-out headquarters site. Lassiter had arrived first with a tough crew and occupied the remaining structures at Rafter H. They had a barn, a bunkhouse and several sheds for cover, and two days of sporadic threats and a few shots fired had failed to dislodge them. Flood had cursed the rider who came to tell him about the Association meeting. There would be no negotiation, he said, as long as Triple-Seven or anybody else sat on Rafter H and claimed possession.

It didn't matter. The real contest would be between Link and Triple-Seven, and everyone except Marcus Flood knew it. So far, Link had held his guns back, not relishing a showdown with Triple-Seven. In terms of men and guns, Link had the edge. But behind Colonel Nelson and Triple-Seven lurked the ominous shadow of the Dominion Land and Cattle empire.

Now Herman Link and Colonel Nelson faced each other across the length of the ranked meeting tables, and the others present didn't matter very much.

"Are you willing to bargain?" Link demanded.

Nelson gazed at the fierce old man with something like distant humor. "I'm here," he said. "I shall listen to what you have to say."

Link scowled at him. "What I have to say is that by rights Link should have right of expansion into Rafter H graze. It's adjoining property and

105

it's abandoned . . ."

"I concede no such rights," the Englishman interrupted. "Dry Creek is pooled range. Contiguity rights are assigned to the pool. Read your charter, sir."

"Let me finish," Link growled. "I'm talking general law, not pool charter. But in any case, it isn't the land that matters, it's the grazing rights."

Nelson shook his head. "To you, Herman. Not to me. Triple-Seven holds the north range. I can expand as far as I want for graze. To me it is the land that matters. I haven't forgotten your threat to push my animals off the water."

"I never threatened!"

"You pointed out that you *could,* Herman. But not if I have a headquarters operation in the south range. So you see, what is important is the land and its location. That's why Mr. Lassiter is out there right now, holding possession of Rafter H."

"He doesn't have possession! He's just squatting there."

"And he intends to stay until Rafter H is declared abandoned. Do you intend to push us, Herman?"

Link's eyes narrowed in the lamplight. Away from the tables, in shadows, gunhands of two spreads watched each other carefully, hands hovering at their hips. "If that's what it takes, Colonel," Link said softly. "But I'd rather talk reason."

"And I told you I'm willing to listen. Once."

"All right. Suppose we share Rafter H, the two of us. You take the spread and give me the additional pool graze that it holds."

106

"Now just a damn minute!" Lou Campion exploded. "What about the rest of us? We're part of this range, too!"

Link and Nelson both glanced along the tables at the other ranchers . . . Campion repping the town brands, the others with their little spreads notched like patchwork into the broader sectioning of the Dry Creek range. Lazy J, Sawtooth, T-Cross—minor spreads, but they were part of the Association.

"If I'd thought you and Nelson was plannin' to split the proceeds, Link," Sammy Lang snapped, "I'd never have gone along with that blackball on Hazelwood. I just thought you was mad about what he done to your kids."

"The rest of you stay out of this," Link growled. "If the Colonel and I can come to an agreement, then we'll see what's in it for you all."

"We can talk," Nelson nodded. "As long as we understand each other."

"Then we better get to it before the gunplay starts."

Link's agreement was interrupted by harsh voices in the street, challenges of those on guard there and a response. The batwings swung inward and a man stepped through. It was Triple-Seven's foreman, Johnny McGraw. He was stained and drawn, and blood dripped from a gash in his shirt sleeve.

"You're a mite late for that, Mr. Link," he said thinly. "It already started. Marcus Flood is dead. So's Whiz Conway. Two-three others are hurt."

Everyone at the tables was on his feet. Colonel Nelson strode around the group to his foreman.

"Who started it, Johnny? Was it Flood or Corky Lassiter?"

"Neither one, Colonel." McGraw's eyes shifted to Lou Campion, accusing. "It was your damn town marshal that started it. He showed up at sunset with a dozen hardcases, said from now on Rafter H is his. Then he started shootin'."

Campion paled. "Pinto? Pinto Boyd did that?"

"He did. And right now he's holdin' Rafter H, and what's left of the T-bar-T and Triple-Seven crews out there are hid out, tryin' to stay out of rifle range. Those men Boyd brought in . . . they're killers, Colonel."

"Where is Corky?"

"He's comin' in. Him and Will Bower are bringin' in Flood and Conway and the men that was hurt. He said he guesses this changes things."

"It certainly does." Nelson stared at Herman Link. "I think it is time for us to make a bargain."

9

Through sheer grit and blind luck—and a large dose of what Samuel T. Price called "plain too ornery to quit"—Rafter H had made it through another day. By driving hard, trail-breaking the stubborn critters the only way they could, they had moved ten million pounds of surly beef another eighteen miles, and it had cost them dearly.

They were all on the verge of exhaustion. They were edgy and grumpy. There had already been one serious face-off between Bo Maxwell and Jesus Maria Gomez. Tired and impatient, Gomez had fallen back on right flank to tighten a bulge there and had pushed too hard. The resulting explosion of cattle on left flank had taken the combined efforts of Maxwell and Stan Lamont to turn. When they were lined out again Maxwell endangered a tired pony by cutting through the herd to deliver some abuse to the Mexican, who immediately drew a knife and threatened to cut off Bo's ears.

If it hadn't been for Gabe Sinclair breaking it up,

they might have tangled then and there.

They pushed the herd off water in late afternoon, made another four miles and bedded them on a rocky flat. Dave Holley and Nacho Lucas had drawn cocktail shift and had a few hours' sleep, so Soapy left them out to night-herd for the first shift and rode out to join them, leaving the others to get a bite to eat and what rest they could.

But Gabe Sinclair ate quickly, dark eyes on the waning daylight, then drew two mounts from the remuda and headed south where Tip Curry waited a few miles out. "Tip's been scoutin' strays," he told Matt Hazelwood. "Reckon we can clean up our drag 'nother time or two."

At the first day's bedding they had swept the backtrail and circled up nearly four hundred head of strayed and bolted stock. The second night it was less than two hundred. They were losing some, but not many so far, and Matt had noticed on this third day of trail that the drags were straightening up, moving better with fewer breakouts. A few more men and ponies and they might be able to hold this herd and move it in an orderly fashion. He shook his head dismally. They didn't have more men and they didn't have more ponies. They had moved seven thousand head of range stock forty-five miles in three days, and not even the skill and grit of his outfit could account for that. It was luck. Three days of good, clear weather with no surprises and no incidents . . . water where they needed it and the courses wide and shallow so they could move the herd onto water and off water each day and bed them dry for the next day's headout. It wouldn't

110

last. The land would change. The weather would change. Watercourses would become far apart and unpredictable. There were so many ways for even the best equipped of crews to lose a herd. Fifteen or twenty top-notch hands could push a couple of thousand cows eight hundred or a thousand miles and stand a fair chance of getting there with most of them. But ten men could not push seven thousand head two thousand miles. Forty-five miles they had made since leaving Dry Creek range, and he was seeing clear sign of men and horses beginning to wear out.

Matt Hazelwood watched the sun go down and dreaded the color of the western sky. Clouds were making up out and there and that was bad news. This time of year there could be storms up in the hills, and that could mean trouble. Flash floods up there meant high-water crossings down here, and bogs in the valleys. And if the storms moved, as they often did, scudding eastward on the prevailing winds, that was worse. Matt had seen herds stampede from lightning and thunder. He had also seen stampedes set off by the flash of a match or the sound of a flapping slicker, but there was nothing more likely to spook a wild herd than a storm.

In last good light he climbed to the chuck wagon's box and looked out across the range. The great herd was less than a mile away, bedded loosely on high ground, a square mile of animals cropping at sparse graze and beginning to settle for the night. As he watched, a rider appeared, coming slowly around the south end of the herd. He squinted. Dave Holley, probably. He shifted his gaze to the

111

north perimeter in time to see Soapy Green appear there, circling to pass Dave at flank. Matt breathed deeply. Three men circling a herd that size, trying to keep the calm. Three men, riding circles that were five miles every time around. There should have been six or eight men out there, at least. But he couldn't even afford three. Soapy was working double shift as it was. He caught himself. They were *all* working double shift. Soapy had just extended his double.

In the far distance south of the great herd there was motion. He could barely make it out, but he recognized it. Tip Curry and Gabe Sinclair had combed the drags and now were bedding a small herd of regathered strays a mile south of the main ground. The light was too poor now to chance throwing them into the settled herd. They would have to be held out until morning.

At a sound from the remuda corral he turned in time to see Sam Price tightening the cinches on a saddled cowpony. Matt swung down from the wagon and walked to the rope corral, where Ollie Sinclair was tending the hocks of hard-ridden stock and muttering to himself about the way they were wearing out his beloved ponies. As Matt approached, Sam Price swung into the saddle, stiffly. In earlier years, the cook had been a top hand, but now his injuries plagued him.

Matt stepped to the rope and looked up at him. "Grub wagon can't tend itself, Sam," he said quietly.

Sam chewed his whiskers and raised a brow. "Then you boys will need to scrub your own plates,

Matt." He jerked a thumb toward the distant stray herd. "Those youngsters yonder have put together a batch that's about my size, and I've got a hankerin' to see if I still know how to sing to cows."

"Which one of 'em do you intend to relieve, Sam?"

Price grinned. "Both of 'em. They're growin' boys and they could use a little rest. Hand me up that Henry over there, will you, Matt?"

He picked up the rifle and handed it to the cook. Price slid it into his saddle-boot. "If you all want breakfast in the mornin', you best send somebody out to chouse those critters about an hour ahead of first light."

Matt stepped back and loosed the corral rope. "You take care of yourself, Sam."

"How many years you been tendin' cows now, Matt?"

"I don't know. A lot."

"Well, whatever it is, you can add six for me."

As he watched the cook ride away, Ollie Sinclair stepped up beside him. "That pony's got a rope burn and slick shoes," he said.

"Then why did you let him take it?"

"Cause it's the best we got, Mr. Hazelwood. I got to tell you, we ain't doin' right by these ponies. We 'bout to wear 'em out. Where'd you say we was goin'?"

"Wyoming."

"Where's that?"

"North."

"Well, if it's more than a week from here, Mr. Hazelwood, I don't know what we goin' to ride."

113

Matt shrugged and turned away. "Just take care of them the best you can, Ollie."

"Yessir, I will. I always do."

Hazelwood rolled in and tried to sleep for a while. He would spell Soapy on the night herd in a few hours, and without a little sleep he wouldn't be worth his salt out there. But the more he tried to sleep the more found himself worrying the problem around in his mind. Like a puppy with an old boot, he chewed at it, tossed it around, looked at it first one way and then another and couldn't put it down.

Basically, it was simple. Either they had to spill some cows or they had to find some help. Ten men with a fifty-horse remuda could not handle a wild herd three miles long on the move. The sheer distances to be covered were impossible. Even half the herd would be too much for any real control.

The idea of cutting the herd flirted around the practical side of his head, but found no place to land. Even if he were willing to ride off and leave several thousand critters with the Rafter H brand, it would be a treachery to his drovers. Those boys had busted their butts gathering this herd, partly out of spite for Link and the Association, partly out of loyalty to the brand and, he was certain, partly out of plain devilish glee at what they were getting away with. And in the process they had showed everybody, once and for all, that when it came to working a range, they were the best outfit in Texas. To trim the deck now would be letting them down, and he couldn't bring himself to even consider it.

So that left the other alternative. Where could he get more drovers and a bigger remuda?

He chewed at it, weighing remote possibilities.

A few feet away, Stan Lamont rolled over, flipped back his blankets and sat up, a burly silhouette in the lamplit darkness. He crammed his hat onto his head, drew up his knees and wrapped heavy arms around them. As though he had been reading his boss's mind he said, "Might be a hand or two ridin' grubline back yonder, that would sign on for a drive if the pay was right."

A faint sound on the wind brought Stan's head up and Matt out of his bedroll, slitted eyes scanning the darkness. Nothing was visible now beyond the chuck camp's lantern light except distant darknesses under starglow. Matt squinted. "Where was that, Stan?"

Hesitantly, Stan pointed, south of west. "There, someplace. Hard to tell." He crouched, saw nothing out on the trail, and sprawled beside his soogans to press an ear to the ground, his hand covering his other ear. Over by the wagons Ollie Sinclair had just finished saddling a second night horse, and was leading Hazelwood's grulla into the light. He stood frozen now, staring out into the darkness. Even at a distance of more than a mile, the sound had been unmistakable. A single gunshot.

Matt gave Stan Lamont time to listen, then crouched beside him. "Is the herd moving?"

Lamont raised himself, then got to his feet. "I don't think so. But it's a long way. Want me to go look?"

"I'll look. You and Ollie get those others awake and put a team on that wagon. You know what to do."

They knew. Somebody out there had fired a shot. If those cows decided to stampede off their bed grounds because of it, there were two options . . . either go after them or get the hell out of the way, depending on which way they headed. Matt scooped up his bedding and ran, tossing the stuff into the open wagon as he passed, pausing to collect his saddle and tack. Ollie led the grulla to him, and went on to boot Bo Maxwell and Jesus Maria Gomez awake. He threw more wood onto the cookfire. Sometimes fire would turn a night stampede. But then again, sometimes it wouldn't.

Stan Lamont caught up the next horse Ollie looped, and began saddling it, directing Bo and Jesus to get leather on some draft stock. Matt Hazelwood hoped the few hours sleep they had managed had washed some of the hostility out of the two, and he shot them a glance. They were working side by side, groggy with sleep but uncomplaining.

Matt swung into his saddle and wheeled the grulla, then paused. "Listen again, Stan."

Lamont hit the ground again, listening. Then he raised up and shook his head. "Nothing I can make out, Boss. If those cows were moving and coming this way, I think I'd know it by now."

Matt relaxed a bit. "Just get ready to move and hold it like that," he said. Then he put heels to the grulla and headed out, south of west.

With the camp light behind him, his eyes began to adjust to starglow. A half mile out he eased off and stood high in the stirrups. Errant wind brought him the distant, hot scent of bedding cattle. But no thunders of stampede. He let out a breath and noticed how tight his shoulders felt. The base of his neck felt like a hot bruise, right on the spine. He angled closer and finally could hear the huge, quiet voice of the resting herd, a sound that touched the ears and the scalp and said, at least for this moment, that the cattle were content. A night breeze washed cow-scent across the prairie to him, and carried the distant voice of Soapy Green, singing, "... *marching home again, hurrah, hurrah, we'll give him a hearty welcome then, hurrah* ..."

Matt grinned in the darkness, rolling his shoulders to relieve the tension soreness. Soapy Green had about the worst voice he ever remembered hearing, but there was a puzzling thing about it. Cattle liked the sound of it.

He eased left on his reins and went on, wishing for moonlight so he could see better. The stars showed only shadows, though he could tell now that the shadow horizon ahead and to his right actually was the herd, a subtly shifting darkness in the night. He wasn't aware of Nacho Lucas approaching him until the shadowy rider was only steps away, but he realized that Lucas had seen him coming. The kid had eyes like a cat.

"It was south of here, the shot," Nacho said. "Dave closed for me and I came out to see."

"It didn't spook them up here?"

"We had some restless in the drag, but Soapy was there and he sang 'em down. Who's out there with the strays, Mr. Hazelwood?"

"Gabe and Tip were. Mr. Price went out to spell them. You think that's where the shot came from?"

"Seemed like." They were riding side by side now, Nacho staying to Matt's right, loose and alert. Like a gunhand, Matt thought . . . staying in position to draw and shoot and to protect the boss. He had noticed how Nacho watched Tip Curry, and how the youngster seemed always to adopt the styles and movements of the gunhand, as though trying each habit on for size.

"How many head in the stray herd tonight?"

"Dave rode out a ways before dark," Nacho told him. "He made it maybe a hundred, maybe a little more. Tip and Gabe were just beddin' them down." The youngster tugged his reins abruptly, heeling his mount in front of Matt's. "There," he pointed. "Riders, goin' toward the wagon camp."

At first, Matt couldn't see them at all. Then he made out dim silhouettes moving against the distance. Three . . . maybe four riders, on line between the stray herd and the camp, going toward the distant firelight. He reined the grulla and touched heels, and Nacho kept pace with him, slightly ahead and to the right. They closed rapidly on the riders, and Matt saw faces turn toward them.

"That's Tip," Nacho said. "And Gabe. I don't know the other two."

As they came up, Matt made out four riders. Two of them rode together, their hands on their saddlehorns, heads down. Tip Curry followed them

118

a few paces back, and Gabe Sinclair rode off to the side, holding a saddlegun which he kept pointed at the pair.

"These two here," Tip gestured, "they came from the west, after dark. They intended to stampede our cows, but I guess they thought the stray herd was the main herd, because that's where they tried."

"Who fired the shot?"

"The skinny one there. I didn't get to him fast enough to stop him from that."

"The cows didn't run?"

"Oh, they bolted, but there aren't that many of them. Gabe just circled 'em in and put them back to bed."

Matt rode forward to look at the two prisoners. Even by starlight he could see that they had been disarmed and their hands were tied to their saddlehorns. He couldn't make out their faces, but that didn't matter. He'd have a look at them in camp. He eased back to where Tip followed. Nacho had closed in on the side across from Gabe, thoroughly boxing the prisoners.

"I don't see how they could mistake the stray herd for the main herd, even in the dark," Matt said.

Tip pushed back his hat. "I don't know either, Mr. Hazelwood. But they didn't go anywhere near the main herd. They just came right at us."

"They made a mistake," Nacho Lucas said.

One of the prisoners raised his head now, his face a pale blur in starlight as he looked around. "You got that wrong, pard," he said. "Me and Pye, we

119

never went for your herd. We seen you fellows workin' strays, we thought we might skim a few and get clean with 'em. I admit to that. We're down on our luck. But we never rode on your main herd."

"Shut up and keep movin'," Nacho Lucas said. "Stampeders hang."

10

Twice they changed shift on night herd, the men grumpy and sullen from too little sleep, slopping down a bite of grub and heading out into the night on horses that Ollie Sinclair fussed over and worried about. Soapy Green came in and sent Stan Lamont and Bo Maxwell out to relieve Dave Holley, and later Jesus Maria Gomez went to relieve Samuel Price on the strays so that he could start breakfast. Through the dark hours Nacho Lucas tended the fire, kept the coffee boiling and guarded the prisoners. His turn to sleep would come when the herd was moving and he could crawl into the chuck wagon for two hours' rest.

As the men came in they looked curiously at the two secured to wagon wheels. Pye and Slater, they called themselves—a pair of down-at-heels drifters by their appearance, grubliners off some distant range too far from home and friends to find a bunk and biscuits at places they were known.

It would be up to the boss what to do with them,

and if Mr. Hazelwood decided to hoist the wagon tongue and hang them there, then that's what they would do. But in the meantime they gave them food to eat and hot coffee and tried to be civil to them.

Soapy Green brought them breakfast in the dark of morning, and questioned them while they ate. Then when Matt Hazelwood came in to swap the grulla for a day horse, he met him at the rope corral.

"I don't believe those two are hardcases," he said. "They spent some time on the wrong trails, but they both been workin' cowhands in their time."

"Then what set them off?" Hazelwood frowned at him.

"Bad luck and dumbness is my guess," Soapy shrugged. "That and some shotgun outfit losin' cows to a blizzard and the boss needin' to blame somebody."

Matt studied him thoughtfully. Two things made Soapy Green a first-class trail boss. He knew cows and he knew cowpunchers. He was a fair judge of character in both.

"Back when you run the Link boys off," Soapy said, "I was for hangin' them, if you remember."

"I remember," Matt scowled. He'd had a feeling ever since that he might one day regret his decision to let that pair go. "What are you getting at, Soapy?"

"What I'm getting at, Matt, is we're pretty short-handed right now."

Matt had the grulla stripped down, and he handed it over to Ollie Sinclair, who clucked at its condition. Matt dusted himself with his hat. "Well, let's take a look at them," he said.

The two had been untied and they stood now beside the chuck wagon. They were both very young, Matt noticed, and so scared they trembled. Still, as he approached, they held their heads up and met his eyes.

"If we're gonna hang these fellers, let's get it done," Sam Price growled. "We're burnin' daylight."

The others gathered around, ready to do whatever Matt wanted done.

Matt placed himself squarely before the two and hooked his thumbs in his belt. "Do you boys know me?"

They looked at him blankly, then the larger one—Slater—shook his head. "Not by sight," he said, "but I guess you must be Matt Hazelwood."

"How do you know that?"

"Those are Rafter H critters out there, and we shared a fire two evenin's back with a couple of jaspers that talked about you."

"They did, did they?"

"Yes, sir. We—Pye and me—we been layin' out in them hills yonder for a time, tryin' to think how to get by. Then these two come along and we shared our fire with 'em. They said they plan to spook your herd one night, for pay. But they ain't in any hurry to tangle with none of you, seems like. They talked a lot, but never did get around to when they aim to do that."

"Did they say who's paying them?"

"Yes, sir. They called him Pinto. A lawman, they said."

"So you boys decided to get the jump on them, is that it?"

Pye shook his head and Slater said, "No, sir. We might be hard up right now, but me an' Pye, we ain't stampeders. We just figgered ... well ... when them two spooks your cows you all are goin' to lose a lot of 'em anyways, and maybe a few head here an' there might not matter. So we thought maybe we could pick up some strays an' maybe cash 'em in for a stake someplace."

"So you aren't stampeders, but you *are* cow thieves."

Slater dropped his eyes. "Yes, sir. I guess that's about how it is. Can't argue that."

"We got hungry," Pye muttered.

"You what? Speak up."

"Yes, sir. Slater an' me ain't had work since last winter, and Mr. Anderson passed the word so's nobody will hire us or grubstake us. It's his right, I reckon. We cost him some cows."

"I heard about that. Those two stampeders you talked to, what were their names?"

Slater shrugged. "Lindahl and Garth, they said. Only names they gave."

Sam Price finished packing his wagon and closed the bay with a thump. Then he walked to the front and raised the tongue and secured it. The heavy pole with its trace rings stood nine feet above the wagonbox, an effective gallows with ropes already dangling from the rings. He began forming a noose in one of them. "Come on, Matt. Time's wastin'."

Pye's adam's apple danced in his scrawny neck, and Slater's cheeks paled.

124

"You boys admit you tried to steal Rafter H cows," Matt said.

The prisoners both nodded, miserably.

Soapy Green edged close to Matt. "Show me a man in this outfit that hasn't swung a wide loop now and again," he whispered.

Matt ignored him, fierce eyes fixed on Pye and Slater. "Do you have anything to say in your defense . . . either of you?"

They looked at each other, then dropped their eyes and shrugged. "Not much to say, sir," Slater's voice quivered. "We did try to do that."

"Where are you from?" he asked them.

Slater had tears on his cheeks, but his eyes were steady. "I'm from Arkansas. Pye's from Nebraska. But we don't either of us have any kin that has to be notified, sir. There's just us. We been pards on three-four spreads, all the way from the Territories to Colorado. We thought we'd come see how things are in Texas." He swallowed, choking.

"I guess we done that," Pye finished.

Up on the box, Sam Price finished the second noose. "All set, Matt," he said. "Get 'em up here."

Matt looked from one to the other of them, then stepped forward suddenly and prodded Slater's chest with a stiff finger. "Do you know the way to Wyoming?" he demanded.

"Y—yes, sir. I reckon."

Hazelwood turned to Pye. "Hobbs trail or Northern trail?" he snapped.

The cowboy blinked at him, then licked his lips. "I s'pose either one'd get you there, but if it was me I'd try to cut the old Western trail up past Ft.

Griffin, then I'd bend over toward the Canadian cut and try to hit Black Mesa up past the Llano. From there I'd just sort of point 'em at Cheyenne and go. Was it me, that's what I guess I'd do."

Hazelwood stepped back, satisfied. "Would you two rather stretch hemp or ride for Rafter H?"

They stared at him, too stunned to speak.

"I'd need your solemn oaths," Matt added. "And if you ever let me down so help me God I'll shoot you where you stand." He looked up at Sam Price. "Quit playin' with those ropes, Sam, and get hitched up. We're burning daylight."

As he strode toward the rope corral to get his day horse, Soapy Green and Dave Holley fell in alongside him. He turned to Dave. "You have any objection to those two being behind you?"

Dave shrugged. "Not as long as they can keep the cows from pilin' up on me. I'm still tryin' to educate Sonofabitch."

"I thought you had that steer leading."

"Oh, he leads, alright. But he keeps wantin' to veer to the left. I think I twisted his sense of direction when I busted him. But he'll work out, I guess."

"I thought for a minute or two that you was fixin' to hang those two," Soapy said.

"And they sure thought Sam Price was going to," Dave allowed.

Matt shrugged. "Try them on swing, Soapy. Or maybe flank if you have to. But spread the word to keep an eye on them. And I don't want them anywhere near the drags until I say so. And by the way, once we get the herd strung out this morning

126

and throw in the strays, get somebody to spell Tip Curry and send him to me. I'll be dropping back to wait for him."

"You goin' someplace, Matt?"

"Yeah. Tip and I are going over into those hills to see if we can find a couple of *real* stampeders."

North of the broad reach of rolling prairie that was the Dry Creek range, the grass flats narrowed, becoming a long corridor between the climbing hills that shouldered in from the west and the scrub breaks which formed a perimeter on the east. For years, since those early days when Rafter H had been the only working ranch on Dry Creek, this long corridor of gentle graze had been called "the outlet." It was the natural road and mustering chute for drives heading for any railhead to the north. But all through the growth of the cattle industry in these lands the range of hills along the outlet's western rim had been a source of trouble.

They were a natural hiding place for predators. Riding up a slant canyon to look for sign, Matt Hazelwood remembered times before when armed men had combed these same hills as outriders for other herds. Sometimes Indians had lurked here, sometimes rustlers, sometimes no one. And sometimes those who went into the hills never came back.

Morning sun was on their backs as they entered the climbing lands, following a game trail that would lead to the ridges beyond. They had angled southward several miles to enter the hills far behind the position of the herd . . . an old trick that Matt had learned in the early years, when the threat usually was from raiding Comanche. A herd out in the outlet could attract a lot of attention. Anyone watching from the hills would tend to stay even with it as it moved.

Meadowlarks called from the ridges above, and an easy breeze lazed down the canyon floor, touching the lacework of brush among the rocks and gullies of its bottom. A mile in from the spreading flats, Matt angled upward toward a sloping shoulder and Tip Curry edged aside to stay at his flank. It was a thing Matt always noticed about the young gunhand, this instinctive positioning for best effect no matter what the circumstances. He wondered sometimes whether Tip even realized that he did it, or whether it was something born into him that all the military manuals in the world could not have equalled. Tip had never been to war, but in a way the quiet young man had been at war all his life.

Approaching the crest of the shoulder, Tip edged his mount slightly ahead for first look beyond. Matt's cheeks twitched in a semblance of a smile. By the time he had a look at what was beyond, Tip would already know and be satisfied with it. He drew gunhand's wages, and he had a definition of the job that went far beyond what Matt might have assigned.

On the crest Tip reined in, and Matt pulled up beside him. To the north and west the hills climbed away, rising to meet the high plateau country beyond. On a hillside a quarter mile away, two tiny flashes of white showed and disappeared as a pair of whitetail deer noted their presence. That meant that there was no one else around, at least not here. Matt scanned the terrain, satisfied that their quarry was ahead of them. Out on the flats—rolling land in fact, but in the distance it seemed flat—he could see the herd, a dark wash on the pale prairie, immense even at this distance. A great, elongated triangle of moving animals, its point barely perceptible in the vanishing miles, the herd crept northward along the narrowing funnel of the outlet trail, and only the perfection of its shape gave indication of the riders out there working it.

From the herd he let his eyes rove across to where the hills began, and he focused on a stubby spire six or seven miles away, a vantage point that the herd would not pass for at least an hour.

"They're up there," he pointed. "At least, I would be if I were them."

Tip nodded, but a hint of worry lurked in his eyes.

"You don't think so?" Matt asked.

"They probably are," Tip agreed. "But there's something else. Look."

The deer had reappeared, specks on the far hillside, not moving. But the white undersides of their tails were plainly visible. They were facing away from the riders, watching something else.

"We ought to take a look," Tip suggested.

Backing off from the crest of the climbing shoulder, they followed its line upward, threading through thickets of horse-high brush. Near the top they turned and went over the ridge and across to where the next little valley sloped away, and again

129

it was Tip who skylined first to see what was beyond. He waved Matt forward and pointed.

"Horses," he said.

The ridge sloped away to a stream-fed bottom rich in tall grass between encroaching walls of brush. Almost a box canyon, but too wide to serve as a cow trap.

And grazing there, knee-deep in rich grass, were nearly a dozen horses. Even from the ridge, it was obvious that these were no mustangs. Most of them were a uniform blood bay in color, with varied white blazes and stocking marks. Two or three were darker, approaching sorrel. Two pairs of practiced eyes took in the conformation of the animals, their size and condition, the way they moved, and Matt pursed his lips in a silent whistle of appreciation.

"Short-tailed," Tip noted. "Saddle stock, every one. Wherever they belong, they're a long way from home."

"Do you see anybody?"

"No. There's downed brush up on that far rise there, like maybe somebody passed that way, but whoever it was was going north, and it was a day or two back. Those horses haven't been on that grass that long."

They rode carefully down the slope, and the horses watched them come and did not run away. When they broke out of brush at the edge of the little waterway, the entire bunch turned to look at them, ears perked and heads up. Several began to wander toward them, curiously.

"This bunch has been educated," Matt observed. "Look how they move! I believe those are

130

cowponies, Tip."

They rode among them, and the animals showed no alarm. Then Matt spotted a brand and his eyes widened. A neat rowel brand, high on the right hip. Star cross! Not in ten years had Matt Hazelwood seen that brand, so placed—not since the day he and Soapy rode out from Abilene to see the place in the flint hills where Jim Tyson intended to build a herd and perfect a working breed.

Two more animals came out from the shade of a salt cedar copse, then another. "I count fourteen," Tip said. "All shod, hand gentled, no mouth scars, no stargazers, no walleyes. Mr. Hazelwood, I believe I'd give three months' wages for a horse like these."

But Matt Hazelwood wasn't listening. Selecting a friendly young mare that stood her ground when he rode near, he built a loop and dropped it over her head. He dallied the catch-line, then stepped down and walked its length to the horse. She stood steady, neither frightened nor hostile, only curious. With a hand on her muzzle he stroked her ears and let her nuzzle him, getting acquainted. He stroked her sleek neck, then ducked under her chin and stroked the other side, resting his arm across her withers. He slipped his loop off her neck and let it drop. She stood content, a schooled, show-breed, five-year-old cowpony just entering her prime, and something like awe welled in Matt's chest. He waved Tip over and looked up at him.

"I don't know how," he said, "but these are Big Jim Tyson's horses."

Curry knew the name. He had heard the older

131

men talk about Tyson. But Tyson was up north somewhere. "Maybe they're some he sold," he suggested.

Matt shook his head. "Do you see any earmarks or overbrands? No, these are Jim's horses. But what in God's name are they doing down here?"

11

There was no choice but to take the fourteen horses down into the outlet, catch up with the herd, and turn them over to Ollie Sinclair. Matt Hazelwood would have it no other way. But when he ordered Tip Curry to drive them there, the gunhand backed away and shook his head firmly. "No, sir. Mr. Hazelwood, I won't do that."

Matt stared at him. Never in the years Tip had worked for him had the young man refused to obey an order, but now he stared back at his boss, morning sun shadowing his eyes, and there was a grim determination there that overrode his obvious concern at the unpardonable thing he had said.

"You what?" Matt squinted.

"I won't take those horses back to the herd, sir. You take them."

"Why won't you?"

Tip's distress was obvious. But he held it in check. "Because you tellin' me to take them means you intend to go on after those two hardcases by yourself. I can't let you do that, Mr. Hazelwood."

"You can't *let* me? By damn, Tip, I don't know what's got into you, but I give the orders here."

"Yes, sir. I know. But you pay me gunhand wages, Mr. Hazelwood, and I have to do what I think is best, or I wouldn't be doin' right by you."

"Well, I swear!" Matt couldn't think what to say, so he scowled and gritted his teeth.

"One of those jaspers is Garth," Tip explained. "He's a known man, and he's mean as a snake. The other one's probably just as bad. So if one of us is going up there to find them, sir, it's goin' to be me."

"I'm not about to tolerate a hand who won't take orders," Matt growled. He caught up the reins on his day horse, stepped into the saddle and retrieved his catch rope. Then he turned blazing eyes on his errant gunhand. "Now you do what I told you to do! Then maybe I'll forget all about this."

But Tip was adamant. "No, sir," he said, his voice shaking. "I just can't do that."

"Well, I sure as hell can fire you here and now!"

The young gunhand went deathly pale, and Matt felt as though he had just kicked a puppy. Damn it, Tip, he thought, you've had your say, now just back down and let's get on with it.

But Curry wasn't backing down. "Mr. Hazelwood, if you fire me right this minute, then which are you going to do, take these horses down to the herd or go after those stampeders?"

It caught Matt off guard. The horses couldn't wait. Maybe the stampeders could, but the horses couldn't. For some reason there were fourteen of Big Jim Tyson's blooded mounts out here in the

Texas hills, and he couldn't bring himself to leave them. He owed a lot to Tyson. He had to look after his stock long enough to find out why they were here.

"I guess I'll have to take the horses," he conceded. "I can't do both by myself."

"Since I'm fired, it doesn't make any difference what I do," Tip said slowly. Then without further pause he wheeled his mount and headed north across the little meadow. At the screen of brush he hesitated once and looked back sadly. Then he was gone.

Matt Hazelwood sat his mount in the morning sun and shook his head. "I swear," he muttered, "I swear." Then, alone, he began rounding up horses. The great cow herd would only travel a mile while he and the horses covered seven or eight, but still it would be noon before he could hand them over to Ollie Sinclair.

Nacho Lucas finished the harnessing of Sam Price's team, then helped Ollie Sinclair dismantle the rope corral and get the remuda started. With his chores completed he caught himself a leggy gray gelding out of the rough string and slipped a hackalea onto it to lead it across to the wagons.

Ollie Sinclair glanced at him from the saddle of his fresh horse. "Mr. Green didn't assign you to the herd today," he pointed out. But Nacho ignored him. He shouted at Sam Price to hold up so he could retrieve his saddle, and walked across to the wagons. He snugged the gray to a rim and climbed

135

the tall sideboard to get his trappings.

"Time was," Price grouched, "when a trail cook's swamper stayed with the wagons to spell the cook with his drivin'."

Lucas glanced at the old man. "They're short-handed out there."

"So I hear," Price muttered.

Nacho tossed down his saddle and trap, then paused, his dark eyes somber with curiosity. "Mr. Price, how come the boss didn't go ahead and hang those two while ago? They admitted to thievin'."

"He decided to hire 'em instead, that's all."

"Well, I was sidin' with you. I'd like to've seen them hang."

Price swung around to glare at the youth. Hardly more than a tad, Nacho was the youngest of all the young men in the Rafter H outfit. Yet in some ways, Price thought he might be the most dangerous. The kid had an intense, insatiable curiosity that seemed too often focused on death.

"Nacho, have you ever seen a man hang?" Price demanded.

"Well, no sir, but I thought I was about to."

"Well, until you know what you're talkin' about, don't talk about it!"

Nacho's eyes widened. "All I meant was—"

"What you meant was, you're always just itchin' to see somebody die. You know why that is, boy? It's because you ain't seen it yet. Once you do, you might see things a whole lot different."

Nacho's jaw tightened, a fierce glint in his hard Mexican-Irish eyes. "Well, you sure were fixin' to hang those two, Mr. Price. You like to've had the

136

ropes around their necks before Mr. Hazelwood changed his mind."

Price shook his head. "Matt Hazelwood didn't change his mind, son. I've rode with that man since before you was born, and we've hanged some men in our times, for a fact. But Matt Hazelwood never was fixin' to string up anybody just for bein' dumb and fiddlefooted and down on their luck. And neither would I. Now you think about that, son. There's just too many ways for good men to die in this country for us to add one more way to the list."

"But I saw you—"

"You saw a couple of mixed-up cowpokes gettin' the kinks straightened out of their perspectives Hangin' is for outlaws."

Nacho hoisted his saddle and tossed it aboard the gray. With his back to the old cook he muttered, "I should'a shot them out there when I had the chance." He tightened his cinches, checked his lashings, swung aboard and put heels to the pony without looking back.

Price watched him go, then shrugged and laced his reins through gloved fingers. "Hard-ass button!" he told himself. "Like to hear how he sees things after he's lived long enough to see some things . . . if he does." He flicked the reins and yelled at the team and the wagons rolled. Ahead, Ollie Sinclair had the remuda on the move, lazing them along, waiting for the wagons to pass so he could follow with his stock.

At an easy lope, Nacho aimed the gray toward the rear of the great herd a mile away. The point had been in motion for nearly an hour, and was almost out of sight. Along the flanks, riders were galloping their mounts in a huge choreography, thinning out the bulk of the herd, making them remember to follow the cows ahead of them, ordering the line of march. And in the drags, still on the bedding grounds, others were bunching great masses of beef, pushing them inward and northward.

Soapy Green had not assigned a position to the young swamper for this day, so he chose one of his own. Tip Curry was away somewhere with Mr. Hazelwood. Nacho Lucas felt the gun resting on his hip and knew where he should be. He would ride tail, the way Tip Curry had been doing. He would work out from the herd, watch for strays and bunch-quitters and keep an eye on the trail behind. He knew they were all expecting trouble, and he wanted to be there when it happened.

He came up on the drags and veered away, staying out of the way of the men working there. This morning the drag riders were Gabe Sinclair, Jesus Gomez and Stan Lamont, and they had their pattern worked out.

Nacho rode a lazy arc behind them, several hundred yards out, and watched the spaces between them. When he saw a hundred head or so beginning to mill at a gap between Gabe's path and Stan's, he dashed in and rode through them to break it up, then circled around and patrolled the gap, swinging his coiled catchrope and shouting cusswords, until he saw Lamont returning to pick up the sweep. He waved then, and backed away again, then turned for a careful scan of the prairie southward.

138

Out there was only distance, receding miles of the outlet sweeping back toward the Dry Creek range. Who would come for them? he wondered. Would it be Marcus Flood and some of the T-bar-T gunslingers? Flood had a reputation on Dry Creek as a troublemaker, and the hands he hired confirmed it. Mostly they were a rough and sullen bunch, and the working hands of neighboring spreads avoided them when they could. And it was whispered that Marcus Flood had never been above a little overbranding now and then to fill out his herd.

As many critters as Rafter H had branded in recent weeks, there must be hundreds with the marks poorly set, marks that a hand with a running iron or a cinch-ring artist could transform into some other brand, given the chance. Rafter H would not easily counterfeit into any of the Dry Creek range brands. The Association was careful about things like that. But most ranches also had trail brands for bought or traded critters, and one of T-bar-T's trail brands was Arrowhead. Musing about it, Nacho could see how a slick hand might turn Rafter H into Arrowhead on the shoulder and then rebrand T-bar-T on the hip and nobody the wiser.

Then again, Link might be coming out to fight, despite what some of the others said about Link being bottled up in a claim dispute—Stan Lamont said he figured Matt Hazelwood had fired his house just to set off a dispute and give Rafter H time to get shed of the whole mess. Nacho wasn't so sure. Herman Link was a bitter old man, and he was used to making big strides and didn't hold with anybody crossing him. But those two cow thieves—Pye and Slater—had said there were stampeders in the hills hired by Pinto Boyd. What would Colter's town marshal have to do with Link?

And somehow he couldn't see Colonel Nelson sending riders out from Triple-Seven at this point. They had been on Triple-Seven home range the first two days of the drive. If the Colonel wanted to tackle them, he would already have done it.

Recalling about the stampeders in the hills drew Nacho's attention to the west, and he found himself studying those hills at every opportunity. Where would they be, if they were there?

Another hour had passed, and now the great herd was strung out and moving at a good pace. Even the slowest of the drags was more than a mile north of the bedding grounds. Several times Nacho had sprinted in to fill a gap between drag riders, chousing animals that tried to turn. But each time he returned to ride far tail, and more and more he studied the hills off there to the west, less than a mile away now from the trail.

If I wanted to lay up there and watch this herd, where would I be? His dark eyes studied the rolling skyline out there, and came to rest on a stubby spire just back of the front canyons. It was like a sheared-off short mesa, offering plenty of vantage for view across the outlet. His hackles rose slightly. If he were them, there's where he would be. With a delicious tingling longing that seemed to pull at him from the hills, he licked his lips and touched the butt of his gun. Matt Hazelwood might forgive cow thieves, but nobody would forgive stampeders. Such men, it seemed to Nacho, were fair game.

Still, he had no call to go riding off out there without a reason. Just because he wasn't assigned, that didn't mean he could just wander off without Soapy Green's approval. And Soapy Green was at least three miles ahead now, working the point of the herd.

Nacho shrugged and dropped the idea. But still his gaze returned again and again to the westward hills and the spire that sat among them.

The sun was high when Nacho Lucas saw movement in the distance. He had pulled away from the dust of the drags again, to study the backtrail, and this time there was something to see. A feather of dust swept across the prairie two or three miles south, and its point was a bunch of horses, approaching at a lope. He checked the loads in his gun, put it away and headed in that direction.

With a mile still between them, his sharp eyes made it out... Mr. Hazelwood, bringing in a bunch of short-tails. Standing tall in his stirrups, he searched the sun-hazed landscape. Tip Curry had gone out with the boss, and they had headed back into the hills. Now the boss was coming with horses and Tip was nowhere in sight. Intuition as deep as the soil of Mexico and as dark as the soul of Ireland crept through him and he turned again to stare at the stubby spire now only a few miles west, among the frontal hills. He knew where Tip Curry was, and he knew why.

He glanced back at the herd, now hazy and

141

distant, then again at the oncoming horses, still far out on the flats, and he made up his mind. Tugging his hat low over his eyes, fingertips swinging down to feel the Colt at his hip, he neck-reined to the right and dug heels into his mount. At a mile-eating run he headed for the low hills and the broken mesa beyond. A nagging worry tugged at him, an uncertainty that bordered on delicious anticipation. In his mind he reviewed all the things he had learned from Tip Curry—from watching and imitating the gunhand—and he knew there was one thing he could never learn from Curry or anyone else. There was only one way to learn to kill. It was a thing learned by doing. Intense dark eyes danced as he watched the rises beginning around him and the hills just ahead. Those two waiting up there had seen him now, and were waiting. Tip Curry was up there somewhere, probably stalking them right this minute, but it wasn't Tip Curry they were watching, it was Nacho Lucas, and the thought carried with it a wild joy that drove him on. Now was his chance to test himself, to find out. . . .

The whip of a rifle bullet past his ear as he rounded a rock shoulder just below the spire delighted him. He had never before heard the sound of a gun from the target's vantage point. It was a tiny, brief scream, abruptly extinguished as the bullet slapped rock behind him and ricocheted away, flattened and howling as it tumbled through the air, and the hard thunder of the rifle's report followed it into the distance. Even as he sorted out the sounds and tasted the sensation of them his eyes found the puff of smoke among the rocks above and he drew and fired, the Colt's roar redoubling the echoes of the rifle's voice. It was a narrow cleft in broken rock, only a few inches wide, but he knew as the hammer fell that his point was dead on. He thought the shot home, as surely as the pointing of a finger, and heard the clatter of a dropped rifle even as his senses probed the rocks for the second man.

His horse was still running, bobbing and leaping like a dancer through the littered gully leading to the crest of the spire. It was one of Stan Lamont's working string, and it was a cowpony.

But now it slowed, heaving, baffled by a maze of jumbled stone, and Nacho wheeled it around, full circle, his dark eyes scanning the broken skyline of the ledge just twenty yards away.

There was another man there. He sensed the presence, searching. Nothing moved. He started to wheel again.

This time the shot was so close that the scream of lead was simultaneous with the rifle's bark, and something vicious slapped at his saddle. He felt the jolt of it and tried to spin toward its source, but could not find the reins. How had he lost his reins? His hand didn't seem to know how to feel for them. He groped and found the saddlehorn and it was slick and hot. In surprise he glanced down. There was blood there.

The world seemed unnaturally bright, as though a second sun had entered the sky. He heard his horse whinny, and lurched to the side as it shied and danced, shifting his weight to stay aboard. Something cold stung his shoulder . . . cold or

143

terribly hot. His head came up and now he saw the man, rising from rocks, a rifle at his shoulder, pointing at him. White glare erupted from the muzzle and Nacho felt the shift of sound as his left ear abruptly went deaf. But then his Colt was out and talking, and he saw the man jerk upright and twist this way and that as .45 slugs tore at him. He heard a peculiar clicking sound, loud in one ear, dimly in the other, and realized he was snapping the hammer on empty chambers. The man collapsed and fell, seeming to have been held upright only by the bullets hitting him, and abruptly there was a profound silence.

Dazedly, Nacho Lucas stared at the body doubled over white rocks just a few yards away, trying to grasp the notion that the inert, scarlet-splashed thing there and the man he had seen just seconds before were the same thing. It had been—he had been—a man with a gun. Now he—it—was a fresh corpse dripping hot blood in the brilliant sunlight.

He wondered where his reins were, and lifted his hand, and the horse backed in response. He looked down curiously. His hand held the reins, but it was a bright red hand holding bright red slippery reins and its shadow wavered on a saddlehorn bathed in fresh blood. And his shirtsleeve was wet and matted at the shoulder, a spreading dark red stain.

Idly he dropped his gun into its holster, thinking that he ought to reload it first, then carefully, with his right hand, removed the sticky reins from his left, and noticed that his bloody saddlehorn had a deep gouge in its leather cap. And something lay

144

beside it, a small curved thing caught in the cleft of the saddlebow. He started to pick it up, and bile rose in his throat. The hand at the bow was minus a finger. What it was trying to grasp was its missing part.

Wild dizziness rocked him, and when it subsided he was on his knees on the hard ground, doubled over his injured hand and rocking back and forth. Rocks rattled nearby and Tip Curry slid down a gravel slope to look at the body hanging over the ledge. With a glance at Nacho he disappeared beyond an outcropping and reappeared higher up where the first man had been. He knelt there, then stood, put his gun away and climbed down to the gully floor. He looked at Nacho's shoulder, then looked at his hand and took out a bandana to wrap it.

Standing beside the pale, trembling youngster he looked again at the dead man on the shelf, then toward the one hidden behind the crest.

"I reckon now you know," he said.

12

Maynard and Rodney lost two more of the money horses, driving down from the hills onto Dry Creek range. It was Rodney's fault for not paying attention, and Maynard fumed and griped until Rodney was exasperated.

"All right, all right!" he shouted. "It ain't but a mile from here to that box-end gully where we used to put our dollar calves. Let's take 'em there an' you can hold 'em while I go back a ways and look."

"If you'd been watchin' your side we wouldn't have lost any in the first place," Maynard pointed out. "It isn't that hard to herd horses, Rodney."

"I ain't cut out for this kind of work," Rodney snarled. "I got other things in mind."

They moved the horses down a runoff slope to the brushy draw where they had learned to shave weaning calves off from branded stock and put a road brand on them with a heated cinch ring. Between them, over a span of nearly two years, they had accumulated several hundred dollars by selling the calves to shotgun outfits at a dollar a head. The money had gone into Maynard's silver saddle, Rodney's fancy Colt and slip-draw rig, and to the poker tables at Colter.

It was a hidden place, largely ignored by the working hands on Link except during spring and fall roundup. A few cows might wander into the gullies now and again, but there was nothing to keep them there and they came out again on their own. Still, the box draw was a handy place to hold a few animals for a few hours.

Maynard counted the horses filing in. Twenty-eight. He frowned and glared at his brother. He was sure there had been more than forty originally, when they took the herd from that big wrangler. But they had lost several right off, and now two more were missing.

"You're just like an old woman," Rodney rasped. "Always fussin' about one thing or another." But he wheeled around and headed for the front hills again, to look for the missing stock.

Maynard stared after him in disgust. He had a feeling that Rodney was going to complicate things again, just like he always did. Rodney was always enthusiastic about getting money, but when it came right down to it, he usually cut out and left Maynard to do the work. Just like now, he acted like he really didn't care whether they got all these horses to where they could sell them or not. But when it came time to get the money, Rodney would be there for his full share and maybe a little more.

Rodney liked to strut and talk big, and he always wanted to be the center of attention, but

148

Maynard couldn't remember him ever having an original idea. It was Maynard who had figured out how to ring-brand calves in the first place, when the old man wouldn't give him the money he wanted for a fancy saddle. And as he remembered, he was always the one who wound up doing most of the work. It had been his notion that the big wrangler who showed up in Three Rivers to talk to Valdez might have breed horses to sell—when Valdez talked business with strangers, what else would it be about?—and his idea to follow the man to see what he had. Rodney had complained about it all the way, though he had done nothing but crow ever since about the slick way he gunned the man down. And then he had turned right around and spooked the horse herd so a bunch of them ran off into the hills and the last they saw of them was their dust.

Maynard had heard the hands on Link whisper from time to time about his brother. Some of them thought he was crazy as a loon. Privately, Maynard agreed with them. He had been tempted for a long time to part company with Rodney and just go his own way. And especially since Rodney had gone to practicing with that gun of his, and thinking of himself as a bad man. Lately it seemed like the more people Rodney shot the crazier he was, and Maynard was about fed up.

Thinking about it, he wondered whether he could take these twenty-eight money horses—right now while Rodney was away—and head off with them someplace and never look back. The problem was, he would have to look back, because Rodney was as likely as not to come gunning for him if he did.

"What we ought to do," he told himself, "is just keep on goin' until we're so far from Dry Creek that nobody ever heard of us, then get rid of these horses and split up. Stock like these, they ought to bring two-three hundred each back in civilized country."

He thought about having three or four thousand dollars, all his own, and he looked at the horses and thought about having twice that much if he didn't have to share with Rodney.

"That's what I ought to do," he told himself. "I ought to just light out of here right now, with these that I've got, and just not ever come back."

He strung a rope across the wash, anchored to brush on both sides, then tied his saddle pony nearby and climbed the bank to look across the wide basin of Dry Creek. There wasn't much to see. Rodney had disappeared into the maze of little draws that led up into the hills, backtracking the way they had come. In the distance, out on the plain, he could see a few cattle here and there. Things looked odd in some way—as though the roundup scheduled for next month had already taken place. It was like all those Link critters he had seen in the hills—odd.

In the far distance east he could make out the house and cluster of barns and sheds that were the headquarters of the Link ranch. Vaguely, he wondered what the old man was doing and whether they ought to stop in and see him. He shrugged the idea off. Herman Link had made it clear to his sons from the time they came here eleven years before and staked out this spread that they had no special

150

place on it and no call to feel at home here. He gave them a roof over their heads and food for their bellies, and he expected them to work for every bit of it. Maynard wondered sometimes if the old man hadn't kept them down just to see what they would do about it, the way some of the Mexican wranglers would prod and push a string of horses just to prove out the bad ones so they could sell them to Hacendados for bucking stock to use in their rodeos. He remembered in the early years, when he was a lop-eared kid of ten or so and Rodney just two years younger, that Herman Link had treated all his hands that way. But he stopped eventually because he kept losing good hands and the bad ones just stayed around long enough to steal from him. But he never stopped treating his sons that way.

"I guess he never had to," the thought occurred to him and he muttered it to himself. "Where were we goin' to go?"

He was pretty sure the old man knew—had always known—when he and Rodney began shaving calves and selling them. He doubted, though, whether his father knew that most of those they shaved were his. They had made a point of it after a while. It served the old son of a bitch right.

Maynard squatted on his heels, relaxing. From here he could see for miles in all directions. The horses were secure and nobody was going to slip up on him and he had nothing to do until Rodney came back.

"I hope he finds those two horses," he muttered. "That's maybe four-five hundred dollars worth of

151

horses right there. He ain't got any sense at all."

No one around for miles . . . just the sun, the heat haze on the prairie, wavering hills to the west and wavering cattle out on the flats, and nobody around but him . . . he jerked upright, his hackles rising. The voice he heard was only yards away, a nasal, irritating voice, singing, ". . . *I spied a young cowboy all wrapped in white linen . . . wrapped in white linen and cold as the clay . . .*"

Eyes wide, Maynard crouched and turned full around. There was an eerie quality about the voice, as though it had been there for some time, singing, and he had only then heard it. Now it trailed off, and he heard the horses whuffing and stamping, down in the draw. Brush rustled, hooves pounded and his saddled mount broke through the brush, clawing to gain the top of the draw, then thundered away across the flats, reins swinging loose and stirrups flapping. He started to go after it, then heard the voice again, complaining, ". . . ought to learn these young-uns to tie a proper knot in a rope . . . don't teach 'em half what they ought to know these days . . . there, that's better."

Drawing his gun, Maynard scuttled to the brush at the shelf-edge, found a break where his horse had come through, and looked down into the box gully. The money horses were backed up against the draw's washout end, and near at hand, almost directly below, a man was coiling Maynard's rope while he pushed brush aside to clear the opening. He finished coiling the rope, hung it carefully on a snag, and stepped into a brush thicket. A moment later he reappeared, riding a scruffy gray horse that had the look of mustang about it. Both the man and the horse looked as weathered and tough as the land itself.

Getting his senses about him, Maynard pushed through the brush, holding his gun ahead of him. "Hey, you!" he barked. "What do you think you're doin' here?"

The man looked up at him, eyes shadowed by the floppy brim of a battered slouch hat. "Howdy," he said. "That your rope there?" He indicated the coiled rope hanging on the snag. "If it is, you ought to practice tyin' a decent half-hitch. That knot was more like a shoestring bow. By the way, your horse run off, but it won't go far loose-reined like that."

As though that ended the conversation, the man turned and started the gray through the brush opening into the penning draw.

Maynard scrambled down the bank, into the gully, trying to keep his gun pointed at the man. "Hey!" he shouted. "Now you stop right there, Mister!"

The man reined in the scruffy gray and turned to look back at him. "You want something?"

"I asked you what you're doing here!"

"Oh. Well, I'm gettin' those there horses out of this draw. You had them all penned up in there. You better stand aside, because I'm goin' to bring them out."

Maynard's face went slack for an instant. This whole thing didn't make any sense. Where had the man come from? And why wasn't he paying attention to Maynard's gun?

Before Maynard could come up with words, the

man continued, conversationally, "Those ponies belong to a feller I know, and he'll feel a lot better when he gets 'em back. Some jasper shot him dead a couple of days back, west of here, and he's havin' a hard time puttin' a loop on what things is all about. I'm tryin' to give him a hand, so to speak, 'cause he knows the way to some places that I don't. That all right with you?"

Confused and irritated, Maynard stepped closer, holding his gun now in both hands. He cocked the hammer and pointed it at the intruder.

The man squinted at him curiously. "Am I botherin' you or anything?"

"I'll shoot," Maynard assured him. "Don't think I won't shoot. You ain't takin' any horses!"

"Yes, I am. Those yonder. They belong to Jim Tyson an' he'll feel a lot better about things once he gets 'em back. You want to stand aside, now? I'm fixin' to bring 'em right through here."

"The hell you are!" Maynard shrilled. He levelled the gun again and squeezed the trigger. The gun roared and bucked in his hands, and he heard his slug ricochet away into the distance.

"My," the mounted man said. "I ain't had anybody shoot at me in a coon's age. Now you best stand aside. Time's a-wastin'." He turned and headed the gray into the box draw at a trot.

Maynard stared after him, stunned. The man rounded a cutbank and disappeared. Maynard heard the money horses stamping and milling just beyond, then a flurry of sound that became the thunder of many hooves. The horses came around

154

the cutbank massed and running, filling the narrow draw. Maynard goggled at them. Then he dropped his gun and ran. He scrambled up the steep bank, slipped and slid to the bottom again, and felt the heat of plunging horses almost on top of him. With a yell he scrambled upward, pulling himself above them, clinging to thorny brush as they passed, a thundering mass of running horses, some of them brushing against his boots as they passed.

Behind them came the man on the gray, chousing them along, singing at the top of his lungs, "... *look away, look away, look away, Dixie land!*"

The thorn brush tore loose in Maynard's hand. He slid downward and a horse shouldered him, knocking the wind out of him. He flailed for purchase, lost his hold and fell backward, rolling. A horse went over him. Another shied aside, its hooves barely missing his head. He lay for a moment, stunned, then sat up. The man on the gray reined up, stared down at him sadly and shook his head. "You ought to go into some other line of work," he said.

By the time Maynard found his gun and his hat, they were gone. He climbed again to the flats above the gully and shaded his eyes. The money horses were lined out in the distance, going away at a steady lope. The rider on the gray was nowhere to be seen, but in the distance someone else was coming—a big man, slumped over the saddlehorn of a long-legged blood bay.

Maynard didn't wait to see any more. Scuttling

155

away, staying low and running awkwardly on fancy boots, he went to find his horse.

Rodney was a half-hour into the running hills when he crossed a low hogback ridge and saw a pair of horses grazing among cottonwoods in a spring-fed swale beyond. He grinned in anticipation and uncoiled a short, knotted reatta. The stupid things had made him go out of his way, wandering off like that. He'd take them back, all right. He'd run them until their coats were lathered and their tongues hung out, and when they slowed down he'd take pleasure in whipping them from head to tail.

He headed for them, spurring his mount cruelly, then hard-reined into a skidding stop as a man on a gray horse appeared in his path. Rodney didn't know where he had come from. One minute there was nobody around, and then suddenly there he was, directly in front of him, blocking his way. He shifted the reatta to his left hand and let his right fingers brush the butt of his Colt.

"Howdy," the stranger said. "You look like a feller that knows where he's goin'."

"I might," Rodney allowed. "What do you want?"

"I was just curious. Do you know the way to Porterville?"

"Never heard of it." Rodney suddenly felt uneasy. There was something about the man facing him . . . something not quite right.

"Didn't figure you did," the man said. "Seems like hardly anybody does. Where you off to?"

"I don't see how it's any of your concern," Rodney glared at him. "But I'm on my way to bring back those horses yonder."

"You don't need to do that," the stranger said, amiably. "They ain't your horses. They belong to a feller that's showin' me the way to some places. I'll take 'em to him."

Rodney's fingers closed on the butt of his fancy Colt, but he hesitated. The man didn't seem to care whether he drew it or not, and there was a chilling uncertainty in realizing that.

"You got a wallet there on your belt," the man added. "I guess I'll take that, too."

Rodney was aghast. "What do you think you're doin', mister? You think you're gonna rob me?"

"You might look at it that way," the man agreed. "But the thing is, that ain't your wallet. It goes with the horses." The stranger touched his reins and the gray stepped forward. With a friendly smile, the man held out his hand, and Rodney's gun came half out of its holster . . . then hesitated. There was something cold and distant about the eyes gazing at him from under the slouch hat. The smile on the weathered face never reached those eyes. "You don't want to shoot at me, Bub. Your brother already did that. It was a waste of time. Just hand over that wallet. It belongs to that feller you boys killed back there and he wants it."

The reatta dropped from nerveless fingers and slithered to the ground. Like one in a trance, Rodney reached around and drew the fold-over wallet from his belt. He passed it across to the man, who smiled again and put it away.

157

The man touched his hatbrim laconically. "Y'all be careful now, you hear?" He clicked his tongue, tugged his reins and turned away. Rodney stared after him, his hand still on his gun. Then he blinked, rubbed his eyes and squinted. He didn't know where the man had gone. He just rode away and . . . then he wasn't there. Rodney sat and blinked, engulfed in a blinding confusion that ebbed slowly as he realized what had happened. The man had never even drawn a gun. He had simply faced him down and got what he wanted, and never turned a hair in the process.

"God damn," Rodney whispered. Then as hot anger blazed up in him he drew his Colt and screamed, "God damn you! Where are you?"

Down in the cottonwoods, the two strayed horses raised their heads and stared . . . but not at him. They were looking at something else, something Rodney could not make out. They stamped and snorted, then turned in unison and loped away toward the low valley that opened out onto the plains of Dry Creek.

Rodney spurred his mount, angling down to head them off. Abruptly, the man on the scruffy gray was there again, and across the distance Rodney felt the shock of those cold, distant eyes. He eased back, started to charge again, then changed his mind. He waved his gun, shouted a curse, then turned and angled back the way he had come. He had never felt so confused in his life . . . and somehow, in a way that made no sense to him, he had never felt so close to death.

*   *   *

Big Jim Tyson sat hunched in the saddle of his blood bay and stared at the thirty horses filing sedately past him, a neat little herd on the way to someplace. Then he recognized them, and through the pall of dull pain in his head he catalogued individual markings and configurations. They were his horses.

"Seemed to me like I'd lost them," he muttered.

The herd passed and he fell in behind it, noticing that he felt a little better because they were here.

Clifton Flowers came from somewhere and rode beside him, whistling a discordant tune.

Tyson counted the breed horses ahead and frowned. "I guess I did lose some," he said. "There's only thirty head here."

Flowers stopped whistling. "How many more was there supposed to be?"

"Fourteen more. I had forty-four head."

"Well, I didn't know that." Flowers raised his head and turned it slowly, his eyes seeming to see distances that Tyson could not comprehend. "Are you sure you know the way to Rafter H?"

"Well, I ought to. Why?"

"Because the direction we're goin' don't seem right. It seems to me Rafter H is up yonder someplace, and gettin' more up yonder by the minute."

Tyson shrugged. He had stopped expecting Clifton Flowers to talk sense.

"So you're still shy fourteen short-tails," Flowers complained. "Is there anything else you're missin' that you ain't mentioned yet?"

"My wallet—"

"It's safe," Flowers told him.

"I don't know what happened to Pepe," Tyson said. "It seems like Pepe was with me."

Flowers scowled thoughtfully. "Mexican feller, was he?"

"Yeah."

"Well, you can quit worryin' about him. He was a lot deader than you were back there. He didn't even try to get over it. Seems to me like we ought to start swingin' north about now, if we want to find Rafter H."

"I thought you said you don't know the way."

"I don't. I just know where it ain't, is all."

13

Law was a tenuous concept in the great, shallow basin that formed the Dry Creek range. There had been no law when first Matt Hazelwood and Jim Tyson put together a crew to chouse wild cattle out of the brush flats and create trail herds for the market. The only law then had been themselves and the guns they carried, and when they staked out a spread and Matt Hazelwood put money into the improving of it, that spread became the center of the law.

On an old Spanish map they found the words *arroyo seco,* and one of their vaqueros told them it meant dry creek, so they named the range that, and the name became the title of the law.

As times and troubles passed, rules of conduct grew from experience, simple standards of behavior necessary for men to live and work and profit in the wild lands. These became the body of the law, and as the markets grew and others came to share the range the law expanded to accommodate the fact of neighboring ranches with common graze. It was Matt Hazelwood who proposed an association to govern the business of the range, and the Dry Creek Association became the force of law.

Few on Dry Creek now remembered—or cared to—that it was Matt Hazelwood and Rafter H who started it all. A lot of the early small outfits had been swallowed up in those early years, bought out or run off by bigger players. What was now the Link spread, with its chain-link brand, covered the land that nearly a dozen early shotgun outfits had developed. And to the north, those vast ranges controlled by Dominion Land and Cattle Company under the Triple-Seven brand included the remains of more than twenty one-time enterprises that had not lasted.

Times changed, and boundaries changed, and what made it all work was the Dry Creek Range Association . . . the law.

But now that law lay broken and in jeopardy, victim of the vacuum left by Rafter H pulling out and the hardcase crew that had moved in to claim possession of the Rafter H share of the range. It was probably the first time in his life that Pinto Boyd had been dealt a full house by the fates, and he ante'd up everything he had.

After Will Bower and some of the T-bar-T hands brought in the body of Marcus Flood, they hung around Colter, uncertain what to do next. Flood's attempt to claim Rafter H hadn't lasted an hour. Backed by a tough crew, he had ridden down on the burned headquarters and run into massed gunfire from a barn and two bunkhouse structures. Pinto

Boyd and his hardcases were playing for keeps. With Flood dead, the T-bar-T crew was left adrift. Martha Flood would have no use for gunhands on her spread. Short of picking up their wages, Bower and the rest—eight men in all who had backed their boss at Rafter H—were now out of work.

So when Johnny McGraw came to summon Will Bower to Paisley's, where the bosses of the remaining spreads were holed up making their plans, Bower was more than ready to hear what they had to offer.

"I didn't think it would happen," McGraw told him, "but Colonel Nelson and Herman Link have decided to work together to drive Boyd's men out."

"I never thought I'd see those two agree on anything," Bower allowed.

"Well, the Colonel knows how to make things happen."

As they approached the guarded door of Paisley's, McGraw paused and stepped aside into an alleyway, beckoning for Bower to follow. He glanced around to be sure they were alone. "Before you go in, Will, let me tell you how the cards are dealt. The Association is puttin' up a war chest to hire gunhands to ride on Rafter H and take it from Boyd's bunch. They made a deal. Triple-Seven gets the headquarters site and Link gets the pool grazing rights, and they said they'll share out with the little outfits in cash."

"So they're hiring riders."

"Yeah. Gun wages. I reckon you boys are interested."

"Probably."

"Well, that's fine. You go on in and hear 'em out, and make your deal. But let me give you some advice. If Herman Link tries to make a private deal with you on the side, I suggest you all shy away from it. The Colonel can make you a better offer."

"What would Link want with us?"

"Just this, Will—the Colonel figures Link intends to go after Hazelwood and that herd as soon as we deal with Pinto Boyd, and he'll try to hire some of you boys to ride for him."

Bower was puzzled. "What difference does it make to the Colonel whether Link goes after Hazelwood?"

McGraw grinned. "It doesn't. Matter of fact, the Colonel is countin' on it. But it will be worth a lot to him if that herd doesn't turn out to be easy to take. The longer Link is tied up tryin' to take back that herd, the better it will suit Triple-Seven. The Colonel's got some plans of his own for how this range gets split up."

Pinto Boyd had planned well for a siege. He had twenty-two men forted up on old Rafter H, and two wagonloads of provisions and ammunition, snaked out from Colter by Joe Bond on a promise of payment and share as soon as the Association recognized Boyd's claim. Which they would have to do, Boyd explained carefully. Not a ranch on the range could mount a force capable of putting him off the property.

The men with him also were there on promises—

cash money for each gun, to be paid from the sum he could borrow from Joe Bond's bank with Rafter H as collateral.

Marcus Flood's raid on the place had been no surprise. Boyd knew either T-bar-T or Link would test his claim. He had expected it to be Link, but it made no difference. Even Link wouldn't have that kind of firepower.

So Pinto Boyd was already counting his money, and waiting for the Association to recognize the fact that he had won.

As dawn of a new day pinked the eastern sky, the former marshal of Colter pulled on his boots and stepped out to savor the aroma of boiling coffee and frying bacon.

"I have a feelin' this is the day," he said to himself and anybody else who cared to listen.

Some of the men by the cook fire moved aside to make room for him. Fell Hankins and Pony Simmons glanced at each other cynically. Older than most of the men here, they had both seen a lot of schemes go awry in their times, and would believe in this one when they saw the money in their hands. If not . . . well, they had other things in mind. Gator Jones, the gunslinger from Bodine, raised a brow that said he agreed with them, and kept slicing side meat into a skillet.

But Yuma Joe Riley was curious. "How do you think it will go, Pinto?"

Boyd grinned. "They've had plenty of time to butt heads about this. Now, either Herman Link or Colonel Nelson will be headin' out here to make a

165

deal. Simple as that. The first Association boss to recognize my claim will expect a piece of the pie. And I'll deal, all right, because once I have either Link or Nelson to back me, the other will have to fold and all the rest will fall in line. It's just a matter of who gets here first."

"How do you know you can trust them after they sign the quitclaim?"

"I can trust them," Boyd said. "Because they got no choice. We're squattin' right here on this ranch until the whole deal is done and we get cash in hand, and meantime they got fall circle lookin' them in the face. If they don't deal, we'll pick them off one by one and they know it. They got no choice, is how I see it."

He was so pleased with himself that he couldn't stop grinning.

When breakfast was done Gator Jones drifted off toward the corrals, and after a bit Fell Hankins and Pony Simmons came to join him.

"I thought Pinto was smarter than that," Fell said. "This whole deal has begun to stink."

"He ain't smart," Gator allowed. "He just thinks he is. You all know as well as I do what them ranchers are gonna do."

Simmons nodded. "So what do we do about it?"

"Just make sure we got horses saddled and ready, and pass the word to the boys you can trust. I don't aim to be strung up alongside the likes of Pinto Boyd. I got better things to do."

"That draw back yonder runs better'n two miles before it breaks out on the flats," Fell nodded.

"Who's standin' guard out there?"

Gator raised a brow, sardonically. "My boys. I seen to that."

"Then that's the way to go."

The sun was high in the sky when a lookout spotted movement on the eastern horizon, and Pinto Boyd climbed the barn to see who was coming. When he came down he was pale and agitated. Something had gone terribly wrong. The riders approaching were not a negotiating party. He counted more than fifty armed men in the bunch.

The former Marshal of Colter had never considered that the Association ranchers would join forces to enforce range law. It simply had never occurred to him.

And by the time he discovered that his force of twenty-two guns had shrunk to six—including himself—it was too late to escape.

The Association riders swarmed over the abandoned ranch, firing as they came, and two of Boyd's men fell in the first assault.

The other three surrendered immediately, and handed Pinto Boyd over to the Association representatives.

"What happened to the rest of your heroes?" Will Bower asked the sullen former marshal.

"I don't know," Boyd said. Hands tied behind him, he slouched between two Triple-Seven hands. "What are they going to do with me?"

"Turn him around, boys," Bower said. The Triple-Sevens swung their prisoner around to face the barn, and Bower pointed at the open loft where other hands were suspending nooses from the upper sill. "Pinto, I don't think I ever heard of a dumber stunt than you pulled here. You shoulda stuck to fleecin' drunks."

Nearby, Colonel Owen Nelson and Herman Link sat their mounts, surveying what was left of old Rafter H.

"Does our deal stand, Herman?" Nelson asked.

Link nodded. "You sign over the Rafter H share of pool rights to me. What you do with this place is up to you."

Nelson dipped his head in agreement. "I intend to begin general roundup in three weeks. Our foremen can work out the schedules." He waved and Corky Lassiter walked his horse across the yard to join them.

"This place is now the south station of Triple-Seven," Nelson told him. "Consider yourself foreman, and talk with Johnny McGraw about what you'll need. Roundup begins in three weeks." He looked around him at the waiting men and raised a hand for silence. Then with Herman Link at his side he walked his horse to where Boyd and the other three prisoners were being held. He looked from one to another of them, then glanced at Link. "Do you want to do the honors, or shall I?"

The old rancher shrugged. "It's your turf."

Nelson turned back to the four prisoners. "You men are charged with criminal trespass, attempted land theft, mayhem and the murder of Marcus

168

Flood. Do you have anything to say in your defense?"

"You got it wrong, Colonel," Boyd's voice was a terrified shrill. "All I did was establish a claim on vacated land, and defend my claim. You can't hang me for that."

Nelson stared at him, ice-eyed. "This range is pool land, Mr. Boyd. Only a representative of the Dry Creek Range Association may exercise claim rights. What representation do you claim?"

"I got my own brand," Boyd blustered. "The Colter town brands are part of the pool, and I'm one of them."

"Colter town brands are considered a unit of the pool," Nelson explained. He turned. "Mr. Campion, did Mr. Boyd act on behalf of the owners of the town brands?"

Lou Campion shook his head sadly. "He did not. He acted entirely on his own."

Boyd looked stricken, abruptly realizing that the law he had expected to break down had not. "I thought I was in my rights," he quavered.

"Unfortunately," Nelson said, "what you thought is of no concern here."

"I didn't do a damn thing that you high-an'-mighties wasn't intendin' to do, yourselves!" Boyd's eyes were huge as he looked from one to another of the ranchers. "If it hadn't been me it would have been Marcus Flood . . . you know he tried . . . or Link there, or you, Colonel. What difference does it make?"

The Englishman pursed his lips thoughtfully,

then tipped his head. "Assuming your allegations were true, Mr. Boyd, the difference is the law. You should have thought more about that. You other men, do you have anything to say?"

The three hardcases didn't look up. "We was just hired guns," one of them said. "We got no part in this."

"That is a shame," Nelson told them. "You really should have stood to gain more, for the price you have to pay." He removed his hat and raised his head so everyone could hear him. "Acting on behalf of the Dry Creek Range Association I declare the prisoners to be guilty as charged. Hang them."

Miles away, sixteen hard men approached the little town of Colter, spreading as they rode to enter from three directions.

"Let's make this clean," Gator Jones said again. "Six of us take the bank, and nobody else moves until we're in. Then the rest split up. Hit Paisley's and the other two saloons, and take the cash box at the general store. Anything else in this town ain't worth takin'."

"It ain't like anybody's goin' to object very much," Fell Hankins grinned. "The only law here was Pinto Boyd, an' he's bein' the guest of honor at a necktie party right about now."

"Yeah," Pony Simmons agreed. "An' every gun-toter available is out there helpin' him learn to sky-dance."

Hankins squinted, shading his eyes. "Two riders

up there, just goin' into town. Anybody know them?"

"I can't make them out," Gator said. "But they won't matter. Just be fast and thorough, boys. It ain't often a chance like this comes along."

"Comes of livin' a pure life," Hankins decided. "We been blessed."

14

Rodney was fit to be tied. Never in their lives had Maynard seen his little brother so wild with rage, and the closer to Colter they came the worse he was. He raved and cursed, he muttered to himself, he abused his horse with spurs and bit and he abused Maynard with words.

"How could you have missed the son of a bitch?" he demanded for the fiftieth time, as the outlines of Colter town grew ahead of them. "Fifteen-twenty feet, you said. How in God's name could you miss?"

Maynard was about fed up. "At least I shot at him," he growled. "Did you? You an' that fancy gun of yours, that you crow about, did you even try? Why didn't *you* shoot the son of a bitch?"

"That don't matter. I had my reasons. But by God had I decided to shoot him I wouldn't have *missed,* for Christ's sake!"

Nothing was going right. With the horses gone, and the money in the wallet gone, they were down to a few dollars. They had stopped in at Link headquarters—Maynard had an idea he might convince the old man to advance them something—but the old man wasn't there. Nobody was there except the cook and a couple of stock hands.

Then they had learned, from the cook, that Rafter H had pulled stakes and gone north, and Rodney came near to shooting the cook just for telling them that. If Rafter H was gone, then Matt Hazelwood and Tip Curry were gone, and Rodney couldn't gun them down in the street at Colter like he'd planned.

So they headed for Colter, for lack of a better plan, and Rodney was so riled that Maynard was afraid of him. He needed to come up with something to do, to take Rodney's mind off his troubles.

He was thinking of a hand of cards at Paisley's, or maybe a visit to one of the sporting houses—Rodney tended to cause trouble at the sporting houses, but not as much as he did at places like the saloon if he got liquored up—but as they rode into town he noticed how quiet the place was. Kids and old folks and a few women on the streets, here and there a merchant at a window, a swamper sweeping a porch, a drummer asleep in a tipped-back chair, an old hound dog sleeping on the shady ground beside him . . . he didn't remember ever seeing Colter so quiet in daylight, not even on a Sunday.

Rodney was looking up and down the street, also puzzled. He angled his horse across the street and sidled up to the porch where the swamper was working—a busted-up old cowboy not fit for anything anymore except swinging a broom.

"Where is everybody?" Rodney demanded.

The old poke looked up at him, squinting in the sun. "You're Rodney Link, ain't you?"

Rodney nodded. "Heard of me, have you?"

"Heard you an' your brother got run off Dry Creek," the oldster shrugged. "Decide to come back now that Rafter H has pulled out, did you?"

For a second there, Maynard thought Rodney was going to gun the old man, but then the door opened and Joe Bond stepped out of the shop. The banker was a florid man with a big belly and galluses, and Maynard had never liked him. He glanced up at Rodney, then across at Maynard, and blinked. "Howdy, boys. I didn't expect to see you two around here anymore."

"What's to stop us?" Rodney growled. "We go where we please."

Bond spread his hands and put on a placating smile. "No harm intended, boys. Glad to see you back."

"Where is everybody?" Rodney asked.

Bond looked worried. "There's a doin's out at the old Rafter H headquarters. Pinto Boyd has took possession, and most of the men are out there. I don't exactly know what's doin' but it ain't good. Seems to me Boyd's in the right, since he got there first, but your daddy and the Colonel and some of the others don't see it that way."

Maynard's eyes brightened. He heeled his horse across the street to join his brother. "Is the bank open today, Mr. Bond?"

"Sure is," the banker assured him. "Seven to five, every day. Why?" His glance suddenly was wary.

Maynard winked at Rodney. "The marshal gone an' all the gunhands gone . . . Rodney, seems to me we ought to do something about makin' up the losses we been takin'."

Bond blinked again. "I don't guess I understand."

"Sure you do, Mr. Bond. You just walk across the street ahead of us, an' we'll go in your bank and make a little withdrawal. Seems to me there won't ever be a better time."

"You can't do this!" Bond's face purpled and his eyes bulged.

"Yes, we can," Maynard told him. "Now walk. And don't get funny or anything. Rodney here will shoot you dead if you do. Go on, walk!"

The swamper had backed off several steps, trying to be invisible. Now he turned and darted for the shop door. Instantly Rodney's fancy Colt was out and talking, its echoes rattling windows up and down the street. The old poke was thrown against a plank wall. He bounced off and lay where he fell. Women screamed and people ran for cover. The hound dog and the drummer got tangled with the tipped chair, then sorted themselves out and disappeared around a corner.

"You see?" Maynard glared at Bond. "Rodney don't hesitate at all."

In the bank, they backed two clerks and a faro dealer against a wall and made Bond open his safe. Maynard cleaned it out while Rodney waved his gun around, grinning. "Why don't you fellows try to come up with a gun? Anybody? You, dealer! Ain't you got something that'll shoot? Come on,

176

now . . . try your luck. Wouldn't you like to be the man that gunned Rodney Link?" He turned to Bond, who had backed away, his hands high. The banker's florid face had gone a deathly gray. "How about it, banker . . . you gonna just let us clean you out? Tell you what, how's if I turn my back and give you a chance to get to that gun under the counter there? Maybe I'll even count to three . . ."

Rodney was getting nasty, and Maynard hurried to fill a currency bag with bills and coin. The trouble with Rodney was, once he got started, there was no stopping him. He worried about that swamper lying dead on the walk across the street. The old man might have had friends. He closed the bag and straightened abruptly, raising his head. "Rodney, I hear horses coming. Look out the window."

Rodney sidled to the front window and glanced out. "Men comin' up the street," he growled.

"Okay, let's get outta here." Carrying the money-bag, Maynard strode to the door and flung it open. Up the street near the livery were mounted men, approaching. He glanced downstreet and saw several more. He didn't recognize any of them, but they were hard-looking men, heavily armed. "Come on, Rodney!" he shouted. "Let's go!"

As he swung aboard his horse he heard the thump of gunfire inside the bank. A shot, then another, and Rodney came running out, grinnng and wild. He sprang into his saddle and turned to level a shot at the nearest group of horsemen.

Maynard ducked low and spurred his horse, heading for the alley beside Paisley's, that led to the north road. "Dammit, Rodney!" he shouted. "Come on, dammit! That's enough!"

The sudden attack had halted the approaching men, but now they were in motion and bullets sang around them as the Link brothers pounded through the shadowed alleyway and past the few buildings beyond, to hit the north road at a dead run.

Behind them was turmoil, but they didn't look back. Maynard aimed his surging mount at the line of thorny growth that marked the beginning of the breaks a half mile past the town, and for once Rodney was content to follow. As wind whistled past Maynard's ears he heard his brother shouting behind him, "Now they'll know who Rodney Link is! Now by God they'll know!"

Ollie Sinclair took one look at the fourteen horses Matt Hazelwood drove to him and his chocolate face resolved itself into a mask of bright eyes and gleaming, grinning teeth. "My, oh my," he marveled. "Mista Hazelwood, these here is some kinda *horses!* Where in the Lord's name did you find them?"

"That's just what I did," Matt scowled. "I found them—*we* found them, Tip and me—up in the hills, strayed."

"I never seen the like of these on this range," Ollie couldn't take his eyes off them. "They's some pretty fair horses around, but nothin' like these. Where'd they come from?"

"I don't know. But I know whose they are. Do you remember talk about Big Jim Tyson?"

178

Sinclair stared at him. "The wrangler? The one you started out with?"

"They're his horses. That's his mark. Star Cross."

"Then they ain't ours?" The dark face sobered. "We ain't gonna use them?"

Matt had puzzled about that all the way across the outlet. "Put them in with the remuda," he nodded. "We need the mounts. No choice that I can see. And tell Mr. Price to list them in the log as bought and payment due, to Jim Tyson."

Ollie's face brightened again. "Yes, sah!" He reined around, then hesitated and turned back. "Only thing is, these here is maybe two-three hundred dollar animals. Maybe more than that. How's it gonna set, puttin' ten-dollar cowboys up on stock like these?"

"Don't put prices on them until they've been worked on cattle," Matt frowned. Privately, though, he knew there was no question of value. These horses had been educated by Jim Tyson. Whatever else they might be, they were cowponies.

For the hundredth time he let the troubling thoughts swirl before him. What were these horses doing down here in Texas? Where was Jim Tyson? Why weren't his horses with him? Was Jim Tyson in Texas? What had happened to him?

There were no answers . . . none at all. But when Dave Holley dropped back a little later to change mounts, and returned to the herd aboard one of the Tyson brands, Matt watched him from a distance and understood the rapture on the young drover's face. Dave Holley had just died and gone to heaven.

179

Matt put his own saddle on one of them—a chesty bay with a blaze and stockings—and rode out to the herd. Cutting across from right drag to left drag, he put the animal through its paces, working a half-mile of recalcitrant beef with ease while the drag riders gaped at him in wonder.

It was a Tyson horse, all right. It had his impress as plain as the brand it carried. No two wranglers educated horses exactly the same, and Hazelwood had ridden with Jim Tyson long enough to know when he was straddling a Tyson mount.

Still, the animal was more than that. It had speed, stamina and the quick response of an intelligent horse. It had those little extra qualities that said high-bred, and the others were like it.

Matt thought back over the years—the campfire evenings on the old trails when young Tyson had talked about his dreams, as they all had. Campfire talk. But Tyson had always had a special thing in mind. Always he talked about Mexican mares and eastern Arabian-cross studs, and the qualities that he thought a good working breed should have.

So he had done it. Matt's cheeks twitched, almost a smile. The kid had found his dream. Arabian-cross cowponies. The all-around horse for cow country.

Working his way to left drag, Matt spelled Bo Maxwell with a wave and a wink. "Go on in and put your saddle on one of these," he told him. "Just don't get used to it, because there's only one of these per man per day."

By day's end and bedding time, each drover on the herd would have forked a Tyson horse. Matt wondered idly whether his cowboys would ever be the same again.

With left drag pushed into reasonable traveling order, Matt hung back and watched the hills. Even to himself, he refused to admit the concern that kept him there in position to watch, but when finally—late in the afternoon—he saw riders in the distance, he felt a great relief. Before he could make them out, he knew Tip Curry was coming back.

When Bo Maxwell returned, wide-eyed and grinning aboard a Star-Cross horse, Matt formed a quarter-mile of drag at a hard run, then headed out to meet the riders.

Four horses. Tip Curry aboard his own, leading two horses with dead men slung across their saddles. Nacho Lucas tagging along, slumped in his saddle, pale and bloody.

"I came to help Nacho bring these two in," Tip explained quietly. "They're his."

"What happened to him?"

"Crease on his shoulder, and he lost the little finger off his left hand. I thought Mr. Price ought to take a look at it. Is that all right?"

Matt edged alongside the youngster to look him over. "You killed those two, Nacho?"

"Yes, sir." Nacho's voice shook, but he held the boss's eyes.

"These are the stampeders those other two told us about," Tip Curry explained. "The big one there, that's Garth. It was him that messed Nacho up."

Matt scowled at him. "Where were you?"

"Up in the rocks. I was thinkin' I might bring you at least one of them alive, but Nacho got

181

there first."

Hazelwood turned again to the wounded kid. "Why did you go out there, Nacho?"

Nacho hesitated, very pale. Then he sighed. "I went out to kill some men, sir. I never done that before."

"Well, you have now. Did they shoot first?"

"Yes, sir. But I guess they had to."

"Why?"

"Because I was there."

Hazelwood thought it over, then nodded. "All right. It needed doing. How do you feel?"

They were angling to pass the huge herd at a distance. A man never knew how wild cows would react to the smell of blood.

"I don't know, sir." Nacho was weaving a bit in his saddle, but his head was clear. "Guess I need to think about it for a while."

Tip was riding ahead, leading the dead men's mounts. With a glance at Nacho, Matt Hazelwood spurred ahead. Riding beside Tip, he asked, "Why did that kid go out there?"

"Like he said, I guess. He never killed anybody before."

They were passing the rear of the herd, and a couple of drovers shaded their eyes to stare at them.

"I brought in those horses," Hazelwood said. "They're remuda stock now. You want to pick one out for your string? Maybe two?"

Tip gazed at him seriously. "I can't afford horses like those, Mr. Hazelwood. It's gonna take most of my back pay just to buy one of your line stock for a travelin' horse. But I thank you for the thought."

Hazelwood took a deep breath, held it for a hand-count, and expelled it. "That's what I thought," he said, finally. "Well, you can forget about being fired, Tip. Things worked out all right. Just for God's sake, from now on let me make the decisions and you follow orders."

"I'm not fired?"

"That's what I just said, isn't it?"

"And I draw gunhand's wages?"

"Of course you do."

"Then I guess you're going to have to go ahead and fire me, Mr. Hazelwood, because if I draw gunhand's wages I just plain have to do what I think is best. Otherwise I'm overpaid."

"Dammit, Tip! Don't you have any give in you at all?"

The young gunhand gazed at him, respectful yet remote. "Do you, Mr. Hazelwood?"

"Oh, all right!" Matt closed his eyes and shook his head. "Damn, but you are stubborn!"

"Yes, sir."

"But a gunhand is a hand first and a gun second . . ."

"I know that, sir."

". . . and when you're punching my cows you punch them the way I want them punched!"

"Yes, sir."

"Good. I'm glad that's settled. How did . . . ah, how did Nacho do out there? I mean, was he all right?"

"I never saw a slicker man with a gun in my life, sir. Both of those two had the drop on him, and both of them fired. But he nailed them both."

"He wants to be a gunhand, Tip. Like you. Will he make it?"

"I don't know, Mr. Hazelwood. Maybe he thinks too much about it . . . but maybe not. See how he does next time, then you'll know."

In the wake of the great herd, a mile north of where it crossed Outpost Road toward its final Dry Creek bedding at the top of the Outlet, evening sunlight slanted across the hills to accent the little mounds of two fresh-filled graves that bore no names, but only rough crosses of kindling wood capped with chunks of sod. As long as they stood, they would serve as warning to any stampeders who followed—two hardcases put under for messing with someone else's herd.

In the receding distance Nacho Lucas, pale and shaky, sat hunched on the tailbrace of Sam Price's trail wagon, dark eyes looking back. He gazed at the mute little graves on the prairie until they were out of sight.

15

Through the last hour or so of driving light, Dave Holley rode far point, scouting for the best bedding grounds in the converging sliver of grassland that was the Outlet's last funnel into the wild country beyond.

His delight at the horse beneath his saddle distracted him somewhat. Even as a top hand, he had never warranted a mount such as this, and he put it through its paces just for the joy of it. It was a strong, intelligent dark bay, superbly educated and proud of itself, and it carried a Star-Cross brand that Dave had never seen. All Ollie Sinclair had told him was that Mr. Hazelwood had brought in a few new horses, and a dark warning that this horse was worth a lot more than he was and he had best take good care of it.

For a long time, Dave had set great store by the quick little steeldust that was his favorite day horse. But now, with the mercurial fickleness of the true cowhand, the steeldust slid into distant realms of his affection and the dark bay between his legs reigned unchallenged as top horse.

He was so enthralled that he almost missed the flicker of motion a quarter mile west, among jutting slopes of closing hills. But it came again and he saw it—a string of riders moving fast, northbound, cresting little rises just at the edge of the plain.

He saw them only for a moment, then they were gone. A tingle of apprehension went up his spine, and he thought about moving back to spread the word to Stan Lamont, who was holding point at the moment, directing the dim notions of Sonofabitch while Dave scouted for bed grounds.

But the herd was coming up fast—he had never seen cows pushed so hard on a drive—and he still had to decide where to put them. A few miles on, just north of the Outlet, were the string of shallow waterholes called Six Tanks. He tested the wind, judging how far they could go before the cattle caught the scent of water. Their plan was to bed them dry each night and push them to water each morning, as long as the terrain permitted. Nobody in the outfit looked forward to the prospect of pushing seven thousand wild critters off water when they were bedded and grazed and full of vinegar. The whole Rafter H crew might be crazy— mostly they had decided in the past few days that they were—but that didn't call for being dumb.

So he ignored the glimpse of distant riders and explored the land. A mile on, he found a swell of high ground a half mile wide and maybe two miles long, bordered by sharp bluffs on the west and heavy scrub on the east. It looked like a fair bet, and he turned in his saddle to wave his hat. Far behind, Stan Lamont caught his signal and waved back, then circled abruptly as Sonofabitch tried to cozy up to his horse. Dave grinned. He could almost hear the big man cursing.

Beyond, a massive carpet of moving creatures, came the herd. A drover beyond Lamont had moved up to cover him on left swing, and Dave saw that it was one of the new men, the one called Pye . . . just this morning a convicted rustler, now a hand working the herd.

The herd bulged to the west as riders on east flank and swing applied pressure to push them clear of the cedar breaks beyond. Instantly Pye swung his mount and rode the line, waving his coiled catchrope, pushing them back into formation.

Dave Holley's eyes narrowed in appreciation. A cowboy down on his luck and taken to rustling, but still a cowboy. Dave turned back to his own chores.

He let the Star-Cross bay have its head, and felt the glad surge of powerful legs as it flew across narrowing flats, northward. For a mile he let it run, then reined in to look at the terrain. This was far enough, he decided. From here the high grounds became broken and erratic, and a shift in the wind might carry the wet scent of Six Tanks, but probably not this far. He glanced aside for landmarks to set the place in mind, and when he looked north again there were mounted men there, filing out of a draw a few hundred yards away, spreading and turning to face him. He hard-reined the bay, his hackles rising. He recognized several of them, hands from T-bar-T. The one in the lead, slope-shouldered and powerful, was Marcus Flood's foreman, Will Bower.

Dave held his ground, counting them. Six riders, he thought. Tough hands. Fighters and brawlers, a hard crowd hand-picked by the blustering Flood because they were like him. As a working top hand on pool range, Dave knew most of the regular hands of the other spreads by sight, and could get along well enough with most of them. But T-bar-T had a reputation for being quarrelsome and contrary. Worse than that, any hand knew better than to spread a line ahead of somebody else's moving herd. It was plain bad manners. He held his ground, rolling his shoulders to loosen them, clenching and unclenching hard fists.

But the line was only momentary. As the riders approached they bunched up, edging slightly aside, seeming to recognize that the herd had right of way here. They hesitated, still two hundred yards away, and five of them stopped. Will Bower rode forward alone, raising a hand.

Twenty feet away, the big man halted and raised his hat brim with a thumb. "Howdy, Dave," he called. "You boys fixin' to bed those critters here?"

"Plan to," Dave allowed. "Any objections?"

"Seems like a good plan to me," Bower said. "Another half-mile and they might get wind of the tanks. Don't suppose y'all have heard what's been happenin' back yonder since you pulled out, have you?"

"What we heard was that somebody sent stampeders out to hit us. We buried a couple of them a few miles back."

"You hear who it was that sent 'em?"

"Heard it was Pinto Boyd. Didn't hear why." Dave decided to push matters. It irritated him that these men were out here, in the way of his herd. "Wouldn't have been any surprise if it had been T-bar-T, though. Your boss never has been above such things."

He half expected Bower to open the ball then, but the big man only shrugged and grinned. "Can't argue with that, Dave. 'Cept I guess you don't know you're speakin' ill of the dead. Mr. Flood is shot dead, and Pinto Boyd and some of his crowd was sky-dancin' off Mr. Hazelwood's old barn loft last we saw. Anyhow, I guess you could say these boys and me are ridin' grubline now, unless you know of any outfits that are short-handed." He grinned again, as at a joke, and his eyes lifted to study the distant, oncoming herd. Seven thousand cows, half of them visible from here, and not more than three riders in sight. "Seems to me, you fellers' cup sort of overfloweth."

Dave relaxed a bit. "I don't do hirin'," he pointed out. "But I reckon the rollin' camp will be along directly. If you boys want to back off an' wait for the boss to show up, that's your business. Just stay away from those cows 'til somebody gives you leave."

Will Bower's eyes studied him, and Dave couldn't tell whether the man was impressed, amused or measuring him for knuckle dusting. Then the man's eyes lifted and Dave heard running hoofbeats behind him. He turned and saw Stan Lamont approaching, still distant but coming fast.

Dave Holley felt a flood of relief. There weren't many men around as big as Will Bower, but there were a few, and Stan Lamont definitely was one of them.

Bower grinned and lfited his reins. "I believe your notion has some merit," he drawled. "And you got a herd to bed and no time to socialize. See you later, Dave."

Bower rode away and the others followed, casting hard grins at Holley as they passed, daring him to push his luck. Dave gritted his teeth and watched them go. They angled eastward, veering to cut a path that would take them far closer to the lead cattle than was acceptable, but still would bypass the herd. A hard-ass bunch, Dave thought. Just spoiling for trouble. Still, Bower said they were out of work, and it was up to Mr. Hazelwood or Soapy Green to make such judgements.

Stan Lamont came pounding up to him, leaning around to watch the riders going away. "Trouble, Dave?"

"They say they're lookin' for work. I told them to stay away from the cows and wait for Mr. Hazelwood to come along."

"Why are they out of work?"

"They said Marcus Flood is dead. Also said Pinto Boyd and some others was hanged. I don't know."

Lamont pursed his lips, thoughtfully. "I guess when Mr. Hazelwood burned that old house, the sparks must have carried."

"Let's point 'em about here to bed," Dave said. "We can push from here to Six Tanks tomorrow."

190

Stan nodded, wheeled and lifted his reins, then stopped, squinting under his hatbrim. "Oh, for God's sake!"

Bower and his riders, crowding the herd out of sheer cussedness, had passed close enough to the point to come within Sonofabitch's limited scope of attention. And seeing no other riders at hand to follow, the steer had homed on them. Suddenly the great herd's point dissolved as first one critter, then a dozen, then a hundred turned hard right, milling back against the tide of their followers.

Pye came around from left swing at a hard run, trying to position himself to stop the swirl, and other riders headed forward from right swing and flank, with too much distance to cover. Lamont and Holley raced toward the herd, wind whipping their hatbrims, while far to the east, tiny with distance, Sam Price hauled up his team and stood in his wagon, trying to see what was happening.

Bower and his ex-T-bar-T bunch had been so absorbed in prodding that they didn't see what was happening until too late. They rode countercurrent past the early animals in the herd, laughing and cutting up, and suddenly found themselves awash in pressing, milling tons of irascible beef, wide horns waving and thrashing as the cattle tossed their heads in abrupt, mindless excitement.

Bower clung to his saddle as his mount crowhopped, swapped ends and spiralled, trying to evade the punishing horns. A few feet away a horse reared, pawed at the air and went over backward, taking its rider down with it. Cattle washed over them, and the mill continued to turn, hitting the oncoming herd, breaking through, picking up more hundreds of cattle in its collapsing vortex. Somewhere a man screamed and another horse went down.

"Damn you, Bower!" Dave Holley shouted as he and Stan Lamont spread to slant into the mill. "I told you to stay away from these cows!"

Close to a thousand cattle had been sucked into the mill now, and others were piling up beyond it, spreading both ways around it, trying to encompass it in their mass. At different points on the north perimeter Dave Holley, Stan Lamont and the young stranger Pye guided their mounts directly into the roiling mass, going counter-current, forcing the cows to veer away, out of their circle. Out of the corner of his eye Dave saw one of the T-bar-T riders break free of the tangle and wheel to do the same thing. Even in the mass of milling, deadly beef, the noise and the dust and the confusion, Dave noticed that the Star-Cross bay he rode was rock-steady, outthinking cow after cow, doing far more than its rider to break up the mill.

Another of Bower's men worked free, both rider and horse bleeding brightly, and wheeled to cut back into the mass at counterflow. Gradually, like blades slicing into a turning wheel, they pared cattle away from the mill, wearing it down, heading for its center. Stan Lamont met Will Bower almost head-on and blocked cattle for him while Bower wheeled his cut and skittish mount around the rump of Lamont's horse and broke free, shearing off more cattle as he went.

In a momentary gap between pressed backs Dave

192

Holley glanced down and saw a welter of blood, bone and churned earth beneath the dancing hooves. He could not tell whether it was man, horse or cow. Then he was at the middle of the swirling mill, and Sonofabitch recognized a leader and fell in behind him. The big brindle steer veered left as Dave's Star-Cross pony changed course, and oncoming cattle clove ahead of them like many-spiked waves on a pitching sea curling away from the prow of a ship.

Dave's eyes stung with dust and descending darkness, and he realized abruptly that the sun had gone down. He wondered how long he had been here, yelling and pushing in a seething hell of circling cattle. Other riders were around him, spreading outward, and again he emerged into open space, the cattle still in massive motion but spreading now, wandering randomly, no longer organized. The mill was broken, but so was the drive. Square miles of Outlet prairie were dotted and clotted with drifting, grazing cattle, and he could see riders out along the edges, packing them back, pushing them inward, keeping them away from the cedar breaks.

Sonofabitch followed him placidly for a distance, then raised his head, sniffed at the dusk and began to graze. All across the Outlet, cattle began the bovine procedure of bedding.

And among them rode tired men on tired horses, identifying one another, searching, stopping here and there to look at something on the ground. A mile away among the cedars, a fireglow signalled the location of Sam Price's wagons and the night

193

camp. After a time, Dave headed that way.

At the rope corral Ollie Sinclair waited with horse salve and sacking, and a scowl on his dark face to express his disgust with men who would bring in horses in such condition. The Star-Cross bay had a horn-cut along its ribs and several other, lesser wounds. It was exhausted, lathered and battered. Yet still, it moved like a dancer.

"Some kinda horse," Dave muttered, wiping it down while Ollie applied salve and dressings and clucked dire murmurings as he worked. Three other mounts were in the rope corral, held there for grain-feeding and tending of their wounds. The injuries weren't serious, but it was likely that one or two—at least—would run cow-shy the next time they were saddled and be useless as cowponies until somebody reeducated them.

From the rope corral Dave walked across to the night camp. Lanterns hung from frames on the chuck and trail wagons, and Sam Price was dispensing stew and biscuits while Nacho Lucas, working grim and one-handed, poured steaming coffee into mugs. Dave accepted a tin of coffee and strode over to the beacon fire, where men stood or squatted, cooling their heels. Dave looked from face to face, wondering if any Rafter H riders were missing.

Will Bower's remaining three partners stood aside, outside the ring of fireglow, sullen and quiet, ignored by the rest. And beyond the fire, Bower himself stood talking quietly with Matt Hazelwood.

Dave watched them, fuming. Finally he couldn't stand it any more. He raised his voice. "Mr. Hazelwood?"

Matt glanced at him across the fire.

Dave sipped his coffee, then emptied the tin cup on the ground. "Sir, are you hirin' these men on for this drive?"

"We're talking about it," Matt raised a brow at the interruption.

"Well, did you hire them yet?" Dave pressed.

"Not yet, Dave. Why?"

"I just wondered," Dave said. Then he dropped his cup and turned a hard stare on Will Bower. "I told you to stay away from them cows," he rasped. With two strides he reached the fire, went directly over it and launched himself at the big intruder.

Bower barely had time to get his fists up before Dave Holley was all over him, a flurry of hard fists and driving legs, carrying him back and down, raining short, hard blows at his face and gut.

In sheer size and brute strength, Will Bower outclassed the smaller cowhand by half. But Holley was going on rage, smashing blow after blow into the bigger man. They tumbled and rolled, Bower trying to grapple, Holley battering him at every move.

Men crowded around, and Bower's guards found themselves faced by the big, crouching form of Stan Lamont. "You want a piece of that, fellers? Try me," he growled.

Pushing and scuttling, Will Bower opened a space between himself and Dave Holley, and

195

unleashed a roundhouse swing that caught Holley on the jaw and sent him rolling. Bower followed, wading in, but Dave got his feet under him and charged, a flying tackle that took Bower in midsection and bore him back and down. His shoulders thudded on the ground and Holley was atop him, smashing hard fists at his face.

Matt Hazelwood watched the brawl curiously until he felt it had run its course. Then he turned to some of the others. "Break that up," he said.

Soapy Green had been waiting. Now he stepped forward with a bucket of water and doused the combatants. While they were still sputtering, others moved in and pulled them apart, heaving and gasping.

Bower tried to pull loose to rush Holley, but Gabe Sinclair was there, pinning his arms. Bower snarled at him, "Get your black hands off me, nigger!"

Gabe's eyes widened. "Oh, my!" he said. "Oh, yassuh, boss, I sho' will. Jes' let me clean a bit of that mud off yo' fine white face, first." Abruptly, the black hand released him, stepped back and bowed, then swung a driving fist that came out of nowhere and collided with the bridge of Bower's nose.

The former top hand and champion brawler of T-bar-T toppled like cut timber and lay where he fell.

Gabe Sinclair looked down at him, sadly, rubbing his knuckles. "Lordy, I wish folks wouldn't talk like that," he muttered.

Aside, Matt Hazelwood told Soapy Green,

"When he comes around, if they still want work, hire them on. I guess they're educated now."

On a rose-gold morning when the rising sun reflected on climbing cloudbanks in the west and everything had two shadows, Rafter H drove through the final mile of the Outlet and passed the outer limits of Dry Creek range, pushing toward Six Tanks.

Dave Holley, bruised and sore, nursing a cut lip and some loose teeth, rode point and held his steeldust close within the perceptive range of Sonofabitch, who tagged along happily at the head of the herd. Soapy Green and Stan Lamont had flank positions where they could keep an eye on their new recruits.

Tip Curry rode ahead now, scouting the terrain with eyes that missed nothing. With Dry Creek behind them now, he felt that if trouble came it would come from the front.

Slowly they narrowed the great herd, drag riders on fast horses pushing the rear critters into motion as the point cleared the range of ridges beyond the Outlet and speared northward into the trailing hills.

A mile from the bed grounds Matt Hazelwood turned to look back just once at Dry Creek range, and his eyes came to rest on the three mute graves with their fresh firewood crosses. Two of them had chunks of sod atop them. The third was a simple cross above the little mound where they had buried what was left of Jesus Maria Gomez. The drover had been on flank, and was caught up in the

197

backwash of the mill. They hadn't found him until morning.

Matt looked at the nearby hills and knew that they were being watched. He felt an odd sadness at leaving old times and old places behind, but it was only momentary.

It's all yours, he thought, feeling the eyes in the hills upon him. You all came late, and when you came it all changed, and it's yours now. But when you come out here to see where Rafter H has gone, look around you. So far we've left five graves behind us, and four of them are sod-marked. You might want to count them before you come after us.

He turned away, tapped heels to his Tyson horse and rode after his herd. Dry Creek was behind him now. Ahead was the way to Wyoming.

16

Ollie Sinclair took down his rope corral and tossed the rigging into the tail of Sam Price's stove cart, then took up the reins of his day horse and swung aboard. He rode among his patients, looking again at their cuts and scrapes, clucking like a mother hen, then he choused them on their way, following the rolling camp. The rest of the remuda had spread during the night, grazing among the cedars, and he worked for more than half an hour bringing them out and getting them started.

Despite the hard work of the past several days, they were mostly in fair shape and when he had them gathered on the flats and swung his coil at them, they broke out in an enthusiastic lope following the dust of the horses ahead.

Ollie had done his stint at punching cows, plenty of times. But given his choice, he would far rather work with horses. He had broke in as a wrangler for Rafter H several years ago, when he followed his big brother Gabe to the western spreads looking for work. Gabe was a top hand with cows. He always had been. But Ollie found his niche the first time he straddled a bucking horse and talked it down. And the day he sacked out his first short-tail, doing it his own way, and heard Mr. Hazelwood tell Gabe, "That boy is a wrangler, sure enough," Ollie Sinclair made up his mind.

Gabe and the others could deal with the cows. Ollie would tend their horses.

He had thought about putting himself on one of the Star-Cross horses today, to get the feel of Jim Tyson's work, but had decided not to. The rough string needed working, so he picked out a dish-headed pinto that the drovers all avoided and put his leather on it. It went to crow-hopping as soon as his foot was in the stirrup, but he talked it down and now it moved along mannerly enough, taking direction from his reins as he eased from flank to flank of the loping remuda, keeping them going where they were supposed to.

Ahead, in the distance, he saw the wagons rolling along. The doctored horses had already caught up to them, and he could see that Nacho Lucas was in the saddle, tending them for him until the rest of the remuda came up.

"That boy ought to stay on his rump in that wagon another day or so," Ollie told himself. "It's gonna be a while afore he heals over." Ollie had watched Sam Price fix the kid's hand—trimming back stub bone with a clasp knife while a couple of the others held him down, then carving a neat flap of loose skin to sew over the end of the stump.

Ollie always liked to watch when there was doctoring going on. He picked up pointers sometimes that he could use when the horses needed attention.

"One thing I never seen," he told himself. "I never seen any horse get its finger shot off. How y'suppose a thing like that can happen to a man."

"Probably had his finger where a bullet wanted to go," the man beside him said, and Ollie swivelled so fast he almost fell out of his saddle. Then he was occupied for a minute or so trying to talk the pinto down again. Neither of them had seen anybody come up on them, but there he was, a long, lanky man under a slouch hat, and riding a scruffy gray pony that looked like a mustang.

Ollie got his mount under control and stared at the intruder. "Where'd you come from?"

"Tennessee, originally," the man said. "More lately, though, I come from Porterville. Do you know the way to Porterville?"

"Where's Porterville?"

"If I knew that, I wouldn't need to ask." The man was studying the remuda ahead, counting. "Where's the rest of them? I only count nine."

"Nine what?" Ollie stared at him.

"Horses."

"What are you talkin' about, mister? There's better'n sixty horses in that bunch. We got seventy-eight all together . . . I think."

"Them with the Star-Cross brand, I came to get 'em."

"You came to . . . mister, you ain't takin' any of

201

these horses without Mr. Hazelwood says so."

"Fourteen of 'em, there's supposed to be. What happened to that one there?" The man scowled, pointing at the dark bay with the horn cut. "What kind of way is that to treat a good horse? And where's the rest of 'em?"

Ollie was becoming exasperated. He yelled, waved his coil and stepped up the pace. The stranger kept pace, riding beside him effortlessly.

"That one got hooked by a cow," Ollie said. "We had a mill last night. One of our drovers got trampled, and a couple of other folks, too. And we lost three horses."

"Noticed the graves back yonder," the man admitted. "How come y'all to get mixed up with cows?"

"This is a drive!" Ollie shouted. "That's what we're doin' out here, is drivin' cows! See, out there? Them is cows!"

The man looked to the west, squinting. "Why, so they are. Land, but you got a mess of 'em, don't you? What outfit is this, anyhow?"

Ollie stared at him. "This here is Rafter H. Who'd you think it was?"

Abruptly the man swept off his hat and howled with delight. "Well, I declare! I told that feller it seemed like he was goin' the wrong way to get to Rafter H. I do declare! An' him knowin' the way an' me not, an' here I am an' he don't know yet where it is!"

"Who?" They were closing fast on the wagons now, and he saw Sam Price and Nacho looking back to see them come.

"Feller that belongs to these horses. Jim some-body. Got hisself killed out in the hills a while back, an' now he's awful confused. He'll feel better when I get the rest of these short-tails back to him an' let him know I found Rafter H. I declare!"

"Mister," Ollie stared at him, eyes huge in his dark face, and tried to edge away, "I don't have any idea what you're talkin' about. But like I said, nobody takes any of these horses 'less Mr. Hazel-wood says so."

"Well, that's all right, because this is where we was goin', anyway. You reckon you can just sort of sit tight with his horses until I get back with him?"

"We ain't gonna set tight no place, mister. We got to take these cows to Wyoming."

"Do you know the way to Wyoming?"

"No. But I reckon Mr. Hazelwood does."

"That's all right. So does the feller I'm ridin' with." He squinted westward again. "Cows. I declare. Long time since I seen a cow herd." He crammed his hat onto his head and flipped a wave at Ollie. "Y'all be careful now, y'hear? We be along directly."

As abruptly as he had come, the man turned his mount and departed, and when Ollie looked back the cloud-light was playing tricks with the dust on the wind and he couldn't see him going away.

The remuda came up with the wagons, and the horses slowed to an easy trot, then to a walk, spreading a little to graze as they moved. Sam Price waved his hat and Ollie went forward to ride alongside the wagon.

Price looked at him quizzically. "What were you yellin' about back there, Ollie?"

Ollie shrugged, gesturing back with a dark thumb. "Oh, that feller yonder. He come up on me and said he was gonna take some of our horses. Peculiarest talkin' man I ever run across."

Price turned to look back, then gazed at Ollie again, his face creased with puzzlement. "What fella, Ollie?"

"That one back yonder. You seen him. Like to spooked me white when he come up like that. I guess he's just plain crazy. He didn't even know we had cows 'til I told him."

Price chewed on his whiskers, looking concerned. "When's the last time you had a night's rest, Ollie?"

"I sleep when I can. Why?"

"Well, because there wasn't any fella back there with you, Ollie. I could see you plain as day. So could Nacho. There wasn't anybody there but you."

The raid on Colter by Pony Simmons and his bunch was a disaster. "Make it clean," Gator Jones had said. A fast raid—into the little town, hit the bank and three saloons, with the general store as a target of opportunity and diversion—then get out fast and fade away . . . that was how it was supposed to go.

But they had heard the first gunfire before they even entered the town. And when they met on the

204

street the Link boys were coming out of the bank, and there was more gunfire. The robbery was ruined. The surprise was gone, and they found themselves in a crossfire from the shops and the hotel windows.

Gator Jones was dead, along with two others, and four of them were injured. Belly-down in brush at the edge of the breaks, Fell Hankins watched riders come into town from the wide flats, and when there were plenty of people on the streets he got his horse and rode back in. He was not a known man in these parts, and he blended among the ranchers and cowhands on the streets. More than anything else, he wanted to know what had gone wrong.

Wandering and listening, he began to piece it together. A banker named Bond was dead. A faro dealer from Paisley's, in the bank to deposit his take, was dead. And an old swamper named Jess Purcell was dead, shot down in the street before the robbery.

There were a dozen witnesses and a dozen different versions of what had happened, but the way it came together was that the Link boys had come back to Colter and brought friends with them. They had robbed the bank and cleaned out the day vault, and got away with more than six hundred dollars, but had missed the deposits in the closet safe.

When Herman Link came into town with his men he was met with hostility, and there was talk in the saloons about making him pay for what his

205

sons had done. But it was just talk. Those who were serious about it would not face Link and his gunhands, and the rest shrugged it off after a time. It wasn't Herman Link who had hit Colter, or the Link ranch. It was those two wild kids of his, the ones Matt Hazelwood had run off the range. A white-faced clerk from the bank told the story over and over of how Rodney Link had screamed at Joe Bond and the dealer as he shot them down . . . how he kept calling them Hazelwood and Curry. How he said—suddenly calm and sober as he looked at the fallen bodies—that this was just the first time and that when he found them again he would kill them again.

They laid out the bodies on a plank walk in front of Paisley's, for people to come and see, and Fell Hankins joined the line moving past them. Gator Jones had been nearly cut in half by a shotgun blast . . . somebody said it was the old swamper's daughter-in-law, Molly Purcell, who shot him. The other two who rode in with him were riddled with bullets, and Fell thought grimly of the crash of guns and the whine of slugs when people opened up on them from doors and windows, alerted by Rodney Link's shots.

But he looked longest at the three townsmen lying there. A fat banker, a faro dealer and a beat-up old cowpoke. All three had died of single bullets. The swamper was back-shot, but the two from the bank had bullet holes through their shirt pockets.

Fell Hankins had been a lot of places and seen a

lot of men who wouldn't hesitate to use a gun. He was one himself. But through the years, just once or twice, he had encountered men who were not like the rest . . . gunmen and killers with a quality about them that made a man's flesh crawl just to think of them. Wild kids gone bad, just like a hundred others, but different. They got a taste for killing the way a bad cougar gets a taste for the blood of domestic stock, and there was no stopping them short of putting them under.

He had seen Rodney Link, in that moment on the street before all hell broke loose, and he wouldn't forget him. Rodney Link was one of those. Looking at the bodies, he knew it now for sure. Probably the kid had just begun his career as a killer. He was sloppy and stupid. How could anybody rob a bank and miss the closet safe? But he had a trademark, and Fell Hankins noticed that old crawly feeling as he looked at the holes in those shirt pockets.

A person or two glanced at him suspiciously and he moved on. It was not a time for a man to draw attention to himself. Suddenly, Fell Hankins was anxious to get away from this place . . . maybe get clear out of this part of the country. He had a bad feeling, and couldn't shake it. He thought about Rodney Link, out there someplace running wild and loose, and the notion of him being out there made him a little sick. He decided he would go out and find Pony and the others, and see if they might want to try some new territory. Maybe someplace north, he thought. Fort Worth, or maybe on up around Tulia or Mobeetie. Or maybe farther than that. Maybe Dodge or Denver. He would talk with them about it.

Once, for a couple of days, Fell had shared a jail cell in east Texas with Billy Shaw. Another time he and some others had holed up with the Rock Creek bunch up in the Llano, when that wild youngster they called Kid Pitch was with them. He felt about Rodney Link now as he had felt about those two then. It just wasn't worth it to be in the same country with them. It was like being in a rattlesnake den at night, or in a dark room with a mad dog.

Across the dusty street from where the bodies lay, in the musty shadows of the little stitchery she had tried to keep up, Molly Purcell wiped an irritating tear from her cheek and stood. She had sat there for hours, it seemed, barely aware of the heavy shotgun across her lap. Not thinking, really, although the image of the blasted man falling away from her as she fired the shotgun was vivid and shrill. There had been other gunfire as well, and men on horseback milling in the street, and Papa Jess lay dead on the plank porch outside the shop door.

And with Papa Jess gone, Molly had no one left.

In the year since coming to look after Papa Jess, after Jude died under a spilled haywagon, she had come to know a few of the people around Colter. But she didn't know any of them very well. Barely nineteen, widowed and alone except for the old man who had been Jude's father, Molly had kept to

208

herself as much as she could, and Papa Jess was not much for socializing. A few of the young cowhands from the big ranches around had tried calling on her, but Papa Jess still considered her Jude's wife so he discouraged them, and so did she.

Only a couple of them had made much impression on her, anyway. She thought sometimes of Bo Maxwell, the way he grinned and the way he laughed when something struck him funny, the way he had of pulling jokes on people so that half the time they weren't even sure what the joke was. And now and then she thought about Tip Curry, handsome and somber, always seeming to be on the alert, with eyes that seemed never to blink but always to be watching everything around him. An intense, private young man . . . Papa Jess said he had killed men, and that idea chilled her. Yet, so had she, now.

The man had seen her and come for her, and the grin on his face was ugly. She had stood there, over the bleeding body of Papa Jess, and the man had not cared at all. He had simply seen something he wanted and come to take it. She had never conceived what a shotgun could do to a man, and the image of it was stark and shocking.

She tried to think about Bo Maxwell and Tip Curry. They had been kind to her, at least, each in his own way. Bo Maxwell had made her laugh, and Tip Curry had told her once—and meant it—that if there was anything she ever needed, all she had to do was let him know.

But they were gone now, too. They were with Rafter H, somewhere far away and on the move, and she had no idea where. Only that they had gone north, and it was said they would not be back.

After a time Molly sighed and stood, laying the spent old scattergun on her sewing table. She glanced out the window and was surprised that it was growing dark. Heavy clouds, building in the west, had swallowed the setting sun and the streets of Colter now lay in dusk.

Across the street in front of Paisley's, men were removing the bodies, piling them into a wagon. They would bury them in the morning, she guessed, out at the graveyard. All those dead men and one of them was Papa Jess and now there was no one left.

Molly barely remembered her father. He had gone off somewhere, years ago when she was little, and her mother had never really said where he was bound. South, somewhere . . . a casual departure of a man going off on business, and they had waited for him to return. But the weeks became months and the months ran into years and there was no word from him, and eventually the time came when Molly couldn't remember exactly how he looked or sounded or smelled. Only that his hands were big and hard and gentle, and he liked to sing sometimes when he thought nobody was listening.

At any rate, with him gone there was only her mother, and she had taught Molly how to read and how to sew a good stitch and sent her to school. Molly had watched her hair grow gray and noted how she paused sometimes, looking south, across the rolling plains, toward Texas.

But by then Molly had stopped expecting her father to return.

Molly had been fifteen when her mother died of fever, and friends in town had taken her in. She cooked and sewed and kept house, and the Johnsons kept her on until Jude came along and they were married.

Jude was from Texas, and wanted to back. So when they had saved a month's wages they took the coach to Newton and another to Kansas City, and Jude signed on as a loader on a riverboat for their passage to St. Louis, then on an old steamboat that brought them to New Orleans, and eventually they had come to Port Lavaca and Jude hired on with one of the ranches for wages to get them the rest of the way to Colter so they could stay with Papa Jess.

But three days later Jude was dead, crushed under a haywagon. And Molly had come to Colter alone because there was nowhere else to go.

Now Papa Jess was gone, and she found herself laying out her things in the darkening little room, getting them ready to pack. Somehow, without even realizing it, Molly had decided what she would do. Maybe she had decided a long time ago, she didn't know.

There wasn't much reason to go home, and she didn't have any clear idea of how to get there, but at least there would be people there who knew her, and she could go out sometimes and put flowers on her mother's grave.

Flowers, she thought. Flowers for Helen Flowers.

The time with Jude had been a dream that just didn't quite come true. It was best to go back and start over, where she had been before.

She would find a way to get there, somehow.

211

There were trade wagons that rolled from Colter to other towns, and those towns had roads that led north. There would be a way.

Molly Purcell would find the way to Porterville, and when she got there she would be Molly Flowers again, and maybe things would work out better next time.

She lit a lamp and looked outside again. Lamps glowed in the windows across the street, and there were a lot of men at Paisley's. Voices floated across with the cool, gusting breeze. Some of the men were trying to organize a posse to go after the Link boys and the others who had robbed the town, but there wasn't much interest in it. A few townsmen, but the ranchers had other matters on their minds. Colonel Nelson was organizing a new headquarters crew to take over the old Rafter H spread, and the smaller ranchers were meeting with him, arguing over their shares in the pool. Herman Link had taken his men and pulled out. They said he was going after the Rafter H herd, and there was hard talk about that. Still, what he did beyond Dry Creek range was his lookout. He had tried to hire extra hands to back him, but without much luck. Not many men were willing to face Matt Hazelwood's bunch in an open fight . . . and somebody had put out the word that Will Bower and some of T-bar-T had gone off to join them. And with Nelson offering wages to man a new Triple-Seven headquarters, the grubline was about weeded down.

Papa Jess had said it would come to this, that the pool would break down and the big outfits would pull apart. Strange, Molly thought, how abruptly things that seemed so stable could change.

She made a little fire in the stove to warm some soup, then went back to her packing and sorting. A fresh, cool breeze gusted through the open window and made the curtains flap. Somewhere in the distance lightning flickered, and after a time she heard the muttering of thunder.

17

Now storms walked through the western hills, and Soapy Green worried as he watched them build. With every able hand on the herd, they pushed the animals cruelly hard during the final hours of daylight, then bedded them on shingled flats above a valley where the last of sunlight showed the pale greens of willow bottoms.

Six Tanks was behind them now, and the last perimeters of organized civilization. Ahead lay two hundred miles of wilderness, before they would approach the settlements ranging the "Scarp," beyond which were the high plains of the Llano Estacado.

The outfit now was sixteen men, counting Sam Price who tended the wagons and Nacho Lucas who wouldn't be able to sling a saddle for a while.

The two young rustlers, Slater and Pye, had worked out well enough. They were capable drovers, and they blended quietly into the outfit, stepping wide around the older hands and making no waves among the younger ones. They were grateful to be alive, and even more grateful to be employed.

Will Bower and his bunch raised some hackles among the other drovers, and Soapy knew there were grudges there and maybe some scores to settle. But whatever else they were, they were also cowhands. Slim Hobart in particular had real cow sense, and Soapy had put him on left swing to take some of the pressure off Stan Lamont over there.

The fourteen horses Matt had found out in the hills—how in God's name did Jim Tyson horses come to be in the hills of Texas?—were a blessing. Superb animals, they carried the unmistakable imprint of Big Jim's special way with critters. The result was a major addition to the remuda. The Star-Cross mounts were worth two ordinary cowponies each when it came to the grinding, grueling task of moving cows, and a rider aboard one was worth two riders.

Despite Tip Curry's constant worry about the trail ahead, Soapy was beginning to feel a little better about the mess they were in. But as he watched tall clouds building in the west, other worries crowded him.

Of all the four men fresh from the war who had first choused wild cattle out of the brush and headed for Chicago—God, how long ago it had been!—it was Soapy Green who took most naturally to the driving of cows. He had done his share of fighting. They all had on those early drives. But it was a thing he would just as soon leave to others, the way he left the planning of roundups to Sam

216

Price, or the conduct of business to Matt Hazelwood . . . the way he readily left the educating and tending of horses to the kid—so he had been in those early times, a big, rangy kid with stars in his eyes and a silly grin on his face when he talked of horses bred and raised the way horses should be.

For Soapy, it was the cows. And as others like him came along, youngsters like Dave Holley and the black drover Gabe Sinclair, Soapy taught them the skills he had learned about pushing cows, and watched them become as good at it as he himself. Something about the ex-rustler Pye said he might be another, and Soapy kept an eye on him. He might make a top hand, with a little guidance. Maybe even Slim Hobart.

Each day now, the herd seemed to take a little better shape. Slowly, the cattle were getting used to the trail, and there already were a hundred or more that Soapy could identify that moved out of a morning without much more encouragement than seeing the backside of Dave's lead critter, Sonofabitch, moving out ahead of them.

In time, he knew, the herd would lose its wild snuffiness and settle down to be a proper trail herd . . . if they had the time.

The clouds were a long way off still, but they grew and banked and formed mushroom tops in the sunlight, and below those tops was a blackness. And they were moving.

For two days he had watched them come and go, forming out there in the western hills and marching away, cutting swaths of storm across the vastness.

217

Now they swallowed the evening sun and were closer, and the wind was from the west.

Now his worry was the weather.

The valley ahead was in shadows, and distances were indistinct, but he judged the watercourse lined by the willows to be maybe four miles out. Another morning drive to water. He pursed his lips, nodded to himself and began the process of bedding the herd.

Riding forward at a lope, he signalled the swingmen to begin waving the herd, watching them respond as he passed. Gabe Sinclair moved forward to close with Slater on right swing, and together they began a push against the massive stream of beef. Riding like parade soldiers they pivoted their mounts and charged the cattle, shouting and waving their coils, an angling attack from front quarter, bringing them into confrontation with a perimeter of beef a hundred yards long. The cattle veered away, pressing those beyond them, and the long line bulged away to the left.

A few hundred yards forward, and across the herd, Pye and Bo Maxwell did the same thing, circling out to swerve and charge the cattle filing by on their side. Now the meandering line of the drive had a distinct S-curve to its neck, and this grew and widened. Beyond the left swingman Stan Lamont galloped ahead, closing on the distant point of the herd. Soapy Green drummed heels against his pony and ran to parallel him, two riders an eighth of a mile apart, neck and neck as they sped past the ambling herd leaders. As they approached point, Soapy waved his hat and Stan Lamont charged the

218

herd, pushing the front leaders off course toward Soapy. As they came toward him he headed them out at an angle, then began to curve them back in a great, slow arc too wide to allow for milling.

Two and a half miles back, the drags of the great herd continued to move, unaffected. But now the point and neck of the drive dissolved as the moving S-curve widened, lost forward momentum, and its members began to encounter the point cattle being turned back by the trailboss.

Once, years before, a tame Cheyenne named Charley Shoes had watched from a high crest as a Rafter H crew had bedded a herd in this manner. Later he had come to the rolling camp for supper and demanded to speak with the "cow-dancer." It was Matt Hazelwood who finally figured out what the Indian was talking about, and pointed him at Soapy. Charley Shoes had walked twice around the cowhand, staring at him blankly, while Soapy pivoted to keep an eye on him and wondered what it was all about. Then the Indian had approached him and handed him a piece of folded deerskin with markings on it.

The predominant emblem was a clear representation of a great serpent coiling itself into an elaborate figure-eight.

It was the sign of peace carried by runners among the plains tribes of the south, very much as their distant cousins to the north carried elaborately-decorated pipes.

"The Wo-haws make the sign of friendship," Charley Shoes told him solemnly.

From a high place the Indian had watched a

great serpent of moving animals twist itself so and then come to rest. It was a thing profoundly moving to the Indian.

Soapy had never understood Indians.

He backed his horse away and sat his saddle, just near enough to the spiral of beef to keep the critters aware of him and paying attention to following one another. A quarter of a mile to the north, Dave Holley had turned Sonofabitch and was bringing him in to join the herd. Somehow, Dave had taught the brute to break the bedding mill by rejoining the circling lead at right ankles and cutting straight through to its center.

Satisfied that the herd was stopped—at least the front of it was, it would be nearly an hour before the drags were all thrown in—Soapy gave the wave to Gabe and Stan, turned and headed out toward where Sam Price was rigging his camp. The wagons were west of the herd now, on the weather side, and about a mile away.

It was the beginning of cocktail shift, the interval between bedding of the herd and the first night guard. Soapy had assigned himself to early night guard since the weather had shifted, and those standing it with him were selected for nerve as much as anything else.

So the first to be fed their supper would be the first night shift, while later shifts bedded the herd and stood cocktail.

From the rolling camp Soapy looked back at the herd, immense and shadowy in the cloud-darkened distance. Far away in the hills, thunder muttered, and the breeze was cool. He shivered. The cattle

220

were a dark carpet thrown over the shingled flats, a carpet that crept and crawled in intricate pattern, and stretched away across the distance, a landscape of its own.

Stan Lamont and Bo Maxwell were coming up the rise toward him, and further back he saw Slim Hobart and Slater quitting the herd to follow.

He rode to the holding corral, stepped down and shucked his rig off the tired horse, then shooed it in to join the cooling string as Ollie Sinclair held the rope gate aside.

"Who's spellin' you for nighthawk, Ollie?" he asked.

The wrangler tipped his head toward the wagons. "Nacho's up to it. His hand smarts him, but I'll saddle his horse for him. All he got to do is stay on top of it."

"Weather's makin' up," Soapy nodded. "Best break out fresh stock for the guards."

"Don't have any fresh stock," Ollie frowned. "Just some that ain' wore down as bad as others." The wrangler paused, still holding the rope gate. "Mista Green, do you know the way to someplace called Porterville?"

Soapy thought, then shook his head. "Never heard of it. Why?"

Stan Lamont and Bo Maxwell rode up and stepped down, grimy and tired, as beat as the horses they pulled their saddles from.

"I was just wonderin'," Ollie said. "If there wasn't anybody out there talkin' to me . . . back yonder . . . then how come him to ask about a place I never heard of?"

221

Soapy stared at him. "What?"

"Well, I mean, if I was just tired an' sort of dreamin' like Mista Price said, well, it jus' seems to me like I'd dream about things I know about, not things I don't."

The story of Ollie's encounter with a ghost had made the rounds the way stories do, and there was mixed amusement and sympathy for him among the men. They were all so tired—and had been for weeks—that it wasn't hard to imagine seeing things that weren't there. But Ollie kept worrying about it.

Soapy shrugged. The workings of human minds was not a matter within his scope. "You just thought it up, I reckon," he offered.

"I don't believe I'd of thought up any place called Porterville," Ollie frowned, stepping back to admit Bo Maxwell's horse into the cooling pen.

Bo glanced aside at him, his eyes twinkling. "Where's Porterville, Ollie?"

"If I knew that I'd of told that fella the other day . . . if he'd been there to tell. That's where he wanted to know the way to."

"I thought he wanted to know the way to Wyoming."

"Yeah, there too. But I know about Wyoming, 'cause that's where we're goin', so I prob'ly could have thought that up. But I never did know about Porterville."

Bo tipped his hat. "I bet Porterville is someplace out around Barsuvia, and if it is, I sure would like to go there. That whole part of the country is full of women and geese."

They all stared at him.

"The women raise the geese," he explained, "so they can make goosedown featherbeds, and no man that ever went there was ever known to come back."

"Where'd you hear about a place like that?" Ollie demanded.

Bo shrugged. "I didn't. I just thought it up."

Ollie was busy then, helping Stan Lamont get his big sorrel into the pen, and when he turned again Bo had gone off to the fire to get his supper.

"I swear I don' know what's wrong with that scutter," Ollie decided.

With the help of Nacho Lucas, favoring his bad hand, Sam Price had turned out a meal of blanket steak, crisped marrow-gut, biscuits and—to the intense delight of the cowhands coming in from the herd—a pot of sucamagrowl. By the time Soapy and the others had stuffed themselves on main courses, Nacho was dropping bits of dough into the simmering pot—a blend of vinegar, sugar, flour and spice—and fishing out the brown dumplings to serve steaming hot.

"Early on to start spoiling us, isn't it, Sam?" Matt Hazelwood asked him.

"Probably high time," the cook turned his head to spit into the fire. "This crew is wore down pretty good, Matt. You can push men a long way if they're well-fed, but I'm seein' some funny things begin to happen here."

"Like Ollie talking to himself?"

"Yeah. Like that. Anyhow, I don't see you passin' up the sweets."

Soapy helped himself to several more dumplings.

223

"I'm puttin' out five night guards, Matt. Might not do any good. If those cows take a notion to spill, a hundred riders couldn't hold them. But I figure with five we can at least circulate twice on the hour."

"Weather worryin' you, Soapy?"

"Yeah. I don't like the way the air feels. It wouldn't take much to stampede that bunch."

"We've handled stampedes before."

"Never with seven thousand cows, we haven't."

Hazelwood shrugged. He was as worried as the trail boss, but it wouldn't do any good to let on. "A stampede is a stampede. Size of the herd doesn't matter."

Soapy didn't bother responding to that. He knew as well as Matt what a mess a spill this size would make. He finished his sucamagrowl and looked around. "Have you seen Tip? I thought he could . . ."

"He rode out about an hour ago," Price interrupted. "Said he was goin' to look at those bottoms ahead. That young'un is gettin' touchy as a badger about keepin' a clear trail."

Matt shrugged at that. The gunhand was going to do things his way, and nobody was going to change him. He noticed, though, that Nacho Lucas turned quickly, looking at Sam Price, then peering out into the dusk, beyond the herd, into the distance.

Yeah, Kid, Matt thought, that's where Tip Curry thinks the danger is. So that's where he has gone. Aloud he said, "Glad to hear you're up to riding nighthawk, Nacho. Ollie said he'd give you a hand with saddling."

The look of disappointment on the square young face said he had hit his mark. For a moment there Nacho Lucas, bad hand and all, had been fixing to go out and look for enemies. Because that was what Tip Curry was doing.

Fresh winds gusted, winds with a cool edge to them, and flattened the cookfire into a momentary comb of writhing blue flames. To the west thunder growled, and Soapy looked at the sky.

"Cocktail's over," he announced. "Let's get some horses forked."

Big Jim Tyson hunkered by a fresh fire at the base of a limestone shoulder and watched his horses grazing in the little walled valley beyond. He had stumbled into the place and decided to bed here for the night. It was as good a place as any, plenty of graze for his stock and a little artesian spring that fed a rivulet stream, and with weather making up it would be good to have a sheltered area where his horses couldn't wander far. He was feeling better, most ways, but he still was in no shape to round up a scattered horse herd.

His chest still ached when he moved, a radiating pain that centered behind his shirt pocket. The deep bruise there and the way he ached suggested a cracked rib or two, but it wasn't the awful shooting pain it had been . . . seemed to have been, from time to time that he could remember . . . the first day or two.

The flesh wound in his arm was healing nicely,

not bothering him much more than the knitting break in the bone there. He found he could use the arm sometimes now, if he was careful.

The scar atop his head was scabbed over and healing. The scab was a long, diagonal cap of hard substance running from just above his left temple to a place almost over his right ear. He had poked and prodded at it, gingerly, and although his touch hurt like blazes he didn't think there was any softness beneath. His skull seemed to be intact.

I'm just damned lucky, is all, he told himself for the hundredth time. A pocket full of brass belt buckle and a head full of hard bone.

He recalled very little now of what had happened, only snatches of memory: a pair on horseback following him, then a young man with wild eyes grinning at him as his gun thundered and the world went out. Obviously, though, someone had done a pretty thorough job of shooting the hell out of him. It was a standing wonder that he wasn't dead the way Clifton Flowers kept saying he was.

Whoopee ti yi yo, git along little dogies . . . Like an old friend, the tune ran around in his head and reassured him. He had been left for dead, but he wasn't dead. His horses had been taken from him, but he had them back—most of them, at least, and Clifton Flowers said he knew where the rest were. His wallet had been gone, but Clifton Flowers had brought it back to him. How had he done that? A lot of things about recent days were very fuzzy, and Clifton Flowers was one of them. The man just sort of came and went, sometimes riding with him, sometimes not, and when he went Jim never knew where he went—or how. He just was there sometimes, and other times he wasn't.

I owe him a lot, he reminded himself. I'm grateful to him. I need to keep remembering that.

It was difficult at times. Jim Tyson didn't remember ever meeting a more annoying person. But even that was odd, considering that Flowers never seemed to be intentionally annoying. Generally, he was cheerful and friendly. He didn't seem to have a care in the world, or to be more than vaguely aware of the cares that other folks had. It was as though the man didn't belong in this world at all. As though he were just visiting, just passing the time.

Most of what he said didn't make much sense. Even when it did, it didn't quite. Like the notion he had that Jim Tyson was dead. Tyson felt the muscles tighten in his jaws. He wished Flowers would just quit saying that . . . or at least explain why he kept saying it. The man acted like the fact that Tyson was riding through Texas pushing a bunch of breed horses—which, he noted again, Flowers had recovered for him and for which he was deeply grateful—had no significance whatever, and no bearing on whether he was alive or dead.

And he kept asking whether Jim knew the way to Porterville, despite the fact Jim had told him a dozen times that he did not. And each time he asked, and Jim said no, the man reacted in the puzzled manner of one who literally wonders what he is doing here.

He had even voiced it one time. "If you don't know the way to Porterville, then how come I'm

227

ridin' along with you?"

Jim had only glanced aside at him then. "I don't have the vaguest idea."

"Oh, I didn't expect you to," Flowers had said. "But it seems to me like *I* should know. Don't it to you?"

It was always like that. Everything about Clifton Flowers, it seemed to Jim Tyson, just missed making sense. Maybe, he thought, it's just how a man sees things after he's been shot in the head.

Whoopee ti yi yo, git along little dogies. It's your misfortune and none of my own . . . and that's right, he thought. A man can get over being shot and left for dead, but a critter on its way to market isn't likely to get out of going to market, and it sure can't get over being a critter.

Cool west winds gusted down the valley and whipped the flame of his little fire. High, dark clouds stood above the western hills, lightning flickering in their feet. He gazed at them and felt lonely. What am I doing here? he wondered. At first, mostly out of his head, he had meant to find Rafter H because he needed help. But now what he needed to do was what he had started out to do in the first place—gather his horses, get down to Three Rivers and sell them, then get on back to Wyoming. Katie was waiting.

"You want the rest of them, don't you?"

He hadn't even realized that Clifton Flowers was there, but there he was, squatting on his heels over by the bluff, staring lazily from under his hatbrim. "The horses," he explained. "I wish you'd make up your mind. Do you want the rest of them or not?"

"Sure, I do."

"Well, Rafter H is where they're at, which is why we're on our way there."

"Yeah, I remember. I was just thinking."

"You sure you're up to it?"

"I'm doing the best I can," he grumped, wishing he had a better class of company.

"Who's Katie?" Flowers asked.

"She's waiting for me in Wyoming. I promised her I wouldn't be gone very long."

"Yeah, I said the same thing one time. That was a while back, I reckon. I ought to have got back before this."

"Then why haven't you?"

"I told you. I don't know the way." Flowers dipped his head, only his chin showing below his hatbrim. "I guess I used to, but somethin' come up and now I don't."

"What came up?"

"I just don't exactly know. But I do know I told Helen I'd be back directly, so I reckon I ought to."

Tyson shook his head. He didn't understand.

18

Stands of willows lined the bottomlands meandering down from distant high hills, marking where various recent channels of a little water-course wound and looped like ribbons thrown down on the flats.

In eerie silence broken by gusts of cool breeze and the sound of distant thunder, Tip Curry guided his tall black upstream, following the valley upward toward its source. When he first began scouting tomorrow's trail, it had been just a feeling, but now it was a certainty. There were people near, crowding in on Rafter H's route.

He had seen tracks of horses, coming down into the watering flats and then turning to head back into the rolling lands above. That had been an hour ago. Now, when a fresh gust of coolness swept down toward him, his nostrils twitched at the scent of smoke.

Ranks of tall, dark clouds stood above him, towering into a sky that still was pale beyond their glowering caps, but no light came through them from the sunset beyond. The clouds themselves were better light, dull fires rippling through their mushrooming heads and flashes of brilliance darting from their lower reaches, obscuring the blackness beneath them.

Prairie storm was on its way, and somewhere in those dark rises at its feet, someone was boiling coffee over a fire.

He slowed the black to pull on his slicker, leaving it open from the neck down, and swept back on the right to keep his gun free.

He had listened, with Matt Hazelwood and Sam Price, to what Will Bower had to say . . . about how Triple-Seven and Link had divided the range rights left by Rafter H, how the Colonel and Herman Link had agreed to a general roundup to start in three weeks—it would be maybe two weeks now—and how Link had gathered his forces to go after the Rafter H herd.

Matt Hazelwood had listened thoughtfully and said nothing, but Tip was puzzled. Why would Link want to bring the herd back to Dry Creek? Was he aiming to claim them as his own? Did he have the power to set himself against range law and take marked animals as his own? Somehow, considering the Colonel and the forces he could call down, it didn't seem likely. Yet, Will Bower was certain. Link was coming for the herd.

The Colonel's actions were a puzzle, too. It was as though he had deliberately pointed Bower and his toughs at Rafter H, had almost ordered them to

232

catch up and sign on. Why would he do that? The most it would accomplish for him would be to detain Link. More armed riders with the herd would make it harder for him to take, but Tip didn't think it would ever occur to Colonel Nelson that Link might not take it if he made up his mind. Even with a few extra riders, the outfit had little chance of defending a big herd on the move against a concerted attack. Men could drive cows or they could fight—and with a small herd they might shift rapidly from one to another. But not with seven thousand wild cows. Just making them line out and move in an orderly fashion in a determined direction was a man-killing task.

So, why think that a few more men might make a difference in the final outcome? Tip tried to put himself in the Colonel's boots, to think as he might think, and could come up with no answer.

But in the meantime the herd, being pushed hard, was getting farther from Dry Creek each day. If Link meant to take it by force and turn it back, he would be in a hurry. Whatever he had in mind would come soon, and Tip Curry intended to find out what it was.

The dusk deepened, and the lightning danced nearer. He could connect each flash now with its own responding roll of thunder. The storm was walking down the hills, and it was only a few miles away.

Where the land rose from the valley in a broad swell and the narrowing bottoms curled away northward, Tip left the lowlands and headed up toward the near hills. The mushrooming peaks of the thunderheads now swept out above him, and a searing, crackling fork of brilliance danced on a ridge ahead. Its voice was like cannon-fire.

Tip clenched his jaws and kept going, aware of the danger in the clouds. More than one rider on high ground had died from a lightning strike. But high ground now was where he needed to be, and he concentrated on the job at hand. Somewhere ahead, nearby now, men huddled around a sheltered fire. The storm could be an ally now, if he used it so. If the fire meant one man, or even two or three, he might get close enough to confront them, to get the drop on them and take them back for Matt Hazelwood to talk to.

Another lightning strike crackled and roared nearby, then two more, and vivid memory flashed in his mind. Years ago, a hillside up in the territories, a storm front like this, and a rider under a tree. He never knew who the rider was, had only seen him coming down the hill toward the old trail where Tip rode. Two drifters in a land of drifters, trails meeting by chance.

He recalled the man coming down the hill, saw him wave at him, saw him ride close to the bole of a standing elm . . . then there was a brilliance, a blinding blaze that left his shocked eyes imprinted with the image of a shining man on a shining horse under a shining tree, all etched in flame against darkness.

Thunder that was like a fist whipped at him and its echoes rolled back and back from the hills

234

around. He rubbed his blinded eyes, and when he looked again the elm tree was a broken thing with blue fire flowing up its stump, and the man and horse were a motionless heap beneath it.

It was not a sight a man could forget. It burned in his mind.

Again the sharp, cool air gusted and again he smelled the cooking fire. He fixed on the direction of the breeze and shifted his weight, knee-guiding the black to angle toward it. Beyond the curve of the rise and climbing back from it was a shelf, and the fire would be below it. Just . . . about . . . there.

Lightning flared again and he shivered, putting the burning image away. He didn't have time to think about it now.

Miles to the south, in a box canyon among the hills, Jim Tyson winced at the approaching thunder. It reminded him of gunshots and blackness and pain. He wished he had a roof over his head, and he stood to look for a good place to throw his bedroll.

A moment before, Clifton Flowers had been squatting on his heels over by the bluff, just a few yards away, but now he wasn't there. Tyson sighed. "I wish he'd quit doing that," he muttered.

He turned, and suddenly he saw Flowers. The man was halfway up the side of the canyon, mounted on his scruffy horse on a narrow limestone ledge, and as lightning crashed nearby both the man and the horse turned to stare at it, wide-eyed.

"Flowers!" Jim Tyson shouted and waved. "What in hell are you doing? Come down from there!"

Another bolt struck, closer, dancing along the rim of the canyon, its crash rolling back and forth between the walls. As though drawn, Flowers and his horse edged upward, toward where it had struck. Out in the canyon the horses shied and whinnied, seeking shelter.

Jim ran toward the near rise, waving his hat. "Flowers! Are you crazy? Come back down here!"

Another blaze, and little swirls of ball lightning floated here and there above the canyon floor, lingering, like little Chinese lanterns hung at random. One floated past his face and he felt a stinging pain on his chest. He grabbed at his shirt and his fingers sensed a jolt as they closed on the old belt buckle in his pocket. Again he shouted, "Flowers! Clifton Flowers! Get back down here!"

The man above turned slowly and stared at him, bemused as one awaking from a dream. Tyson waved at him frantically. "Get down here! Come back!"

Both the man and the horse seemed confused. Then, abruptly, Flowers squared his shoulders, flipped his reins and the mustang came down the slope in a cascade of gravel and sod that was lighted by instant flashes and drowned by thunders.

At the bottom, Clifton Flowers reined hard and turned to look up at where he had been. He seemed intensely puzzled.

236

"I ought to have been up there just then, but I wasn't," he said, and Jim Tyson had the feeling the man wasn't even aware of him. "That there is just how it was . . . except I should have been there . . . Helen, I declare, I didn't know . . ."

"What in hell were you doing up there?" Tyson shouted at him. "Are you crazy? You could have been killed!"

Flowers looked down at him, as though seeing him for the first time. "Howdy," he said. "What did you say?"

"I said you might have been killed."

Again Flowers turned to look at the canyon wall above. He rubbed a hand thoughtfully across his grizzled face, and the mustang stamped and shivered.

"You know," Clifton Flowers said, "that's the smartest thing you've said yet. And I got to admit, I might have been."

At first the storm was a liveness on the horizon, flares and blackness in the hills hurling mutters and gusts of cold down across the living carpet of cattle on the shingled flats.

The five riding first guard pulled on their slickers and worked closer to the herd, snugging in those random bunches that had separated from the rest, pointing them toward the bovine security of their peers. Walking their horses, holding them to a constant, soothing pace, they rode the fringes of a vast circle, some of them talking to the critters near

237

enough to hear, some singing to them. And as the storm advanced, others rolled out of their beds and came out from the wagon camp to join them.

Stan Lamont came up on the herd carefully, peering into windblown murk that was darkening by the minute. As he made out the mass of dark forms that was the perimeter of the herd, he angled aside, keeping his distance for fear of spooking them. The wind at his back was erratic and chill, with the ozone sweetness of distant rain, and in the sporadic calms it fairly crackled with pent energies. Lightning danced on the hills behind him, great running webs of brilliance branching and zagging crazily, and the hills echoed its voices.

A rider passed in front of him, paralleling the edge of the great herd, and paused, leaning to peer at him. Lightning flared, highlighting the dark face of Gabe Sinclair. The drover recognized him and waved. His voice was thin against the wind.

"Mr. Green needs men yonder, on the downwind side! If they spill, try to fight shy of them bottoms yonder!"

Stan nodded and waved, turning to begin the long ride around the bulk of the herd, to the downwind side. Glancing back from a distance he saw Gabe directing two more riders. He couldn't see who they were.

He hoped Tip Curry had showed up. At thirty-three years, Stan Lamont was the oldest of the regular hands on Rafter H, as well as the biggest, and despite owing his life several times over to the young gunhand, he still thought of him as a kid and he worried about him. It came of being in some scrapes together, he supposed.

Curry had gone out to scout the bottoms ahead, but he had plenty of time to get back and so far Stan hadn't seen him. The kid was doing more than scouting trail, he knew. He was scouting enemies. And it just wasn't in his nature ever to let a body back him up . . . if he had a choice. There had been times when Stan Lamont didn't give him that choice.

Stan was no gunhand, and didn't want to be. But there were those who walked wide around him, and he felt that sometimes Tip took senseless risks, out of pure pride.

It gnawed at him that one day the kid would walk into something he couldn't handle alone, and not come back. And Stan would regret that. In a lot of ways, Tip Curry reminded him of his kid brother. Johnny had been full of that same quiet, inflexible pride. It had killed him.

He met Bo Maxwell coming around the herd. The curly-haired puncher was walking his horse, pressing close against the herd and singing to them. Lightning glares lit his face, and his voice sounded thin against the gusting wind, but those cattle near him as he passed stopped tossing their heads and seemed to listen. A hundred yards beyond him, though, the flaring skies showed cattle on their feet and churning nervously. The wind had whipped up a dust devil near the herd, and several hundred animals were lowing, stamping and beginning to mill. Stan put his mount to a lope to get there before the agitation spread further.

Ignoring the tossing horns, he headed in, trying to find the middle of the churn. Dust and animal heat welled up around him, and cattle parted as he passed, backing away, their eyes wild in the brief bursts of light.

He couldn't think of anything to sing, but a spiked horn skidded along his saddle fender and bruised his leg, and started him to cursing, and that seemed to work as well. Gritting his teeth he kept at it, his voice a deep monotone, calling the cows every bad thing he could think of to call them. Gradually, the bunch subsided, and he turned and worked his way back out of the herd, still cursing.

Past the perimeter he looked back. Some of the cattle were beginning to bed again, momentarily pacified.

"Stupid, slab-sided boneheads," he muttered. Ahead, another rider was coming toward him. He couldn't see who it was, but he pulled aside and went on.

Someone was beside him then, going the same direction, and he glanced around. Will Bower grinned at him. "Heard you discussin' philosophy with them critters back there," he said.

"They're plenty snuffy," Stan admitted. "Thunder's got 'em riled."

"Might pass over, I guess."

"Might."

"Hazelwood's crazy a a loon, tryin' to move this

many cows."

Stan looked at him, a beefy shadow against the dim cloud-glow of the rising hills. "You signed on."

Bower shrugged, a motion frozen by lightning glare. "Yeah. We signed on. Crazy, but we did."

"If you can't cut it, Bower, then you better pull up stakes right now. That storm's movin' in, and nobody's got time to hold your hand for you."

"I never said I couldn't cut it, Lamont. You hold up your end and I'll hold up mine."

Whatever Stan Lamont might have said was lost in a bone-rattling clap of thunder that seemed to be directly above their heads. Lightning sizzled around them, exploding puffs of dust where it danced along the ground, and for a moment they were blinded. Bower's horse went into a pitching fit, and Stan backed his mount away, blinking dazzled eyes, trying to see. Off to his left the edges of the bedding herd erupted with bawling, scrambling animals, then collapsed inward as the cattle crowded and pushed, setting off a rolling wave of activity diminishing toward the bulk of the great herd in the distance.

Once again, though, the commotion subsided, and Stan squinted and shook his head. There was just no predicting cows. A herd as big as this, in a way, was its own anchor. A few hundred head, pushing inward, might not set off a general panic . . . there was just too many to start moving easily. Yet Stan had seen stampedes, had seen them start from the flapping of a slicker in the wind, from the flash of a match, the distant bark of coyotes, from most anything or from nothing at all.

That lightning discharge . . . it had been directly overhead, a forking, flaring explosion that by all rights should have brought every cow on the bed grounds to its feet and set them all to running blindly in the night.

It had done no such thing. Dimly he could see the vast bedding herd beginning to resettle itself.

Will Bower had his horse under control and came up with him again. "Well, if that didn't spill 'em I sure don't know what will," he said.

Lesser lightning, higher up, flickered and rumbled, and Stan felt the hair on the backs of his hands stand up. Suddenly the air seemed to be charged, and it was hard to breathe. He pushed back his hat and squinted at the flickering, lowering sky. It seemed to shimmer, a greenish rippling that wasn't in the clouds, but hung in the air below them. He turned, looking around, and his fingers brushed past the gun at his hip. Sparks jumped, inch-long threads of bright blue connecting his fingers to the steel frame of his gun. He jerked his hand aside. Suddenly he could see the cows more clearly, dark massed shapes against a green glow that came from the ground beneath them.

"What in God's name—?" Will Bower muttered.

The shimmering in the air brightened and crept downward, rippling and coalescing as the ground-glow rose to meet it. Cattle bellowed and came to their feet, eyes white-ringed in the eerie light, horned heads tossing, and their horns burned with green fire that danced from one to another, crackling like burning wet wood.

242

The thunder that came then was not like the thunder before. It was a growing rumble that began a long way off, far across the packed bed ground, and rolled back as first dozens, then hundreds, then thousands of bawling cattle began to run, ball lightning trailing from their horns in the gloom.

19

Dave Holley had just arrived at the northeast quadrant of the bed grounds when the spill began. He was circling the herd, crooning against the wind, and watching the advancing storm play its bright games in the distance. He couldn't tell from here how close the storm might be to the upwind edge of the herd. At least a mile, he guessed, though it might be closer. A brilliance of bolts splayed and webbed all along the dark hillside out there and he waited for their thunder. It came promptly, and he revised his guess. A blazing pitchfork speared across the sky, low down, and for an instant he could see entirely across the bed ground. The lightning seemed to be just at its far edge, and the huge drumroll of its thunder followed it by seconds. Even as the following flares faded he could see motion in the herd, little ripples far away.

He kept moving, sensing as much as seeing the near fringes of the square mile of packed-in beef that he circled. He and his horse together, in

245

combined weight of bone and muscle, more or less equalled one cow. And there were seven thousand of them there, the nearest of them only yards away as he passed, evil horns and blinking eyes shimmering in the stormlight.

They stared at him as he passed, and he glared back. "God never made no cows," he assured them, making a croon of it. "God made heaven and earth and birds and horses and varmints and folks, but God never made cows." He thought about the notion, then expanded on it. "The devil never made cows either. The devil made sidewinders and chiggers and flash floods and cardsharps . . . and prickly pear and skeeters and ticks, but the devil's way too proud to have ever made cows. Cows just grew. Even the devil'ud have done a better job than designing the likes of you!"

It made him feel a little better.

Thousands of dull eyes followed him as he passed. Polished, sword-curved horns bobbed and glinted in the flickering light, shifting in unison to follow his passage, dumb momentary awareness of the presence of a comforting familiar thing.

"As I was out walkin' one morning for pleasure," Dave sang, *"I spied a young cowboy all ridin' alone . . ."*

Wind gusted and stilled for a moment, and he heard another voice singing, somewhere ahead. Soapy Green, he thought. He squinted. There were two riders out there, coming toward him, one following the other at a space of fifty yards.

"More the better," he told himself. Holding cows on bed on a night like this took some doing. If some

246

of them decided to break and run, the only thing standing against them was a few men on horseback . . . like himself. A thin cordon of non-cow shapes to keep the cows confused and amused. Presences to occupy their meager attentions. Familiar figures . . . dark shapes moving steadily around the herd, each a ton or so of combined man and horseflesh, cajoling, comforting and intimidating thousands of tons of horned brutes.

"That's the difference between cowboys and cows," Dave crooned, nodding at the mile-long perimeter of horns and eyeballs. "The cowboy is a little bit smarter."

The huge burst of fork lightning a few moments before, with its tooth-rattling roll of thunder, had shaken him. He had seen herds come unglued for far less reason. Now, though, they seemed somewhat placid again. Flares danced in the advancing black sky and glinted on dull cow eyes and a vast sea of gently waving horns.

Dave shifted his weight in his saddle, reached to lever against his saddlehorn, and little threads of crackling light shot from the horn to his fingertips. He jerked his hand away, noticing that the crackling, sizzling sensation continued. It seemed, abruptly, to be all around. His eyes lifted and went wide. Far off across the herd, a greenish glow had appeared, and it washed toward him at great speed, patterns of weird light running ahead of it, green fires dancing on the horns of the animals, leaping from one to another, brightening as they came. Balls of cold fire swirled and skittered through the air, just above the horned heads, and the ground underfoot began to glow.

An animal bawled and a hundred answered it, then a thousand more, and abruptly there was no perimeter to his right. Cattle bawled and lurched upright and the tattoo of their hooves was a thunder greater than what the sky had produced. Before Dave could react, cattle were passing him fore and aft, and a solid mass of them was coming at him, broadside. The horse beneath him was a cowpony. He barely kept his seat as it spun, dug in its heels and ran, bounding into eerie darkness alive with glowing, electrically-charged cattle and a faintly green land and sky no more than ten feet apart.

Sheet lightning was heaven and earth in a world abruptly short but incredibly wide, a world engulfed by a thundering tide of bawling, racing, crackling animals, and Dave Holley ducked low over his shining saddle and raced its pounding crest.

Before dark, Matt Hazelwood had saddled a Star-Cross horse and loped eastward from the wagon camp, angling wide of the bedding herd, aiming for the slopes of a long ridge that would give him a view of the darkening bottoms ahead. Tip Curry had gone out there, to have a look at tomorrow's trail, and Matt had a gnawing worry chewing at him.

The more he thought about what Will Bower had said—about how things were shaping up back on Dry Creek—the more he felt he had underestimated somebody, and he brooded about it. Colonel Nelson seemed to have taken charge, and the word was that Link was out after the Rafter H herd . . . and there was a general roundup starting soon. Something about it all just didn't make sense. So Link intended to take his herd. What did he intend to do with it? Rafter H might be a blackballed outfit, but that didn't mean Rafter H brands were up for grab. If Link intended to return the cattle to Dry Creek, then what? Was he going to throw them in with the pool stock? If he intended to claim them for himself, how was he going to make it stick?

He had a feeling the one he might have underestimated—the one they all had, in fact—was the Englishman. Nelson was a slick customer, and not above playing his neighbors for fools if they would let him. But Link was no fool, even though he seemed to be falling right in with Nelson's plans.

Unless—the thought had beem worming its way around, and now he considered it—unless Link had no intention of taking the herd back. And unless Nelson had figured that out and was playing the hand that way.

And that had started him to worrying about Tip Curry. If Link was coming, he was out in the hills someplace by now, maybe watching them. And if he was, that might be where Tip was going.

The slope of the ridge, where it faced the bed ground and the wide bottom lands beyond, was a series of wide ledges. He rode to the first one and cut back, finding a point where he could look out across the great herd—the drags were just now crowding in, beginning to settle for the night—and the ranging lands beyond. Far out in the bottoms a meander of dark growth indicated the course of a stream, willows and cottonwoods growing along its path.

He looked, but could see no sign of movement out there. In the distance, upstream, the stream lost itself among rolling hills where lightning was beginning to show. Soapy was right. There was storm in the air and they might have their hands full tonight. As the light began to fail he saw a rider heading for the wagon camp, and a bit later he saw others coming out, going toward the herd. Soapy was putting out extra men . . . maybe every hand.

Darkness came quickly then, as banked clouds marched from the west to swallow the evening light and replace it with the pyrotechnics of storm.

Tip, dammit, he thought, get back here. I need hands right now more than I need gunhands.

He hoped he was right.

Except for the advancing, erratic flares of lightning coming through the hills beyond the wagon camp, he could see little. But he read the wind and watched the path of the electrical storm and knew where Soapy would be, and most of the others. There were riders this side of the herd, one circling counter-clockwise . . . Bo Maxwell, maybe . . . and others coming from the windward curve toward him. Stan Lamont was down there, and Will Bower, heading for the downwind edge of the bed ground, to give Soapy additional manpower. He guessed that Dave Holley was over on the other

250

side somewhere, also heading for the lead.

The storm strode down on the flats and rattling flashes illuminated the land. A low, jagged fork of multiple bolts cut across above the herd, low down, and crashed near where the riders had passed each other.

Another, smaller bolt seemed to leapfrog from there and sizzled against the ridge above and behind him. It was time to go to work. He heeled the Tyson horse and angled downslope, heading for the downwind side of the great herd.

A fireball the size of a man's fist, glowing with an eerie greenish light, floated toward him from the shoulder of the ridge, bobbing in the air, and swerved aside, narrowly missing him. He felt the hair rise on his head, under his hat, on the back of his neck, on his hands. In front of his knee, where his catch-rope rode coiled, the silvered brass concho at the base of his dally-string glowed and shimmered, and little pulses of sullen light ran toward his iron saddle horn to build a glow like a halo around it. Bluish sparks ran up and down the horse's headstall and seemed to trail their glow behind the swivels of the bit.

Where the animal's hooves struck the dry ground, they splattered sparks in the gloom. All around was a faint, sizzling sound almost like bacon in a pan.

Flares danced overhead, and he saw riders off to his left cutting into the herd, trying to break a mill. They were dark shapes above a sea of glowing horns. Fireballs waltzed here and there, bright glows in the murk swimming slowly about, tantalizing one another.

He hoped Sam Price would remember to stay clear of the stove wagon. The camp was on higher ground, and the stove wagon would draw lightning quicker than anything they had.

He felt the static of his revolver in his holster at his hip, the steel drawing a charge from the air and pulsing it outward, and he winced, remembering the waddy who had lost his leg one year when his six-shooter discharged all the loads in its cylinder during an electrical storm. A freak occurrence, but then that was the nature of electrical storms—assembled freak occurrences.

He had seen storms before. There were no two alike.

So far, the herd was still on its grounds. Horns tossed and the bawling of cattle was a raucous chorus on the wind, sung to a staccato of stamping cloven hooves, but there was as yet no concerted movement.

He let the horse make its own best pace in the stuttering light, guiding toward the east.

A cannon burst in his ears and something hit him with stunning force. Blinding light was all around him and he seemed to float in it, then it was gone and there was darkness and something else hit him. Slowly he identified it. It was the hard ground, and he was lying on it. Yards away, the dark silhouettes of horned cattle milled about, lowing and bellowing. For a moment Matt Hazelwood couldn't move. He lay paralyzed and wondered how he had come to be here. Then there was light— an eerie, murky green light that seemed to come

252

from everywhere at once, and that sang and hummed and crackled and was like fire and ice in his lungs. He pushed himself upright, and his hands on the ground were dark hand-shapes outlined against a green glow that rose around them.

Something nudged him and he jerked, whirling and backing away. It was a horse. His horse. The Tyson horse with his saddle and gear.

God bless Jim Tyson for a wrangler!

He got his feet under him and caught the trailing reins, sparks shooting from his finger tips as he reached for the saddle-horn. He got his foot into a stirrup and swung aboard, ducking his head as he mounted because the sky had turned green and had descended until it was almost on top of his hat. Thunder rolled and he swung around, dazzled eyes ranging the distances of a rolling, shifting sea of running cattle, a sea that bobbed and thundered and clattered and was awash with glowing whitecaps where foxfire danced crazily from point to point and trailed behind like tatters of bright silk.

"Stampede!" He yelled it and the word was lost in the din. Matt Hazelwood slapped reins and the Star-Cross bay bounded away, running parallel to the flowing thunder of the herd, heading forward, toward the front.

Pye and Slater had saddled together after their supper, glancing back over their shoulders at the lightning storm moving in. The trailboss had sent word in that all hands were needed on the herd.

Both of them felt strongly a need to prove themselves in the eyes of the rest of the outfit. They had come as rustlers, after all, and it was only by the grace of short-handedness that they hadn't danced at the end of ropes. Thus they made a race of it when the word came for riders, catching out mounts under the watchful eyes of the black wrangler, slapping their saddles on them and heading out.

Slater had the faster animal, so he was a hundred yards ahead when he approached the herd and was pointed to the left, to head around to the north side of the herd and work the circle there. But Pye saw which way he was being sent and hauled left, shortcutting, and thus got ahead of him.

The land sloped away toward the north, shingled flats spreading out toward wide bottoms in the distance, and they both understood their task. Should the big herd spill, spooked by storm, the boss would want them to spill toward the east and not the north. They would be easier to recover out there than spread over those wide bottoms. And should that storm have rain behind it and be dumping it in the hills, flash floods could cost the outfit a lot of beef.

Dimly, in the failing light, they saw another rider ahead of them, going away, beginning to curve around the mass of the bedded herd. They followed. Where he put himself, they would spread back from him and work the herd.

Pye held his horse to a steady lope, staying out from the herd so they wouldn't be alarmed by his passage. Dusk had turned to the rumbling gloom of

254

advancing storm and he could tell that the cattle were aware of it, in whatever dim way cows are aware.

Pye had never seen a trail herd this size before, would not have believed that a one-wagon outfit could move such a mass of critters. But these past days he had seen it done, and had developed a certain pride at being part of it. Folks would be talking about this in years to come, and he enjoyed the idea that when they did he could step right in and say, yes sir, I was on that drive, let me tell you how it was.

And how it was, was hard. He had never worked so hard or covered so many miles or slept so little as in these days since he and Slater signed on. But it felt good. He and Slater both had been stung and humiliated by their treatment up on the Canadian, when Anderson blamed them for losing some of his cows to blizzard. What had cost Anderson his cows was him being a skinflint. Only the two of them were out there, and there should have been more hands. As it was, they had managed to save most of the cows . . . but not all.

He wished Mr. Anderson could see them now, see the work they were doing with this outfit. Running them off like that, the old rancher had left them both wondering if they really couldn't cut it. Mr. Hazelwood had given them a chance to prove they could.

Beyond the herd, behind him, brilliance flared and he looked back to see fork lightning striking and skipping up the ridge. It was close, almost at the edge of the bedding ground, and its voice when

255

it came was a roar of thunder rolling away into distance. He saw critters rising in the herd, and slowed and swung toward them, seeing out of the corner of his eye that Slater, a hundred yards back, was doing the same. They pushed in against the cattle, being noticed, taking it slow, giving the cows something different and reassuring to think about. The wave that had begun subsided, and they worked their way northward, crooning and talking to the animals in a dark world of flares and flashes and drumrolls.

The cool, gusting wind that had been on his left began to quarter, more behind him now, as they rounded the curve toward the north perimeter. In the flickering light he couldn't see the rider ahead of them, so he pushed on, aware of Slater coming along behind.

To his left and ahead now, far off in the stormlighted gloom, were the wide bottom lands, stretching away under a layer of dark cloud that had lightning in it. Out there in the distance there were moving lights, as though folks were walking around, carrying lanterns of different colors. Some of the lanterns came toward the herd, and one seemed to fly just above the brush, hop up over the last shelf of the bedding flats and come directly at him. It was a bright ball of light, bigger than his head, and it bobbed up and down as it came. He felt the hair rising on his head. The ball soared away, then came back, spiralling and dancing, and curved around to come at him from behind. He shifted to watch it, and there were cattle there, between him and Slater, a knot of panicked critters

on their feet and running, breaking from the herd
as others followed. The green ball swooped and
dived and they turned, cavalry forming for a
charge, and thundered toward him, a wall of horns
and hooves. He spurred his horse and felt the jar in
his rump as it missed its footing on broken ground,
going to its knees. Cattle swept past, great horns
hooking at both man and horse. The pony neighed
fearfully, got its feet under it and tried to run with
the flow. Pye loosed his catch rope and flogged
desperately with its coil, trying to make some space.
The fury of hooves almost deafened him. For an
instant there was clear space ahead, then the cattle
beyond and to his left turned again, pushing back
toward the herd, and he was cut off.

Green light grew above and below, and now all
the cattle around him were moving, pressing in at
him from both sides.

Then Slater was there, beside him, yipping and
shouting and flailing a coiled rope, all the trappings
on his mount aglow with cold fire.

Their combined attack sundered the press of hot
flesh immediately around them, and Pye saw a
momentary break in the running mass to his left.

"Come on!" he yelled at Slater, and spurred his
horse in that direction. The bobbing, tossing horns
around him now had fire dancing on them. He
didn't look back, but thought he heard Slater right
behind him, and he prayed as he rode for his life. A
moment, and then another, and there were fewer
cattle around him. He fought and yelled and let the
horse have its head . . . and then he was past the
stampede, and it flowed and thundered behind him,

a huge living thing that went on as far as he could see. Shimmering green light pressed down on it, and the ground where it passed was green, and the running herd was a vast thudding darkness with fire in its horns that filled the space between.

He looked around for Slater. He had thought he was behind him. But there was no one there, and nowhere in that sea of glowing, stampeding beef was there any sign of a rider.

20

As abruptly as it had begun, the crackling green glow was gone and in its place was a thundering darkness ripped and sundered by lances of brilliance striding across the land. Raw ozone burned in the lungs of men and beasts, and a wall of driving wind sliced down from the hills. Behind it came the rain.

Layer by layer, ring by bellowing ring, the great herd unwound itself and ran, rank after rank of cattle scattering and pounding away, mindless and blind, clearing space for others to follow. The leaders, those on the downwind face which were the first to spill, had gone a mile or more before the entire herd was in motion, so close was the crush on the upwind drags.

They put their tails to the wind and ran, wild with panic, and there was nothing the riders of Rafter H could do but try to stay clear of them, keep up with them and let them run themselves out. In better circumstances, and with a smaller herd, riders might have managed to narrow the front of the stampede into a point, and turn it back on itself. But this stampede could not be turned or controlled. Only the wind and the dancing storm pointed the way.

Dub Newton, late of T-bar-T, found himself alone and racing crazily against a tide on the north side of the mass. Moments before, about the time the spill began, he had been aware of riders behind him at a distance—two of them coming around the north curve. But now there were only himself, his horse, and a world of flaring darkness and pounding brutes. By lightning's light he saw the bottoms looming ahead and to the left, and he spurred the horse for more speed. He shouted and waved, pushing the nearest cattle toward those beyond them. The bottoms were closer. He drew his gun and fired into the air, then fired again. A moment later he saw a flash ahead, dimly heard the crack of another pistol. Sluggishly, slowly, the running herd edged inward upon itself, to the right. With a howl of triumph Dub fired a third shot and a fourth.

The flats were narrowing now. The thrust of the ridge from the right, a prow of rocky ledges pointing northward, funneled the stampede closer and closer to the ragged little cliffs that dropped to the sloping bottomlands below. Dub found himself walled by cattle on his right, the nearest ones only yards away, and blind shelving encroaching from the left. The man ahead, he knew, was even closer to being pushed over the edge. He heard him fire again.

His shouts were drowned in the thunder of the herd. He glanced around as lightning flickered crazily overhead, and saw hundreds of cattle, shoulder to shoulder, blocking his way back.

In desperation he pulled the little brass flask from his coat pocket, then peeled off his coat, pulled the flask stopper with his teeth, dropped the cork, got the reins in his teeth and leaned aside to empty the flask onto the whipping coat. He tossed the flask aside, found his matchbox and struck a light. The wind whipped it out. He struck another, shielding it against the soaked coat. Flames sputtered, grasped hesitantly at vapors, then surged up the alcohol-wetted fabric, dim blue flames that scorched his hand and whipped in the wind, then brightened to a flare of red and yellow as the fabric caught. Like a demon horseman wielding a hoop of fire, he swung the coat in great arcs and pushed against the wall of cattle. The animals bellowed, some stumbling and going down as others bolted away from the fire thrust at them.

Pushing and blazing, packing cattle back toward the ridge, Dub Newton howled with rage and pain and drummed his horse's flanks, surging ahead.

Dave Holley rode desperately, blindly between erratic pales in the gloom, using every trick he knew to crowd the cows pressing him toward the shearing edge of the low cliffs. Flecks of hot moisture flew back at him as his horse heaved and lathered. He had been directly in front of the herd when the stampede began, had gained some distance and veered off to the left to get into position to turn the leaders when the chance allowed. But his horse had stumbled in the gloom, and both of them went down. By the time he was up again, a thousand cattle or more had passed him and he had lost his chance to swing the leaders toward the ridge.

He had lost track of time and distance. He had no idea how far they had come, was aware now only of the noise and heat of running cattle crowding him nearer and nearer to the vaguely-seen edge of the flats. The drop there might be two or three feet, or ten or fifteen. There was no way to tell. But it would be enough. Once over the edge, he and his mount would fall and roll, and a hundred cattle would tumble down upon them.

Lightning flickered and the horse danced to the right, barely missing a cut wedge in the cliff. A horn hooked him brutally in the thigh, almost throwing him from his saddle. He fired his last shot, not into the air but into the spine of a steer veering to cut him off, and heard it fall almost under him. A pummeling behind him told him of others piling into it.

Lightning danced again, and he saw the herd edging nearer to the cliffs ahead. There was no space left. In the blackness that followed he gritted his teeth and braced himself.

Bright heat smote his face and a blazing thing like a huge wing whipped past his head, an arc of fire in the night that burned images into his eyes. Someone shouted at him, almost in his ear, and a rider shot past swinging a blazing cloth, hazing crazed cattle back away from the edge. The man's whole arm seemed to be afire.

Dave demanded more speed from his mount and

fell in behind, shouting insanities, flailing brute backs with his coil.

Ahead of him the blazing rider smoldered down to showering sparks and flung aside a thing of embers. Tossing horned heads bawled and sheared aside, and the lightning flickers showed open space ahead. Almost side by side they surged through. Now the stream of cattle to the right was thinner, more strung out. They had found the point of the herd. As one they galloped past and wheeled back, hauling up hard on their reins, shouting and waving. The leaders veered aside, still running but now in a slightly altered direction, others following.

While the other man held his position Dave spun, got some distance on them and wheeled again, veering them more. Not far away there was a shout, and another rider came at an angle, cutting through the line, passing him with a wave to wheel farther ahead and bend the run again. Surging cattle arrowed past, turning, following those ahead.

Dave held his place while the man behind him dashed past, on past the new rider, and wheeled to bend them again. Dave still couldn't tell who the man was—the one who had hazed them with fire— but the rider between them now was Matt Hazelwood.

Jagged lightning limned the sky and he saw the rancher point and wave his hat. Beyond the turning leaders were open flats, and for a moment Dave felt disoriented, trying to get his bearings. With next light he spotted the ridge, far back and away in the distance.

It was time to handle the stampede.

The line of lightning was dimmer now, going away to the east, and for the first time Dave noticed that he was soaking wet. Somewhere along the line it had begun to rain.

Slowly, agonizingly, they worked to bend the lead around, to throw the cattle back into those following. Cold rain sluiced from hatbrims and steamed on the rumps of tired horses. The cattle had slowed, mostly from exhaustion, but they remained wild and skittish even as the men began paring away small clusters of them to throw into reverse mills.

What light there had been from the storm was failing, replaced by a drumming, soaking darkness in which there was no moon and no stars, only black clouds above a black land, unseen rain and unseen mud underfoot.

Matt Hazelwood was in the lead when they finished arcing the herd, forcing the leaders back the way they had come. By distant stormlight he removed his slicker and swung it like a catchrope, flogging it around the heads of lowing, panting cattle. Stan Lamont and Will Bower came up from the right, barely visible and then only at brief intervals, and joined in the hazing.

Matt knew they had thrown the stampede back on itself when he heard cattle colliding in the darkness ahead of him, and he sagged in his saddle, replaced his slicker and shouted for whoever could hear, "All right, it's checked! Back off now and give 'em room!"

The herd might continue to mill for hours. But they were tired, and if left alone they would simmer down.

One by one, tired men on exhausted horses found their way to the place where Matt Hazelwood waited, some distance away from the main body of the circling herd. And as they came, some drawn by shouts in the darkness, some brought in by the brief flickers of matches held high, he counted noses.

Dave Holley came leading a horse with a groaning rider clinging to its saddle. "This is Dub Newton," he called in the darkness before realizing that he was within feet of others. "He's hurt," he continued more quietly. "I can't tell much, but his right arm is burned pretty bad. He set his coat on fire."

Stan Lamont and Will Bower helped the waddy down and sat him on the wet ground with a blanket over his shoulders. Bo Maxwell showed up afoot, leading a horse that limped so that they could tell even in the darkness which leg was lame. An hour or so later Gabe Sinclair found them, and sometime after that, when stars showed here and there among the breaking clouds, Slim Hobart and Clyde Burns showed up. They had stayed with the drags until they were certain the run was checked, a thing difficult to know in darkness. Slim had ridden a hundred yards or more into the herd before realizing he was there.

"Them cows ain't goin' anyplace else tonight," he assured them. "I bumped square into several of them, tryin' to find my way out, and I don't think they'd have cared if I was a pack of wolves. They just grunted an' moved over."

265

Matt waited out the hours of darkness, surrounded by wet and miserable young men he could barely see, horses so tired they just stood with their heads down and, out on the prairie, a huge spattering of dark forms that condensed in the distance toward solid shadow. The herd.

Pye came to them, across the night prairie, just when a dim gray line was forming on the eastern rim of the world. He had been looking for his partner, Slater. He hadn't found him.

Another who didn't appear, during all the long hours of dark vigil, was Soapy Green.

At first light Nacho Lucas helped Sam Price hitch up the team, then he went with Ollie Sinclair to gather in the remuda and the three of them headed eastward, aiming for the point of the jutting ridge.

There were cattle everywhere, strays and laggards from the stampede grazing placidly in the dawn, here and there a cripple and—dotting the trampled flats like anthills—the carcasses of those that had gone down and been overrun.

With the remuda moving in good order, tagging after a lead mare tied to the stove cart, Ollie and Nacho fanned out and began gathering cows as they went, chousing them along slowly, ignoring those that balked. They could be gathered later. But those that would move they moved ahead of them, plodding along over land torn and muddied and littered with death.

When the sun was high they were near the point

266

of the ridge and Nacho rode ahead to see what was beyond. The trail was a swath a half-mile wide, curving in the distance, its outer fringe sweeping the rim of the banks that stepped down to the bottom lands beyond. From a high place on the sweeping shoulder Nacho saw the herd several miles away, thousands of head of cattle scattered over four or five sections of land, riders here and there among them. One rider was coming toward him, less than a mile away. Nacho saw him wave as he spotted him on the rise. He didn't return the signal, just gazed at the wide land, the cattle, and the huge track of devastation that had occurred in the night. This would be a good place to make a count, he thought. A man with a tally string could spend a few hours up here, spying out the fallen cattle, and could tell them what they had lost. He let his eyes range the land below and saw another rider, off to the north, tiny in the distance. As he watched, the rider stopped and seemed to study the ground beneath him. Then he dismounted and studied it some more.

From where he sat, his injured hand thrust into his coat with its buttons serving as a sling, Nacho could see back across the bedding grounds. Ollie was coming along with the few cattle they had collected, and the remuda was moving with the wagons, and the hills beyond were crisp and bright with morning sun.

"Nobody caused that stampede," he said aloud, fixing on the notion. "It just happened." It seemed to him at that moment that folks had their hands full, just keeping up with things that were nobody's

267

fault and trying to get a little ahead in the process. People had enough to say grace over without going out of their way to cause grief to one another . . . didn't they? He pulled his bandaged hand out of his coat and clumsily removed his hat—a hat like Tip Curry wore, a gunhand-looking hat. Back there on the trail, a long way back, it seemed, were two graves of men who had Nacho's bullets in them. He had thought a lot about those graves, had even dreamed about them. But he guessed now that he wouldn't any more. They had come to cause grief.

He looked out on the stampede path with its litter of little mounds of death, and when he put his hat on again he set it carefully on his head, low over his eyes, the way Tip Curry wore his hat.

Stan Lamont saw Nacho on the shoulder of the ridge from maybe a mile away, and waved at him. Nacho didn't return the wave and Stan supposed he hadn't seen him. He rode on, tired and gray-minded, scarcely noticing the littered trail, the scattered cattle, the dark mounds that were dead stock. There would be time enough later to think about all that. In the distance, north across the stampede's path, he saw Pye dismount and stand staring at the ground. When he looked again, the youngster was on his knees.

Somebody ought to go see about him, he thought. All through the night, Pye had searched for his partner. Stan guessed now that with the coming of light, he had found him.

The tightness in his throat remained, not

changed much by the sight of that kid out there on the prairie, a hard-luck young cowboy down on his knees . . . was he crying? Maybe. Stan Lamont had been on the range most of his life. He had seen men cry. And he had seen boys become men. Those that lived to.

But the tightness in his throat had already been there. Matt Hazelwood had sent him to find the wagons and the remuda and the rest of the outfit. They were to gather several miles east, beyond the ridge, and would regroup the herd and start again from there.

Hazelwood had said very little, but the look in his eyes had said enough. A long time ago, four men had started Rafter H. They had begun with nothing more than the horses they rode, the guns at their hips and a dream about gathering up wild cattle and pushing them to market. Matt Hazelwood, Sam Price, Soapy Green and a kid wrangler named Jim Tyson.

Stan Lamont hated to be the one to tell Sam Price that another of the old four was gone . . . that Soapy Green was dead.

21

Soapy took too long to die, Matt Hazelwood told himself. Corded muscle stood out on his forearms as he pried up the last spadeful of sod to form a neat three-by-six foot hole one spade deep on the crown of a featureless little rise in the prairie. He set it aside carefully, with the other cuts of sod, then stepped back to the shallow hole and began to dig in earnest.

No man should take that long to die. Not like that. Pinned under a rolled horse, his hips and spine shattered, one arm trampled into the ground and half his chest caved in by a cow's hoof. To be like that through the long night, and still live . . . He bent to his task, oblivious to those around him, the cowboys who hung back and pretended to ignore him and kept glancing at him with deep concern. He relished the work. It was something he needed to do.

Gabe Sinclair had started to dig the hole, until Hazelwood took the spade away from him. He hadn't questioned how the black drover came to have a spade with him, way out here. Gabe was nearest the camp when they started to run. So he'd picked up a spade because when cows spill sometimes there are folks to bury. Or maybe he'd had it with him before that, when the lightning danced in the hills. Whatever the reason, it was a spade and Matt needed to use it.

He dug and felt the morning sun on his back. Soapy had always liked the morning sun, was always the one who rode out to meet it on a drive.

All the years . . . all the drives. Soapy's wheezing voice lingered in his years, speaking to him again and again. "My own doin', Captain . . ." How many years had it been since any of them—or anyone at all—had called him Captain? "My own fool doin', Captain. I tried to take point."

He lay where he had fallen, a crushed and distorted body with a voice wheezing from its lips. They had put ropes on the dead horse and dragged it off of him, but there was no way to move him . . . not alive.

"Even when they hit me that horse stayed up," the lingering voice said. "Sure was some horse. Thought for a minute or two we'd make it."

"You damn near did, Soapy," was all he could think of to say.

"Some kinda horse . . . but there wasn't any room . . . and no light . . . they busted down his legs, is what done it . . . tell Big Jim he done fine with that horse, Captain. Tell him . . ."

The short-handled spade creaked and protested in hard hands and the deep gray soil of Texas mounded toss by toss beside the neat hole.

"You recollect that first time out, Captain? Chicago . . . that's where we was goin'. We damn near made it, too."

"We damn near did, Soapy. Sure enough."

"Told you we'd get a price for them up yonder, didn't I?"

"You sure did, Soapy. And you were right."

"Shoulda throwed in with you right then, not wasted it all at Cairo. Never thought anything about bein' rich, but I guess I damn near was that time."

"Damn near, Soapy."

"Where's Sam, Captain? And Big Jim? They here someplace?"

"They'll be along directly, Soapy. Sam's bringing the wagons out." *They*. None of them had seen Jim Tyson in years, but Soapy wanted to hear the best he could tell him. "They'll be here soon. You just hang on, now."

They thought he was gone, then. Long minutes passed and they couldn't even tell if he was breathing. But then he spoke again, and Matt leaned close to hear the words.

"Tell Sam he can keep that shotgun of mine, Captain—"

"I'll tell him, Soapy."

"Tell Big Jim he can have my Sunday saddle . . . no, Big Jim ain't here, is he? But those Star-Cross horses . . . he'll be along directly. You tell him."

"I will, Soapy."

"Funny thing . . . seems like Big Jim has found

273

hisself some help . . . that's a right good thing, you know."

Some of the words made a kind of sense. Some were just ramblings of a dying man. Matt crouched, listening.

". . . Can't wait around any more . . . time to move on . . . maybe I'll stop off at Cairo, there's a gal there . . . did I ever tell you about that, Captain? Can't remember anything any more, seems like—"

"It's all right, Soapy."

"Damn near made it . . . so many times."

His hat was gone and Matt noticed vaguely how gray his hair had become, how deep the creases in his face. When had all that happened?

Soapy sighed, a bubbling, rattling sound. Then his eyes opened wider and sought Matt's face with a strange intensity. "Let's take these cows to Wyoming, Matt. Damn near just ain't good enough any more. Let's take them all the way to Wyoming."

The mound of soil grew and the neat hole deepened as Matt worked, sweat glistening on his brow. All the way to Wyoming, Soapy. Just like we decided, you and me and Sam, after we read Jim Tyson's letter.

The grave was waist-deep now. He raised himself to look at the prairie around. Cattle were everywhere, grazing placidly, without memory of a stampede in the night. In the distance he saw Dave Holley putting a loop on a critter that had got itself trapped in a cedar motte. The big brindle steer, Sonofabitch, stood near, watching balefully. The steer had followed Dave around all morning.

He thought about making Dave trail boss, but discarded the idea. Dave was a top hand with cows, but bossing men wouldn't set well with him. Stan Lamont would be a better choice.

Out on the flats, Gabe Sinclair rode guard on the little patch of ground where Soapy had died. They would bring the body up here for burying when he finished the grave.

He bent to his work again, and the clean breeze of morning whispered across the mound of dirt, *"O bury me not on the lone prairie . . . where the wild coyotes will howl o'er me. In a narrow grave, just six by three . . ."*

It wouldn't matter to Soapy. He had breathed his last, and there had been a contentment on his bloody face in those last seconds. Almost like a man who knew where he was going and was anxious to be on his way.

I reckon you knew the way, all right, Soapy, Matt thought bitterly. You had all night to think about it before we found you this morning.

Better, when a man's time comes, if he never knew what hit him. Be a sight easier, it seemed to him, if a man could get it done with and never even know he was dead.

Bo Maxwell rode up the rise on Matt's horse, and pulled off his hat. "Wagons are in sight, Mr. Hazelwood, about four miles back."

"All right," he said. "Any sign of Tip Curry?"

"He might be with the wagons. We can't tell yet. Do you want some of us to head back and start pushin' cows this way? It looks like we spilled 'em

275

all the way from the bed ground to yonder."

"They'll keep. Wait for the wagons. I want to know where everyone is before we start the gather."

"Yes, sir."

What became of a man who died and didn't know it? The thought was so strange that he stopped his digging and looked up. Bo Maxwell had ridden away, going out to meet the rolling camp. But someone else was there, slouched in his saddle, hat in his hand, watching him dig. The sun was behind the man's head and Matt couldn't make him out for a moment, then realized he was not one of the outfit.

"Howdy," the stranger said. "Had yourselves a spill, seems like. Lightnin'?"

Matt nodded.

"What I was thinkin'," the man said. He tapped his mount and eased around to where Matt could see him better. A weathered, rawhide man, with some years on him. His face was deeply-lined and intelligent. He ran a hand through graying hair, looking at the hole. "My name's Flowers," he said. "Clifton Flowers. Do you know the way to Porterville?"

"Matt Hazelwood," Matt introduced himself. "No, I don't guess so. Where is it?"

"Surely don't know," Flowers said. "How come you're plantin' that feller so deep?"

Matt looked down. He had dug until the grave was shoulder deep—deeper than was customery except in civilized graveyards where they usually went six feet. Generally, on the trail, four feet was considered more than adequate. "Got carried

276

away," he said. "It's for an old friend." He wondered how the man had ridden in on them unchallenged. "Are you from around here, Mr. Flowers?"

The man looked puzzled for a moment. "I don't think so. I'm just passin' through, ridin' with a young'un named Tyson. He knows you."

"Jim Tyson?" Matt's jaw dropped. "He *is* here, then? In Texas?"

"Sure. He'll be along directly. He's got hisself a herd of purely fine horses an' a notion that he needs to find Rafter H, so I been stickin' with him. He knows the way to Wyoming."

There was something strangely aslant about the man's words, but Matt wasn't analyzing them. He tossed the spade out of the hole, got his hands atop it and levered himself up. Standing on the mound of earth put him almost face to face with the stranger. "Well, I declare! That's just what Soapy said. He said Big Jim would be along directly."

"That who this hole is for?" Flowers indicated the grave with his hat.

"Yeah. Stampede got him."

"Dead folks generally don't lie."

The comment caught Matt off guard. He found it intensely irritating, but couldn't think of a response. Obviously, the man had no sensitivity.

"The feller with the horses got hisself killed a while back, but he's gettin' better. That there is one of his horses, yonder." Flowers raised his head and pointed his hat. A couple of hundred yards away Gabe Sinclair sat his mount, guarding the body of Soapy Green, and watched them as though waiting for a signal.

277

"Mighty fine animal," Flowers allowed. "Had forty-four of them originally, he did, but now he's down to thirty head not countin' the one he's ridin'. You fellas got the other fourteen."

Matt squinted at him, trying to sort out what he had said. "He was . . . killed? You mean Jim Tyson was killed?"

"I believe so. Or at least pretty near it. But he's better. He called me down yesterday evenin' about ridin' into lightnin'. Gave me a mite to think on, for a fact. How do I look to you?"

Matt stared at him. "How do you *look?*"

"I mean, can you see through me or anything? Tyson said he could, but he's still a little bit wobbly north of his ears. Comes of bein' killed, I reckon."

Matt gave up. He couldn't make sense of what the man was saying, but somehow he knew Jim Tyson and apparently Tyson was on his way to join them. "Where is he right now?"

Flowers looked around, seemed a bit confused. "Where are *we?*"

"I mean, which direction is he coming from? You said he'll be here directly."

"If he don't get lost, he will. But don't worry. I'll go back and get him. I found the way to him several times already."

The man nodded in a friendly manner, clamped his hat on his head, reined the mustang-looking horse around and loped away, southwestward. Matt stared after him, then turned and waved his hat at Gabe Sinclair. When he looked back, Clifton Flowers was out of sight.

278

Gabe came up to him. "You ready, Mr. Hazel-wood?"

"Gabe, I want you to follow that man that was here. He says Jim Tyson is with him, seems to know him, but he sounds like a loony. See if you can find out what's going on."

Gabe looked at him blankly. "Yes, sir. Uh, where is he?"

"I don't know. But he went off that way. You saw him. His name is Flowers."

Gabe frowned. That was the same name Ollie had been babbling about. He stared out across the cattle-pocked land, then back at Matt. "I didn't see anybody, Mr. Hazelwood. When was he here?"

"Just now, damn it! You were looking right at us."

"No sir, I was lookin' at you, but I didn't see anybody else. Uh, I was wonderin' if you're ready for us to bring Mr. Green up here."

Will Bower came in from somewhere and rode to the rise. He still showed the bruises of the pummeling he had taken from Dave Holley, and he couldn't resist a sidewise glare at Gabe as he approached, but he only stepped down and picked up the spade. "We need another grave, Mr. Hazelwood. I rode a ways out to meet the wagon bunch, and Stan Lamont met me halfway. They got another dead man. The one called Slater. Cows stomped him." He paced off a few steps and began another grave.

Matt Hazelwood watched the big man for a moment, noticing his slow movements, the stoop to

279

his shoulders. Gabe looked drawn and beat-down, too. If I'm as tired as these men, he admitted to himself, maybe I *am* imagining things.

"Who all do they have with them?"

Bower shrugged. "Everybody else, I guess. Mr. Price, the Lucas kid, Lamont, the other nig—" he glanced at Gabe and changed his mind. ". . . the wrangler, and that drifter kid, Pye."

Matt turned away. Everyone accounted for, then, except one. Tip Curry had gone out to scout, yesterday. He hadn't returned.

"Dig it deep," he told Bower. "Like this one here. We're putting some good men under today."

An hour or so later the wagons were in sight, and an hour after that they gathered on the rise, a tough, tired outfit with hats in their hands. Sam Price got out an old Bible and read some words over the two graves with their blanket-wrapped contents. Matt knelt for a moment over Soapy's grave, then picked up a handful of fresh earth and tossed it in. So long, Corporal Green, he thought. So long, Soapy. He stepped to the other grave and picked up earth there, then paused and waved Pye forward. He handed the soil to the young drover. "You go first," he said. "You were partners."

One by one, the men filed past the two graves, each depositing a fistful of the good earth on those who rested below. Spades were handed out, and the work of filling began. Matt put on his hat and picked up his gunbelt. As some of the men worked and others watched, he buckled it on, drew his Colt and checked its loads. Then he thrust it into its holster.

"Listen to me," he told them all. "If any man here wants to ride away from this job right now, he can do so and no one will think the worse of him. But for those who stay, I want you all to know this . . . before Soapy Green died, he had words to say. He said to take these cows to Wyoming. He said damn near isn't good enough. And that's what I intend to do. Right now we have critters scattered from here to yonder, but they'll shape to trail again, and then we'll go on. Stan Lamont is your new trail boss, and if anybody's got objections to that he'd best say them now or hold his peace.

"And another thing, if anybody here has any objections to anybody else, I want them put to rest here and now. Some of us started this drive as Rafter H and some didn't. But we're all Rafter H now, and that's how it's going to be. We bury our dead and we bury our grudges, and we circle up every head of Rafter H stock that's still walking around, and we head north. All the way to Wyoming, boys. All the way."

The remuda was fresh and fit after a day of simply following the wagons. Matt looked them over, then looped out a tall Star-Cross bay and put his saddle on it.

From atop the Tyson horse he told Stan Lamont, "Take charge, Stan. Gather them and count them. I'll want a tally. Get the men fed and rested. Then, if I'm not back, put them on the trail from here. And don't let anybody stop you."

With that done, Matt headed southwest against a

lowering sun, in a land littered with the swelling carcasses of dead stock. Maybe he had imagined Clifton Flowers. If so, he had imagined him going southwest.

Besides, he wanted to look at the bed grounds where the spill had started. And besides that, he wanted to know what had become of Tip Curry.

22

Molly stayed in Colter just long enough to see Papa Jess properly buried, then she packed a trunk and paid a teamster to carry her east to Windom, where the transit stage line had a terminal and coaches going north twice a week. From Windom she rode a coach to Harperstown on the old Butterfield Road, and from there northwest to the rebuilt little town of Speed, an outpost on the edge of the wild lands that had been Comancheria until just a few years ago.

Out there, beyond, were the central ranges of running hills where the cattle trails pushed northward toward the Kansas railheads and, further west, the great open ranges stepping up toward the Llano Estacado.

No regular stage line presently operated beyond Speed, and the clerk at the little hotel—who sometimes booked passengers for the immigrant trains coming up from the Gulf and the occasional wagon traders heading for the Llano and No Man's

Land—shook his head when Molly asked for a way to Porterville, and shook it more emphatically when she explained where Porterville was. "That's a long way, Miss," he explained. "And it's the wrong way. I don't believe you can get there from here."

"Why not?" she frowned, tired and disgusted.

"Because there ain't anything much between here and there except several hundred miles of miles and miles, and it sure ain't anyplace for a young woman to be out in. You ought to head east and go around. I might could get you hauled up to Fort Worth, by way of Waco. There's roads and things over there that go north. There ain't any out here . . . none that you'd want to travel."

The well-dressed man in the nearest settee lowered his newspaper and glanced at her. Catching her eye, he removed his hat and nodded politely.

Molly drummed her fingers on the counter, trying to imagine the mounting fares of various passages by commercial coach. She had little concept of the geography entailed by her venture, but it struck her as absurd that a person should have to go east, then north, then west again, to reach a point somewhere north of where she was. She told the clerk so and he shrugged. That was just how it was.

"But there are towns and things between here and there, aren't there?"

"Yes'm," he admitted. "A few, I guess. I heard there was some Germans had a town up yonder a ways, if it's still there, and maybe a few folks up at

Ft. Griffin, but past that . . ."

"Mobeetie's up that way," the man in the settee offered.

The clerk looked surprised. "Is it still there?"

"Last I heard, it was. Somebody was talking about a railroad through there, I suppose from Fort Worth."

"Through there to where? There ain't anything past there."

"West, maybe . . . toward Santa Fe."

"But this lady is wantin' to go north, clean up into Nebraska—"

The door swung open and a man strode in. Quick eyes darted about the dim lobby and settled on the well-dressed man. The newcomer reminded Molly of a burly ferret. He strode across to stand in front of the settee. "Gambler, I got table stakes. Now I intend to win my money back from you."

The man with the newspaper only glanced at him. "Sorry, mister. The game is closed."

"Well, we're fixin' to open it again. You're into me for better'n four hundred dollars, and I intend to have it back."

Now the man lowered his paper and gazed at the man standing before him, a level gaze with ice in it. Molly noticed that, in addition to nice clothes and nice manners, the gentleman had a nice face— lean and thoughtful-seeming, eyes set wide apart, a face that hid exciting mysteries behind it. "I'm sorry, Mr. . . . ah . . ."

"Speed," the ferret spat. "You take my money and don't even know my name? Well, it's Speed. Just like the name of this town. And in this town when I say we play cards, we play cards."

The man put aside his newspaper and stood. He was taller than Speed, but not as wide. "Haven't you lost enough, Mr. Speed? If we play again you may lose again, because cards aren't your game. Why not just take my word for it? I don't want trouble . . ."

"You already got trouble, gambler. Nobody takes my money and just walks off."

"You lost fairly, in a game you chose to enter."

"Maybe it was fair and maybe not. But I say we play some more. Now!"

The man called gambler took a deep breath, then sighed. He turned to smile at Molly, and tipped his head in a somehow very formal manner. "It appears I must play cards," he said. "I wish you good fortune in your travels, Miss. Good evening."

He put on his hat and left the lobby, Speed trailing behind him.

"Nothin' good's gonna come of that," the clerk said. "I told him he oughtn't to gamble with Toby Speed. Toby can't stand to lose."

Molly returned to the subject at hand. "I guess I need a room for the night. Maybe in the morning I can think a little better."

The room was small and spartan, second floor rear with a window that looked down on a dirt street no wider than an alley. Several men entered a side door there, and a window glowed with lamplight in the dusk. One of the men, Molly noticed, was the well-dressed man from downstairs.

She took off her bonnet and shawl and sat on the bed to rummage in her purse. Before leaving Colter

286

she had sold what she could—her fabrics and forms, scissors and patterns, and Papa Jess's little house and its contents. All of it together had produced a very little bit of money, and she was just now becoming aware of how far she had to go and how much it would cost.

She had no doubt that the clerk was right. He had shown her a printed map which was hard to understand, and had traced on it the known roads, had pointed to the location of Speed, and then to the area in which Porterville might be found, far to the north in western Nebraska. Between the two points, the map was virtually empty. Scattered dots identified as Ft. Griffin, Dodge City, Abilene and Oglalla had lines through them indicating roads or rails, but all the lines seemed to go east and west. And the distances north and south were daunting.

She was going to need more money.

Lighting the room's single lamp, Molly poured water into a bowl on the nightstand and washed herself, enjoying the refreshing coolness after a day of travel. It tended to revive her spirits a little. She had come almost a hundred miles in the wrong direction, only to run into a dead end. The anger she felt, directed at the clerk downstairs, was uncalled-for, and she knew it. It wasn't his fault. It was hers for not knowing the routes, and for not planning ahead as she should have. But the real problem, seen now in its stark reality, was how much it would cost her to backtrack, find passage northward through the more settled lands, and then head west again across the cold plains. If she reached Porterville at all, it would be as a pauper.

How much had the burly ferret accused the gambling man of taking from him? Four hundred dollars, he said. The number floated before her. A fortune. Men played at cards, and money in large amounts changed hands.

Cards aren't your game, the gambler had told the ferret man, and the implied meaning was clear. *Cards are my game.*

The thought that struck Molly then was so bold and so unseemly—so unlike her—that it almost took the wind from her. Molly knew nothing of the playing of cards. But she had gotten by at Colter because people who couldn't sew as she did brought their fabrics and patterns to her to sew for them.

I don't play cards, she told herself. But he does. Again she sat on the edge of the bed and counted her money. One hundred and forty-four dollars and seventeen cents. It had seemed like a great deal. Now it did not. It was not enough to take her to Porterville, even if there were direct routes to that place from this.

Armed with a resolution that astonished her, Molly dressed herself again, went downstairs and approached the clerk. "The man who was here earlier, the other man called him 'gambler,' can you tell me his name?"

"Yes, Ma'm." The clerk peered at a room register. "That was Mr. Fallon. Mr. Timothy Fallon."

"Does he . . . ah . . . reside hereabouts?"

"Oh, no, Miss. Mr. Fallon is a traveling man. He comes and goes. He makes his living by gambling."

"He must be quite skilled at it, then."

The clerk grinned. "You might say that. He came here once before, for a few days, and a lot of the local boys were poorer by far when he left." The grin faded. "Been best if he hadn't won from Toby, though. No good can come of that."

"I gather they are playing cards again, now?"

"That's where they were going," the clerk shrugged. He pursed his lips and leaned his elbows on the counter, deciding to confide in her. "Best thing Mr. Fallon could do now, would be to let Toby win back his losses . . . and maybe a bit over. Otherwise he's gonna be in real trouble."

"But he wouldn't do that, would he?" Molly frowned. "He appeared to me to be a proud man."

"That kind of pride has got folks killed," the clerk said, his eyes flicking around the room, empty except for the two of them. Molly felt he immediately regretted having said such a thing, and realized that the man was afraid of Toby Speed. She wondered if everyone around here was.

But there had been no indication of fear in Timothy Fallon. Confronted by the burly man, he had seemed . . . amused, possibly. Maybe a bit irritated in the way a person can be irritated at the intrusion of a foul odor on the breezes of a pretty day, but nothing more.

She made up her mind.

The side door across the narrow street was closed and barred, but Molly rapped at it with a trembling hand and after a moment it was opened. The smell that came from it was of cigar smoke and raw liquor, and she had a quick impression of men sitting around a lamplit table beyond, before her view was blocked by a large man who peered at her in the deepening dusk.

"You got the wrong door, Miss," he said. "This is a closed game."

"I would like to speak to Mr. Timothy Fallon," she told him.

The man hesitated, scowling, then stepped back and closed the door to a crack. Beyond, she heard his voice. "Toby, there's a woman out here that wants to talk to the gambler."

"He's busy." It was the ferret man's voice.

Molly heard voices in discussion, too low to make out the words, then Speed's voice again, raised in anger, "All right, but finish this hand first. You ain't walkin' away from this table with those cards."

And the gambler's smoother voice, sounding amused. "They are your cards, Speed. Not mine."

The door closed and Molly waited. Minutes passed. Then it opened again and Timothy Fallon stood there, tall and handsome, a rough-looking armed man at his shoulder.

"Well," he smiled. "Hello. Were you looking for me?"

"Y—yes," her voice quavered and her hands shook slightly. She wondered what he must think . . . what he certainly would think in just a minute. "Yes. Mr. Fallon, my name is Pur . . . ah . . . Flowers. Molly Flowers. Ah, could we speak privately?"

The tough-looking man beside him grinned. "No, Miss, he can't. Just say what you have to say. This feller has folks waitin' on him inside."

Molly swallowed. So be it. "Mr. Fallon, I understand that you are playing cards in there . . . for money."

"Yes, we certainly are."

She tilted her head, looking directly into his eyes. "Mr. Fallon, are you a good player . . . at cards, I mean? Are you very good at it?"

She saw a flippant answer begin to form, saw it echoed in the smile that creased his cheeks, and saw him change his mind about flippancy. "Yes, Miss Flowers," he said. "Card playing is a skill, and I am very good at it."

She reached into her purse and brought out a roll of notes. "Mr. Fallon, I have one hundred and forty-four dollars here that I would like to invest in your skill. I would be willing to pay you a commission on the profits, if you would . . . ah . . . gamble this money for me."

Surprise, amusement and delight all managed to show themselves in his expression. "Well!" he said. "Well, I must admit, I have not had such an offer before. Are you sure?"

"I'm quite sure," she nodded. "I need the money."

He glanced at the man beside him. "You place me in an interesting position, Miss Flowers. There are people here who would prefer that I not win. Do you understand that?"

"I understand," she nodded. "I also feel that you are a person I might trust. Will you do it?"

The rough man chuckled and turned his head. "You hearin' this, Toby? You ever hear such a thing in your life?"

"Send her away," the ferret man growled from inside. "We're busy."

Molly stared at the tall gambler, sudden qualms clenching her stomach. She was asking this man—a total stranger—to risk his life for her. "Will you . . . *can* you do it?" she asked again.

His smile had not altered. He held out his hand, a casual motion that pulled his coat open at the waist, and she understood that he had intended it. There was a gun there—a small revolver, concealed.

"I hope so, Miss Flowers," he said. "I would be honored to try."

She handed him the money. He stepped back and the rough man closed the door. Inside, she heard laughter.

Molly went back to the hotel and back to her room. She repacked her traveling bag, set bonnet and gloves on top of it, placed her shoes beside it, and lay down on the bed to wait, ready for whatever happened next.

She slept. At first she had no dreams, and then they came in a tumbled mass, crowding and overlapping: dim dreams of her father whom she barely remembered, of her mother's hair growing gray, of tending and sewing for people who were sometimes kind and sometimes not . . . of Jude and journeys and Papa Jess bleeding . . . gunfire dreams where men ran and fired in the street and a leering man fell backward again and again as she triggered a shotgun . . . she awoke trembling and confused. Someone was pounding on the door. When she opened it there were men there with guns. They peered past her, their eyes searching the empty room.

"He ain't here," one said.

"Have you seen him, Miss?" another asked. "The gamblin' man?"

"I . . . no, I've been asleep. What—"

"Toby Speed's dead," the second man said. "Him and Spike both. Toby was winnin' until you came to the door, then his luck went bad and that gambler about cleaned him out. Toby accused him of cheatin' and drew on him, and the gambler cut him down. Cut down both of 'em, just like that. I seen it."

She stared at him blankly, still half-asleep, trying to understand.

"Come on," the first man said. "He ain't here. Let's get men out on the roads. We'll find him."

For a time then, the streets outside the hotel were alive with activity. Molly watched from her window as men carried bodies from the door across the way. Why, she wondered, did so many men gather to the cause of a brute such as she had seen downstairs. Then she recalled something Tip Curry had said one time, in that quiet, watchful way of his.

"Men do what they're paid to do, Molly. The good ones do, anyway. Pay's more than money. Pay's trust. A man takes pay, he rides for the brand."

Eventually the little town settled into night-touched silence, and Molly sat on her bed, waiting. She was not surprised when she heard a rapping at her window.

Timothy Fallon entered quickly and stood over her, smiling in the dim lamplight. He handed a bundle of notes to her . . . at a glance, more money than Molly had ever seen. "Lady Luck's share," he winked. "Enough to travel on, I imagine."

She put the money in her purse. "There still aren't any roads north of here," she said.

"Can you ride a horse, Lady Luck?"

"I can if I have to."

"The roads are crowded this time of year," he said. "But if you'd care to go where there are no roads, I'd be honored to have Lady Luck at my side for a while."

23

Trussed like a calf waiting for the iron and the knife, Tip Curry had spent a miserable night under a tarp. With morning, though, they freed his ankles and let him hobble around the encampment. They kept his hands tightly secured and he held his tongue about that. In their place he would have done the same.

He counted eight men in and around the little camp in the hills, and guessed there were a few more though he hadn't seen them. At least three of those he knew were Link gunhands, and two others he recognized as drovers on Link payroll.

His mistake had been walking into a camp that was not one camp but two. Only three men had been huddled around the little fire when first he saw them, and he hadn't investigated far enough beyond them. The storm, the distraction of dancing lightning and rolling thunder, had been too much of a temptation. The three had not seen him until he was among them, gun in hand, explaining to them how they were all going back to Rafter H for a talk with Matt Hazelwood. They hadn't seen him, but others from the second—and larger—camp beyond the shoulder of the draw, had.

They had caught him fair and square, and it did no good to fuss about it.

In the early light, while he rested under his tarp, he had heard riders going east, toward the trail. Going out to look at the herd, he supposed.

Through the day he was treated decently enough. The hands fed him breakfast and held water for him to drink, and even loosed his hands long enough for him to go into the brush—with three guns pointed at him all the time. Then they had bound him again, but he could still walk around. Given the situation, he couldn't complain.

Frank Harrel drew gunhand wages and had ridden for Link for several years, and he took it upon himself to see to the care and feeding of the prisoner. "It was just bad luck that we snagged you the way we did, Tip," he said. "Good luck for us, but bad for you. But that's how things work out sometimes."

"Some win and some lose," Tip agreed. "I sure would like to know how the herd made out, though. I feel bad about not being down there last night, the way that storm went through."

"Well, I expect they spilled," Harrel told him. "But I don't know yet. Mr. Link and some of them have gone to look. They'll be back directly. What's Matt Hazelwood tryin' to do with a herd that size, anyhow, Tip? Some of us have been wonderin' about that."

Tip lowered his eyes. "All I know is, we're pushin' them north. Mr. Hazelwood doesn't talk a lot about his plans."

Harrel nodded. "I didn't expect you to tell me. I wouldn't have, either, was it me. The way I got it figured, though, I think maybe Rafter H is bound for a new spread somewhere. Maybe up on the Llano. I can't hardly see Matt Hazelwood tryin' to push seven thousand cows to the Kansas railheads all at one time. Why, he'd ruin his own market . . . along with everybody else's. That just don't figure."

"For that matter," Tip cocked his head at the older gunhand, "I don't understand what Herman Link in doin' up in these hills, with a general roundup fixing to start on Dry Creek. Seems to me like if he planned to take this herd he'd already have made his play so he'd have time to move 'em back. But you fellers are just taggin' along, like he's waitin' for something special to happen. How do you account for that, Frank?"

It was Harrel's turn to look away. "All I know is, we're keepin' a close eye on that herd and waitin' for Mr. Link to tell us what he wants done about it. Mr. Link doesn't talk a lot about his plans."

"There's just a whole lot neither one of us knows, isn't there, Frank?"

Harrel poured coffee for him, fanned it with his hat to get the heat off it, and held the cup for Tip to drink.

"Obliged," Tip said. "Any notion what you all are going to do with me?"

Harrel shrugged. "Up to Mr. Link. If he says

297

shoot you, we'll shoot you. If he says hang you, we'll hang you. If he says to turn you loose we'll do that and no hard feelin's."

He gave Tip another slug of coffee and grinned amiably. "Hell of a way to make a livin', ain't it?"

Late in the day, Herman Link and his riders returned to the camp. Link conferred with his men, a few at a time, then came to where Tip Curry sat on a cedar stump. Tip stood, embarrassed that with his hands tied he couldn't remove his hat in the old rancher's presence.

Frank Harrel noticed his problem, and removed it for him. "Mr. Link, this here is Tip Curry. He's Matt Hazelwood's gunhand. What do you want us to do with him?"

"I know him," Link said. His eyes were cold and expressionless in a bulldog face that seemed to have almost no neck under it. Tip recalled someone saying that before Herman Link got rich and went to ranching, he had worked in coal mines back east. He was about sixty years old, but seemed ageless— a tough, stocky old man who did what he felt like doing and answered to no man.

"Why did Hazelwood send you out here?" he asked. "What were you supposed to do?"

"He didn't send me, Mr. Link. I just sort of came."

"Then why did you come?"

"Because I'm Rafter H's gunhand, and it's up to me to take care of problems."

Link glanced at Harrel, frowning, then looked back at Tip. "You're saying you don't take orders?"

"No, sir . . . well, yes, sir, I . . . I'm saying I didn't

298

have any orders not to take. I just knew you all were up here and I came."

"To do what?"

"To look. And maybe to take one or two folks back with me so Mr. Hazelwood could find out why you're following his herd, so he could decide what to do about it."

Link thought that over. "Suppose I tell Harrel here to take out his gun and shoot you with it. Then what?"

Tip scuffed his feet and dropped his eyes. "Then I guess I'll die, because Frank Harrel is a good man and if you tell him to do that he sure as hell will do it. Though I wish you wouldn't."

"Why shouldn't I?"

"Because Frank Harrel would feel terrible about gunning down a man with his arms tied and no gun in his holster. If it was me, I would, too."

"You telling me you aren't afraid?"

"No, sir . . . I mean, yes, sir, I sure am afraid. Fact is, I'm scared about half to death right now, but that doesn't have much to do with anything, is how I see it. Mr. Link, what happened to the herd last night? Did they hold?"

"Hold, nothing! They spilled. There are cows scattered over about half a county out there right now."

"That's goin' to make them kind of hard to take, isn't it?" Somehow, Tip found that idea very cheering.

Link scowled at him. "I have half a mind to shut that mouth of yours for keeps."

"Yes, sir. I know." Tip squinted at him, deep in

299

thought. "Mr. Link, if you found out that it wasn't Mr. Hazelwood that run those no-good sons of yours off Dry Creek, would you go on home and let Rafter H alone?"

"My no-good sons have nothing to do with it!" Link shouted. "This is business!" He paused, then asked, "If it wasn't Matt Hazelwood, then who was it?"

"It was me."

"Why?"

"Doesn't matter. Somebody had to. Meaning no disrespect, Mr. Link, but that Rodney is mean as a snake and Maynard is a schemin' little weasel and the only saving grace either of them has is they're both just plain dumb."

Link's face seemed to turn to stone. "Curry, are you trying to die?"

"No, sir. I'm just saying it like it is and everybody knows it. But you shouldn't keep blamin' Mr. Hazelwood—"

"Shut up!" The old man swung his eyes to Frank Harrel. Harrel shrugged and drew his gun. "Put it away," Link growled. Harrel put it away. "I don't want him killed," Link decided. Harrel sighed with relief. Link spun on Tip Curry and thrust his bulldog face up at him. "Boy, what would it take to get you to work for me?"

"I already have a job," Tip told him. "But I sure appreciate you thinking about me."

Link turned away, exasperated. "Cut him loose," he said. "Let him go on back and wetnurse Hazelwood. I'm through with him."

For a time, Tip Curry walked around the raider

camp swinging his arms and rubbing circulation back into his hands. Frank Harrel handed him his gun and helped him saddle his horse.

"I'm more than a mite sorry we're on different sides in this thing, Tip," the older gunhand admitted, "because Mr. Link intends to have that herd, no matter what."

When he was mounted, Tip hesitated. Instead of turning the black's head toward the flats, he reined around and rode to the main camp, making mental note as he went. He found Link.

"Mr. Link, was anybody hurt when those cows spilled?"

"How the hell should I know? Get out of here before I change my mind."

"Yes, sir. Mr. Link, will you all turn around and go on home now?"

Link just stared at him. Among the others, many gawked and some fingered their guns. Frank Harrel hurried up to him. "Tip, get out of here."

But Tip kept his gaze on the old rancher. "Be better all around if you did," he said.

"Get out of here," Link growled. "I have half a mind to tell Frank to shoot you yet."

"I hope you don't do that, sir."

"Why shouldn't I?"

"My hands aren't tied now, sir. And I have my gun. Frank Harrel is a good man and I don't want to have to kill him."

With a low sun quartering behind him, Tip rode down from the running hills and out along the ledges beyond which were the bottomlands. He was tempted to double back and try again to take a prisoner or two, but he knew they would be watching now. After a time, he had the feeling he was being followed.

The sun squatted atop the hills and gave them skirts of shadow when he saw movement far off, ahead and to his right. Another half mile and he recognized Matt Hazelwood.

Well, my fat's in the fire now, he told himself. The herd was spilled, and he should have been there. Maybe another hand might have made the difference. Mr. Hazelwood was right. He drew wages to punch cows first, to carry a gun second.

He was sure now that he had been followed, though he saw no one behind him. Why had Mr. Link had two camps up there. The three men at the first one, the ones he had surprised, didn't have the look of cowhands, nor had he known them.

Finally he topped a rise and looked out on the shingled flats where the herd had been bedded. Nothing moved there now. But out across the wide flats and beyond, trailing and curving away into blue distance, the stampede's path was plain. And those little dark dots out there . . . he knew what they were. Calves would have gone down first, then the weaker cattle, then just whatever animals happened to stumble or collide or turn the wrong way.

Somewhere out there, by now, they were picking up the pieces, starting a new gather, sorting things out, repairing the herd.

But Matt Hazelwood was going the other way. A mile or so distant, the rancher was skirting the south side of the old bed ground, angling away

302

toward the southwest.

"He shouldn't be ridin' out in this country by himself," Tip muttered. "A man could get hurt out here." He eased the reins over and spurred the black horse, stretched it out to a mile-eating lope.

Tip Curry wasn't completely happy with himself. He had not learned for sure what Herman Link was up to, and he certainly hadn't talked him out of anything. He did know now, though, how many of them there were and which ones would be the most dangerous. He knew what animals they had and what supplies they carried. And he knew why Herman Link was in no hurry to take the herd. Link had no intention of taking those cows back to Dry Creek.

"What I think is," Tip explained to a glaring Matt Hazelwood an hour later, "Mr. Link intends to set himself up a new spread up on the Llano, and put all our cows to grass there to fatten them, then drift them on up to Kansas a thousand or so at a time at prime prices."

"And you figured all this out," Hazelwood rumbled, curling his lip so that his moustache seemed to writhe. "All by yourself. Amazing."

"Yes, sir. I had plenty of time to listen to those boys palaver, and it all kind of fit together."

"How come you to decide the Llano is where he plans to squat?"

"Well, sir, it was Frank Harrel that suggested you might be thinkin' about somethin' like that, so I figured he got the idea from someplace, so maybe

303

Mr. Link might have mentioned it to him. Then I got to thinkin', with Rafter H pullin' stakes on Dry Creek and all the ruction that come of that, well, that was too good a chance for those big ranchers back there to pass up to try and put somethin' over on one another, like ranchers do . . . beg pardon, Mr. Hazelwood, present company excepted, but if I was a rancher I wouldn't any more trust another rancher than I would a boar hog not to waller."

Despite his irritation, Matt turned away, stifling a smile. Generally, Tip Curry didn't say more than seven words on a given day. But now the young gunhand was wound tighter than a snagrope on a saddlehorn.

"Anyhow," Tip continued, his eyes studying the deepening blue of dusk across the miles ahead of them, "we heard that T-Bar-T is out of the picture, so that leaves Link and Triple-Seven to notion out how to do each other a disfavor. And Triple-Seven is Dominion Land and Cattle Company, which claims about half the grass in No Man's Land, and the nearest place a man could stake a legal claim to there would be the high Llano. I reckon Mr. Link figures to throw our cows over onto Dominion's graze and take root while Colonel Nelson is still down in south Texas settin' things up to cheat Mr. Link out of his headrights when he misses the roundup. That's how I see it."

Dusk deepened around them as they plodded southward side by side, and stars came out in a deepening sky.

Matt Hazelwood gave thought to the best way to explain to his errant gunhand that he had known all that for a week. He decided to take another tack. "Well, you told me one thing. Now I know there are only about a dozen of them. But it's just a Lord's wonder you didn't get yourself killed, boy. Come time I decide I want a dead gunhand, I'll kill you myself. I declare."

Having delivered himself of his final word on the subject he rode in silence for a time, with Tip tagging along, chastened. By last light he led them to a stand of runty cedars. "We'll sleep here. You fix the fire. I could use coffee."

"Yes, sir."

They stripped their gear from their horses and rubbed them down, then hobbled them to graze and Tip built a little fire and started the coffee. He squatted on his heels and watched the flames lick around the black iron of the pot, hoping it would boil soon. The only sounds out here now were the mournful whispering of prairie breeze and the distant call of a coyote. They were sad sounds. They reminded him of people dying.

Mr. Hazelwood had told him, in terse words, about the stampede and the lost cattle . . . and about the deaths of Mr. Green and Slater. After that he had talked as long as he could think of anything to say, just to keep from thinking about it, but finally Mr. Hazelwood had shut him up, and now the regrets stood in his mind, holding it the way the twinkling fire held his eyes.

He forced himself to look away. Matt Hazelwood had walked out away from the fire, alone with his own thoughts. But now he turned and came back. His eyes were distant when he knelt by the fire.

Tip poked the fire with a stick, chewing on his lip. He knew the boss was brooding about his old friend, and he tried to think of a way to take his mind off his misery.

"Mr. Hazelwood, do you mind if I ask you a question?"

Matt blinked, returning to reality. "What?"

"Where are we going?"

The rancher's eyes went distant again. "All the way to Wyoming, Tip. Just like Soapy said. All the way to Wyoming."

Tip tried again. "Mr. Hazelwood?"

"What?"

"I meant right now, sir. Where are we going right now, you and me?"

Hazelwood gazed at him and the sombre spell was broken. "We're looking for a man with horses. Another old friend, that somebody told me is dead."

"Who told you that?"

"I'm damned if I know, but I aim to find out."

A quarter mile north, two riders stepped down from their saddles and ground-reined their mounts. Only starlight lit the land around them, but they knew where they were going. Ahead, they could see the little campfire.

"You suppose that was Matt Hazelwood he took up with?" Snake asked.

Charlie Joe's teeth gleamed. "I sure hope so. Wouldn't ol' Link pay a bounty for his hide?"

Snake's nod was hidden by darkness. "I don't quite see why he didn't just shoot the kid when he had him. Why let him go like that, then send us to peg him?"

"That's easy. The kid faced him down back there, even hog-tied. Killin' him then would have took the old man down a notch with his hands. They'd have lost respect. He don't want that. But then, be dumb to leave him alive to face later."

"So he turns him loose, then after a while he sends us out to get him, and nobody the wiser. Slick."

"Well, that's what he keeps us on for . . . to do odd jobs. You ready? Let's nail 'em both."

"Yeah. I'll enjoy puttin' lead in that smart-ass kid. Him walkin' in on us like he done."

24

"I wish you'd quit doing that!"

Big Jim Tyson felt a moment's vague regret at snapping like that. He knew Clifton Flowers was preoccupied and not paying attention. It was just that Flowers could come up with more ways to irritate a body than anybody he had ever encountered, even when he wasn't paying attention.

Flowers jerked and looked around. "Doin' what?"

"That little cedar tree there," Tyson pointed. "You just rode right through it."

Flowers glanced back at the lone cedar, a thickly-boughed, weathered little tree about eight feet tall. "I must've went around it," he said. "I didn't notice."

"No, you didn't. You went right through it. I saw you. Not the first time you've done that, either. I wish you'd just stop it."

"Sorry." Flowers shrugged. "I got a lot on my mind."

"Well, it would be a mercy if you'd help me tend these horses. I mean, it isn't like I mind the company, and I'm obliged to you and all, but two men pushing a horse herd is a lot easier than one doing it."

"I don't think they'll pay me any mind," Flowers said. "They're your horses, not mine."

The sun had set behind the hills to the west, leaving rose echoes in a flawless dome of sky where the evening star already gleamed brightly. Tyson had lost track of how many days they had travelled together, much of it jumbled memories knocked askew by the violence of lasting concussion. But just in the past day or two he had been feeling better. Mostly now his mind was clear of confusion, except for the persistent, irritating and puzzling confusion inherent in being with Clifton Flowers.

There were things Flowers said that just never made sense. Like the fixation he had, that Jim Tyson was dead. Tyson knew better. He might have *almost* died, back there in the hills, but he hadn't, and he wished Flowers would quit harping on it.

As though reading his mind, Flowers looked around at him. "I got to admit you don't seem dead to me," he said.

Tyson shook his head. They had covered this ground as much as he cared for.

"That's kind of what's chewin' on me," Flowers went on. "Seems to me like there's *somebody* dead here, and if it ain't you, who is it?"

He had been like this all day, preoccupied and thoughtful and not making any sense at all. In fact, he had been like this since the evening before, when

310

the lightning storm went through. Tyson really wondered whether one of those lightning bolts up on the slope—maybe just a little sliver of one— had hit him and left him more addled than usual.

The horses were moving along at a good pace, covering ground that showed plentiful evidence of recent passage of a large herd of cattle. Despite his words, Tyson found no problem in driving and guiding the little herd alone. All thirty were top-notch cowponies and responded to him perfectly. All he had to do was zigzag now and then to flank them first on one side and then on the other. It simply puzzled him that Clifton Flowers didn't just ride one flank himself, the way a civil person would naturally do.

It was part of the left-over confusion from his head wound that left him uncertain as to how much about Clifton Flowers was just the way the man was, and how much was his own perceptions having been scrambled.

Like the funny way Flowers and his horse both had of—just now and then—becoming slightly transparent, so a person could see right through them to whatever was on the other side. He had mentioned that a time or two, but he didn't make an issue of it. Chances were, he himself was just imagining that. And if he wasn't, then it didn't seem like the sort of thing a person ought to notice about another person.

Or the way Flowers would talk about things that just couldn't be. He insisted, for instance, that this herd they were following was Rafter H. And that was well and good, Tyson hoped he was right. But then he would say he had been talking with Matt Hazelwood just this morning, and come up with some far-fetched thing about there having been a big stampede the night before, and two men killed, and that just didn't make sense. Flowers did sort of disappear now and then, go off somewhere on his own, but that herd was still enough miles ahead that nobody could just pop back and forth between the two places. He didn't understand why Flowers would say such things.

Oh, well. It was much more pleasant, now that his aches were subsiding and things at least beginning to fall back into place in his head, to think about Katie Toliver.

Promise me, Jim, her sweet voice murmured in memory. Promise me you'll come back.

I promise, Katie.

I've had a few problems, and things haven't gone just like I had in mind . . . so far. I haven't made it to Three Rivers just yet, to sell my horses to Valdez. And that's because somebody sort of interrupted me. And now instead of heading south with forty-four horses I'm heading north with thirty, and maybe the others are where I'll be tomorrow and maybe not, and maybe I'll get the chance to visit with some old friends who might help me get things sorted out.

But you wait for me, Katie. I'll be there by and by.

Whoopy ti yi yo, git along little dogies. We know that Wyoming will be our new home.

Darkness was settling down, and he edged the horse herd to the right, off the path the cattle had

312

followed, aiming them at a little pocket between rises where there would be good graze for them for the night.

Clifton Flowers was lagging behind, deep in thought. Something really seemed to have been troubling him, all day. Jim felt a twinge of guilt at having snapped at him. In a way, he had grown fond of Flowers. It was hard not to like the man, even if he *was* aggravating as a bedbug.

The pocket was a little meadow with high grass and a fresh water seep swelled by rain. By last light he herded the stock into it with little concern that they would wander. He wondered for a time whether it would be worthwhile to build a fire—he had been out of coffee and flour for days, just existing on a dwindling pack of jerky and hardtack, and whether there was a fire had never seemed to matter in the slightest to Clifton Flowers. But there was something about a fire that gave a man comfort out in the wide lonelies, and he decided he would have one.

And then, maybe, over a crackling fire, with nothing else to do, Flowers might open up and tell him what had been bothering him all day. Even at his best, Flowers could be remote and changeable. But for the past twenty-four hours, the man had acted like he had the miseries.

Still in his saddle, Tyson turned and started to say, "Hold them here while I go get some—" but Clifton Flowers was not there. He had gone off again, somewhere.

". . . firewood," Jim finished. "I wish he'd quit doin' that."

Not far away, the shadowy bulk of a cedar copse promised deadfall. Leaving the horses to graze, he headed that way, enjoying the freshness of evening breeze on his face. Last night's storm had washed the air clean and left a sweetness in the land. It exhilarated him, made him feel strong and alive, and he knew it was the first time he had felt so since the day a young hardcase had shot him down on the rocks beside a limestone tank.

Near the cedar clump was a little knoll and he rode to the top of it to breathe the clean air and look out on the starlit landscape.

His fevers had come and gone, the dizziness and light-headedness that had plagued him seemed less by the day, and pieces were falling into place. There were things still that he could not remember, snatches of memory like pieces of dreams melting in the morning sun, and he still carried the ache of cracked ribs that would take more weeks to heal. But the crease along the top of his head was mending and the headaches were mostly gone. He hadn't worn a sling on his arm in a week now, and found he no longer needed it if he was careful. For the first time in a time that seemed forever, Jim Tyson felt whole.

He reached a hand to his shirt pocket to touch the old buckle he carried there, that had saved his life—a buckle salvaged from a pile of bones. I've come through it, pard, he thought. Whoever you were, I was luckier than you. Maybe you left your luck to me.

Beyond the knoll, starlight silvered the great trail where cattle had passed no more than two days before. The trail stretched away northward, and he wondered if Rafter H was out there, like Clifton Flowers said. If so, they weren't far away.

A pinpoint of light caught his eye. Not far away—less than a mile it looked—a little fire twinkled in the night. Then abruptly there were other twinkles near it, brief flaring sparks of brighter light, sparks that were answered by other sparks.

Sweet prairie breeze whispered on the knoll, and after a time brought the sound of distant gunfire.

Carrying saddleguns, Snake and Charlie Joe worked their way afoot to within a hundred yards of where Matt and Tip hunkered over their little fire, sipping coffee.

"It's him, sure enough," Snake whispered as they crouched in brush. "That's Hazelwood. You think we ought to try to take him alive?"

Charlie Joe chewed on the notion for a moment. "Naw. Kill him."

"You kill him," Snake said. "Me, I want to put some lead in that smart-ass with him."

"All right. I'll take Hazelwood. But let's get just a mite closer. I ain't interested in a gunfight. I just want to shoot 'em dead."

Belly-down, they worked their way another thirty yards before Snake put a hard hand on Charlie Joe's arm. "This is close enough," he whispered. "Hell, from here you can pick which eye you want to shoot him through."

By the fire, Tip Curry froze in the act of raising a

tin cup. His head lifted, his eyes slitted and nostrils flared. Slowly he turned, looking toward the two killers. As one, they sank to the ground, hugging it. Voices drifted to them: "You hear something?" ". . . don't know. Something . . ."

"That kid's got ears like a wolf," Charlie Joe hissed.

Snake didn't answer. Carefully he raised his head, and grinned in the darkness. "They can't see us," he whispered. "You ready? Let's take 'em out."

Silently then, the two lifted themselves to their knees, raised their rifles, and gawked. Directly in front of them, a silhouette against the night sky, was a man on horseback. He was looking at them curiously.

"Howdy," he said. "I don't suppose you gents know the way to Porterville?"

Snake fired first, swinging up his gun, and Charlie Joe's shot was an instant echo. They levered the rifles and both fired again.

"Didn't aim to rile you," the mounted man snapped. "If you don't know the way, just say so."

Snake fired again, directly at the shadow rider. His eyes were wide with disbelief.

"Jesus," Charlie Joe shrilled. "He don't fall."

Beyond the rider was the little campfire, but now there was no one there. Snake heard the rustle of boots on dry sand off to his left and swung that way. Another shadow, crouching, coming at him. He levered and fired, wildly. A flare of light answered him and thunders burst forth in his chest, throwing him backward against Charlie Joe. They both went down.

316

Charlie Joe had lost his rifle, but he rolled and came up with his Colt in one hand, staring around. A voice from the darkness rumbled at him. "Drop it!" He fired at the sound.

Matt Hazelwood barely felt the bee-sting of the bullet scoring his side. His answering shots were fast and sure. The silence that followed was punctuated by the spasmodic rustling of a man twitching on the ground.

From somewhere beyond came Tip Curry's voice. "Don't shoot, Mr. Hazelwood. They're both down."

Lying on his back, bleeding his life away under the cold stars, Charlie Joe heard the words too. But they meant nothing to him. He didn't know where he was or why he was there. He only knew that there was a man on a horse, a dark pattern against the stars, and the man was over him, looking down at him, as the stars beyond him faded away.

"You're dead," the man said, a long way off. "That's somethin' you need to know."

Tip Curry brought fire and they knelt beside each of the dead men in turn. "This one's called Charlie Joe," Tip said. "That one is Snake. They're two of the ones I told you about. Not regular hands for Mr. Link. They're hardcases."

"Gunhands?" Matt studied them.

"No, sir. Not gunhands. Just gunmen. I think they kept their distance from the Link hands because those boys wouldn't tolerate them. I know Frank Harrel wouldn't."

"You were expecting them."

"Yes, sir. Kind of. I knew somebody followed

317

me. I guess Mr. Link had second thoughts about letting me go. These kind here, they're back-shooters mostly. They come cheaper than a good gunhand."

"Well, they weren't very good at it. What were they shooting at?"

Tip just shook his head. There was no way of knowing. "They probably left their horses back there a ways. I'll bring them in."

He stood, then paused. "Wait," he said. "Back off from the light, Mr. Hazelwood. Somebody's coming."

The breeze eddied from the south and Matt Hazelwood heard it, too. Scuff of hooves, and somebody talking.

"Where we goin' now?"

Jim Tyson tensed and jerked around. Clifton Flowers had come up beside him in that spooky way of his. One moment he wasn't there, the next he was.

"I wish you'd quit that," Tyson muttered.

"I only asked where we're goin'."

"Over there, where the firelight is. I heard somebody shooting over there."

"Yeah." Flowers' voice was thoughtful. "Couple of old boys got theirselves killed yonder. I just come from there. I made sure they knew they was dead, because that's important."

Jim gritted his teeth. He wondered if he would ever get used to Clifton Flowers. "I thought I saw people moving around there, after the shooting."

"Couple of 'em. One's that Rafter H feller that I told you about. Him and his outfit have the rest of your horses."

"Matt Hazelwood? You're telling me you think Matt Hazelwood is there at that fire?"

"Was a minute ago. I reckon he come out lookin' for you. I told him you'd be along directly, but sometimes folks fidget."

Big Jim peered ahead at the light. There were two fires, one a built-up campfire with trapping around it, the other flickering a little way beyond, as though someone had dropped a burning stick. He heard horses nearby, beyond the little cedar copse, and his blood bay responded with a nicker.

The voice from the darkness then was a voice he had not heard in many long years, but it was unmistakable. "Hold it right there, mister. Who are you?"

He hadn't really believed Clifton Flowers. But now he did. "Matt? Matt Hazelwood, is that you? My lord, Captain! Come out where I can see you."

There was a pause, then Matt Hazelwood stepped out of the shadows of the copse, peering up at him in the starlight. "Jim? Big Jim? Boy, is that really you there? I declare!"

Another, darker shadow moved off to the right and Matt waved an arm. "It's all right, Tip. This is an old friend of mine, and the best damn wrangler that ever slapped his butt onto a saddle."

While Tip built up the campfire Big Jim and Matt pummelled each other, exchanged meaningless comments and in general began the process of becoming reacquainted. There would be a lot to tell, and it would take time.

Tip Curry prowled the perimeters for a time, then approached Tyson. "Sir, pardon, but who was with you out there?"

"That's right!" Matt remembered. "Where's the other fella?"

Jim looked around. "That was Clifton . . . now where did he get off to? That's the strangest man I ever met, bar none. You know, Matt, he told me he talked with you this morning."

"Well, I reckon he did, though I can't put much stock in what he had to say, even the parts of it that I understood. You know, he told me you'd been killed? Seemed plain set on it."

"Yeah." Jim sighed. "He's been telling me that, too. And for a fact, I guess I durn near was. Some young hardcase had me dead to rights out around Three Rivers. Shot me three times that I can count. The only thing that saved my life," he reached into his shirt pocket and pulled out the dented old buckle, "was this."

Abruptly, Tip Curry jerked around in a half-crouch, his hand poised at his gunbutt. At the edge of the firelight, Clifton Flowers stood, holding the reins of his mustang gray. His features were drawn, his eyes bleak. "You was lookin' for me?"

"I sure don't know how you do that," Tyson admitted. "Mr. Hazelwood . . . Mr. Curry . . . this is Clifton Flowers. I'm a whole lot in his debt."

Flowers glanced at the other two, sadly. "Howdy," he said. Then he fixed Tyson again with a thoughtful gaze that had a coldness in it, a longing. "I think I been wrong about you. When I

320

said you was killed. It ain't you that's dead, bub. It's me."

They gaped at him, and even Jim Tyson didn't know what to say. Flowers sighed, turned and swung to his saddle. "See y'all around," he said. He touched heels to the mustang, reined around and was gone, into the night.

"What did that mean?" Matt asked after a time.

"Your guess is as good as mine," Jim told him. "That's the strangest man I guess I ever ran across."

Tip Curry went with Tyson to move his horses closer to the camp, working by clear starlight, while Matt Hazelwood unpacked provisions and cooked their supper. They would bury the two gunmen, he decided . . . with cuts of sod on sticks to mark their graves. But they could wait for morning.

If Jim Tyson wanted to sell his Star-Cross ponies, Matt would buy them. If Tyson would consider shares in the herd, they would work it out. Wyoming was where Rafter H was bound, and Wyoming was where Big Jim Tyson was bound, and even with the stampede losses it was still a huge herd for a few men to move.

By the time he heard them coming in with the horses, Matt Hazelwood had made up his mind. Big Jim Tyson was back with Rafter H, and it was just a matter of working out the details. And he could bring his strange friend along, too. Flowers had gone off somewhere and had not reappeared, but if he did, any friend of Big Jim's was a friend of Rafter H and he was welcome.

They ate over a little fire, and talked for an hour while they watched the coals dwindle.

321

Tip Curry just listened, enjoying the good talk between old friends. But when Tyson described the owlhoot who had gunned him down, Curry pressed for details. He and Matt exchanged glances.

And when Tyson showed them the belt buckle that had saved his life, Tip looked at it carefully in the firelight and his eyes went thoughtful. An old, handmade brass shield buckle, scarred and weathered. And yet, except for the marks of age and the imprint of the bullet, it was a match for the one Clifton Flowers wore on his belt. He wondered if either of them had noticed that, but he didn't say anything. It seemed to him, though, to be something worth puzzling about.

25

The regather required four days, working from the southwest and pushing them north as they went. Behind them, cow carcasses bloated where they had fallen, and two new graves stood side by side on a little rise.

Before the rolling camp passed, moving on to new ground, the outfit gathered one more time to stand, hats in hands, while Sam Price said a prayer for Graham Wallace Green, and threw in some words as well for a hard-luck youngster who rested beside him. Only Pye had known him well enough really to miss him, but they all shared the bittersweet assurance that, whatever Slater had been, he was buried in good company. And whatever else any of them were, they were all drovers. To a cowhand, nothing is more profoundly moving than a little mound of fresh sod where a cowboy has met his maker.

No one sang. Such would not have occurred to them. But the rambling breeze whispered it for them. *O bury me not on the lone prairie-e-e . . .*

Working as teams, Stan Lamont and Dave Holley leading, the men scoured the land from the shingled flats to the wing draws back of the long ridge, from the breaks to the bottoms, and drifted their finds northward toward the chuck wagon camp. Ollie Sinclair and Nacho Lucas circled further out, picking up strays from the spill and bringing them in. Ollie Sinclair worked with Jim Tyson to throw the rest of the Star-Cross horses— they were all Rafter H now—in with the remuda. It was a process similar to introducing and consolidating separate political parties, and the wranglers trusted the job to no other man.

On the evening of the final gather, Matt Hazelwood and Tip Curry rode out to the foot of the hills and saw smoke from the encampment there. The Link crew now was making no effort to hide its presence. They simply watched and waited.

"They're in no hurry," Matt decided. "They don't have any more men than we do, and as long as we're going their direction they will just tag along and bide their time. But I want no man riding out alone from this point on . . . and that means you, too, Tip. We won't give them any chance to shave the odds."

When finally the herd was gathered and bedded for travel, Jim Tyson went with Sam Price to look it over, and the sight made his eyes widen.

"You should'a seen this bunch when we had seven thousand," Sam allowed. "Not many folks ever seen a herd that size . . . and damn few outfits would be crazy enough to try to trail 'em."

They would break out the tally strings later, when the herd was on the move. But for now, Stan Lamont estimated that they had lost maybe a thousand animals. Mostly calves and the weaker critters. The herd was still massive, and it was fairly weeded now, and snuffy. Six thousand tough, wild creatures barely adjusted to trailing but with the will to stampede now fully alive in them.

"We are just plain crazy," Sam Price assured Jim Tyson. "Ever' one of us, crazy as a bunch of loons."

"At least," he added later, "the odds are better'n they was. When we started there was eleven of us—countin' me and Ollie—and seven thousand cows. Now there's fifteen of us—countin' one rustler an' four brawlers—and only six thousand cows. We keep improvin' the situation at this rate, I figure we ought to have a manageable herd about the time we get to the north pole."

They rode along the flanks of the great herd, staying far out, watching tiny men on tiny horses patch up, pull in, settle out and bed down a great, undulating carpet of cattle that lay like a living mantle across three hillsides and the little valley in their midst. Miles of cattle, miles from anywhere, with long miles yet to go.

"If Link does decide to take the herd," Jim Tyson asked, "can we stop him?"

Price shrugged. At fifty years of age, he was twice the age of most of the drovers and six years senior to Matt Hazelwood himself. But the shrug was the same shrug Jim Tyson recalled from so many pasts. Aside from some superficial differences, he decided, Sam Price had not changed at all over the years. From quartermaster sergeant, CSA, to brush-busting wild stock drover in the wild old days of Comancheria to the dour, ironic old top hand and *cocinero* cook who rode beside him now, it was as though time had overlooked him. He shrugged and Jim saw a thousand Sam Prices shrug exactly the same way, in as many times. "I reckon we'll just have to stop him," he said. "When he comes he'll have the advantage. We might have a few more men now than he does, but when this herd moves every man has his hands full and we're all spread out over half of Texas. But then, Big Jim, when did we ever have the advantage . . . and we're still around, ain't we? Most of us, anyhow." His eyes went sad at thought of Soapy Green, and Jim saw him put the memories away.

Another quarter mile and they were still on the flank of the bed ground. "We've made out before, Jim. Who else but us ever took the notion to take Texas cows to Chicago?"

"We didn't make it."

"Naw, we didn't make it to Chicago. But lordy, didn't we get rich?"

"We sure did, Sam. We surely did."

Jim was thinking about Clifton Flowers . . . wondering about him. He hadn't showed up since the night out there on the prairie, when those men had died and he had said that *he* was dead. Maybe he had changed his mind about going to Wyoming . . . or about going to Porterville, wherever that was.

Sam Price's poultices and good food the past few days had made a new man of Jim Tyson. His wounds, already mostly healed, were now no more than minor annoyances. The headaches were gone, and much of that time spent coming up from the limestone country seemed vague and dreamlike. He had imagined some weird things out there, such as Flowers and his old horse riding through a cedar tree. And that appearance of becoming transparent now and then. A head wound can do funny things to a man, and a character like Clifton Flowers would be a natural magnet for fever pictures.

Maybe he had gone on, to wherever he wanted to go. Maybe he had just tired of the company. But, oddly, Tyson had the feeling that Clifton Flowers would show up again. Since the first day he had met him, he had always had the feeling that Flowers was not far away.

"Did Matt tell you it was your letter that got us to thinkin' about Wyoming?" Sam asked.

"Yeah. But I never heard back, so I didn't know."

"The decision was kinda sudden, you might say."

"Yeah. He told me that, too."

"Got yourself a gal waitin' up there, do you?"

"Sure do. Her name's Katie. Katie Toliver. It was her father who got me thinking about a horse spread up there. That's horse country like you never saw, Sam. And it was seeing it, and the mining and all, that got me thinking Rafter H might want to put some beef up there."

"Real market, is it?"

"A real market, Sam."

Price's eyes twinkled. "Like Chicago, would you say?"

"Better'n Chicago ever was, Sam. Better by far."

Price turned off then, to head back to the rolling camp. Come sundown he would have grub waiting for fifteen hungry bellies, and Jim had a notion the grub on this day would include biscuits baked in Sam's dutch oven. It was the way to start a drive.

In the evening, men came from the east, riding wide-eyed around the great herd to arrive at the camp. They were from a place called Speed, a hard day's ride to the east, and they were looking for a man.

"Slick-lookin' feller," the leader told Matt Hazelwood while others standing around, eating their supper, pretended not to listen. "Name of Timothy Fallon. Got a price on his head."

"What for?"

"Mainly," the leader grinned, "for beating Toby Speed fair and square in a card game. But mostly for murder. He shot two men, then got clean away. Might have a woman with him, nobody's sure. But she'd be a brown-haired filly named Molly Flowers. She was put up at the hotel, lookin' for a way north. When Fallon come up missin' so did she."

Flowers?

Jim Tyson stepped closer, eyeing the three. "Any idea where she was wanting to go?"

"Hotel clerk said she was tryin' to make connections to someplace up in Nebraska. Not too far from Oglalla, I guess. Place called Porterville."

Abruptly, Jim Tyson had the feeling that Clifton Flowers was near. Very near, and keenly interested.

The Speed men stayed around to share chuck

and coffee, and to bed by the fire. In the dusk they gazed off into the distance, where night herders were beginning their rounds on the edges of a section or more of solid beef.

"I seen some herds go through these parts," one said, "but I never seen a herd the like of that one."

"Is that right?" Bo Maxwell glanced at him innocently. "How's that?"

"I mean so many cows all in one trail herd," the man explained. "That's four-five times the size of any herd I ever seen."

"Oh," Bo pursed his lips and shrugged. "That ain't the herd. That's just the culls. We'll go back an' pick up the main herd later."

The man frowned at him. "What kind of spread has your boss got, anyway?"

"Real nice little place," Bo assured him. "'Bout an acre an' a half altogether, but most of it's in vegetables."

"If any of you boys are looking for work," Matt said, "I'm hiring."

They were not. They had heard the talk, of another outfit tailing after this one, and few men were interested in involving themselves in a trail war. They would, however, spread the word around Speed.

Dave Holley came in from cocktail shift and reported the cows down and steady. Sam Lamont handed him a plate and a mug.

"You got your lead critter located?" he asked.

"Sonofabitch is right out front. I'll take him out on long point first thing, then you all bring the cows to us. You know we're gonna have to

329

trailbreak them all over again after that spill."

Stan sighed. "If there's anything on God's good earth that's stupider than a bunch of cows, I wish somebody'd tell me what it is."

"A bunch of cowboys, maybe. Anybody else'd have better sense than to associate with cows."

Stan called them together then, told off the night shifts and set places for the morning. Dave Holley would take long point with his lead steer, so when the herd came up they could get the notion again of seeing Sonofabitch's heels ahead of them. Stan would point the herd, with Gabe Sinclair and Will Bower at right and left swing. Dub Newton and Bo Maxwell on forward flank, with Clyde Burns to back Bo, and when Nacho Lucas finished helping Sam Price lash down he would come out and back Dub. All those remaining would work the drags.

"All except Tip," Matt Hazelwood put in. "You might as well put him out on forward scout, because that's what he's going to do, anyway."

For a time, at least, Jim Tyson would work the remuda with Ollie Sinclair.

Tip Curry came to Matt Hazelwood as he was throwing his bed. "You changed your mind about nobody riding out alone," he said.

"Does it make any difference?"

Curry shook his head. "Not while I draw gunhand wages. But I'm obliged, Mr. Hazelwood. I feel better about it now."

"We need a scout, anyway. We're several miles off the main trail. You see if you can't angle us back that way so we hit it again in a few days without losing any more ground."

330

"Yes, sir."

"And Tip, you stay away from that Link crew. We know all we need to know about them."

"You think I'm right?"

"I thought so all along. Why do you think I burned the house?"

He turned away, and Tip knew he had all the explanation he was going to get. But a little later he saw Matt talking with Jim Tyson, and then the boss came over to him and held out his hand. He had the old, dented belt buckle.

"Put this in your pocket, Tip. It's brought luck to one man, maybe it can bring luck to another."

In the dark of morning, Sam Price rolled out, washed his face, kicked up his fire and began clanging skillets while Nacho Lucas carried wood and sliced bacon.

He fed the point and wakeups first, then Dave Holley saddled his steeldust and rode out to find Sonofabitch by first light. Gabe Sinclair, Bo Maxwell and Will Bower were right behind him. They would relieve the last night guards, then begin rousing the cattle and pushing them inward to drive.

By the time Dave was well away with his lead steer, the head of the herd would be pointing northward and thinning out, beginning to move.

And by the time the leaders were looking at Sonofabitch's rump, two or three miles away from where they started, every drover in the outfit would be on station and getting the kinks out of his first day horse.

It was like starting all over again, but this time, God willin' an' the crick don't rise, maybe some of the cows would eventually remember why they were there and what they were supposed to do. It was a wish shared by every man who ever punched cows.

They rolled their beds and ate their breakfast, drew their mounts from the remuda and cinched their forks down snug. They flexed their catchropes and checked their gear, and headed for the herd where wakeups already had the leads moving.

Dawn touched the eastern hills and Stan Lamont swung his hat over his head in signal. "Get 'em up! Move 'em out!"

Behind them Sam Price cleaned his wares while Nacho Lucas loaded bedding, and Big Jim Tyson and Ollie Sinclair began moving the remuda. With the Star-Cross horses now a respectable part of the crowd, the animals tended to cluster and drift apart, casting wary glances at their neighbors.

"Horses are a lot like women," Tyson told the black wrangler. "Being formally introduced doesn't mean they approve of one another. They'll keep right on choosing up sides until they've tea-partied together enough to decide to gang up on somebody else."

"*Just* like women," Ollie agreed. "Onliest reason a man ever gets in charge of one is because it plain decides to let him."

Big Jim hid his grin and watched with approval as Ollie reached down to pat his mount on the neck. It was a casual, automatic thing, a touching for the

332

sake of touching.

Matt Hazelwood was right. Ollie Sinclair was a wrangler.

Astride a Star-Cross bay, Matt Hazelwood watched the rolling camp move out, with the remuda following. He watched Nacho Lucas head for the herd to take up rear flank, and he watched the distant herd begin to move. Like a great, fat snake arousing from torpor, it began with slow and massive flowing to uncoil itself and slither away. Its head was already out of sight, lost among the running hills to the north.

Matt circled once past the rise where the two graves were.

"All the way to Wyoming, Soapy," he said.

Then he turned away, spurred the bay and headed for the herd.

26

The more he thought about it, the more sure Tip was that the owlhoot who had gunned Jim Tyson and left him for dead was Rodney Link. He wasn't sure why he thought so, considering how brief was Tyson's description. But there was something about how it happened, so sudden and mean, that went with the description of a young man with a wide hat and stringy yellow hair, a scrawny kid with flat eyes who grinned and fired, and that something said Rodney Link.

It was purest chance, of course, that the victim lived to describe his assailant . . . purest chance that there had been someone there to help him, to encourage him to live—Tyson said Clifton Flowers had *aggravated* him into staying alive—but Tip's observation was that in a wide land with not too many people travelling around in it, chance was not such an uncommon thing. Coincidence that the same owlhoot Rafter H had run out of Dry Creek had gone off and shot a man who was one of the founders of Rafter H. (Had he known that? Probably not.) Coincidence that the injured man wandered cross-country and made his way to Rafter H on the trail. Coincidence that Tip had been there to hear the part about the shooting. And yet, the coincidences were orderly and seemed proper. If chance had no pattern, he thought, then how would anything have any meaning? Chance is all there is, when you get down to it.

And chance was, the outlaw who shot Jim Tyson was Rodney Link. That first shot, placed so precisely—right through the shirt pocket, which as it turned out was why it didn't kill him—was the kind of thing Rodney would have thought about trying to do. And he had done it, and that was what Tip worried about.

Rodney Link had been a hell-raiser and a nuisance. But now Rodney Link was dangerous. Like a panther that has been raiding stock, then gets a taste of human blood.

Right through the shirt pocket. That was intentional. And that said to Tip Curry that the shooter was Rodney Link.

Chance saved Jim Tyson's life. Chance and an old belt buckle retrieved from a sand wash littered with the bones of a man and a horse.

Dawn was full in the sky, and Tip rode to a hilltop to meet the morning sun. In that moment, just as the sun broke out from under the east, the land seemed a vast blue bowl under a fiery sky, a world where the last shreds of night shadow faded in the valleys and draws, and each hill wore a halo of rose and gold. From here he could see the herd, several miles back now, a plodding dark carpet whose contours were those of the land it covered. And just at the spear-point of it were tiny separate dots—Dave Holley and Sonofabitch, maybe a couple more riders, and a scattering of cattle stretching out ahead of the rest.

He wondered where the Link boys were now, certain in his mind that they had graduated to full outlaw status and that Jim Tyson had been their victim.

The old belt buckle was a tangible weight in his shirt pocket, and it pleased him that Mr. Hazelwood had gone to the trouble to borrow it for him . . . that he had thought of a lucky charm at all for his errant gunhand.

Well, if Rodney Link was taking to shooting people through their shirt pockets, then a brass shield buckle wasn't a bad thing to carry there. Jim Tyson was still alive.

The voice beside him sent his hackles rising and his hand to his gun.

"Where we goin'?"

He spun, tensed, and recognized the weathered, saturnine features of Clifton Flowers.

"Howdy," Flowers said. "Where we goin'?"

Tip stared at him. "How did you get here?"

Flowers shrugged. "I don't know. I just come. Where we goin'?"

"*I'm* scouting trail," Tip told him.

"Suits me," Flowers raised an eyebrow. "Do you know the way to Porterville?"

"Not exactly. I heard it's up in Nebraska."

"That sounds right. How's about we go there?"

337

"You'd have to talk to Mr. Hazelwood about that. I go where he says." Tip stepped his horse out to an easy lope and headed northward. Clifton Flowers rode by his side. Tip scowled and touched spurs to his animal. He rode one of the Star-Cross bays, a leggy, spirited mount with the gate of a racer. The horse responded joyously and ran. Down a long hill and up another he flew, glorying in the crisp air of morning, and Tip glanced around. Clifton Flowers was only a pace behind, matching his gate, the scruffy mustang seeming hardly to touch the ground as it ran.

A mile passed, and part of another, and Tip sighed and reined to a halt. Beside him, Flowers' pony circled and pranced before settling down. Tip scowled at the man, vague suspicions building within him. "Where are you going?"

Flowers seemed to think about the question, as though it were a puzzle. "With you, I reckon."

"What do you want?"

"What I want is to get to Porterville, but I hate to be a nuisance about it."

"Then why don't you go?"

The man leaned on his saddlehorn, regarding him with eyes that seemed very old and very sad, and a chill ran up Tip's spine. Just for a moment, it had seemed as though he could see through both the man and the horse, as though they became slightly transparent. But only for an instant.

Flowers sighed deeply. "I would if I could. I need to be there. I promised somebody. But I can't go, not without somebody helps me. I tried, sure enough. Ever since I figured out what's wrong with

338

me, I been tryin'. But I just wind up back here."

"What do you mean, figured out what's wrong with you?"

"I don't know much about it," Flowers said. "But you got a notion what I'm talkin' about. I can tell. You done some thinkin' about it yourself."

"You mean—"

"Yeah." Flowers nodded. "I mean I'm dead. I ain't alive any more, probably haven't been for a long time and just never knew it."

Tip stared at him, realizing he was perfectly serious. "But that's crazy!"

"Time was, I'd have thought so, too. But not any more. I don't recollect it at all, but I kind'a think lightning got me. Seems like it must have been a long time ago. I never thought much about it. Fact is, I don't guess I paid much attention to anything at all 'til that feller Tyson showed up. All along, I thought it was him that was dead. But it was me. Don't you see?"

Tip felt disoriented, almost dizzy. As though the world had just changed faces and nothing quite made sense the way it ought to.

"Whole notion takes some chewin' on," Flowers said, sympathetically.

"But I see you! Big as . . ."

"Big as life? Thing I don't understand is, how come I'm out here with you?"

"I don't—" Tip paused. Then he reached into his pocket and drew out the old belt buckle. "Mr. Flowers, is this yours?"

Flowers' eyes didn't shift. It was as though Tip's hand and what it held didn't exist. "What is it you

339

think you got there, son?"

"This! Can't you see it?"

"I don't see anything. What do you think you have?"

"It's a belt buckle. Tyson was carrying it. It saved his life. Is it yours?"

"Seems to me I'm wearin' my buckle on my belt. But there's just a whole lot that don't make sense to me right now."

"Then if this isn't yours, it won't matter to you what I do with it."

"Don't see how it would."

"I don't believe any of this," Tip glared at the man.

"I can see how you might not."

With a curse, Tip flung the buckle to the ground, wheeled his horse and rode away. He went a hundred yards or more, then looked back. He was alone. On open, rolling prairie with a view in all directions, Clifton Flowers had disappeared as though he had never existed.

Reining the bay, Tip turned full circle, shading his eyes in the morning sun. There was no one there but himself. No man, no horse, nothing. Just himself and his mount and the endless land.

"I'll be damned," he muttered.

"I've been talking with a ghost," he said.

"Out here all by myself, nobody around anywhere, and I've been keeping company with a ghost?" he shouted the question at the empty sky.

Just like Ollie Sinclair, that time. And like Gabe had said about Matt Hazelwood, when he was digging Mr. Green's grave. And like all the odd

340

things Jim Tyson had related.

Hell, it just couldn't be.

Could it?

It took him more than an hour, searching on foot, to find the old belt buckle where he had thrown it. It was under a prickly pear stand, out of sight. But finally he held it in his hand, turning it over, studying it. It was scoured by wind and water and time, deeply patinaed. Bones, Tyson had said. The bleached-out old bones of a man and a horse, and this belt buckle. Maybe other things, buried under the sand. Maybe Clifton Flowers' old gun was out there someplace, thick with rust. And maybe the fork of his saddle, and the shanks of his boots, and the mustang's bit and curbchain and iron shoes.

Could a man not know he was dead? Could a man just overlook a thing like that . . . maybe if it happened so quickly that it didn't register on his awareness . . . could a man just go on like nothing had happened if he didn't know anything had?

Morning breeze touched the hillside and tiny brush-voices whispered sad old songs just at the edge of hearing.

I'm sorry, Mr. Flowers. I didn't know.

"It ain't easy to wrap around a notion like that, is it?" Clifton Flowers was right there again, up in his saddle, looking down at him with eyes that were the color of time gone by.

Big as life.

Tip could only think of one question at that moment. "If you really are dead, aren't you supposed to . . . well . . . go someplace?"

341

"Seems like," Flowers said. "Seems like I'm supposed to go to Porterville."

"Why? Why Porterville?"

"I promised Helen I would."

From Speed they headed west, riding the rolling land by starlight until they were past the first hills.

"There will be people looking for me," Fallon told her.

"I know," she said.

"I'm afraid I killed two men back there," he admitted.

"I know. I heard."

"I didn't cheat them, but they would have it no other way."

"I understand."

"Well, Lady Luck, I hope you have chosen wisely in selecting your company for travel."

Molly was awkward on horseback, unsure of either her animal or herself, but she held the steady pace he set and beyond the first hills—where the land surged upward once again, this time a maze of canyons and draws reaching toward shadow heights against the sky—they stopped to rest.

"No such comfort as a fire this night," he said. "It's best we not be seen."

But there was water for the horses, and it was a place to rest. Molly slept, and when she opened her eyes first dawn was in the sky.

Timothy Fallon came down from a flat-top rise and paused to smile at her. "Good morning, Lady Luck." Then he saddled the horses and they rode again, still westward.

"They say there are no roads out here," he said. "But where men have gone there are always roads. Out there beyond those far hills is a road that's two miles wide and a thousand miles long, and beyond it is another, longer still. The Western Trail, some call it. And beyond that is still another, though it takes sharp eyes to see it. It's a road where no road is. The buffalo found it, and the Indians learned it, and there's talk now of men putting cattle on it to deliver to the mines in Wyoming. Some say it will lead all the way to Canada."

"Will it take me where I want to go?" she asked.

"Lady Luck goes where she will," he chuckled. "But roads are a convenience."

In high morning, before the heat of day set in to haze the distances, he led her to the top of a hill. He looked around, then pointed. "See there."

Far off to the north, no more than slow-moving specks at the edge of vision, a line of riders crossed an open hillside.

"Are they looking for you?" she asked.

"It's best to assume so. And there will be others, too. They'll think of the cattle trails when they don't find me on the roads. They won't stop looking soon."

"Who were they . . . the men you killed?"

"One was Toby Speed."

"Who was he?"

"A bad man, Lady Luck. A bad man who surrounded himself with proud men and could not bear to lose, even at cards."

"Would you have let him win, but for me?"

343

He shrugged. "It would have been the easy thing to do."

"But you didn't."

He smiled at her, the easy smile of one who is very sure of himself. "I had a change of heart."

Late in the day they topped a lazy ridge and the valley beyond was broad and flat, a great trail coming up from the south and disappearing to the north.

"The first of the roads," he told her. "Abilene is at the end of it, and the flint hills."

Molly looked at the rising distances. "Is this my road?"

"If you choose, Lady. But I can't go this way. There's settlement now, north of here, and there'll be posters on me."

"Then let's find a farther road."

They crossed in the evening, in fading light, and wound their way into hills beyond. He led them to a place where sheer walls hid a meadow with an inch-deep stream of sweet water and rich graze for the horses. Then he made a fire, and from the packs he prepared food rich with spices.

"The last time I met Lady Luck was in New Orleans," he said. "She was taller than you, and had long hair as black as a raven's wing. She gave me luck and laughter . . . for a time. Then she took it away. But she left me her taste for fine things, and the skills to pursue them, and I recall her fondly."

With warm food inside her and stars overhead she wrapped a blanket around her shoulders and sat with him by the fire.

"How do you feel about those men you killed?"

344

she asked.

He smiled. "They weren't the first, Lady Luck. Nor, probably, the last."

"I killed a man. In Colter."

His eyes twinkled in the firelight. "Did he need killing?"

"He left me no choice."

"Then you know how I feel about those others."

She watched the living coals, embers glowing, brightening with each touch of breeze, ebbing as it passed. Like people, she thought. Brightnesses that flare in the darkness, and writhe and burn and cast their light around them, but when the flame is gone the darkness remains just as it was before, and all that's left is ashes.

"Is that all there is," she asked, "just bright times and ashes?"

For a time he didn't answer, and she thought he had not heard. But then he said, "For some of us, that's enough. But there are others whose fire leaves its traces. Some bring iron to their fire and forge things that will last. Others make their fire a torch, and light other torches so that those who come after them can see. We choose the fashion of our flames, Lady Luck."

"I've needed a torch. Sometimes it is so dark."

"Will you find a torch at Porterville?"

"Maybe I can light one there."

27

The bank money was gone, and Maynard had been thinking for several days of how best to get rid of Rodney. He had thought several times of shooting him in his sleep, had actually had his gun in hand twice to do that, but had hesitated. What if Rodney wasn't actually asleep? He was greased lightning with that fancy Colt of his, and if he got in the first shot Maynard was a dead man.

Or what if Maynard actually managed to shoot him, but didn't kill him? Rodney would shoot back, he knew.

There hadn't been all that much money to begin with—not nearly as much as he had expected—and Rodney had insisted on carrying it all. They had stopped off in some little two-bit town, and Rodney had gone to drinking. Then he had gone to playing with his gun, daring other men in the saloon to take him on, throwing his name around. Maynard had gotten fed up and gone to the stables to sleep. In the early hours of morning he had found Rodney, passed out behind the saloon, all the money gone.

And if that wasn't bad enough, after Rodney had sort of sobered up he had gone crazy. He had shot up the town in broad daylight, and at least two people were dead.

I ought to just get clear away from him, Maynard kept telling himself as they traveled westward across the open lands. Even if I don't kill him, I ought to just ride off and leave him.

But if he did that, he knew, sooner or later Rodney would take it in his head to come looking for him. And Rodney would probably kill him then.

They rode stolen horses, and concentrated on putting distance behind them. Twice, in the distance, they had seen parties of riders.

"They're after us," Maynard assured his brother. "They ain't going to stop lookin' for us. An' all because you couldn't let well enough alone."

Rodney glared at him. "If I was as chicken-livered as you, I'd go hide in a hole."

"Well, I didn't get us in a scrape where half the country is out lookin' for us. It was you that had to go and shoot up that place."

"Yeah," Rodney grinned. "Did you see them two fall? I think I got me another one, too. But did you see them two? Did you see where I shot 'em? Right through their shirt pockets, is where. Man! That was pretty."

They kept to the low ground and pushed the horses.

"What I ought to do," Rodney declared after a while, "is turn around an' go back there."

"What for?"

"Somebody in that place has still got all my money."

Our money, Maynard thought, but he kept his peace. Rodney had that hot look in his eyes again, and when he got like that there was no telling what he would do.

They swung wide to bypass a little town, and watched from cover as armed men passed on the road. "They know about us," Maynard hissed. "Look at that, they know we're around here someplace."

"I bet they know who they're dealin' with, too. I bet they know the name Rodney Link all over Texas by now. I got a notion to go into that town there an' get me some whiskey."

"Hell, Rodney! You just tryin' to get yourself killed?"

"Ain't anybody gonna kill me, Maynard. You know why? Because first they'd have to get the drop on me, and nobody gets the drop on Rodney Link. Besides that, we need money. Maybe there's some money there. What town is it, anyway?"

"Sign said Speed. Maybe that's its name."

Rodney snorted. "Speed! That's about the slowest-lookin' Speed I ever saw. Let's go in an' see if we can have ourselves some fun."

"Rodney, you can't just . . ." Maynard snapped his mouth shut at the look in his brother's eyes. "Maybe it'd be best if just one of us went in."

"Yeah? Which one?"

"You go ahead if you want to. I'll wait out here."

"Chicken-livered," Rodney spat.

Maynard watched him go, with a mixture of hatred and relief. Maybe they'd be waiting for him there. Maybe they'd shoot him down on the street. Maybe Maynard would be rid of him once and for all.

He tried to imagine how it would be, without Rodney. He could go back to the Link ranch, he thought. Without Rodney kicking around he could probably talk the old man out of a stake . . . maybe a good one. Maybe enough to get him to St. Louis or someplace where he could make his way by his wits. All he needed was a chance, he knew. With a stake in his poke and a place he could work things, nobody would ever outsmart Maynard Link.

His eyes aglitter with anticipation, Maynard watched the little town and listened for gunfire.

Rodney rode into the little town, walked his tired horse the length of its main street, turned and went the entire length the other way. The sun was low, the air hot and there were few people on the street. Those that were paid him little attention, and his eyes slitted with anger. He knew they were faking. He was a wanted man . . . a bad man. They were pretending not to notice him. Then it occurred to him that they were afraid of him, and he felt better. With the thought came the realization that there were probably a lot more people behind those doors and windows, watching him. For good measure, he turned and rode the length of the street one more time, his hand near his gun, a happy sneer on his face.

Finally, he reined in at a hitch-rail in front of a run-down little saloon, rein-tied the horse and went to lean against an awning post. Let them have a good look at Rodney Link, he thought. Let them sweat a little, wondering at the audacity of a famous outlaw who would ride right into town and dare them all to do something about it.

Minutes passed and the sneer on his face faded into a frown. People came and went and did not seem particularly to care that he was there. And that didn't seem right.

It dawned on him then that maybe they didn't know who they were looking at. After all, no one here likely had ever seen him. All they would know would be a name. He strode to the saloon doors and pushed them open. "You folks looking for Rodney Link?"

There were only three men inside, a fat man with a stained shirt lounging behind a plank bar and two old men seated at a table, playing dominos. They all looked at him.

"I seen men ridin' out from here," he said. "I could tell they was lookin'!"

"Yeah," the barkeep shrugged. "Lookin' for a gambler fella that gunned Toby Speed and one of his bunch. He's got a bounty on him. Five hundred. You seen him?"

"Crap!" Rodney spat and turned away. He went to stand by the awning post again, glaring at any who passed. If the town had a bank, he couldn't identify it. The place was barely a town at all, just a collection of buildings set out at the end of the farmer roads where the narrow ranges began which butted against the old trails—a place for farmers to trade their produce for goods from a couple of stores so that they could farm some more. Another year or two and there would be more farms, spreading layer by layer toward the west.

Across a narrow street that might have been a wide alley was a two-story building with a hotel sign. As Rodney watched, a man with a wilted cravatte came from there and approached, glancing at him without recognition. The man went into the saloon. A little later three rough-looking men on tired horses rode in from the west. They stopped in front of the hotel, dismounted and went inside. Then they came out again, all of them frowning, and strode to the saloon. Each of them glanced at Rodney as they passed, and he returned their glances with a stare of challenge. But they ignored him and went inside.

Rodney heard voices from within, and stepped to the batwings. A rearward door was just closing. Only the three he had seen before were visible.

On impulse, Rodney walked to the corner of the building and turned to walk along the narrow street. Fifty feet from the corner was another door, the window beside it partially open.

Crouching by the window, he heard men talking inside.

". . . on, Herb," one said. "We think you know where he went. He had horses, and Steubner says you rented 'em for him. Now why don't you just tell us about it."

"Service of the hotel," another voice said. "Customer wants to rent a horse, we rent a horse

352

for him. I don't ask where he's goin'."

Another voice: "You know we could beat it out of you. You and that gambler was thick as thieves. You know which way he went, anyhow."

"I don't know anything. Leave me alone."

"And that woman, too. You talked to her. I bet they both told you where they was goin' to, didn't they, Herb?"

"I don't . . ." Rodney heard the sound of fists on flesh and someone whimpering and gagging.

"Come on, Herb. Just tell us which way, that's all. Look, with the head start they got, it won't matter much anyhow."

Again the scuffling, the thuds and the whimpering.

"Now dang it, Herb, we ain't enjoying this, you know. But we could use the money."

"I told you, I don't know," Herb wheezed.

"See if he'll talk with a gun in his gut," someone suggested.

"Oh, sure. And what do I do if he doesn't? Shoot him? Hell, Clem, it ain't worth that. Maybe he really don't know."

"Oh, he knows, all right. Bump him again, Tom."

More scuffling, then a silence broken by someone wheezing and gasping.

"Well," one of them said, "it was worth a try. Sorry, Herb. No hard feelin's."

Boots on a plank floor, sound of a door opening and closing. Beyond the open window, Herb still whimpered and gagged.

Rodney had an inspiration then. He eased the outside door open, peered into the gloom, then

353

stepped inside and closed the door behind him. There was a gaming table, several chairs, and Herb. The man with the wilted cravatte sat in one of the chairs, his head resting on the table. He had blood on his face.

"You didn't tell them fellers," Rodney told him. "But you're fixin' to tell me because if you don't I *will* kill you."

At the edge of town, Maynard heard a single gunshot, muffled but clear. He held his breath. Maybe somebody had killed Rodney. He crossed his fingers and wished as hard as he knew how.

But a few minutes later he heard a running horse, and Rodney appeared from between outbuildings, covering ground.

"Mount up," Rodney said as he reined in. "We got things to do."

"What did you do in there, rob somebody?" Maynard hurried to climb into his saddle.

"Get movin'," Rodney growled at him. "We ain't got all day."

"I'm comin'." Maynard heeled his horse and followed his brother, the low sun in his eyes. When he came abreast of him, a mile out of town, he said, "I heard a shot. Did you kill somebody?"

"Sure did," Rodney grinned. "Shot hell out of him."

"Well, who was it?"

"Hotel clerk. I took six dollars and a gold watch off him."

"You killed him for six dollars?" Maynard's eyes

widened. Rodney would kill for money, he knew. Or for no particular reason at all. But to kill a man for six dollars—

"I killed him because I felt like it. Don't worry about it. We got things to do."

"What things?"

"We're in the bounty business, Maynard. There's a bounty back there on a gambler name of Fallon, an' we're gonna collect."

"What makes you think so?"

"Because I know which way he went. Straight west, the man said. Has a woman with him, too."

"How much bounty?"

"Five hundred dollars."

"How do we collect? Take him back?"

"Bounty's on his head. That's all we got to take back."

"What do we do with the woman?"

"Depends on what kind of a looker she is," Rodney leered. "But afterwards I guess we'll take her head back, too. I bet I can get them folks to pay double."

Another mile passed beneath them, and Maynard pulled abreast again. "I can't get used to you killin' a man for six dollars, Rodney."

"I didn't kill him for six dollars. I killed him because I felt like it. Man, you should've saw the look on his face! He really didn't think I was gonna shoot him, not after he told me what I wanted to know. He thought we was all through. When I cocked that hammer he looked like he'd swallered a frog.

"An' I got him right through the shirt pocket,

too," he added proudly. "Folks are gonna learn to respect Rodney Link."

Ahead in the distance, low buildings were visible beyond a rise.

"We're gonna get ourselves some fresh horses," Rodney pointed. "These are about used up."

"Whose place is that?"

"Old Dutchman named Steubner. He rents horses through the stable in town."

"So I suppose we're gonna rent some horses?" Maynard sneered at him. "For six dollars?"

"Rodney Link don't rent anything!" his brother snarled back. "I didn't say rent, I said *get.*"

"I saw a man killed by lightning one time," Tip Curry explained to Matt Hazelwood. "It was awful sudden . . . just he was there and then he was dead, him and his horse both. But the thing is, I always figured the light played tricks with my eyes, because right after that bolt hit I could still see him there, up on his horse like he had been and both of them shining bright, and at the same time I could see what was left of both of them, right there underneath them."

"That doesn't mean he *was* still there," Matt shook his head and reined in. "Bolt of lightning can leave an image in a man's eyes. Just like looking into a fire at night. When you look away into the darkness, you can still see the flames." He turned the bay and slouched in his saddle, looking back at the herd, the point of it a mile behind them. Two thousand cattle were visible from the ridge where they had stopped. Beyond, nearly a mile past the point of the herd, the ground rose to block their view and only the dust haze above it showed how the herd extended onward, back and forth, for another pair of miles.

Tip had scouted the land ahead, then Matt had ridden out with him to look at the route and plan the next day's drive. If they could make ten miles they would rejoin the main trail less than a day short of where the bypass veered off toward the Escarpment and the Llano Estacado beyond. One day at most on the known trail, then the great herd would bear west into lands that had seen few trail herds and none like the size of this one.

Link would know then. Rafter H wasn't following the Western trail to railhead. Rafter H was going its own way, and Herman Link be damned.

Two more days. His plan called for getting them up the plateau ranges and into high plains before Link had time to react. After that they would all be committed.

Tip Curry reined alongside, studying the surrounding hills. They were in rolling land, but here the terrain began to open out, to widen. The distances were greater, and it would be harder for someone to spy on them unseen. The Link crew couldn't trail close as they had in the tighter lands to the south, and Tip felt a measure of relief. They were still out there, he knew—still watching. But now they were watching from maybe ten miles off, and there was comfort in that.

"You don't believe it, do you, Mr. Hazelwood?" he asked. "About Mr. Flowers, I mean?"

357

"I think there are better explanations," Matt said. "No, I don't believe in ghosts."

"I just keep thinking about that rider I saw hit by lightning, and how I could still see him there . . . well, how it *seemed like* I could. And I keep wondering . . . suppose he *was* still there, and didn't know he had been hit, and didn't see himself lying there dead, and just rode on."

"Did you see him ride away?"

"No, sir. I didn't. But sometimes I don't see Mr. Flowers, either."

Matt saw the bedding of the herd begin, flank riders coming forward to turn the spear of cattle back upon itself while Dave Holley threw Sonofabitch in with them. Shading his eyes then, he looked north and west at the widening land.

Another day and they'd be back on the Western trail. Tip had scouted the route.

Then a day or less along that trail. Then at a place he and Sam Price knew, they would turn and strike northwestward for the high lands, on a trail that was not a cattle trail at all—not a trail of any kind except that to follow it one must go where the buffalo had gone, cross rivers where they had crossed and find the way into and out of vast valleys that cut across the featureless Llano Estacado . . . at the right points to hit water when they needed it, and the caprock breaks that were passes and not traps.

And then Herman Link would know, and would react as he chose.

For the hundredth time, Matt Hazelwood tried to put himself in Link's place. What would I do if it

358

were me? He knew the answer. He would attack.

"Mr. Hazelwood," Tip Curry's voice interrupted his thoughts. "Do you recollect Molly Purcell? She kept a shop in Colter. Her maiden name was Molly Flowers. She told me that."

The evening sun rested on the horizon, seemed to settle there, supported by the land but sagging under its own weight . . . a great orange oval elongating at the rim of a sky without clouds to reflect its glory. Like a tired old man dimming at the end of a long day, it lay down to rest.

"We'll bed on the main trail tomorrow," Matt said. "Then we'll head north. But we're going to need supplies. There'll be moon tonight. I'd like for you and Jim Tyson to ride over to that town those people came from. Sam will give you a list of what we need. And if there's a doctor there, get him to take a look at Big Jim's head. He's still a little foggy sometimes."

28

While the boys made camp in the hills, thirteen miles north of their camp the night before, Frank Harrel helped Herman Link string a rope corral for the stock. It was a task the boss liked for him to do, because it gave them a chance to talk in case Link had any talking he wanted to do.

What he wanted this time was an appraisal of the Rafter H situation. The old man had been hard to live with since those two backshooters of his had disappeared. Frank Harrel was reasonably sure that Link had sent them after Tip Curry, and privately felt that in such a case he had deserved to lose them. But even more, the old man was still on the prod because he believed Curry had found out more about them than they had from him. Privately, again, Harrel believed he was right.

"They're anglin' back to the regular trail, that's obvious," he said as he slipped a double half-hitch over a post to snug his rope. Having no wagon to work from, the holding corral was anchored in a stand of scrub oak with a patch of graze beyond.

"They're pushin' those cows hard and smart," he added. "They're scouting trail like folks used to do in the old days and they're usin' the lay of the land pretty good. That's a top crew, for sure."

"Admiration, Harrel?" Link's voice suggested a sneer.

The gunhand shrugged. "Pays to know about folks if you're fixin' to do business with 'em."

"They've been lucky."

"Not my place to ask, Mr. Link, but wouldn't it be easier to maybe just make Hazelwood an offer for those cows, delivered where you want them?"

"You're right, Harrel," Link snapped. "It's not your place to ask."

They worked in silence for a few minutes, then Link paused to wipe his face with his sleeve. "I didn't get where I am by mollycoddling those people who crossed me. Matt Hazelwood pulled this stunt all by himself, and he's not going to walk off with my money for doing it. The way I see it, I have fair claim to that herd. If he didn't want a fight, he should have just accepted the Association blackball and laid low for a season. It wouldn't have killed him."

Harrel glanced at him, wondering: had it been you, Mr. Link, would you have done that? But he didn't ask.

But Link, once started, wasn't through talking about it. "I might have looked the other way if he'd just gone ahead with his shotgun roundup, gathered maybe a thousand, fifteen hundred head, and made his drive. But he cleaned the range,

Harrel. He slapped us all in the face when he did that. It was a deliberate insult."

And a hell of a gather, Harrel thought, holding his tongue. But that isn't the reason we're out here. Are you going to say the real reason?

"And the most deliberate act of all was abandoning his spread—the way he did. Do you know what it means when a rancher pulls up stakes in a pooled range and leaves his holdings contested? It means range war, Harrel. Matt Hazelwood knew that when he did it. He even burned his house to make sure it would start right away."

And left Link standing toe-to-toe with Triple-Seven, Harrel thought. Is it because he put you at a disadvantage? Is that why we're here?

"That Nelson," Link said, scowling. "A strutting Englishman with English money behind him. Didn't he ever step in and sew things up just the way he wanted them? Three weeks deadline on a roundup! I know how he thinks. 'Let's just put the squeeze on old Herman and break him down,' is what he was doing. Probably thinks he got the job done, too. But he never set foot in a mine, Harrel. He never learned how to fight, unless it was out of a book. Let him strut and preen while he wraps up Dry Creek for his own little nest. By fall, I'll have every acre of claim his owners thought they had up past the Texas line, and a legitimate base for it all in Texas, and a half-million dollars worth of cows to market. Then we'll see who outsmarted who at Dry Creek."

Harrel had turned away, unable to control the expressions on his face as the plan became clear.

So that was how it was! Link didn't care about Hazelwood or Rafter H. Link was at war with Colonel Nelson and the Dominion Land and Cattle Company. And Rafter H had started the ball by pulling stakes, so Link was getting even with everybody . . . letting Rafter H push a herd to the Territory for him, a herd he would then take and use to push Dominion out of its biggest operation.

Sometimes Frank Harrel wasn't proud of the brand he rode for. But, he had to admit, it was a slick move.

If Link could pull it off.

In the back of Frank Harrel's mind was just a trace of a doubt. Somehow, he couldn't quite imagine Matt Hazelwood not figuring out what Link had in mind. And somehow, he couldn't see the Rafter H boss doing what Link planned on him to do.

"Country opens out from here on," he said, finally. "We won't have a chance to keep close watch on that herd again 'til they get up by the Scarp."

He wondered, abruptly, whether he should tell Mr. Link about the old buffalo road that took off up there and ran up across the Llano country. Link might not know about that. He didn't make his market drives. He always sent a hired boss for that.

But when he thought it over, he could see no reason to discuss it. The Western Trail went straight on north, staying below the Scarp, to eventually cross the Red River at Rock Falls. People didn't drive cattle across the staked plains.

There were easier ways to reach the railheads in Kansas.

"This is sort of like old times, ain't it?" Clifton Flowers grinned as both Tip Curry and Jim Tyson jerked around in their saddles at the sound of his voice. High moonlight silvered his slouch hat, its shadow hiding all of his face except his grin.

"Howdy," he said. "Where we goin'?"

Curry and Tyson glanced at each other. They had talked about Clifton Flowers, and they were both believers . . . whether anybody else believed or not.

"Town called Speed," Tip said. "We need supplies. Mr. Hazelwood sent us to get them."

"Nice night for a ride," Flowers allowed. "Makes a man feel like singin'."

"No need for that," Tyson told him. "Nobody here needs aggravatin' at the moment."

"That's all right. I wasn't fixin' to, anyways. This Speed, is that where the feller said Molly was?"

"That's what he said. Molly Flowers. I wondered if that was somebody you know."

"Molly Flowers is what Helen and me named our baby. I don't reckon there's too many Molly Flowerses around, though what that child is doin' 'way off out here is beyond me. She ain't any bigger'n a button."

"She's a grown woman," Tip told him. "Last time I saw her she had a stitchery at Colter and was taking care of her Papa Jess . . . her father-in-law.

Her name was Molly Purcell."

They rode in silence for a time, Flowers holding pace between the other two and slightly behind. His being there sent occasional little chills up Tip's spine, although he had never felt the slightest threat from the laconic ghost. It was just the situation, he supposed—riding by moonlight with a dead man.

"If there's a doctor yonder," Tyson commented, "I hope he isn't one of those that tests a headbone with a mallet. I knew a wrangler up in Kansas who got thrown and landed on his head and they took him to a doctor in Wichita to see if his skull was all right. That doctor sat him down and had him open his mouth, then started tappin' his head with a mallet and listenin' to see what kind of sounds came out."

Tip stared across at him. He had never heard such a thing.

"We always figured that doctor had an ear for music, and thought he could tell by the tone if the bone was cracked. But he sure never heard bells ringin'."

"I wouldn't think so," Tip allowed.

"All he heard was that wrangler's yell before he bit him on the ear."

The half-moon above barely paled the clear sky, though its light lay silver on the hills. Night birds were flickering occurrences against the burning stars.

"I declare," Clifton Flowers said, softly. "Little Molly, all growed up. An' a married lady, too. I declare."

"Widow," Tip told him. "Her husband died.

Haywagon tipped on him, she said."

"Poor little thing. I hope she's all right."

"She's tryin' to get back to Porterville," Tyson said. "Right now she's out travellin' with some gambler. That's who those fellows were after. He has a price on his head."

"Bad company," Flowers allowed. "I've knowed some gamblers in my time. Some of 'em was real gentlemen, but ever' last one was fiddlefooted. Woman can do better than to take up with a fiddlefooted man."

"You said you were fiddlefooted," Jim Tyson reminded him.

"I said folks always said I was."

"Were you?"

"Yeah. I always was, and that's a fact. Fiddlefooted. I told Helen I'd change my ways, an' I guess she believed me. Would have, too, I guess, if I'd had the chance. But no, there I went, fiddlefootin' off one last time, and that time I guess I got killed an' never made it home."

His voice had gone soft again, and Tip glanced around. He would have sworn the man had a tear on his cheek. "I'll stand you to a drink when we get to Speed," he offered.

"Obliged," Flowers said.

Jim Tyson breathed a quiet sigh of relief. He was glad the young gunhand had managed to change the subject. "Did Matt Hazelwood say why we're resupplying out here, instead of just makin' do 'til we get to Fort Griffin?"

"No."

"Oh, I just wondered."

367

"Well, it's because we aren't going to Fort Griffin. Mr. Hazelwood counted on everybody thinking we were, but when we get up to the Scarp we're going to cut off on a buffalo trail that goes up over the Llano. We'll be leaving the Western Trail."

"Anybody ever drive up that way before?"

"Not that I heard of, but that's where we're going. Up the Scarp to the high plains and all the way to Wyoming."

Clifton Flowers was ignoring them, lost in his own thoughts. "I declare," he muttered. "Little Molly a growed-up woman. Time flies when you're dead."

Again, Tip felt the little chill in his spine. It wouldn't be polite to say so, but he wished Clifton Flowers would stop talking about his condition.

"I think I know who shot you," he told Tyson. "I think it was Rodney Link, from the way you describe him."

"Link? Kin to the outfit that's following the herd?"

"The old man's son. There are two of them. Rodney and Maynard. We ran them off the range."

"That's right," Clifton Flowers said. "There was two of them. They had your horses, 'til I went and got 'em back. Havin' had the honor of meetin' them two, I wouldn't give you a nickel for the both of 'em."

"Like to get my hands on them," Big Jim grated.

"If you ever do, be careful," Tip said. "They

aren't smart, but they're mean. Anyhow, they're probably out of the country by now."

"I wished you'd said somethin' earlier," Clifton Flowers said. "We passed them just a while back."

Both of them swivelled to stare at him.

"Passed who?"

"Them two. The ones you're talkin' about. I didn't know you all wanted them, or I'd have told you. You won't catch them now, though. They're on fresh horses, and goin' the other way hell for leather."

"I'll be damned," Tyson snorted. "You're sure?"

"'Course I'm sure. I know about things like that, sometimes."

"I'll be damned," Tyson swore again.

Tip Curry swung around, dipping his head to look at the silver-shadowed man pacing at his flank. "Mr. Flowers, do you remember ever shining?"

"Not so's I noticed it."

"I just wondered."

It was past midnight when they saw lights ahead. A cluster of low buildings sat on a little rise, a house and barn and a few outbuildings, situated among trimmed scrub oak trees.

The light came from the windows of the house, from lamps in the barn and from a pair of lanterns on gate posts beside the trail. As they rode into the light men came with rifles and shotguns to stare at them.

"Who are you?" one asked.

369

"Jim Tyson."

The lantern turned. "And you?"

"Curry. Tip Curry. We ride for Rafter H. Comin' into town to buy supplies. What's going on?"

"Horse thieves," the man said. "You see anybody out yonder, two of 'em, one ridin' a sorrel and one on a three-stocking black?"

"Didn't see anybody, but we may have passed somebody at a distance. They stole the horses?"

"Stole 'em and killed Harry Steubner. One of them jaspers shot him. No reason to it. Harry wasn't even armed. Just plugged him, right through the shirt pocket. Mrs. Steubner saw it from the window, then she fainted. Prob'ly just as well."

Jim Tyson squinted at the man. "Any idea who they were?"

"Oh, yeah. We know who one of them is. A strutter name of Rodney Link. He told half the people in town his name, then he killed the hotel clerk and robbed him. Some of the boys think he wanted a line on that gambler they put the bounty on."

"You think they're after him . . . the gambler?"

"Stands to reason. Funny thing is, the town people are gonna have a meetin' at first light. They're gonna take that bounty off the gambler an' put it on them two that killed Harry Steubner. 'Course, them two don't know that."

"Maybe one good thing will come out of this," another said. "Lot of folks are thinkin' it's about time the town had some law. Maybe they'll do somethin' about it now."

Some distance from the farm, Tip noticed that

Clifton Flowers was no longer with them. He started to say something about it, then looked again and Flowers was there, a few steps back, halted and turned, staring westward. Jim Tyson noticed him, too, and drew rein. Something in the way Flowers sat, the tense set of his shoulders . . . Tyson turned and rode back, with Tip Curry following.

"I got a bad feelin'," Flowers said as they came up to him. "Real bad feelin'." He turned, looking from one to another. "We ought to go back. Right now."

"You think there's trouble, Mr. Flowers?" Again, Tip felt the tingling chill in his spine.

"Fixin' to be. Surely fixin' to be. Somethin' bad."

"I'll go," Tip told Tyson. "You got the list and the draft. Do you feel all right to go on in and arrange for supplies?"

Tyson nodded. "I'm fine. What do you think is going on?"

"I don't know. But I trust what he says." Tip glanced at Flowers, who was still peering westward into the night. "Mr. Tyson, let me have that old buckle again, would you? I don't think he can go with me unless I have it."

Tyson handed it over and Tip dropped it in his shirt pocket. "Come on, Mr. Flowers," he said. "Let's get back to the herd."

"Tell Matt I authorized you to go back," Tyson called. "That way it's my responsibility."

Tip waved and touched spurs to his horse, liking Jim Tyson for the thought. But it didn't matter. As long as Tip was Rafter H's gunhand, he didn't need

371

authority to do what seemed best.

Side by side, Tip Curry and Clifton Flowers sped westward by moonlight, back the way they had come, and the chill in Tip's spine was a lingering thing. Something was very wrong. He was needed at the herd.

29

From a hilltop four miles away Tip first spotted the great herd and knew that his instincts—or Clifton Flowers'—had been right. Dawn was in the sky, its tints touching the tops of ridges above the shadowed range, touching that part of the mass of cattle that blanketed two hilltops. But the cattle were not moving. No riders worked at point to stretch them out for the day. Instead, slowly as they came awake, the cattle simply had begun to graze outward.

The Star-Cross horse he rode was nearly spent, but Tip's drumming heels urged it to run once more and it stretched its long, driving legs in response. He was aware of Clifton Flowers keeping pace, the scruffy mustang as inexhaustible as its rider. For a half-mile between hills he saw nothing but the unfolding land and the brightening sky, then he crested another rise and saw riders gathering between him and the herd, coming out.

From a distance he recognized Stan Lamont, Gabe Sinclair and Bo Maxwell. He ran to meet them.

The fierce lines of Lamont's heavy face, the paleness of Bo Maxwell and the gaunt, sad features of Gabe Sinclair told him the story even before they spoke.

"Mr. Hazelwood is dead," Lamont grated. "Somebody shot him."

"Where is he?"

"We brought him to the wagons. Everybody else is there. We saw you on the rise yonder. Didn't know who you were."

It had happened in the last pale hour of moonlight. Matt Hazelwood had ridden out early to look at the herd and the trail ahead. Dave Holley, some distance behind, had heard the gunshot, had seen two shadows fleeing northward. He had found Matt Hazelwood where he fell, dead on the dusty ground.

"One shot," Bo Maxwell said. "Right through his shirt pocket."

Tip glanced around, his eyes glittering beneath his hatbrim. Clifton Flowers was nowhere in sight. "I know who shot him," he told the others. "It was Rodney Link."

"Rodney?" Stan's eyes widened.

"Or him and Maynard, but it was Rodney's bullet. I know."

At the camp he handed a tired horse over to Ollie Sinclair and walked to the chuck wagon. Most of the outfit was gathered there, hats in hands. Sam

Price knelt and pulled back the blanket from a form lying on the ground.

Someone had closed the rancher's eyes. Someone had crossed his hands on his chest and brushed back his graying hair. Tip removed his hat and wished he knew how to pray. Strains of one of Bo Maxwell's songs drifted through his mind. *O bury me not on the lone prairie* . . . Why didn't you leave me fired back there, Mr. Hazelwood? If I was fired, I wouldn't have to be here to see you like this.

He knelt beside his employer and lifted one of the hands crossed on his chest. Death had come suddenly to Matt Hazelwood. The bloodstain around the bullet hole in his shirt pocket was small.

Tip replaced the hand, gently. Then he drew Hazelwood's revolver from its holster and looked at its loads.

"He never fired," Dave Holley said. "There was only one shot. I doubt if he even saw them until it was too late."

"Nacho's gone," Stan Lamont told him. "We think he went after them."

Sam Price replaced the blanket. "Where's Jim Tyson? I need to talk to him, I guess. Him and me are the owners now. Matt had it set up that way."

"He went on into town to have supplies sent out. We . . . I decided to come back. We heard the Link boys were headed this way. They killed a couple of men back yonder. Mr. Tyson will meet the herd this evening, up ahead."

"Then I guess we need to get 'em moving," Price shrugged, still looking at the covered body of his partner.

"We bury him first," Tip said. "We bury him deep, just like he did with Mr. Green."

Stan Lamont nodded his agreement. "Break out a pair of spades, Gabe. We'll all take a turn at the diggin'."

With the grave started, Sam Price called Tip Curry and Stan Lamont aside. The old man's grizzled beard was whiter than they had noticed before. Maybe it was because of the angry flush which had settled into his face and seemed to mean to stay. "Did Matt tell you boys his plans?"

"We try to make the main trail again today," Lamont nodded. "We planned to bed them on that stretch of high pasture Tip found up there. We can push them onto water from there the next day."

"Is that all?"

Stan shrugged. "I reckon from there we go north."

Price glanced at the gunhand. "Tip?"

"We go north, but only a few miles. Mr. Hazelwood said there's a place up there where an old buffalo road heads northwest, up the Scarp. He said you know where it is. He meant to throw those cows onto that trail and head right up into the staked plains with them. He said the buffalo road would take us to the high plains past No Man's Land, and from there we would make trail if we have to. He said you and him talked about it."

"We talked about it. Do you think we can do it?"

"Mr. Hazelwood thought so. But we'll have to fight. When we turn off the main trail up there, that's when Link will jump us, because we won't be goin' where Herman Link wants us to go any more."

"Do you think the boys will stay with the herd, now that the boss man is gone?" The question was for both of them.

Lamont shrugged. "I will."

"Why don't you ask them?" Tip suggested.

It took an hour to dig the grave to everyone's satisfaction. It was a proper grave, cemetery-deep and cleanly cut, on high ground where a clump of scrub oak would shade it in the afternoon.

They rolled Matt Hazelwood into his blankets and tarp, lashed him securely with bed ties and lowered him into the ground. They gathered around the hole, and Sam Price got out his old Bible.

He thumbed it open, tried to read the print, blinked and wiped his eyes. He tried again, then closed it and put it in his pocket. He raised his eyes to the morning sky and every man among them could see the moisture that gathered there.

"Lord, it may be your doin' that this old man can't see to read the scriptures right now. And maybe that's how you want it. But a good man died this mornin', and there needs to be some words said about that.

"Matt Hazelwood would have been forty-five

years old if he'd lived another month. Lord, you and I both know that ain't so many years for a man to have on this earth, but I knowed this man for twenty-five of those years and I'm here to testify that he used 'em well. We went to war together, Matt and me, and I never served a better captain. Then when it was done, Matt said to me, 'Sam, let's do somethin' useful now. There's folk up north that needs beef. Why don't we take 'em some.' And Soapy Green, he was there, and Big Jim Tyson, too, and we all decided that would be the thing to do.

"What we done must of been right, because you blessed us in our efforts—though you never made none of 'em easy—and by an' by Rafter H grew up and opened up the whole Dry Creek range, so's just a lot of folk could share your bounty. An' all the time, it was Matt Hazelwood that studied things out an' said how to do 'er so's we could get 'er done.

"And down the years I seen Matt Hazelwood suffer, like good men always do. I seen him marry an' I seen him bury, and I seen him walkin' among the graves on that hillside by the light of the moon, with his hat in his hand an' his heart so sore it was like to bust, and never say a word to anybody but maybe them that was gone."

Sam's voice quavered and he paused, head down, his eyes closed and the muscles working in his throat. Beyond him, a respectful distance from the members of the outfit, Tip saw Clifton Flowers standing alone, his hat in his hands.

Sam Price found his voice again, and raised his

face. "Anyhow, Lord, I reckon all the family Matt Hazelwood had left was just his friends. And since he was a man who never stepped aside for those that pushed him, he never had a lot of friends, but those he had was good ones. An' I guess I speak for them . . . for all of us here . . . when I say you ought to fix a place up in your kingdom where a man can ride all the miles he wants to, and gather up wild cows and get a good price for 'em, an' never have to have any truck with Comanches or Mexican bandits or city lawyers . . . or range associations. And you ought to slap Matt Hazelwood on the back an' say, 'Matt, I'm glad you got here when you did because this spread needs a man to run it that knows how it's done.'

"You ought to do that, Lord, an' you'll never make a better bargain. Because Matt Hazelwood won't never let you down. And you can have the guarantee of every man here on that."

He was silent then for a time, and finally he lowered his head. "That's all there is to say, I reckon." His voice was hoarse and shaky. "Rest in peace, Matt Hazelwood. There's folks that will miss you."

Sam Price dropped the first spadeful of earth, then they all took turns . . . all except Clifton Flowers, who walked off alone to stand beside the chuck wagon, looking north.

Stan Lamont hitched up his britches and looked around at the lot of them. "We got a herd to push, boys. If there's any man here that has changed his mind, he can draw his wages now. Otherwise,

379

everybody pick your best day horse and saddle up. We ain't stopping until we hit the main trail, even if we have to drive those cows by moonlight."

Clifton Flowers sought out Tip Curry at the rope corral and beckoned him aside. The man's face was gaunt and drawn, his eyes moist. "You said you knew my girl, back yonder. Said you talked with her."

"Yes."

"She needs me now, an' I ain't much good to her dead. Will you help her? Will you help my baby?"

"Where do you think she is, Mr. Flowers?"

"Somewhere yonder," he pointed north.

"That's where I'm going. You're sure?"

"Surest I ever was," Flowers said. "She's gonna need help."

Tip saddled a fresh Star-Cross horse, the one that had the look of racer about it. He waved at Sam Price and headed north, and after a time he looked back and Clifton Flowers was with him.

Fifteen miles north, Nacho Lucas approached the crest of a hogback ridge. He rode slowly now, watching the ground ahead, reading sign. His square face was set with resolution, a hard intensity that was much older than his seventeen years. Dark eyes under a low-pulled hatbrim glittered with reflected light as he read the land and understood its message.

He was near them now. Through the hours of stalking, sometimes reading trail, sometimes going on instinct or hunch, he had held his horse to a steady lope, conserving its strength. They could run themselves out if they chose. He would still be there behind them, coming on.

Nacho had asked no permission to pursue the killers. He had simply looked at the body of Matt Hazelwood when they brought him in, then saddled a strong horse and headed north, where Dave Holley said they went.

If Tip Curry had been in camp, Tip Curry would have gone after them. So Nacho went, instead. Curry had told him, a man rides for the brand. Matt Hazelwood was Rafter H. He was the brand, and now he was dead. Someone had made the worst kind of trouble, and that someone must be found.

With light he had found their trail and held to it. Scuffs on the rocky ground here and there, sometimes a clear hoofprint or two, droppings, grass bent down from the weight of a hoof, all these he saw, and they told their story.

Now he neared the top of a ridge and slowed, looking ahead. Instinct as sure as the gun at his hip told him they were near. Abruptly, a gunshot cracked the morning, quick echoes rolling away. He drew rein and listened. The sound had come from just ahead, beyond the crest. Now someone over there was shouting.

He stepped down, ground-reined his horse, and ran to the ridgetop, staying low. Beyond, the downward slope was broken and rutted, a washboard span of jutting rock strata drooping toward distant runoff breaks. And just below him, not a hundred yards away, were two men, one mounted and one on foot with a gun in his hand. A horse lay on its side there, kicking and bleating as blood spurted from a hole in its neck. The mounted one was shouting and cursing. The one on foot seemed to pay him no attention. He stepped around the writhing, dying horse and kicked it savagely.

Nacho knew them. He had seen them before. Maynard and Rodney Link.

Idly, he wondered which of them had killed Matt Hazelwood. Not that it made a lot of difference. They were both there.

Backing from the crest, he retrieved his horse and led it up to a motte of scrub oak screened by wild vines. It would be secure there. Then he crawled over the ridgecrest, rolled behind a foot-high ledge and worked his way along it to one of the runoff gulleys leading down the slope. He disappeared into it.

Within moments he was near enough to make out their words. Maynard was still complaining. "We needed that horse, Rodney! I just don't see why you had to—"

"You saw it!" Rodney's voice was a snarl. "Fool thing stumbled and threw me off! I wish you'd just shut up!"

"But what the hell are we supposed to do now? We only got one horse!"

"Well, maybe there's one too many of *us,* Maynard. Had you ever thought about that?"

"Don't talk crazy, Rodney. I'm your brother."

"Sure you are. My chicken-livered brother. If you'd shot that cowpoke like I told you to, we wouldn't be in such a hurry now. There wasn't anybody else close enough to see which way we went."

"All right! I told you he was haulin' out his gun. There wasn't time to get to him. Besides, what could he see?"

"He saw me shoot that bastard, that's what." He hesitated and his voice took on a new tone. "Then again, maybe that's just as well. It's high time people started knowin' about Rodney Link. Maybe if he recognized me that's just so much the better. Did you see Hazelwood fall? He was dead before he hit the ground. Right through the shirt pocket! That's how Rodney Link does business."

Nacho had heard enough. He worked his way another twenty yards down the brushy gully and raised his head. Maynard stood not ten feet away, his back to him. Beyond, maybe twenty yards, Rodney stood above the dead horse, looking down at it. He still had his fancy gun in his hand, but as Nacho watched he flipped it in his hand, letting it roll back and drop into its holster. A showy move, Nacho thought. Dumb, but showy.

Neither of them knew he was there until he prodded Maynard's back with his Colt and said, "Just stand real still, both of you." He drew Maynard's gun from its holster and thrust it into his own belt. Then, pushing the shocked Maynard ahead of him, he advanced on Rodney. "You just keep those hands high, Rodney. In plain sight. And turn around and face away from me. Easy!"

Rodney stared at him and Nacho was startled at the madness in his eyes. He blinked, and in that instant Rodney drew and fired. Maynard was just lowering his arms, and Nacho felt the impact of the bullet as it struck Maynard's arm and flung it back against him. Maynard screamed, turned and they both went down. Rodney fired again, too quickly, and his shot splattered rock almost at Nacho's ear. Maynard screamed and writhed atop him and he pushed him away, violently, struggling to keep his eyes on Rodney, to bring his gun into line. But the horse, Maynard's horse, had bolted at the gunfire and was between them. Maynard screamed again and rolled against him, and he had a glimpse of the horse pivoting, fighting the cruel bit in its mouth as its head was pulled around. Then Rodney was in its saddle, racing away, and Nacho lined his Colt for a moment, then lowered it. He was too far away.

He stood, and Maynard writhed on the ground at his feet, moaning and clutching his bloody arm. The bullet had shattered bone, just below the shoulder, and the arm flopped uselessly.

For a moment Maynard's eyes cleared and focussed on the man standing over him, the gun in his hand. He tried to scuttle backward, keening and blubbering. "Don't kill me . . . don't . . . it wasn't me . . . Rodney done it, not me . . . please."

Nacho felt a loathing that was like a pain in his gut. He raised the gun, pointed it at Maynard's head and cocked the hammer. Maynard's eyes went huge in a pale, tear-stained face.

"Please . . . not me . . . kill Rodney, not me . . .

oh God—"

Nacho shook his head slowly, almost sick with disgust. He let down the hammer on the Colt and put it away. He put his foot against Maynard's face and pushed him down on his back.

Then he crouched beside him, stripped off his belt and began fashioning a tourniquet and splint.

30

Timothy Fallon heard the sound of a distant gunshot, and drew rein, beckoning for Molly to halt as well. A hundred yards up the little valley where they rode, scrub oaks veiled a hillside. He pointed. "Ride over there, Lady Luck. Wait among the trees while I go and have a look."

She nodded, and he turned away, heading for the valley rim.

The day was clear and fresh, the morning sun high, and the rolling lands had lulled him with a feeling that he and the girl were the only two people on earth. Indeed, it was two days since they had seen anyone else or even the traces of other people. Still, he knew he should be careful. There were men who would ride far to hunt down a man with a bounty on him, and he had no doubt that Toby Speed's associates had arranged that.

Riding up the slope, he drew his gun and checked its loads, then put it away again. Whatever the sound, it had been far off, barely carried on the morning breeze.

At the crest of the rim he found a high place and reined in to look around. He had no idea what direction the sound had come from, but as he studied the land it came again, this time two shots, close together. Somewhere south, he thought. Maybe half a mile away, by the sound. He saw no one. The little hills rolled away, creases in the distant landscape that could hide people, or might hide nothing. For long minutes he watched, assuring himself that there was no one visible out there.

Far off, much further than the gunshots had been, was just a hint of something, movement on a hilltop, he thought, but then was not sure.

"Whatever it is, it has nothing to do with us," he decided, grinning as the old habit of speaking his thoughts aloud reasserted itself. Habits of a man too often alone. The past days, travelling with Molly Flowers, were the best days he had known in a very long time. The young woman was intelligent, attentive and quick to respond to his thoughts. She was good company, and he was delighted by her. And she had an interesting stubborn streak that fascinated him, as though they were opposites in some strange way. She knew exactly where she wanted to go, and she was determined to get there.

"It's the determination," he told himself. "That's the part of her that allures me, I think. Had I that sort of determination within me, what kind of man would I have become? Certainly not what I am, God forbid."

He smiled, an ironic turn of the corners of his

mouth. It had amused him for a long time to realize that having nothing to go back to, anywhere, did not in any way motivate him to have somewhere to go. Oddly, it seemed that it should have.

But Molly had somewhere to go, and Molly was Lady Luck, and it pleased Timothy Fallon to escort her as far as she cared to have his company. Together, if she wanted it so, they might find that place of hers. Porterville. If so . . . he shrugged and grinned . . . maybe it was time he took a look at another part of the country.

The land went out and out, endlessly, and there was no further hint of movement or sound. Finally he tapped heels to the horse and rode back the way he had come.

She was waiting among the trees, still mounted, and he tipped his hat to her. "A winsome scene," he said. "Lady Luck among the leaves. A picture to carry in the fond parts of the mind."

She guided her horse out to join him and they headed westward again. "I shall keep a better watch than I have done," he told her, "but I think we are safe."

The sun was directly overhead when they topped out on a cedar-lined ridge and looked across several miles of rolling open land that ended abruptly at what, from here, appeared to be a great wall rising hundreds of feet in a nearly vertical incline. To the north and south the wall swept away into the hazing distance.

"The Scarp," he told her. "It's not as fierce as it looks from here, but there are places where few horses could climb it. Beyond are the high, flat lands that the Spanish call Llano Estacado."

"Must we cross?" she asked.

"Not unless you want to see the Llano."

"Then where is the road northward that you told me about?"

"You are looking at it," he chuckled. "Right down there, where you see the flat expanse between the hills. The Western Trail. It goes due north from here, all the way to Oglalla."

"To Porterville?"

"Indeed, Lady Luck. Indeed, to Porterville."

"When we come to it, then, and I turn north . . . would you ride with me for a while, Mr. Fallon?"

He took off his hat, smoothed back his hair and seemed to lose himself in bright distances. Then he turned and smiled at her, his eyes holding hers. "I am a gambler, lady. And a gambler always rides with Lady Luck, as far as she will have him."

She returned his smile. "I believe I would enjoy your company, Mr. Fallon."

She looked past him, then, and her eyes widened. "What on earth is that?"

He turned to look. Far in the distance, miles out from where they sat, dust haze gathered and was flattened away by errant breeze. A huge, dark arrow lay on the land, stretching away to the south, out of sight. It carpeted the land, creeping northward.

"A herd," he said. "A herd of cattle, coming up the trail . . . no, coming from somewhere else, I believe, but angling to join the trail. But such a herd! Why, there must be thousands of them.

390

Thousands upon thousands."

"Then they have come so far," Molly breathed. "Oh, Mr. Fallon! Just look! How magnificent!"

He turned. "Do you know who they are, then?"

"I think it must be Rafter H. They left Dry Creek with seven thousand head, some of the men said. But everybody said they would never make it past that range. Oh, but look! It must be them."

In the distance the cattle crept along, a rippling, slowly flowing dark fabric of intense life, seeming barely to move yet always moving.

Molly felt she was watching a pageant—a great, slow story unfolding upon an immense stage, the actors so small in the vastness as to be invisible, yet by their efforts making an indelible mark upon the world. The sheer grandeur of it caught in her throat. So many dire predictions she had overheard, back in Colter. Such cynical assurance that Rafter H would never succeed in moving so many cattle. Even Papa Jess had said they were all madmen, and that they would all wind up dead or lost and their cattle scattered to the winds within a matter of days.

Suddenly she wondered whether Tip Curry was out there with the herd. Where would he be? At its head? Or maybe guarding its flank? And Bo Maxwell, where was he?

"Magnificent," she breathed, watching the distant herd begin to curve at some contour in the land.

"It is, indeed," Timothy Fallon said.

Neither of them heard the approaching rider until he was just behind them, yards away. Gravel

391

crunched, and Fallon looked around. The man was young and lean, pale eyes seeming to glow beneath a slouch hat from which long, corn-blonde hair fell untended. He rode a three-stocking black horse, poorly kept and grimy with traces of prior days' sweat.

"I do declare," he grinned. "Howdy there, Missus Purcell. You sure are a long way from home. An' keepin' company with a wanted man, why, you just ought to be ashamed of yourself." His eyes shifted. "I reckon you *are* the one, all right. You look like a dude gambler, sure enough."

Molly gaped at him. "Rodney? Rodney Link? What are you doing here?"

The grin was evil, she thought. Humorless and chilling. She noticed that his hand hovered above the fancy gun at his belt.

"Why, mam, ain't you heard? I'm doin' here just like I do anyplace I go. I'm doing exactly as I please."

Fallon reined around to face him. "And what does that mean?"

"Step down from them horses," Rodney rasped. "Both of you. Right now!"

When they were dismounted he had them stand aside from their horses and drew his gun. Keeping it pointed at Fallon, he stepped down and faced him. A grin spread across his face as he replaced his Colt in its holster.

"I heard you was a real bad man, gambler. I heard you hauled out a gun from underneath that frock coat, and you killed two men with it. But them two weren't Rodney Link. Now I want to see

392

just how fast you are, so I'm givin' you a chance to draw on me. Any time you're ready, gambler."

Fallon's muscles tensed. "I have no quarrel with you."

"Oh, yes, you do," Rodney spat. "Because I'm fixin' to kill you, gambler. And when you're dead I'm goin' to have me some fun with your lady friend here, then maybe kill her, too."

Timothy Fallon was fast. But Rodney Link was faster. The gambler's gun was barely out of his coat when Rodney's bullet slammed into him, knocking him backward. He sprawled, twitched and died.

Rodney grinned, holstering his Colt. "Right through the pocket," he giggled. He turned to Molly, who stood in shock, her hands to her mouth. "Come here."

When she didn't move he stepped before her, looked her up and down and, as suddenly as a striking snake, hit her in the face. The blow dropped her to her knees.

"You're fixin' to learn," he said. "When Rodney Link says do somethin', you do it."

Abruptly then, as though remembering something, he turned away and crouched beside Fallon. He picked up the gambler's gun and dropped it into his coat pocket, then he went through Fallon's pockets, emptying them on the ground. A roll of bills, a pocket watch, a small clasp knife, a few coins, some other odds and ends. He put the watch in his own pocket and counted the money, his eyes widening. There was nearly two thousand dollars. "My, oh my," he muttered.

Molly was still on her knees, dazed and sick. A

rivulet of bright blood ran from her lip and dripped soddenly off her chin. Still holding the money in his hand, Rodney went and stood over her. "You got any more of this?"

She looked up with eyes that refused to focus.

"Money," he growled. "You got any money?"

When still she didn't respond he kicked her in the side, toppling her to sprawl on the rough ground. Then he went to the horse she had ridden, opened a saddle pocket and found her clutch purse. He dumped it on the ground. "My, oh my," he breathed. He added the money to the roll in his hand and counted it all together. Now he had more than three thousand dollars. His grin was pure delight. "All this an' bounty, too," he told himself.

Remembering something else then, he went to the stockinged black and dug into its saddle pockets. "Wonder what all Maynard had in here. Ah, here it is."

He drew out an old sheath knife and pulled it from its scabbard. The blade was foul with rust. He tested the edge of it with his thumb and cursed. It was very dull. He flung it down, walked back to Fallon's body and retrieved the little clasp knife. He opened it and tested its edge. It was small, but razor sharp. "That's more like it," he said. He raised his head to leer at Molly. "Get up off the ground, woman," he ordered. "Get up and take off that dress."

Molly felt as though she were caught in a nightmare. Everything seemed to run together, and nothing made sense. But the voice brought with it the certainty of more pain and she struggled to

394

her feet.

"That's right," he said. "Now the dress. Take it off and bring it to me."

She wanted to run, but fear paralyzed her. She wanted to scream, but her voice wouldn't work. Nothing seemed real—the cedars whispering in the wind, the three ground-reined horses cropping at grass, the stillness of Timothy Fallon, the mad eyes of the young man crouched beside him—all of it seemed to be only a bizarre dream, nothing more.

All those miles away, the great cattle herd crept along, shrouded by its writhing dust, coming on with infinite slowness. Nearer, yet still far away, a line of three loaded wagons had appeared from the hills and was rolling westward toward the place the herd would be many hours from now. Like the distant cattle, Molly's world was shrouded and indistinct.

Take off her dress, he had said. He would hurt her again if she didn't do what he said. With numb fingers, she began unbuttoning the bodice.

He had turned from her. Now he crouched astraddle of Timothy Fallon's body, his hunched back to her, his shoulders moving. Vaguely she wondered what he was doing. He paused and lay the handful of money aside, with a rock on it to keep it from blowing. Then his shoulders were moving again. The dress fell loose and she stepped out of it. She walked toward him, holding it in her hand, and he turned and reached for it. His hand was bright with blood, and beyond his shoulder . . . she gasped and began to retch, feeling the world sway beneath her feet.

With a bloody little knife, Rodney Link was working to cut off Timothy Fallon's head.

He saw her sway, saw her begin to fall, and grabbed the crumpled dress away from her. Let her go ahead and faint, he thought. Keep her quiet 'til I'm ready for her. Tied off, her dress would make a poke to carry a head in . . . or two heads, maybe. Three thousand, plus five hundred for the gambler, plus another five hundred he would make them give him for her . . . four thousand and some would stake him for a while. He could go anywhere he wanted to go, do anything he wanted to do, from here on. People would know about Rodney Link.

He went back to work, cursing the stubby blade. It made the task difficult. He wiped his face with a bloody hand.

The sound of running hooves was almost on him before he noticed it. He spun around, still crouched, almost falling as his spur caught in the gambler's coat. His eyes went feral. Beyond the cedars a rider was coming at him. Rodney drew his gun with blood-slick fingers, braced his legs, held it in both hands and pointed. As the cedars parted and the rider came through he held on his shirt pocket and fired. The rider pitched backward off his horse and Rodney had a momentary glimpse of his face, shocked and surprised.

"By God!" he muttered. "I killed Tip Curry."

He couldn't believe it, but as the horse pranced past, the evidence was there before his eyes. The man sprawled on the ground was Tip Curry, and Rodney felt a surge of pride like nothing he had felt before. Matt Hazelwood . . . and now Tip Curry. A sense of power washed over him, an exhilaration so profound that it made him dizzy. Nothing . . . nobody . . . ever could stand against Rodney Link.

"I killed Tip Curry," he said again, walking on stiff legs toward the downed gunhand. "I killed Tip Curry."

"I doubt it," a voice said, freezing him in his tracks. He turned. The man facing him, up in the saddle of a scruffy gray mustang, was the one he had seen before . . . the one who took the horses and the money away from him . . . the one who had made him think of death. And he was holding Rodney's money in his hand.

"Just can't quit takin' things that don't belong to you, can you?" he asked mildly.

Rodney raised his gun and the man looked at him as though he held a toy. The eyes under the slouch hat were the coldest, most distant he had ever encountered. They made him want to back away, to turn away, to run away. Panic and anger struggled in him. "I'll kill you," he said.

The man chuckled. "That's one thing you sure won't do, boy. Never in a million years."

He tried to squeeze the trigger, but hesitated. There was something about the man . . . an absolute certainty . . . that frightened him.

"You can't even keep that thing pointed my way," the man said, and Rodney's eyes went wide. He blinked and turned. Somehow the man had moved. He wasn't where he had been. He was farther away now, maybe thirty yards away, and off at an angle. Rodney swung the gun to point again.

"Pathetic," the man said, his voice carrying as

397

though he were only a step away. He looked at the money in his hand. "My, oh my," he said. "This is a lot, ain't it."

Still holding the gun outthrust, Rodney ran toward him. He ran, and seemed to come no closer. Without seeming to, somehow, the man kept backing away, taunting him. He stopped and leveled the gun . . . but now the man was almost out of range.

Rodney looked around, wildly. One of the horses had wandered over this way and stood a few yards off, looking at him. With an oath that was like a scream of rage, Rodney ran to it, caught up its reins and swung himself into the saddle. "I'll kill you!" he shouted. "You'll see!"

"Sure you will," the man drawled, his voice much closer than he was. "Just like you killed him." He pointed and Rodney turned. He hadn't realized how far he had run. The cedar grove was distant, though he could see it clearly.

He saw the girl, the body of the gambler . . . but Tip Curry no longer lay dead beyond them. The Rafter H gunhand was on his feet, swaying slightly but very much alive . . . and looking back at him.

Rodney felt a chill. He couldn't be! He was dead! He was shot right through the shirt pocket. Tip Curry *had* to be dead!

"No, he ain't dead," the man on the mustang said. "You know somethin', Bub? You just ain't very good at much of anything."

Rodney looked around, dazedly, and something tenuous within him—something that never had been strong—snapped and was gone. Mindless red rage burst forth, a blinding fury that had no meaning and only one purpose.

"I'll kill you!" he screamed. He spurred the horse and charged, and the man on the mustang ran before him, always just out of range, mocking and taunting him with a voice that ran in his ears.

On the crest, Tip Curry watched Rodney raging off toward the distant trail, unsure what had happened. The pain in his chest tortured him with each breath, but he found very little blood there. Only an impacted cut where the edge of the old buckle in his pocket had scored the flesh behind it. He fumbled the buckle out and looked at it. It was almost unrecognizable, deeply dented and scored with stress marks, its shape destroyed.

He hurt each time he moved, the pain intense. He knew he had cracked ribs, but for now he ignored the agony, willing it away.

First he covered the nearly-decapitated body with a blanket. Then he got water and cloth and went to see what he could do for Molly.

31

A Link spotter saw the wagons rolling toward the trail and relayed the word. Three wagons, going out to meet the Rafter H herd. Provisions.

Provisions for what? Herman Link paced and muttered, turning it over and over in his mind. Within hours—well before sundown—the herd would be back on the Western Trail and moving north. Ahead, only a few days' driving time, lay Fort Griffin. There, or at Rock Falls, was where the outfit logically would provision for the drive through the territories toward Kansas. Why would they have gone to the trouble to provision out here?

Finally Frank Harrel came to him with an idea. "They'd stock provisions if they weren't goin' to Fort Griffin, Mr. Link. If they were goin' somewhere else instead."

"Where else can they go?" Link demanded. "The trail only goes north and south. There are settlements east . . . you think they'd buck the grangers? And west is the Scarp. So where?"

"There's another way," Harrel said. "I've been thinkin' about it. A few miles ahead—less than a day's drive—there's an old buffalo road that cuts up through the Scarp. It's a migration path, is all, but they say it winds clear up across the Llano to the high plains and the foothills. I don't know of anybody drivin' cows up that way, but maybe they could. And if they did that, they'd need supplies. It's a long way to anyplace up on those plains."

"I never knew about a buffalo road," Link said. "Nobody told me."

Harrel held his tongue. There were probably a lot of things nobody had ever told Herman Link.

"That's what they're planning, then. Hazelwood said they were going to Wyoming. Nobody believed him. But if he's crazy enough to start out at all with a herd that size, then he's crazy enough to head for anyplace." He squinted at the sun, quartering in the west. "Break camp and mount up," he said. "They'll be bedding the herd in two or three hours. They'll be strung out around three sections. By the time those cows are down I want every Rafter H hand either disarmed or dead. Then we'll dicker.

"But one way or another, when those cows move tomorrow, they'll be mine."

"Hazelwood's not going to hand them over easy," Harrel pointed out.

"Easy or hard, it's up to him."

"Yes, sir." Harrel headed for the rope corral. Link will have his herd, he thought. A forced quitclaim at a token price, probably . . . Link would like the semblance of legality in that.

He hoped the Rafter H outfit wouldn't put up

too much of a fight. He, personally, had nothing against those boys.

Fifteen minutes later they came out of the hills, a fighting force of fourteen armed men, more than half of them experienced gunhands and all riding for the brand. Every one of them knew that there might be shooting. But each of them knew as well that Rafter H had already lost. Those cows would be Link cows by morning.

They had marked where the supply wagons went . . . where the herd would bed. They held to low ground and rode hard, Link hoping that Matt Hazelwood was with the supply wagons. It would be nice, he thought, to take him first, then let him watch the humiliation of his outfit and the transfer in fact of his herd. After that, Link could call the shots any way he pleased.

From the heights, spotters had scouted the terrain carefully. A wide draw wound out across the trail flats to within a quick run of where they estimated the herd would bed, and they held to the draw, wanting the element of surprise. As they neared the rising wall of the Scarp, the sun sat on top of it as though supported by its towering crest. Beyond, where the shadows began, Harrel sent a man up to the bank to look around. He was back within a minute.

"Those wagons are right out there on a rise," he said. "Not a quarter mile from here. And the herd looks to be maybe three miles off."

"How many men with the wagons?"

"I counted four. Three may be hired drivers. I don't know the other one. Never saw him before.

Big feller, maybe taller than Will Bower or Stan Lamont, but not so wide."

"You didn't see Matt Hazelwood?"

"No sir. He ain't with the wagons."

"Did anybody out there see you?"

"I don't think so. I was careful."

Herman Link glanced at Frank Harrel. "Any problems?"

"Guess not," Harrel shrugged. "Those wagons are as good a place as any to wait for the herd."

Sitting on the stacked wagons, watching the distant herd draw closer, Jim Tyson and his hired drivers were unaware that they had company until the Link riders were on them. Expertly, the gunhands ringed them, stepped them down and disarmed them.

Surrounded by guns, Jim Tyson glared at first one and then another of them, then gave his attention to the man who seemed to be in charge—a blocky, aging man with humorless eyes and an imperious manner. He knew this must be Herman Link. And that tears it, he thought. He has the jump on us now.

Link stepped forward and looked him up and down. "Who are you?"

"I'm Tyson. I'm with Rafter H."

"I don't know you."

"I don't know you, either, Mr. Link. But I believe I've met your sons." He paused, then realized that Link probably knew nothing about what his sons had done over by Three Rivers. "How about explaining to me what's going on here?"

"Oh, I think you know," Link said. "You boys

404

have pushed those cows far enough. I'm going to take them off your hands now."

"Thought that was the case." He glanced at the throng of armed men around them. They had put their guns away, but they still had them. "I suppose it runs in the family."

"What does?"

"Robbery and murder. Your sons shot me, Mr. Link. Out by Three Rivers. They stole my money and my horses and left me for dead, and I can't see one whit of difference between what they did to me and what you're aiming to try to do to Rafter H."

"You look all right to me."

"Do I?" He removed his hat and lowered his head, pointing. "Did you ever see a scar like that, Mr. Link? Doctor over in Speed told me the only thing that saved my life was having a hard head. And that wasn't the first shot, Mr. Link. It was the third, after I was already down."

The gunhands exchanged glances and Link's face darkened.

"Whatever they did is their lookout, not mine," he said.

"But what *you* do is."

"What I'm doing is strictly business, Tyson. Nothing more."

"That's probably how they saw it, too. Mr. Link, why don't you just go home and leave decent folks alone?"

The older man's hands balled into fists and Tyson thought he would strike him. But one of the gunnies was pointing eastward. "Somebody comin'," he said.

In the distance, approaching at a run, a single rider crested a swell. Even from here, they could see that the horse he rode was near to exhaustion. It ran erratically, its steps faltering, pitching its head, seeming sometimes almost to stumble. Yet he pushed it unmercifully, spurred heels drumming it. He had no hat, and corn-blonde hair whipped about his face. Sunlight glinted on the bright gun in his hand, and as they watched he levelled it and fired, then came on.

"Who is it?" one asked.

They peered and squinted, trying to make him out.

"What's he shooting at out there?"

Jim Tyson saw his chance, and took it. As Herman Link turned away to look, a long arm looped about his throat and lifted him to tiptoe. He felt his gun pulled from his holster, its muzzle thrust against his cheek.

"Everybody hold it," Jim Tyson said. "No, don't try it, or your boss is a dead man."

Two of the hired drivers backed away and then dived for cover under the wagons. The third vaulted to a seat and burrowed into his load.

Tyson tried to watch all the Link men at once, tried to count them, to remember how many there had been. "Easy, boys," he said. "Let's just be sensible about this." Something wasn't just right, though. The numbers didn't tally. He started to turn his head and something crashed into his temple. The world swam before him for an instant and then went dark.

As Jim Tyson sagged to the ground, Frank

Harrel removed the gun from his limp hand and put his own gun away. "That doctor was wrong," he said. "This feller's head ain't all that hard."

He looked curiously at Herman Link. "Are you all right? Did he hurt you?"

Link tried to swallow and almost gagged. Tyson had nearly crushed his throat. He took several deep breaths and tried again. "I'm all right," he croaked. He looked at the limp form on the ground at his feet, drew back a booted foot and planted it, hard, in the man's side. "Kill him," he said.

Frank Harrel's eyes narrowed. "He's down, Mr. Link. He won't do any more damage."

"Hell!" Link exploded. "Where's my gun? I'll do it."

Another gunshot sounded from the east, nearer now, and the sound of a voice shouting and raving. As one they looked around. The weird rider was still coming, squalling at the top of his lungs, brandishing a bright handgun. His path was erratic. He veered this way and that, shouting obscenities with each breath, pointing his gun wildly one way and then another. As they watched he fired again, and the bullet kicked up dust fifty feet from the rearmost wagon.

"What in the livin' hell—?"

"Who is that?"

Frank Harrel shaded his eyes, then lowered his hand to stare in amazement. "Mr. Link . . . I think that's your son. I think it's Rodney."

Pure red rage now drove Rodney Link. Only one

407

thing was in his mind, driving out all other thoughts. The taunting man on the gray mustang must die. Rodney must kill him. Nothing else mattered.

He spurred the heaving horse and veered to the right as the man somehow shifted to there. He was as elusive as a shadow. First he was one place, then another, but always there, always grinning, smirking it seemed, egging him on with taunts and insults. Rodney tried another shot. He felt the Colt buck in his hand, but the man somehow had edged aside—just as before.

"I'll kill you!" Rodney screamed it, and the words went on and on.

"Child, you keep sayin' that," the man taunted him, the voice low and close to his ear. "But you surely ain't doin' a very good job of it so far. You suppose everything you think you ever done is a lie? You suppose you just never done nothing at all, and just made yourself think you had? How does it feel to lie to yourself, boy? How does it feel to believe it?"

"I'll kill you! God damn you to hell, I'll kill you!"

"No, you won't, boy. Takes a man to kill a man, and you ain't a man. You ain't anything at all, far's I can tell."

"I'll kill you!"

Vaguely, as from far away, Rodney had the impression that there were other people there now. Men and wagons and horses. But it meant nothing. It had no part in the red realm of his fury. There was no one. Only himself and the taunting man.

408

"I'll kill you!" He shouted it again, then stopped. He hauled on the reins and the horse beneath him lurched and trembled, its sides heaving. The man was no longer backing away. He sat there now, in his saddle, motionless except for the humorous glinting of his eyes, the movement of his lips.

"You figured you killed Tip Curry, didn't you, boy? Shot him right down, didn't you? But there he was. You saw him. Standin' on his own two feet, as alive as you. Minds me of the time you killed that horse trader out yonder. Got him for sure, didn't you? Three shots, an' all good ones. But you know somethin', boy? Jim Tyson ain't any deader than Tip Curry. That's him right over there, just gettin' up off the ground. You see?"

In the fog beyond the veils there seemed to be men and horses and wagons. Rodney squinted. One of them was a tall man, just getting up off the ground, his hand to his head. It *was him!* The same one!

"I killed him!" Rodney shrieked.

"No, you didn't, boy. You just thought you did. Why, it wouldn't surprise me none if Matt Hazelwood was to step up right now and look you in the eye. And maybe that hotel clerk back yonder, and the man you stole the saddle horses from, too. All your dead men are comin' after you now, boy. Look around. You'll see 'em everywhere you look, an' they'll be lookin' at you. Comin' to get you, boy. They'll be comin', every one."

Rodney could stand no more. Like a striking snake the gun in his hand rose, levelled and fired.

The taunting man was only a few feet from him now, and he fired directly into him.

Men scattered before the racing, bloodied madman when he raised his gun. He was shouting gibberish, and seemed not to be looking at them at all, just facing them. The shot was sudden and loud, and then he lowered his gun slowly and looked around, puzzled.

He was still sitting there, a blank-eyed madman on a heaving, half-dead horse, when one of the men said, "My God. Look."

Frank Harrel turned. Herman Link was sprawled on the ground, arms and legs spread-eagled. His eyes were wide open, as one mortally surprised. And a stain of blood was seeping outward, forming a neat little pattern around the bullet hole in his shirt pocket.

For a long time, Tip Curry knelt on the ground, his arms tight around the trembling, sobbing shoulders of Molly Flowers. It was all he knew to do for her, and in fact it seemed to be what she needed. He held her away from the cooling body of the gambler, blanket-shrouded nearby. She had seen enough of that. Eventually, there were things he needed to do. But right now the most important thing was to comfort her, and he rocked gently, soothing her, stroking her hair. Where her face was buried against his shoulder was a warm wetness from her tears.

He sensed movement and glanced up. Clifton Flowers stood some distance away, holding the reins of his horse. The man nodded at him, removed his hat and crooked a finger at him.

"You just stay here a bit, Molly. I'll be right back. You're safe now. Just wait."

He felt her nod against his shoulder and pulled himself away. He got to his feet, his breath catching at the sharp pain of cracked ribs. With a glance to be sure she was all right, he walked across to where Flowers stood.

"You got my baby here, Bub?" the man asked quietly.

"Right over there, Mr. Flowers. She's kind of shook up, but she'll be all right."

"That's good," Flowers nodded. Then, hesitantly, "Where is she, exactly?"

Tip turned and pointed. "Right there. With my coat wrapped around her. See?"

He turned back, puzzled.

"No," Clifton Flowers said. He sounded very tired, and very sad. "No, I don't see her. I've waited too long to look."

32

The sun was down behind the standing Scarp when Dave Holley choused Sonofabitch around and threw him into the herd. Gabe Sinclair rode forward from swing and Slim Hobart and Bo Maxwell from left flank to turn the leaders while Pye quartered through them to stop them from milling.

Sam Price drove the rolling camp out to where the supply wagons waited, Stan Lamont and Will Bower riding alongside.

Only eight Link riders remained at the site, older hands who had stayed around to bury their boss and see what happened next. The others, with no brand to ride for now, had simply gone their own ways.

With trace chain and bolts, Jim Tyson and Frank Harrel had shackeled Rodney to a wagon wheel. He sat there alone and ignored, huddled like a child against the spokes, sometimes giggling, other times weeping and gibbering to himself. Now and then he would cry out, his eyes darting around in fear, seeing ghosts that no one else could see.

When Sam Price told Jim Tyson that Matt Hazelwood was dead, Tyson walked to the wagon and stood over Rodney, simply looking down at him for a time. Then he turned away. Rodney had recognized him, and the fear in his eyes was sickening.

Some of the Link hands had dug a shallow grave, and there they buried Herman Link without ceremony. Stan Lamont wanted to decorate the grave with sod on a stick, but Sam Price was against it. It would mean nothing. There was no one for it to mean anything to. And it would shame the eight Link men who remained.

By ones and twos, riders came from the bedding herd to change shifts, eat their suppers and marvel at the story of Rodney Link. They went to look at him and turned away in disgust.

Sam Price had his hands full at the chuck wagon for a time, then a pair of the Link men pitched in and gave him a hand. Tom Campbell knew how to cook, and Wiley Jones had scrubbed a pot or two in his time.

"Don't suppose you fellers have decided yet what to do with us?" Jones asked.

"Thinkin' on it," Sam Price told him. "Mind how you temper that skillet. I'd hang the man that fouled it."

The moon was up when Tip Curry brought Molly Flowers down from the ridge. He had taken the time to clean her dress for her, and to bury Timothy Fallon among the cedars where he had fallen. The roll of money he had found there, weighted with a rock, was now in her purse.

He turned her over to Sam Price, who frowned as he looked at her bruises by lantern light.

"Rodney Link did that," Tip told him. "Tend to her and feed her, then make up a bed for her in the trail wagon. She's goin' along with us." He turned, wincing at the pain in his chest, and scowled at the ring of curious, concerned faces. "You all let her alone. She needs rest."

Sam raised an eyebrow. "What's wrong with you, Tip? You hurtin'?"

"Rodney shot me, Sam. Just exactly the way he shot Jim Tyson. Right in the belt buckle." He pulled out the old artifact and it was passed from hand to hand with exclamations of "I declare" and "Ain't that the beatin'est?" and "Never seen the like."

"I got some cracked ribs, Sam. I'll need a bind."

"We'll tend to it. But first, you might want to take a look over there by that wagon."

Men followed him, bringing lanterns. At the supply wagon he stood silently, looking down at Rodney Link. Rodney glanced up, saw his face clearly and began to whimper and moan, gathering up trace chain in his hands, trying to hide behind it.

"You can shoot him if you want to," Stan Lamont said. "We've all been thinkin' about doin' that. We just haven't done it yet."

"Waste of a bullet, seems to me," Frank Harrel said, and Tip turned quickly, wincing. He hadn't noticed the Link hands hanging back out of the lantern light.

415

"He shot Herman Link, too," Harrel explained. "His own father. We been talkin' about maybe he's rabid. He's been droolin' a lot."

Jim Tyson came into the light. "Do you want to shoot him, Tip? You have as much cause as anybody."

Tip nodded and drew his gun, then remembered that Molly was over by the wagon. She had heard enough shooting for a while. He put the iron away. "Not now, I guess. Sound might carry to the herd."

"Yeah. Most of us have said that. Do you have any idea what made him like this?"

Tip edged away from the crowd and Tyson followed. "Pretty good idea," Tip told him. "He's haunted."

Matt Hazelwood. And Herman Link. And at least two more that they had heard about. Tip looked around. "Where's Nacho?"

"We don't know," Tyson said. "He hasn't come back."

"What are you going to do about those Link hands, Mr. Tyson?"

"Well, Sam and I talked about that, and it seems we have three choices. We can hang them, run them off or hire them. Any suggestions?"

Tip considered it. "Well, I expect the ones that needed hangin' have already run off. And if you run off those others, we'll still be short-handed. It's a long way to Wyoming."

The moon was high and the third night-guard shift was just going out to the herd when Nacho

Lucas showed up. He rode a horse with a strange brand, his own saddle on it, and led a Star-Cross horse which he turned over to a sleepy Ollie Sinclair. Then leading the saddled horse, he went to the chuck wagon for a plate of cold stew and a half-dozen biscuits.

As he rattled pans, Sam Price crawled out from under the wagon. "Keep it down," he grumped. "There's a lady asleep back yonder." Then he turned up the wick of the pole lantern and rubbed his eyes. "Nacho? Where you been, boy? We been worried."

"I went to Speed," Nacho said.

"Speed? Why?"

"Maynard Link took a bullet in his arm and I remembered Mr. Hazelwood sayin' there might be a doctor there. So I took him."

"So you caught Maynard." Sam was impressed. "Is this his horse?"

"No, sir. It's mine. They paid me bounty money for bringin' Maynard in, and I bought this horse." He chewed and swallowed, hesitating. All the way out from Speed, he had been trying to decide how to say this. The only way he could come up with was straight out. "Mr. Price, I'd like to draw my wages if it's all right with you. I'm clearin' out."

It was Price's turn to hesitate. "You can draw your wages if you want to, Nacho. You want to tell me why?"

"I reckon. I ain't much of a drover, Mr. Price. And I made up my mind I don't want to be a gunhand. It just doesn't suit me, I guess. So anyway, with Mr. Hazelwood dead and all, well, I just decided to try somethin' else."

"Where will you go, Nacho?"

"Back to Speed. For now anyway. They got Maynard Link locked in a shed over there, an' there'll be a trial when they can get a judge out from Jefferson, an' I want to be there to see it. After that, well, a lot of folks over there are talkin' about needing law. They're gonna put up a town marshal job, and I think I can get it. It's worth a try."

Using Matt Hazelwood's ledger, Sam paid off Nacho Lucas. "You could at least stay to mornin'," he said.

"I'd better not." Nacho squared his hat on his head and mounted up. "If I stay around I might change my mind."

Sam Price watched him for a time, out on the moonlit range. Then he crossed a knoll and was out of sight. Finally Sam realized what was different about the youth. He no longer slanted his hat the way Tip Curry did, or wore his gun at knuckle height—the way Tip Curry did. And somehow, for that, he seemed much older.

The wakeup crew was already out the next morning, and the final night shift heading in, before anybody noticed Rodney Link. But when Bo Maxwell went to the supply wagon to take his breakfast to him, he returned wide-eyed.

"Y'all better come see this," was all he would say.

Rodney lay where he had been, still chained to the wagon wheel, the blankets they had put over him thrown aside. His feet were braced against the rim of the wheel, the trace chain clasped in both hands.

Maybe he had fought with his dreams in the night. Maybe he had fought the chain. Maybe his madness had attacked him. They would never know. The chain was cable-taut from his hands to the wheel, and the loop of it around his neck had indented the flesh there as deeply as the width of a link. Sometime in the night Rodney Link's ghosts had caught up with him. He had strangled himself with a twelve-foot chain.

"Herman Link should be here to see this," Frank Harrel said. "He would have said it's the boy's own lookout, and he would have left him where he lay."

"This isn't Herman Link's outfit," Jim Tyson told him. "This is Rafter H. Matt Hazelwood at least would have buried him."

They buried Rodney Link next to his father. To mark the grave they left his fancy Colt there, its muzzle stuck in the ground.

"Let's get 'em movin'," Stan Lamont shouted. "Mount up!" He turned to Frank Harrel. "You fellas pick yourselves some day horses and fall in on the drags. We got to line 'em up early, because by the time the drags are walkin' the leaders will be halfway up the Scarp, headin' for the staked plains. You ain't worked cows until you've worked a herd this size."

He headed for the herd, and Sam Price looked after him. In the distance the cows were up and the leads were already in motion, stringing out a half mile beyond the bed ground, a tentacle of flowing, bobbing motion extending itself from a dark carpet

419

of warm, smelly animals that seemed to cover half the world. Light dew of morning steamed off seven hundred acres of close-packed cowhide and blended with the dust haze already beginning to rise. Horns glinted in the morning sun, and when the breeze shifted the sound of them—like distant thunder just at the edge of hearing—carried clear to the rolling camp.

"We're all crazy," Sam Price told himself. "We're crazy as a bunch of loons, ever' one of us. But I declare, maybe that's the only way for a man to be."

A mile ahead of the herd, Dave Holley swung his coiled catchrope and yelled at Sonofabitch, "Get the kinks out of your stupid skull, damn it! I'm sick and tired of havin' to head you off every time you take a notion to turn left! I never saw a stupider critter in my whole life!"

Snuffy and sassy from a night's sleep, Sonofabitch tossed his head and bellowed, long horns doing figure-eights in the sunlight. He stomped, raked sod with his hooves, and stepped up the pace. When Dave Holley was three lengths back he veered to the left.

Four hundred yards back, at lead shift, Bo Maxwell chuckled at the sight. "Kick him in the runnin' gears, Dave!" he called, though Holley was too far away to hear. "It ain't true that cows are God's critters! What they are is mechanical contrivances in disguise, and I believe that one has a bent axle!"

His shout had caused the plodding line of beasts near him to bow to starboard, and across their line he saw Gabe Sinclair race to push them back and straighten the line. Even at this distance, he could see Gabe's glare.

The leads were more than two miles out when riders pushed the last of the drags off the bed ground, forming a cordon behind them that to anything but a cow would have seemed ridiculous. Spaced out at three hundred yard intervals, six men on six horses—by their sheer presence—began to trim and shape the moving bulk of a mile-wide drag of cows that must be thinned down to no more than twelve cows wide before they reached the buffalo road where it wound up the side of the Scarp.

Stan Lamont rode down the line, getting the thinning started, then stopped to wipe dust and sweat from his face and look upward at the top of the standing wall. There they would bed tonight, probably not more than four miles from where they left the Western Trail. But tomorrow—and for a lot of tomorrows after that—they would make ten or more miles a day. And they would have plenty of elbow room.

"Nothin' to stop us now," he told himself. "Barrin' a few minor inconveniences, like stampedes and flash floods, and dust storms and rattlesnakes and dry holes, and rain and wind and wrong turns and blind canyons, and maybe throw in a few rustlers and granger posses and about a hundred different varieties of just plain misery . . . barrin' them things, there's nothin' to stop us or even slow us up. It's just us and the cows an' God's good earth, all the way from here to Wyoming."

Jim Tyson worked with Ollie Sinclair to get the remuda started, then he hung back a little and looked back the way they had come. Matt Hazelwood's grave was miles back now, but he knew where it was and his eyes held on the distance.

O bury me not on the lone prairie, where the wild coyotes will howl o'er me. In a narrow grave just six by three . . . He removed his hat. We'll take them to Wyoming, Matt. And who's to say you won't see it with us. I'd like to think you will.

Leaving Molly Flowers in Sam's care, Tip Curry saddled his choice of the Star-Cross bays, clung while it worked out its morning kinks, then headed north at a mile-eating lope. He swung wide of the herd—they had their hands full lining them out without somebody spooking the silly things—and came eventually to the old, pounded slope that sliced upward into the climbing Scarp. He followed it, angling northward for nearly a mile in a gentle rise, then making the switchback where it cut the rim to emerge in a land subtly different from that below. Here the wind sang of distances, horizons of horizons beyond and the sky was so high and clear that it humbled a man just to look at it. Caprock country, climbing away toward the high plains.

From the rim he could see the herd, a flowing dark ribbon three miles long creeping toward him, tiny riders like specks of motion along its edges, dashing here and there in intricate dance. Far out alongside, the rolling camp and the supply wagons paced the great herd's flank. Today Molly could rest in the little nest of bedding they had fashioned for her. Tomorrow, or whenever she felt up to it, he would cut out a mount for her and she could ride.

The endless wind of caprock rose and fell,

striking minor-key whispers of song from the resonant blades of coarse grass, and he felt that Clifton Flowers was nearby, though he saw no one.

Your baby is just fine, Mr. Flowers, he thought. Somewhere yonder we'll pass close by where you left her, and if she wants to go back there I'll see she gets home safe.

The wind sang its secret song and coarse grass bent and bowed along the old buffalo road that would lead them to Wyoming.

33

Nine days east of Fort Laramie, Tip Curry reined in the buckboard team on a high bluff that overlooked the North Platte. Beside him on the seat, Molly snugged her heavy coat about her and pointed.

"It's still there," she said. "The rise there, where the elms are . . . I see the chimney just beyond."

Tip saw the house clearly, and the town a mile beyond. There was no telling from here what shape the place was in, but they could fix it up. It was the way she had described it, a small house nestled in the curve of a crested knoll with pasture on both sides and a woodlot down by the river.

"We'll have to find out who owns it now," he said. "We'll make an offer and see what happens."

"We'll get it," she said. "I know we will. Can we go down now and look?"

He flipped the reins and guided the team toward

a path that wound toward the house . . . the house Clifton Flowers had built more than twenty years before, the house where Molly grew up.

The buckboard was a gift from Sam Price, and the two Star-Cross bays tied on behind were a gift from the Tysons—Jim and Katie. The rest of it, what they had brought from Wyoming and what they would build with the life ahead of them, was up to them.

"We'll just look," Molly said. "Then we should go on into town and call on the Johnsons. They can tell us who to see. I hope the house is all right, Tip. It's been empty for a long time."

"If we can't repair it we'll build another. It will be fine, Molly. Either way."

The path entered a road, and the road curved down toward the river. But a short way along it another path led off, this toward the house. Coming around the knoll, they had a better view. The house was small, but sturdy and well-crafted. Closed shutters and a boarded-over door spoke of long disuse, of a great deal to be done to make it livable again. But the roof looked sound and the chimney stood like a beacon.

"I remember summer evenings here," Molly said. "Mama and me would sit on the porch and talk about ever so many things, and she would look off there, to the south, and even when she didn't say so I knew she was waiting for Papa to come home."

"Where is your Mama buried, Molly? In town?"

"No." Her eyes grew solemn. "No, people came out here, and they buried her there, where the little rock fence is. Mrs. Johnson said at the last—when she was so ill—she asked that. So they did."

He pulled up in the dooryard and helped her down. They walked around the house and Molly chattered and peered and pointed and planned while Tip began a mental list of the tools he would need. Despite his cautious words, he knew it would be their house. It was a feeling too strong to ignore, as though benign hands had been spread in reassurance and all he had to do was follow through.

He looked at the barn and shook his head. Clifton Flowers might have been a house-builder, but he had not put such loving attention into his barn (*I was always fiddlefooted* . . . fine barns were not the mark of fiddlefooted men). The best thing to do with the barn, Tip decided, would be to tear it down and start over.

But the house surprised him. Empty for years, it stood sturdy and strong. A fire in the hearth and a good cleaning out, and it would be as though it had never stood alone. Clifton Flowers had put his efforts where his heart was.

After a time they sat on the porch and sipped cool water fresh from the well, and Molly snuggled close beside him. "Is it home, Tip? Can it be home to you?"

It brought back images from a long time ago. A squat, ugly ranch house on the south Texas plains, a place of men and leather, of boot-tracks on unswept floors and the smells of bacon and coffee always lingering. That was the only home Tip Curry had ever really known. He had made no comment when Matt Hazelwood put the torch to the place. But he had felt a regret.

"It *is* home, Molly. It's all the home I guess I'll ever want."

Some day he would tell her about how it was. About Rafter H and the pulling up of stakes, and about Matt Hazelwood and Soapy Green and all the rest of it. Some day he would tell her about Clifton Flowers, too. Jim Tyson knew, and so did he, but little had ever been said. To tell her about her father—as they knew him—would mean talking about Rodney Link, and about her Papa Jess and Timothy Fallon and all the rest of it that was better forgotten, at least for now.

He stood, looking up toward the rock fence. "I'd like to walk up there," he said. "Just to sort of look around."

"All right. I'll come with you."

"No, please. I want to go alone. You just wait here for me, Molly."

It was only a hundred yards from the house, a pleasant little plot set aside for the burying of people who were cared about. Inside the fence was a single marker, barely legible. Weather had done its work on the face of the chiseled slate. But he knew the name on it. Helen Flowers.

He knelt there, aware that Molly was watching him from the porch, wondering idly what she might think. Then he pulled out the old belt buckle that he had carried for so long and laid it gently atop the grave, at the foot of the headstone.

Rest in peace, Clifton Flowers, he thought.

Embarrassed then, he stood, put his hat back on his head and walked back down to the house.

Molly stood on the porch waiting for him, but as he approached she was looking beyond him, her eyes wide with awe. She gripped the porch rail and her hand went to her mouth. She was trembling.

"Mama?" she whispered.

Tip turned.

Beside the rock fence stood a handsome woman, a sunbonnet thrown back from her face, her hand up to shade her eyes. And just above her on the gentle slope a weathered-looking man was stepping down from the saddle of a scruffy gray horse with the look of mustang to it.

Leading his mount by the reins, he walked toward her and she raised her skirts and ran to meet him. He caught her up in a hug that lifted her off the ground, and for a long moment the two figures were one. Then they separated as he set her on her feet, and the prairie wind seemed to sing the sound of laughter.

Tip removed his hat and put his arm around his wife. She was trembling, and her cheeks were wet with tears.

Up on the rise, the pair walked hand in hand toward the rock fence, the mustang following behind. He held the gate for her and followed her through, and the mustang shouldered up to the fence to rub itself against the stone.

Lazy clouds drifted overhead and shadowed the little plot, and Tip blinked his eyes. There was no one up there now. Just a rock fence around a little family graveyard, just as it had been.

One day they would talk about it all. Right now, though, it was enough for Tip Curry to put his arms around a girl who had seen a miracle, and hold her like that until her trembling subsided.